Latchkey Ladies

Also published by Handheld Press

Latchkey Ladies

by Marjorie Grant

with an introduction by Sarah LeFanu

Handheld Classic 25

First published in 1921 by William Heinemann.

This edition published in 2022 by Handheld Press
72 Warminster Road, Bath BA2 6RU, United Kingdom.
www.handheldpress.co.uk

ISBN 978-1-912766-62-8

1 2 3 4 5 6 7 8 9 0

Series design by Nadja Guggi and typeset in Adobe Caslon Pro
and Open Sans.

Printed and bound in Great Britain by Short Run Press, Exeter.

FSC
www.fsc.org
MIX
Paper from
responsible sources
FSC® C014540

Contents

Sarah LeFanu, who is distantly related to the Victorian Gothic novelist Sheridan Le Fanu, is the author of *Dreaming of Rose. A Biographer's Journal* (2021), *Something of Themselves: Kipling, Kingsley, Conan Doyle and the Anglo-Boer War* (2020), *S Is for Samora: A Lexical Biography of Samora Machel and the Mozambican Dream* (2012), *Rose Macaulay: A Biography* (2003), and *In the Chinks of the World Machine: Feminism and Science Fiction* (1988), which won the MLA Emily Toth Award. She has taught creative writing for many years, was Artistic Director of the Bath Literature Festival for 2004–2009, was a senior editor at The Women's Press and has presented programmes for BBC Radio 4. She lives near Bristol in North Somerset.

Introduction

BY SARAH LEFANU

If a novel has been out of print for a century or more, what makes it worth reprinting? Is it of significant historical interest? How does it stand within the literature of its period? Does it have anything to say to readers now? *Latchkey Ladies* is not only significant in terms of both social and literary history, but also, through the experiences of its 25-year-old protagonist, it speaks intimately across the intervening years to readers today.

This is a novel that bridges two distinct literary traditions. It looks back to and modernises the nineteenth-century novel of the 'surplus' woman, exemplified by George Gissing's *The Odd Women* (1893). It simultaneously looks forward to the pregnancy/single motherhood novels, such as Lynne Reid Banks's *The L-Shaped Room* (1960) and Margaret Drabble's *The Millstone* (1965), of the later twentieth century. But *Latchkey Ladies* is of more than historical interest: the intricate latticework of individual choice and social constraint within which its predominantly female characters move is as pertinent to women's lives today as it was when the novel was first published in 1921. And its depiction of the experience of unplanned and unwanted pregnancy still has the power to move us.

Set in London during the final year of the First World War and the war's immediate aftermath, *Latchkey Ladies* brings into vivid focus a period of rapid social change. The 'latchkey ladies' of the title were women living independently of male support, whether by choice, or, increasingly in the war years, out of necessity: single women in rented rooms getting by in one way or another as best they could. The novel provides a lively and compassionate picture of a group of these women, and goes on to show us the harsh the next two decades Marjorie and Rose were frequent visitors to the O'Donovan household, welcomed into it by Gerald's wife Beryl. They played the role of family friends while Rose and Gerald were engaged in a love affair that lasted until his death in 1942. Gerald died slowly, of self-imposed starvation after an unsuccessful operation for cancer. At Beryl's invitation, Marjorie nursed him through his final days. Readers of *Latchkey Ladies* may be surprised, as I was, by the strange foreshadowing of this event, more than twenty years before it happened, in a scene in which Anne Carey is invited by her lover's wife to go and help in the household when her husband, Anne's lover, is close to death.

I first came across Marjorie Grant Cook in the early 2000s, when I was doing research for a biography of the considerably better-known Rose Macaulay. In the finished biography I speculated about the shifting relationships between the two women and O'Donovan. I wondered whether, and to what degree, *Latchkey Ladies* was, to put a different spin on the latchkey of the title, a *roman à clef*. I still cannot offer a definite answer.

Marjorie Grant Cook remains elusive. That quality is nicely reflected in the variety of names under which she was known during the course of her career. Pen names, pseudonyms or heteronyms – I like 'heteronym' for its suggestion of alterity or 'otherness' rather than fakeness – have always come in handy for writers. Perhaps the Brontë sisters would not have achieved publication if they had not presented their work disguised as the brothers Currer, Acton and Ellis Bell; nor Mary Ann Evans had she not signed her writing as George Eliot. In the nineteenth and early twentieth centuries an initial instead of a first name could perform a similar trick, helping deliver a readership free of patronising preconceptions about 'lady novelists'. Rose Macaulay, for example, published her first novels in the early 1900s as R Macaulay. There have been, and remain, other reasons for writers to hide their identity: political, personal, or financial; serious, mischievous, or out of a writerly joy in naming and names.

When *Latchkey Ladies* came out under the name M Grant, was this in order to hide the fact that the author was a woman? I think probably not, for on the title page M Grant was credited as 'Author of *Verdun Days in Paris*', which had been published only three years earlier under the name Marjorie Grant. Two years after *Latchkey Ladies* came *Another Way of Love*, published under her full name of Marjorie Grant Cook. That seemed to be her final novel. A full decade later, Caroline Seaford published a debut novel, or so it was assumed to be by reviewers, called *Glory Jam*. Caroline Seaford went on to publish a further four novels. No-one, it appears, made the connection between Caroline Seaford and Marjorie Grant Cook, Marjorie Grant or M Grant. Why would they have?

While as a writer she may have preferred to conceal herself in the chinks of the literary machine, Marjorie Grant Cook was, of course, also a living, breathing woman who led a life outside of literary circles. I discovered something of her from Mary Anne O'Donovan during my research on Rose Macaulay. Mary Anne and her sister, granddaughters of Gerald and Beryl O'Donovan, were god-daughters of, respectively, Rose Macaulay and Marjorie Grant Cook. Mary Anne spoke affectionately of the two women. She lent me copies of two of the 'Caroline Seaford' novels, *The Velvet Deer* and *Dear Family*, that I had been unable to source from any library; they were Marjorie's own author copies, each one inscribed on the first page with 'M G C / own copy', dated a few days before publication. The only picture I have ever seen of her hangs on Mary Anne's wall: a semi-profile sketch that shows her elegant, long-necked and pensive, with something of Virginia Woolf's mix of inwardness and hauteur. It is signed 'Gill' and dated 1924, and is believed by the O'Donovan family to have been drawn by one of Eric Gill's daughters.

Three years after my biography of Rose Macaulay was published, I received a letter from a reader in Montreal, Rosina Fontein, who told me that her mother's family had been close friends of the

Cooks in Quebec, and that Marjorie's sister – known as Molly – had been god-mother to her, Rosina's, sister. She wrote that Marjorie had been a 'courtesy aunt' and, in a subsequent letter, a 'good fairy' to her and her sister, staying in touch while she was in England, sending them presents of books every Christmas. In 1949 Rosina and a friend had been in England and had visited Aunt Marjorie in Pulborough, where she had made her home. Rosina had known that Marjorie reviewed books, but until she read my biography of Rose Macaulay, she had had no idea that she also wrote them (private correspondence, 15 April and 30 October 2006).

※

Latchkey Ladies opens in 1917, in the basement dining-room of central London's Mimosa Club, where 25-year-old Anne Carey and her friends are discussing what it means to be a latchkey lady. The Mimosa Club provides 'simple comforts' for single working women; its members, latchkey ladies all, are some of Britain's surplus, superfluous or redundant (as they were variously known) women, whose numbers were increasing daily in this, the third, year of the First World War. Three-quarters of a million British men were killed or gravely injured in the years 1914–1918. The great majority of them were aged between 18 and 30: they were not only the brothers, sons and husbands of the women at home, they were also potential husbands who, had they survived, would have married and created families of their own. The census of 1921 – the year in which *Latchkey Ladies* was published – showed a particularly large gap between the male and female populations aged 25 to 34: 1,158,000 unmarried women and 919,000 unmarried men (Wall nd; Nicholson 2008, vi, 89).

A great deal of breast-beating and soul-searching went on in the pages of the popular press over the question or problem of all these extra women. 'Problem of the Surplus Woman – Two Million Who Can Never Become Wives' ran a typical headline (quoted in Nicholson 2008, xvii). Spinsterhood carried a heavy stigma.

'Spinster' was used in casual parlance to describe 'a disagreeable woman of advanced years, preferably unmarried,' as Rose Macaulay – a spinster herself as was Marjorie Grant Cook – caustically pointed out in a 1925 essay on the use and misuse of language (Macaulay 1925). Anne Carey is actually in possession of a boyfriend, Thomas, who works in the Army Service Corps. Yet although she harbours occasional fantasies of a rural idyll of marriage and children, she knows that at heart she is bored by him.

Britain's gender imbalance was not new: surplus women had been a noted phenomenon in Britain since the middle of the nineteenth century. George Gissing's novel *The Odd Women* was followed by a number of other fictional explorations of the lives of 'odd', that is, unpaired or single, women in a world in which women's existence was validated only by marriage and motherhood. These include novels by F M Mayor, May Sinclair and Dorothy Richardson, as well as by Rose Macaulay and, with *Latchkey Ladies*, Marjorie Grant Cook.

In Gissing's novel, his splendid duo of odd women, Mary Barfoot and Rhoda Nunn, set up an institute to train girls in typing, shorthand and other office skills. At the turn of the twentieth century office work was increasingly offering women an alternative to the manufacturing or retail trade, and for middle-class women an alternative to governessing or paid companionship. In *The Tunnel* (published in 1917 but set pre-War), the third volume of Dorothy Richardson's astonishing stream-of-consciousness multi-volume work *Pilgrimage*, Miriam Henderson, Richardson's protagonist/ narrator/central consciousness, ecstatically embraces the independence achieved with the one pound a week she earns as a dentist's secretary in Wimpole Street.

In 1914 the massive bureaucracy of wartime – the countless lists, classifications, checks and cross-references; the tallies of all the men and machines and provisions; the logistics required to move them from one place to another – demanded a greatly increased clerical workforce. Young men went to the Front; young women, if to consummate their love affair. They take separate trains down to Devon and spend a perfect week together on Exmoor. It is worth remembering the necessary veil of reticence about sex and sexuality employed by novelists of the early twentieth century writing under the threat of the UK's obscenity laws, in order to fully appreciate Marjorie Grant Cook's boldness. Here, on the first night in the low-ceilinged bedroom of the remote farmhouse where they are staying, Anne and Philip's silk dressing-gowns – hers yellow, his dark blue – hang side by side on the wall at the foot of the bed. Anne, sitting on the edge of the bed and looking at them, 'was like some little boat, tossed on the tide beneath an immeasurable sky. She had lost all sense of her personality, and the beating of the tide and the sound of her heart were one.' Dampier has yet to climb the stairs to join her. The text reveals nothing more, but by a clever sleight of hand Marjorie Grant Cook has already given us the metaphoric images for the love-making that follows.

Back in London the relationship continues, and as the war ends Dampier becomes 'the whole of [Anne's] life' (181). In the early months of the new year, she is forced to consider the dreadful possibility that she might be pregnant. There is nothing abstract about this dread. As with Marjorie Grant Cook's handling of the depiction of sexual union, the feeling of dread is rooted in physical sensation: 'fear, actual and cold, woke her at night and lived unsleeping in her mind by day' (223). At Easter, while Dampier is away with his wife and children, it 'woke her in the defenceless hour of dawn. She sat up in bed and faced it at last, shivering so that her teeth chattered, but valiant. She was certain that she was going to have a child'. This is an unusually visceral, urgent account of the recognition that one is pregnant.

Anne decides: 'Dampier must not know' (224).

To whom, then, can she turn for help? She thinks of Aunt Max and her friend Miss Mollond, who had given her work at their school when she walked out of her office job. They are intelligent, cultured, committed to each other (if to no-one else), and capable. But Anne recognises something 'hard' at their core (240). Tellingly, they do not notice when their long-serving parlour-maid, Emma, becomes pregnant. On discovering she has given birth, alone in her attic room, they feel outrage, and immediately throw her out of the house. A similar case of cruelty features in May Sinclair's elliptical, proto-modernist novel of 1922, *The Life and Death of Harriett Frean*.

Anne turns to the other aunt, her Aunt Minnie in Norfolk. Now another woman is introduced into the story, briefly but significantly. Dr Scott, who attends Anne, believes that every woman who wants a child should have one, and that those who do not, should not. She wishes to 'teach [them] how not to' (275). This was at a time when the advocation of birth control even within marriage – the context for Marie Stopes's contraceptive advice in *Married Love* and *Wise Parenthood* (1918 and 1919) – was widely considered scandalous. Yet here we have a woman – her 'mannish, short grey hair' hints at an unorthodox personal life – who holds views that remain under attack a century later, when women still have to argue the case for reproductive rights and a woman's right to choose. Anne's later reflection on her relationship with Dampier also carries a curiously modern ring: 'He gave up nothing for me' (290).

The lives and experiences of single or odd women continued to interest novelists throughout the 1920s and into the 1930s. Published alongside *Latchkey Ladies* in 1921, and referring in its first few pages to the topic of the surplus woman, Rose Macaulay's novel *Dangerous Ages* explores, through the lives of three generations of women in one family, questions about marriage, motherhood, independence, work, love and sex. In the middle generation are three sisters: one is a writer who chooses to live abroad with her married male lover; another, a social worker in London's East End who sets up house with a woman friend. Only one of the sisters leads a conventional life as wife and mother. Macaulay offers no particularly happy endings, but two of her characters find a form of contentment in unconventional places. Throughout the decade Macaulay would continue to explore in her novels (as well as in her journalism) the issue of single women. She worried away at the dichotomy between marriage and its domestic freight, and female creativity.

Other novelists of the 1920s explored these questions in a variety of ways. In Sylvia Townsend Warner's delightfully fantastical *Lolly Willowes* (1926), for example, the eponymous heroine throws off the role of maiden aunt and moves to the countryside where she becomes a witch, spurning family ties for a fulfilling relationship with the Devil. In fiction as in real life, there have always been women who spurn the opportunity to marry, and thereby claim a different meaning of oddness, in a heteronormative society's eyes, from that of unpaired, surplus, left over. Towards the end of the decade, seven years after the publication of *Latchkey Ladies*, Virginia Woolf launched her *Orlando* into a life of gender-bending time-travelling independence. And in 1930 Dorothy L Sayers introduced, in *Strong Poison*, her own clever, independent, strong-minded heroine, Harriet Vane. (Five novels later, Harriet Vane does agree to marry Lord Peter Wimsey, but very much on her own terms.)

How single women survive, and do more than survive, in the modern world of post-war Britain was not a theme to which Marjorie Grant Cook would return. She published only one other novel during the 1920s, 1923's *Another Way of Love*, which is set in turn-of-the-century rural French Canada. It is a family saga that opens with a triple drowning and moves on through male brutality, death in childbirth and another drowning, to conclude in a Gothic finale of madness. In its moving depictions of grief, and of unfulfilled maternal love, you can hear echoes of Anne Carey's fear and grief from the earlier novel.

Marjorie Grant / Grant Cook then appeared to fall silent. However, when the *Times Literary Supplement* opened up its archive in 1999 and uncovered the names of the people who for its first seventy years had been writing anonymously (the tradition of anonymous reviewing was dropped only in 1974), she was revealed to have written hundreds of reviews, fifty or sixty or more each year throughout the 1920s and 1930s.

This is how she is described in the introduction to the *TLS Centenary Archive*:

> Among the most prolific of those who first began writing for the *TLS* in this period was Marjorie Grant Cook, who reviewed more than 1200 books in the 1920s and 30s, including work by many of the leading women writers of the day both in Britain and the USA. Cook was an early advocate of Willa Cather, wrote discriminatingly about the first novels of Rosamond Lehmann, and also reviewed books by Radclyffe Hall, Storm Jameson, Naomi Mitchison, Vita Sackville-West, Edith Wharton and Rebecca West. Her tastes were catholic: she also covered the work of popular authors such as Richmal Crompton and May Sinclair ... But beyond what she wrote, we know next to nothing about her. (*TLS Centenary Archive* 1999)

No wonder she herself had no time to write fiction.

At some point – in the 1920s?, or 1930s? – Marjorie moved from London (where she had a flat near Sloane Square) to Pulborough in Sussex; throughout these years she made regular trips back to Canada to visit her family (appearing on the passenger manifests variously as Marjorie Grant Cook and as Marjorie Cook). In 1934 she published her debut novel as Caroline Seaford, *Glory Jam*, and the following year *More Than Kind*. They are both set in England, as is 1938's *Dear Family*. All three could be described as domestic or family comedies; none of them have lasted well. 1937's *The Velvet Deer*, set in French Canada, is an illustrated children's book with a distinctly morbid streak. In her final novel, *They Grew in Beauty* (1946), she returned once more to French Canada. A powerful family saga like the earlier *Another Way of Love*, it is less Gothic, more disturbing and transgressive by virtue of its everyday setting. At its heart are two sisters, one of whom runs away at the age of sixteen with the family cook (a woman), while the other marries a man she comes to hate and is worn out bearing his children.

In a letter to her publisher Jonathan Cape, in the September following the publication of *They Grew in Beauty*, she referred to it as 'that deadly book, which I now detest and despise'. 'It really is frightful,' she went on. 'How clever of you to sell so many copies.' It is impossible to tell how serious she was being: perhaps she was like Rose Macaulay, who took every opportunity to disparage her own work (even to the extent of asking for her early novels to be removed from the shelves of the London Library and destroyed. The staff of the London Library acceded to the first request but not to the second.) 'I have a new book all but finished,' Marjorie Grant Cook told Jonathan Cape. 'It is melodrama. Nobody is pious or pregnant in it' (MGC to Jonathan Cape, 29 September 1946).

I have found no trace of this or any further novel by Caroline Seaford, or Marjorie Grant, or Marjorie Grant Cook. Marjorie died in Sussex nineteen years later, in 1965. Perhaps there are other novels waiting to be discovered, published for whatever reason under yet other names.

Works cited

Cook, Marjorie Grant (writing as Caroline Seaford) to Jonathan Cape, 29 September 1946. Jonathan Cape archive, University of Reading Library.

Macaulay, Rose, 'Some Enquiries: Into Human Speech' in *A Casual Commentary* (London 1925), 101–106.

McVea, Deborah and Treglown, Jeremy (eds), '*TLS Centenary Archive* 'The second tranche'. *The Times Literary Supplement*, 15 October 1999 (5037), 33.

Nicholson, Virginia, *Singled Out* (London 2008).

Wall, Rosemary, '*Surplus Women*': a legacy of World War One?* [nd], http://ww1centenary.oucs.ox.ac.uk/author/rwall/, licensed as Creative Commons Attribution-Non-Commercial-Share Alike 2.0 UK: England & Wales, accessed April 2021.

Reynolds, Barbara, *Dorothy L Sayers: Her Life and Soul* (London 1993, 1998), 131–178.

Richardson, Dorothy, *Interim* (1919, 1938).

Sayers, Dorothy L, *Strong Poison* (1930, 1988).

Novels by Marjorie Grant Cook

Verdun Days in Paris (Marjorie Grant) (William Collins, 1918)

Latchkey Ladies (M. Grant) (Heinemann, 1921)

Another Way of Love (Marjorie Grant Cook) (Heinemann, 1923)

Glory Jam (Caroline Seaford) (Victor Gollancz, 1934),

More Than Kind (Caroline Seaford) (Victor Gollancz, 1935)

The Velvet Deer (Caroline Seaford, illustrated by Eirene Rowntree) (Lovat Dickson, 1937)

Dear Family (Caroline Seaford) (Victor Gollancz, 1938)

They Grew in Beauty (Caroline Seaford) (Jonathan Cape, 1946)

Note on the text

The text for this edition was digitised from the first edition and then proofread, with typographical errors silently corrected. Some words were modernised by removing hyphens and character spaces no longer in use today.

Author's Note

The characters in this book are entirely fictitious, but the children's poems are genuine and untouched. They were written by little girls under ten years old. If any of the writers should chance to see their forgotten work, I acknowledge my debt to them, and tell them now what pleasure they gave, not only by their poems, but by their affection, their little eagernesses, and their gifts of flowers — slightly faded — stolen off the dinner-table the day after their mothers gave a party.

M G

'… Latchkey ladies, letting themselves in and out
of dismal rooms, being independent and hating it.
All very well for people with gifts and professions,
artists or writers. But for us, the ordinary ones …'

Anne

1 The Mimosa Club

'What the serpent really tempted Eve with,' Anne Carey said gloomily, 'was a latchkey.' She had been too tired to eat the boiled beef — with plentiful greens — that the Mimosa Club provided for members on Thursday nights. But by the time the hot, burnt coffee was handed round, and she had taken the large cup that Dolly the fat-cheeked maid had remembered to bring her — large cup a penny extra — she began to emerge from the physical languor that had kept her silent, and a faint colour came into her face.

Anne when looking into her glass in times of depression was accustomed to condemn herself as plain and pale. Tonight certainly she was both. Feeling a definite ill-temper with life, she entered into the conversation of a group of girls at the next table, who were discussing, half in earnest and half in fun, what on earth could tempt any woman out of the 'sheltered life' provided she were lucky enough to be sheltered.

These girls, buffeting with the world as they did war-work, or any work that would support them, were apt to have moments when independence seemed the most forlorn ambition on earth. A prolonged struggle for a tram or bus in a sleety wind after a long day in an office induced a state of gloomy self-questioning that was not adequately met by boiled beef, with plentiful greens and treacle roll (very little treacle).

'A home and someone to fuss over one would be better,' Lynette Mason, a deaf girl with a thin, throaty voice, said querulously.

'Well, *I* don't know that it would,' broke in Maquita Gilroy with an effervescent laugh. 'At home there were too many of us for much of a fuss, and we got really even less treacle than this. And we weren't allowed to eat off the sticky part and leave the stodge, and dear Mrs Templeton lets us!'

Maquita's words followed one another so swiftly that even to her intimates she seemed to be speaking a foreign language, and Lynette with her deaf ears could not quite follow.

'I mean a luxurious, really comfy home. Fires in your bedroom, and early tea even in wartime,' she repeated on a note of plaintive greed.

'Nonsense, my dear! Why Queen Mary doesn't indulge in such effete vices these days. No fires before lunch-time in the Palace now. And, anyhow, most of us have homes of some sort — why don't we go to them?' Maquita asked.

'Independence. The pleasure of earning money. The desire to escape interference,' Anne suggested. 'The latchkey claims us, and we become slaves of the key! We turn it, and hope it will open a garden of magic to us. Does it?'

'Oh, my dear, it does!' Maquita insisted vivaciously. 'You must see how it does. By the way, I shall work that phrase into a paragraph in the "Odds and Ends" column in the *Fireside* — five shillings on the side, no joke intended! The man who does that page is a dear, and a great pal of mine, Gregory Ames, so nice-looking, but unfit — only you'd never know it — heart.'

'Why is a latchkey irresistible?' Anne pursued, her eyes becoming amused. 'I believe we got it direct from Eve. The apple was not an apple, all great theologians agree about that, but I seem to be the first to discover that it was a key. Eve had been prospecting outside Eden with the serpent before the Fall, and liked it. He probably knew a little side door where no angels were posted, and let Eve into the secret. How else did he get in? He wasn't part of the garden furniture. She had time while Adam was talking politics and history with the angel to slip out and back. I could enlarge on this subject, but I think Lynette and Sophy are too young.'

'The actual Fall was being found out of course,' Maquita said with a sudden high-pitched laugh that made the Hon Mrs Bridson at the far end of the room shudder at finding herself beneath the same roof as anyone so noisy and ill-bred.

'Maquita,' Anne said warningly, 'you're fearfully noisy. Do try and remember that ordinary as we all are, at the other end of the room there is the first cousin of one of the Ladies of the Bedchamber! The Hon Mrs Bridson very nearly goes off in a faint when you screech like that. She is looking so upset now that I'm sure she'll send Miss Spicer to the top of the house for her smelling-salts if you do it again. Do consider poor Miss Spicer.'

'Poor dear, I will,' Maquita promised gaily.

'I think Mrs Bridson is such a handsome old lady,' Sophy Garden said sweetly, glancing reprovingly at Maquita, and then fixing her eyes on the two elderly ladies who sat at the other side of the room, ignoring as markedly as possible the group of girls.

'Of course she is, Sophy. How could the cousin of a Royal lady's maid be anything else?' Anne asked, glancing with faint contempt that was not without a touch of jealousy at Sophy, and speaking with a clever imitation of Mrs Bridson's impressive tones. 'She goes to tea every week at Hampton Court — in the palace, not as you and I go — and somebody from Buckingham Palace takes tea with her once a year. And if you aren't in Debrett don't imagine for a moment that she will smile on you.'

'Oh, Anne, she doesn't really talk like that,' Sophy said colouring a little, but turning off Anne's malice neatly enough.

'More or less,' Anne said a little ashamed. Sophy revered what she called 'the right people', but her snobbishness was more her mother's fault than her own. Besides, she was her guest at the Club for the weekend, and Anne hated to feel that she had been rude. After all, Sophy's mother was far more snobbish than her daughter, and to a love of the peerage added a frank eagerness for the acquaintance of rich people, yet Anne adored her, and put up with Sophy only for her sake. But Mrs Garden had a singular charm which she had not been able to transmit or graft on to her daughter.

'I haven't a real home,' Lynette said rather tiresomely. 'A sister-in-law's house at Penge isn't the same thing, and that's all I've got. The baby cries all night, and my brother's out in Palestine with Allenby.'

They all laughed at her melancholy.

'Well, look what a latchkey did for you,' Maquita said. 'Took you away from a teething baby and put you into a nice cosy Government office at thirty bob a week. You *are* lucky, Lynette! Fancy if you had to get up at night and make the baby's food.'

'I go to Penge on Saturdays,' Lynette said darkly.

'I've got a large, enormous, frequent family,' Maquita said ardently. 'I love every one of them dearly, but I don't go to see them very often. Once you've broken away you don't. What have you got, Anne?'

'I have twin aunts, which is most unusual,' Anne replied seriously. 'With incredible names that I won't disclose. And a married brother, and a young brother at the war. I'm quite popular with them all, but even before the war I took to a latchkey life. I like it.'

'I hate it,' sighed a pretty little girl called Helen. 'I'll never leave home again the minute I've finished my war-work.'

'If the war ever ends,' a frail-looking war bride said sombrely twisting her wedding-ring round on her thin finger. 'Over three years already!'

'Oh, it will soon,' Anne said impatiently. 'Have you any cigs, Maquita? Let's smoke down here and then I'm going straight to bed. Mrs Hickey's in a vicious temper, and the wind is blowing down my chimney so I can't have a fire. Bed for me.'

The dining-room of the Mimosa Club was a warm and cheerful place made out of two basement kitchens of adjoining houses, the kitchen in the third house, also part of the Club, maintaining its original purpose. It was warmed by an old range — on which the Club members were not allowed to heat the water for their hot bottles, much to their indignation — and the walls and lamp-shades were yellow. The small tables set for two, four, and at most six people, carried yellow lustre pots and green ferns kept fresh and pretty and not allowed to fade off into dusty death. Mrs Templeton, the founder and owner of the Club, supervised each detail of its management herself. She was a remarkable woman of sixty, tall and amply proportioned, with a fine face and a character that combined strength and sweetness. Her marriage in early life to a man who had dragged her all over the world, in civilisation and out of it, in his efforts to cover up one failure with another, had inspired her with a passion to have a home of her own in London. When her family had married off and she was a widow, life was suddenly and permanently eased for her by a legacy, not a fortune, but a matter of substantial comfort. She made her home. Then her desire to give women who were working the simple comforts that she had had so frequently to do without led her to turn it into a club. She called it the Mimosa Club to remind herself of the generous warmth and light of Australia, and she charged so little that her original house was soon quite full, and she was obliged to spread beyond its walls. She could not resist the appeals of drifting ladies longing for wholesome meals and enough warmth and light, so she let her club grow. She had meant it chiefly for girls, but she could not refuse older people who begged for admission. Hence the Hon Mrs Bridson and her friend Miss Spicer who had spent each winter at the Club for years past. Mrs Bridson indeed felt that war-work girls should be excluded in favour of the elderly and well born, but she could not convince Mrs Templeton of this.

'What shall I do, Anne, if you go to bed?' Sophy cried dismayed. 'I'm not a bit tired.'

'I'm sorry,' Anne said in apology, 'but really, my dear, I'm all in tonight. I couldn't go out. Why not stay over here with the others for a little and tomorrow we'll racket.'

'I'd take you to the Victoria Palace to see Beatie and Babs, only I've no money,' Maquita said regretfully. 'But I could just manage a movie. Let us go to the Poly and see the film for adults only, 'From the Unknown into the Night,' shall we? — I'm on!'

'I've never been to the theatre without a man,' Sophy said disdainfully.

'Well the men aren't all at the Front. We'll easily pick one up, Sophy,' Maquita promised at the top of her voice, laughing again in the manner that horrified Mrs Bridson, who at the moment passed their table and heard every word.

Anne lifted her eyebrows. Sophy looked angry; Mrs Bridson would think she was one of these common Club girls. Though she was a visitor and not in the least like them she would be judged with the rest. She was indignant. Anne was a dear, but she certainly had noisy, vulgar friends. She looked angrily at Maquita, and then in spite of herself she softened towards her.

Maquita did not look in the very least vulgar with her heavy dark hair brushed in a smooth wing across her forehead, and knotted high and smartly on her head, and her flashing dark eyes and high vitality. Everything she wore was shabby, but had been chosen with care and was worn admirably. She gesticulated with clever and graceful hands like a Frenchwoman. Still, her manners were rowdy, Sophy concluded, half admiring in spite of the smart of Mrs Bridson's cold stare which she had taken as entirely personal.

'Let's all have more coffee to restore us from that appalling chill, my dears,' Maquita said, thumping on the table for Dolly. 'Dear me, how awful it is to have a Lady of the Bedchamber in the family.'

The Hon Mrs Bridson and her friend Miss Spicer made their way up to the general sitting-room in silence and switched on the light. The two plump chintz armchairs in front of the economical fire were unoccupied, and there was no one in the room except an unobtrusive lady who worked for Queen Mary's Needlework Guild writing letters by the light of a small reading-lamp in the corner. Mrs Bridson sank massively into the chair which had all its castors and no broken spring, and drew her skirts off her booted ankles, leaving Miss Spicer to pitch slightly forward in the other chair, which was defective, and to poke the fire into a cautious blaze.

Mrs Bridson was a handsome old lady in the solid British manner of well-cut large features and excellent health. She had the blank expression suitable to a member of a family of which nothing had ever been required but loyalty to King and Church, and which had fulfilled this obligation. Her family on three sides, as she was apt to say in her lighter moments, thus including her husband, had always had one member at least who held a respectable position at Court or in one of the services and qualified later for something rent free and royal in the way of a dwelling.

'That young woman!' Mrs Bridson exclaimed heavily. 'Really I do not know that I can stay here if she continues to do so. She is dreadful. What a manner! What a laugh! I have never before been obliged to associate with such people. Mrs Templeton owes it to the older members of the Club to show a little more discrimination in the admittance of new members. Had I been consulted, Miss Gilroy should certainly have been excluded. Do not destroy the fire, Honoria. I should leave it alone now — I should leave it. These substitutes for wood and coal won't burst into a blaze as I know! But few people poke a fire judiciously. Do pray leave it; I am not remaining in the room long and it will suffice. I was saying that Miss Gilroy's manner is quite shocking.'

'I think she is just high-spirited,' Miss Spicer said defensively. 'It is quite a possession in wartime, don't you think?' She sighed. 'She comes of a large family and must be used to noise.'

'She comes of a very ill-bred one,' Mrs Bridson, said positively, 'She is a constant annoyance to me in the dining-room.'

'She is unconscious of that I am sure,' Miss Spicer said, slightly tart.

'Unconscious! And what business has she to be unconscious? She might learn something in the way of manners — the small outward things at least — were she to pay a little attention to her opportunities,' Mrs Bridson said. 'You are friendly with her, Honoria, and you have beautiful manners. She might imitate you. Your pupils are all distinguished for the same thing. The present Duchess of Swanage — what charm! And Isabelle FitzAlmeric, and the Booth-Pollings, and so many others who have been through your hands. Quite delightful girls, all of them.'

'If the Booth-Pollings have good manners it is the only good thing about them,' Miss Spicer observed drily. 'They were always little liars and thieves — and worse. I could do nothing with them. Virginia married brilliantly the other day, and I almost felt it to be my duty to interview the young man and warn him. But I reflected that after all he was of her own world. Virginia! What a misnomer.'

'Oh well, Honoria, that will do,' Mrs Bridson said uncomfortably. 'Sometimes sad things occur of course. Now that little
Miss Carey is nobody I daresay, and yet she looks a thorough
lady and has excellent manners.'

'She is a lady,' Miss Spicer said, 'and of very good family I
believe, but so is Miss Gilroy. I've always known Gilroys — I
taught the FitzMartin Gilroys for six years.'

'I doubt that girl being related to anyone of birth,' Mrs
Bridson said. 'She has no air of it, no instinct — bouncing
into the dining-room the first thing in the morning, ignoring
me totally, "Oh, Dolly, bring me my breakfast first like a dear,
I'm so awfully late!" What a way to talk to a servant! And
she gets her breakfast first, though I may have been seated
at my table for ten minutes, and simply gobbles it down and
bounces off! What a manner! I can't think why that nice,
aristocratic-looking Miss Carey is so intimate with her.'

Miss Spicer, well-born and highly accomplished, worn
out by training the minds and morals of half Debrett — the
feminine half, to whom she had been governess — retained
in spite of years of disillusion an unconquerable interest and
sympathy for girls, and for girls who made so much of so little
as Maquita, a special warmth of feeling. Maquita's strength
and vitality, her untiring energy and spirit had an appeal for
the tired-out elderly governess that Anne's tranquillity and
reserve had not, though she liked her too. Maquita's sparkle
and colour enchanted the faded delicate woman. Her courage
was amazing to her. She too had struggled, but never in the
actual competition of an office, the hurry of the streets. She
felt old, very far from modern, quite, quite left behind now ...
with her beautiful manners.

'Let us go up to bed,' Mrs Bridson said ponderously, rising.
'I hear those young women coming. I cannot accustom myself
to the feeling of living in a menagerie, which is the air they
give to any room they enter. All but Miss Carey!'

'I shall follow you, Charlotte. I must speak to Mrs Templeton.'

'Tell her what I said,' Mrs Bridson said in a portentous whisper as the room was invaded by a rush of voices and laughter, and she sailed past Sophy, Maquita and the others like a stately frigate, ignoring even the inoffensive Lynette who politely held open the door for her, and said good night in her thin, low voice. She had meant to single out Anne and mark her approval of her aristocratic profile by saying good night pointedly to her, but Anne was not there. She had gone home to bed.

'Being related to an LBC at Buckingham Palace does give you pig-like manners,' Maquita said to Miss Spicer with a high scream of laughter that reached the outraged ears of the poor lady climbing slowly and rheumatically up to her ten-and-sixpenny bedroom.

Most of the girls lived out and came to the Club for meals, and Anne and Maquita had rooms in a house in Belgrave Road. Anne fitted her latchkey into the lock, hating the dark depression of Mrs Hickey's immaculately clean hall as she opened the door. A dim gas-jet burned at the head of the linoleum-covered stairs, and the sound of the coughing of the invalid gentleman who lived on the first floor broke the stillness, A superannuated nurse, visited often by her old 'families', lived in comfort on the second. Higher still were the rooms of Anne, Maquita, and for the weekend, Sophy.

Anne trudged up the three long flights reflecting on the drawbacks of the latchkey life when you couldn't light a fire. She found her voluble landlady in her room, ostensibly turning down the bed, but actually, Anne knew by experience, taking an interested look through her letters.

'It's too bad about the north wind,' Mrs Hickey began at once with plausible sympathy. 'And you coming in tired and wanting your fire, poor young lady! But anyway here's a nice handful of letters you'll be glad of. I brought them up with the hot water, thinking maybe you were in.'

'Thank you,' Anne said coolly. 'I hope the water is really hot as I can't light the fire. And what about coal, Mrs Hickey? I'm not going to pay a shilling a scuttle for stones and dust.'

Mrs Hickey, a spare Irishwoman with an emaciated face lit by ill-tempered dark eyes and crowned by a wild top-knot of black hair, instantly flashed into temper.

'Indeed, complaints is my only lot it seems! You can thank Madeline Duchess of Swanage that you've any coal atall then, Miss! If I didn't know her housekeeper, how would we be off atall? There'd be more than the north wind to keep you from lighting your fire then.'

'Very well. We won't quarrel, Mrs Hickey,' Anne said. 'Good night.' She knew and dreaded the intrusion of the duchess into the conversation. Mrs Hickey had been her lady's maid for some time before she married a lifeguardsman, and drove her lodgers mad with her reminiscences of great company. Mrs Hickey threw her a baleful glance, hesitated, and then decided to descend to the kitchen and finish bullying Alice the slavey, and to engage in combat with Miss Carey at some future date. It was part of her creed to have one devastating quarrel with every lodger, and as yet Anne had maintained a calm neutrality. Mrs Hickey knew no neutrality. The world to her was a battleground, and everyone conspired against an unfortunate widow who let lodgings. Bitter greed contended with a laborious cleanliness in her soul. When she had time for the amenities of life they took the form of gossip with Mrs Pocock the old nurse on her second floor, and indulgence in a brand of port wine decocted from prunes at Twickenham. Her top-knot became wilder and her eyes glittered above her sharp red nose, and her voice was shrill in the basement at such times, and she was apt to weep hysterically, but usually she had the sense to keep out of the way of her lodgers. Anne disliked her, but she liked her room and the cleanliness and order of the house, and as she couldn't endure looking elsewhere for rooms, she endured Mrs Hickey. Maquita, who loved variety even in lodgings, flitted over wide areas, alighting sometimes in Bayswater or further west, and sometimes in Bloomsbury, but after some odd experiences she was now trying Mrs Hickey for the third time, cleanliness and respectability balancing — for a time — a few temperamental storms.

Anne undressed and got into bed as rapidly as possible. Then, wrapped warmly in a yellow quilted silk dressing-gown that had seen better days but which, owing to its comfort, was to see worse, she lay on her side with her arms thrust up under her pillow, making up her mind what to say to Thomas. It would be a great effort to sit up presently and write a letter to him, but with three of his letters to answer something must be done.

'There's really no interest in writing to Thomas,' Anne said, speaking aloud to herself, one of her habits, and yawning. 'And not much in talking to him. Why do I do both so often? Heaven knows — but so do I know of course. He's a man. Oh, how silly women are!'

She yawned again luxuriously, stretching deeper into her warm bed. She looked about her fireless room comfortably. Its orderliness pleased her. She had neat and dainty ways, and wherever she lived her possessions took on a home-like and charming air. Maquita's room looked as if a young tornado swept it once a day.

Anne lay still and her eyes closed. She was twenty-five, but she looked small and childish in bed with her pale golden hair tumbled unbrushed over the pillow. Her face became speculative and sweet. She began vaguely imagining Thomas quite different, and rather richer than he was ever likely to be, and — supposing she married him — their house in the country, and their — possible — little boy. He would be two or three years old, an age Anne adored. She could see him running over the grass. He did not look in the least like Thomas. Anne caught him in her arms.

She sighed and sat up suddenly. Not for worlds would she have disclosed to her latchkey friends that she cherished secret ambitions to live in the country and have a baby two years old.

She took her writing-case off the table and resolutely addressed an envelope to T R Watson, Esq, Lt ASC, at Folkestone. Thomas, unfit for active service on account of his eyesight and a touch of lameness in his knee, was toiling manfully in the ASC. He was unselfish and conscientious and good, and Anne expected to marry him when the war was over.

'Goodness, it is dull, writing to Thomas,' she grumbled, dipping her pen in the ink. 'And how I used to pour out pages about Meredith, and Henry James, and de la Mare's poems, and Lord Dunsany, and Algernon Blackwood. I never can again. I never want to read any of them again, much less write letters about them. The war has killed reading for me. I used to think, like Thomas, that it was exciting to know writers, even by sight. Now they all seem silly and tiresome, and I wish they'd never write again. Well, Henry James and Meredith I needn't complain of. Here goes.

"My dear Thomas, I'm afraid I've taken a long time to answer your last letters, but you know I am awfully busy in the office —"'

2 Simon's Pretty Ladies

'I'll tell you what we'll do, my dears,' Maquita said eagerly. 'We'll all go up to Simon's. His house is such fun — you never know who you'll meet there. Actresses, writers, models, goodness only knows! He'll love Sophy. Do be a sport, Anne, and come.'

They were dining as usual at the Mimosa Club. On Saturdays it was roast mutton with onion sauce.

'I'm willing to be a sport and dodge an air raid,' Anne said, 'only I don't like your Bohemian friends, Maquita. They make me feel mentally dowdy. They dazzle me, and yet I can't see why they should. Really they're as much an imitation as the bowl of goldfish that the men in the street sell. It's only a circle of tin and a paper fish, but it deceives the eye like your friends do, by spinning round.'

'You are rude,' Maquita said without a trace of resentment. 'But Simon isn't exactly a Bohemian. He's got the loveliest house in Clifford Street, and a housekeeper, and servants, and he never goes unshaved. And he is as placid and slow in his movements as a tortoise. Simon doesn't spin. You'll like him, Anne. He may be unconventional, but he's not in the least like all the dears that live at Brook Green and Chelsea — in the short-hairish, queer-meals, studio way I mean. Simon's aesthetic, he loves beauty. He's foreign, exotic — like a big, beautiful panther.'

'Well really, Maquita!' Anne protested. 'I think I prefer the little goldfish dears at Brook Green.'

'Anne, you and Sophy must come,' Maquita said firmly. 'I've known Simon Meebes all my life, and I hadn't seen him for years till I met him by accident in the street last week. I said we'd drop in one night.'

'Why isn't this big, beautiful panther at the war?' Anne demanded.

'Oh, he is, my dear. He's something quite important on the Staff or somewhere, only he's often on leave. He's on leave now. That's why I want to go while he's in town.'

'Is he a gentleman, Maquita,' Sophy asked distrustfully, 'or on a paper or something?'

'He's on a horse most of the time in France,' Maquita screeched with amusement. 'My dear infant, he is certainly a gentleman, though of course he doesn't always behave like one. That's to say he's not an Englishman — but you'll see for yourselves. He's beautifully rich — West Indian plantations, place in Devonshire and interests everywhere.'

'Married?' asked Anne. 'And what is he if he's not English?'

'Technically he is an Englishman — no he is not married — he has a dark streak though. Perhaps it is Italian or Spanish,' Maquita explained rapidly and mysteriously. 'Anyhow he is fascinating.'

'Can we walk into his house? Is it done, Maquita?' Anne asked.

'Oh, there'll be crowds of people, Simon's never alone. His sister, Lady Malloch, is often hostess for him. But anyway any one of us could go to Simon's alone. He is a perfect old dear, and *well* over fifty.'

'You disappoint me very much,' Anne said, as a sudden blight fell on Sophy's face.

'Simon is very fond of actresses — young ones,' Maquita said hesitating. 'He's so good to them — nothing wrong of course, but just to help them on, because he is a thorough artist himself. There are sure to be crowds at his house, and they are fun! They may not be — oh, well, Sophy, you'll enjoy it. Tell Simon about going to see Dorina Daly as the Cash Girl last night. She's one of his protégées. Oh, there you are with the coffee, Dolly. Do let us have it first, like a good child, we're all going out tonight.' She deftly intercepted the tray that was being carried over to the older members of the Club, an action that was not lost upon Mrs Bridson.

'What next, I ask, Honoria, what *next*?' she demanded indignantly. 'This time I shall make a point of seeing Mrs Templeton directly after dinner. The line shall be drawn somewhere. The idea of the servants taking orders from Miss Gilroy!'

The girls went over to their rooms to 'tidy-up', Sophy slightly excited in spite of Mr Meebes' age. Sophy was twenty-one, and very pretty in the apple-blossom and golden style. Her infantile blue eyes were a trifle close together for perfection, and her lips sometimes had a pinched look when she wanted to slip out of her share of expenses, but when she was at her best these slight defects did not show. She had delightful frocks, and she put Anne's old powder blue and Maquita's russet and orange into the shade with her French cornflower and gold. Maquita, generous and unconscious, admired her warmly, and Anne, with the pang of jealousy that Sophy always roused in her, refrained from asking why she had put on her best frock, but refrained also from praise.

Sophy and Anne had been at school together, and though Anne was four years older she had felt a sort of envy of Sophy's 'luck' even then. She always had, and did, nice pleasant things that meant money. Then Anne grew up, and more or less out of necessity took to a 'latchkey life', and knew a good deal about the hard side of such an existence — if not penury and imminent temptation, at least the sharpness of deprivation — by the time that Sophy's mother was planning and carrying out, in spite of the war, a careful campaign for her daughter of amusement and success, with the object of a good settlement in life kept well in view. Anne had worshipped Mrs Garden from her schooldays, and she envied Sophy her mother more than all her amusements and her pretty possessions. Mrs Garden had so much social charm and cleverness that what she wanted she achieved even for a daughter who had looks without a vestige of charm.

When they were shown into Simon Meebes' drawing-room Anne was irresistibly reminded of a scene from a play.

'Peaseblossom — Mustard-seed — Cobweb — Moth!' she said to herself. 'And Bottom has fainted.'

A large fattish man lay on a settee, his head on a pile of silk cushions, his eyes closed, while a group of young women about him ministered to him. One seemed to be massaging his head and eyes with light finger-tips, and one was holding his hands. The others all looked concerned, but not so much concerned that they were not able to smoke.

'Hullo, Simon — hullo, girls,' Maquita called out cheerily, evidently in no way surprised by the group. 'Simon, what is wrong? Do you know what a *perfect* background that tiger head makes to your own?'

'Simon has one of his nervous neuralgic headaches,' said the girl who was massaging him. 'Better now, Diana,' the fat man said in a slow, dreamy voice, pressing the hands of the other ministering child. He opened his eyes and sat up, and gathering energy, rose to his feet.

'Dear Maquita, glad you have come. And these are —?' he said.

'Anne and Sophy,' Maquita said, indicating each one. 'Simon never bothers with surnames,' she explained rapidly to Anne.

'Quite certainly not. Call me Simon, my dears,' the big man said gently. 'I am glad to see you. You must come often. Diana, try that new fox-trot on the gramophone, and Amabel, where are the cigarettes? Maquita, what charming hands you have.'

He patted them, and then walked noiselessly across the room to find the record he wanted. Anne saw the likeness to a great cat that Maquita had indicated. Simon was a curious, heavy-looking man, yet with a feline grace in his movements and a large ease of gesture. His head was striking in an odd, foreign way, with large, very dark eyes, an expressive mouth, and hair worn incongruously long for khaki. He was in colonel's uniform.

He started Diana, a warm-coloured blonde, doing steps with a small dark girl to the tune issuing from the gramophone, and then turned to the three new-comers.

'Sophy, you talk to Lucille,' he said, beckoning a pleasant girl in green over and introducing her, 'and Maquita and Anne come with me. I have something very beautiful to show you. What, Felicity and Alice going? Oh, the rehearsal, yes; run along. Mustn't be late. Good-bye, dears. Come, Maquita.'

He guided her lightly by the shoulder out of the room and up a stair, Anne following slightly bewildered. Mr Meebes was certainly very queer she thought, something between a stage-manager and the chairman of a charity committee. He interested her, but she could not see that he was fascinating. He gave her in fact a feeling that was quite the reverse.

'My latest find,' he murmured, stopping at the door of a large bedroom brilliantly lit by a fantastic number of lights. 'In the chorus at the Dramedy. And not even in the front row. A perfect creature. Astonishing.' His voice faded away. 'Tell me what you think, Maquita and Anne. Look at her.'

They looked.

A girl, straightly built as a slender athletic boy, stood posing before a long mirror for a second girl who was squatting on the floor sketching her. She wore a jade-green tunic falling just below her knees, without sleeves, and her hair was bobbed and turned back from her face in loose, separate curls of rich, shining brown. She was as beautiful as a Greek boy, an acolyte perhaps to some priest of antiquity, and she stood like a statue, but her curved, scarlet lips, her delicate, artificial colouring, her faintly shadowed, long-lashed eyes suggested the decadent air of a tinted statue of Byzantium.

'This is Petunia Garry,' Simon said, looking at her with the greedy expression of a collector who has found a new specimen.

'How is the sketch going, Lorraine? Ah, good! But you haven't done justice to this lovely line.' He stroked Petunia's neck and shoulder with a large soft hand. 'Maquita, have you ever seen a more lovely thing to draw? Look at the lines, at the flow of the whole figure — the wrists, the poise of the head! Petunia, we must get a big artist to paint you.'

The girl, who had been standing with a bored and sulky expression, broke into a smile as audacious as a gipsy, and stretched herself, yawning.

'That's all right, but I'm tired of this, Simon,' she said in a soft, oddly toned voice. 'I want to put some clothes on and have a drink.'

'Of course you shall, dear. I want both of you downstairs now; there are some people coming in. But I specially want you to know Maquita and Anne. Isn't she a clever girl, Anne, to wear jade against that perfect skin? You are clever, Petunia, clever as well as beautiful.'

'Dear old Simon,' Petunia said softly, looking pleased. She threw a glance at Maquita. 'Don't be horrified, will you? I've often sat to artists, so it seems all right to pose like this. But perhaps you think it horrid?'

'My dear, why *not*?' Maquita exclaimed enthusiastically. 'In a nice warm room! And you are so classically beautiful.'

'Lovely child!' Simon murmured in his impersonal, caressing manner. 'Now get into your frock and come down. Diana is dancing. Lorraine, show your Titian hair, dear.'

The girl who was frowning over her drawing-board, glancing from her model to her sketch and back, rubbing out and retouching with charcoal, obediently threw everything aside to unpin a floppy black velvet hat and display a head of gorgeous plaits and waves, arranged to suit her curious Rossetti face and long white neck. She looked adoringly but watchfully at Simon like a dog.

'Do you act too?' Anne asked Lorraine when Simon had gone and Maquita was helping Petunia to dress.

'Me? No,' the girl replied with an accent that did not match the refinement of her face. 'I'm a mannequin for hats and cloaks at Nesbit's. Used to draw fashions for them, but they put me in the show rooms. Red hair is always smart, and you should see the queer colours they dress me up in. Flame velvet, and red hats, and frightful blues. Left to myself, I wear brown and green, but I do light up the salons at Nisbet's and no mistake. You should see the old hags with their faces wrinkled into cracks that no paint will hide buying my frocks, dazzled into thinking they'll look the same in them! It's a funny game! Well, I'm off home. You coming tomorrow?' she said abruptly to Petunia.

'Yes, I think so,' Petunia said.

'Be sure then, and I'll finish the sketch. Otherwise I'm not coming to Simon's every night,' the girl said, turning sulky. She departed.

'I hope you two will be my friends,' Petunia said childishly, looking from Anne to Maquita as they went downstairs. 'I've just come to London, and I'm quite alone. I know some of the girls at the theatre of course, but they are — not quite —'

'I know, my dear, of course not. We'll look after you, won't we, Anne? You are a child, a baby,' Maquita said warmly if vaguely.

'I'm eighteen,' Petunia sighed. She smiled wistfully at them, and then at once left them to speak to a young man in the room, and appeared to forget completely her need for feminine friendship.

Watching her, Anne saw a strange charm in her. She was

thin to the point of fragility, and her young face looked a little worn as if she had lately been deprived of proper food and sleep, but this, added to her youth, was in itself pathetic and charming. There was obviously no occasion for the make-up on her face. Her manner was an odd mixture of natural gentleness and stage tricks of gesture outrageously common. She took little tripping steps across the room on her toes, swinging her hips from side to side in the alluring manner of some footlights favourite, but there was something wistful in her expression. Petunia was so pretty that the rest of Simon's pretty ladies — each one with some quality of beauty — looked like lit candles in the sunlight of her vivid shining.

Their looks were not friendly, but Petunia seemed unconscious of coolness. She was shabbily dressed, and was frankly envious of the other girls' frocks, which were very smart.

The room began to fill with people, and Anne, withdrawing from the inner circle that surrounded Mr Meebes, was content to look on and to talk to such casual guests as drifted by. It amused her to see how naturally Maquita became part of the crowd — her eyes, her hands flashing, her laugh pealing above the other voices. She adored people without discrimination — a party of any sort delighted her, and these chorus girls, and mannequins, and young soldiers were exciting to her. Sophy too seemed to be very happy, and Petunia, when she was not claiming Simon's attention, was charming a Flying Corps officer with his arm in a sling.

Simon, with his noiseless tread, his un-English look and his undisguised preoccupation with the hair and colour and carriage of his young women, was a curious study. Anne disliked him definitely, and thought he wore khaki as if it had been velvet. There was a soft and sinuous something of the jungle about him. It struck her that his dark eyes resembled

Petunia's; she decided that their sadness was an accident of setting and colour. They were wide and brilliant eyes, acute and constantly observant she felt sure. He talked to Anne for a few minutes, but she recognised that in Maquita's phrase she was not his type, and he soon melted silently from her side, after he had introduced her to his sister, Lady Malloch, who came in quite late. Anne was surprised that she should be a plain, elderly woman with an agreeable manner, and a turned-up nose that was almost comic, and more of the market than the jungle about her. She looked at Petunia pleasantly but casually, and took no special notice of the other girls, but greeted some of the young men as if she were glad to see them, and was cordial to Maquita and Anne.

'My brother writes plays, you know,' she said, 'and is very much interested in the stage — always looking for new talent. Miss Garry is his latest discovery. Pretty, isn't she? By the way, Simon tells me he wants her to find new quarters. She's living in a rather rough place, I understand. Would it be possible to get her into your Club, do you think? Simon's idea is that she should leave the stage for a time. She has just finished an engagement. He says she needs training. She looks in need of a rest to me. Oh, so Simon has already spoken to you about it, Miss Gilroy? Well, he is not to impose on you. But if you could help that girl —'

'I'm almost sure there's a room just now, and of course we'll do everything we can,' Anne said. She liked the idea of having Petunia with her oddly mixed manners and her undeniable fascination at the Club. It would be piquant to watch the Hon Mrs Bridson discover her. She was only ignorant, poor little thing, she decided indulgently as she saw Miss Garry pirouetting, with an exaggerated play of eyes, in front of a young soldier she was calling 'Bing dear,' and feeding with spoonfuls of ice with the endearing invitation, 'Eat, little tiger!'

After Lady Malloch had drifted amiably away to play dance music on the piano, Anne suddenly wished that Maquita would come home. The lights, the chatter, the high voices of the girls, the braying gramophone accompanying the piano seemed to have been beating on her nerves for hours and hours, and to be harsh to the point when she could endure it no longer. Anne without warning found herself shivering and then trembling, a way her nerves had of betraying her.

'I can't faint or anything,' she assured herself reasonably. She clutched the edge of her chair and closed her eyes for a moment.

'You look very tired. Would you like to go home? Let me get you a taxi,' a voice said beside her. It was a quiet voice, and it sounded concerned and very kind. Anne, looking up dizzily, saw a man she had noticed come in late and talk for a time to Simon. He was in khaki, but had no look of a soldier. She thought fleetingly that his eyes were as kind as his voice, and wondered if he were a doctor. Her own voice seemed to have vanished when she tried to reply.

'You've had too much of this noise and heat. I'll get a taxi in a moment and take you home, if you will let me,' her friend said. 'You'll feel all right in the fresh air.'

'I'm all right now — thank you very much,' Anne said, sitting up. 'I'm just tired. The Saturday feeling, you know, after the kind of work you hate all the week. The war has invented such imbecile jobs for women, hasn't it? and yet we go on doing them. And I go out so little that I don't seem able to stand a crowded room at night. In the office all day I have to.'

'Why not go home if you are tired? It is late, you know,' the man said, looking at her with penetrating, kind eyes. 'Let me take you.'

It struck Anne that he was very tired himself. She thought he was 'oldish', well over forty probably, and that he had a striking face that was sad and at the same time eager. She gathered up her energy and looked about for Sophy and Maquita.

'I do want to go home,' she admitted, 'but I'm with two other people, and I'll have to see if they're ready. Will you ask them — that tall, dark girl is one — oh!' She dropped back limply, the lights suddenly dipping in a sickening way before her eyes, and her hands turning cold and wet. A window was opened beside her, and she saved herself by leaning out and drinking in the cold air in gasps. Her friend crossed the room, spoke to Maquita, and was back with a glass of wine in his hand.

'Your friends are ready to go,' he said. 'Take a sandwich with your wine. Simon's parties go on till dawn. Better now?'

Anne smiled gratefully at him, but could not eat.

'If you *don't* mind, dear,' Maquita said sympathetically in the dressing-room, helping Anne with her cloak, 'I'll just see you to your taxi and come on with Sophy in half an hour. Dorina Daly is going to sing, and Simon wants to tell me about Petunia — he's anxious for us to be kind to her. But you go home, Anne; Mr —, whatever his name is, Simon's friend, will look after you all right. He looks a dear, doesn't he?'

He may have looked a dear or not, but Anne in the taxi was only half aware of a pleasant, deep voice that talked quietly — about the Zoo, as far as she could make out, and how the animals were standing the war rations and the air raids. Somehow she was so tired that she could hardly make any effort to reply. The taxi went slowly through the dark and foggy streets, and she was almost asleep in her corner.

Actually Anne was almost at breaking point without knowing it. The difficulties of her ordinary day, too long hours, too little food and fresh air, no free time almost, and the common anxiety of the war weighed her down, and the heaviest part of the strain was, as she had said, that she hated her work. Her friend in the cab guessed at much of this, and wondered at more. He had been watching Anne for some time before he had crossed the room to speak to her, thinking that she looked singularly out of place in Simon Meebes' house. Anne had a deceptive look of having been born in a rather delicate and exclusive environment. Actually she had an enquiring spirit that roamed in a most friendly fashion beyond the limits that her reticence and rather shy manner suggested. She loved people even more than Maquita loved parties. She was never shocked except by a hurt to her spirit, and her toleration was remarkable.

'I was wondering,' her companion said as they turned into Belgrave Road, 'if you would come and see us some day? My wife would like so much to know you. She's in Scotland just now, but will be back in a day or two. Like most people, we're generally at home on Sundays. Do come in whenever you are free. We live in Montpelier Square.'

'Oh, are you married?' Anne said dreamily. 'And so am I engaged — to Thomas Watson. How funny, isn't it?'

Her friend laughed. 'I can see that it would be useless to tell you the number of the house,' he said, 'as you're nearly asleep. Here we are at your door, anyhow. Careful with the step.'

'You are so awfully kind,' Anne said, trying to rouse herself. 'I'm ashamed to be so stupid. I must be a little ill I think.'

'Don't work too hard,' he said seriously. 'No office is worth it. Take care of yourself — good night.' He opened the door for her, and watched her into the house.

Anne, stumbling up the long stairs, thought gratefully how soothing his voice had been in the cab talking of the Zoo, and how very kind he had been to her. It was so long since she had had anyone to look after her, even to the extent of taking her home in a cab, that she was touched, in spite of the drowsiness that overwhelmed her.

Later on, waking suddenly and lying in bed with all desire to sleep gone, she remembered that she did not know the name of the man who had escorted her home nor the number of his house in Montpelier Square. Her distress was quite disproportionate to its cause.

'Oh, why was I so stupid,' she said, restlessly tossing about. 'I've lost the chance of making a friend, and I liked him so much.'

Perhaps she was a 'little ill', as she had said. Anyhow, at that hour of the morning, lying unable to sleep, it seemed to her such a calamity not to know the name and address of someone who had kindly driven her home in a taxi, that she began to weep feverishly into her pillow.

3 Anne Walks Out

'Is that the Government's work, that you are paid to do, or private letters, Miss Carey?'

Anne looked up, startled by the insolence of the voice, and rudely recalled to the realities of a Government office. She had forgotten her surroundings for the moment and was jotting down the outline of a one-act play on strips of buff paper. She thought she had a sense of drama, and hoped some day to write a play. At present she seldom got further than the outline. To-day she had an idea for a pantomime play for Petunia Garry, and she was scribbling with a satisfaction that was rudely shattered. She had finished checking her pile of papers and had passed them on to the next table, but now she observed that a new and bigger pile had sprung up at her elbow. She folded her buff slips together. Actuality claimed her.

'Are you going to tell me that's the work you are paid for doing?' repeated the Canadian sergeant who had addressed her.

He lolled against the side of the table, his tunic unbuttoned and both hands thrust into his pockets, a short, coarse-looking man of about thirty-five, his eyes reddened from drink. He stared impudently, and moved his chewing-gum to the other side of his jaw.

'You're taking the Government's time for your own work. You don't come here to write your letters,' he said in a bullying voice. 'I've been watching you, Miss Carey, and your average of work is rotten — just rotten! See! You'd better keep your mind on your job and your love-letters till you get home, see?'

Anne stared at him, shaken by an inward fury that kept her from speaking. Her hands began to tremble, and her temper was so evident even to the partly obscured senses of the sergeant that he moved off and said in a slightly less truculent tone, 'Now mind what I say, and I won't report you this time.'

Anne watched him speechless, her throat dry, as he picked his way unsteadily down the long room, stopping now and then to exchange jocular remarks with the women clerks and soldiers who were all managing to appear very busy at the other tables. As he reached the door and was fumbling uncertainly for the handle, she found her voice.

'Who is that disgusting little object, Mr Keith?' she asked deliberately.

The room looked up startled, but the sergeant thought discretion the better part, and got himself somehow on the other side of the door.

Mr Keith, a red-haired Scottish-Canadian private with bony, raw-looking knees beneath his kilt and a perpetually open mouth, sat two places down the long table from Anne, and did the same sort of work. He looked resentfully at her for drawing him into the publicity which it was his sole aim to avoid. He had passed the entire three and a half years of the war cosily in the office and meant to stay there for life if necessary. He put in his days at present cultivating the affections of a doll-like young person opposite to him who had 'acted in the pictures' and had only been forced by the dearth of men in that profession to seek distraction in an office full of them. Miss Bayly wore a low-cut chiffon frock and a double string of pearls round her plump neck, and giggled coyly at Mr Keith's jokes. He brought her offerings of chocolate and maple-sugar and literature, and was teaching her to chew gum.

Miss Bayly despised but feared Anne. Mr Keith disliked her extremely. He turned his protruding, spectacled eyes on her.

'Do you mean Staff Quartermaster-Sergeant Peters?' he asked impressively. 'He is inspector of Department B.'

'And what authority has he to come in here and speak so insolently?' Anne asked.

'You don't seem to understand that Staff Quartermaster-Sergeant Peters is responsible for this entire floor,' Mr Keith said, feeling this time he had succeeded in snubbing the proud Miss Carey, who seemed to be incapable of understanding military discipline or the importance of the Canadian army. 'It is his business to see that the work is carried on properly.'

Anne laughed, with the mocking look that Mr Keith particularly disliked, and that made him turn uncomfortably redder and subside in his place; he knew that Miss Carey had acquainted herself with his military history, and he resented the fact. He had heard her opinion of what she called the 'Great Imitationary Force' in the office.

'She's a conceited thing,' Miss Bayly wrote soothingly on a scrap of paper and tossed it over to him. Mr Keith returned gallantly, 'Yes, she is, and I wish she was reprimanded oftener,' and tossed it back, and they smiled into each other's eyes.

'Can no one make the Canadian army dress properly or stop chewing gum in office hours?' Anne enquired amiably. 'That little creature would be arrested if he went into the street. I hope he will be!'

'We must get on with the work,' Miss Wilkinson, the head of the room, interrupted fussily. 'Has everyone plenty to do? Be careful how you check the new files, won't you, Miss Carey, dear?'

'Yes,' Anne responded pleasantly.

She did not dislike Miss Wilkinson of the high cheekbones and red-geranium colouring, who had spent her life as a shop clerk but thought it more ladylike as well as more patriotic to be in a Government office in wartime, and meant to aim for 'head bookkeeper in the wholesale' after the war. She was the support of her family at Balham, and she sang; 'Sweet Dreamy F'ices', 'The End of a Perfect D'y', and 'Rowses are Growing in Picardy' were three of her favourite songs.

She melted into sentimental transports when she spoke of these gems, and frequently hummed one or other of them, if it was not Handel's *Largo*. Miss Bayly and Mr Keith had been to musical evenings at Miss Wilkinson's mother's house.

Anne, outwardly calm and inwardly shaken by the attack upon her, turned to the dreary pile of officers' files. She had to check the papers and see that they ran in sequence of dates. Bills, duns, appeals to the P M for an advance of pay, hospital records, claims for lost kit, made monotonous reading. She had to keep count of the letters that were wrongly filed and of those she moved. Eight women and Mr Keith were similarly occupied at her table, each checking the other. It was trivial and silly to a degree, and no one attempted to keep actual count, but wrote down numbers at random, giving in any total from five to eight hundred to Miss Wilkinson at the end of the day. Anne was ashamed to be occupied in 'war-work' so meaningless.

It was the morning of a winter day. A thick fog pressed darkly against the windows and penetrated the room, irritating eyes and throats and producing incessant coughs and sniffs. Electric lights — placed much too high for efficiency or comfort as is usual in Government offices — burnt in extravagant numbers. At each of the three tables sat ten people working at files and indexes and ledgers; others — soldiers and girl clerks — stood beside the cabinets that lined the walls sorting papers and putting them into the drawers. The room was heated insufficiently by hot-air pipes, and was both cold and stuffy. Anne shivered and yawned.

At half-past eleven a whistle blew, a signal that the men might smoke for a quarter of an hour. A notice in conspicuous letters on the wall said, 'Any Woman Clerk Found Smoking Will Be Instantly Dismissed.'

The room was full of noise though conversation was supposed to be subdued, and the door was constantly banged as people came in and out. From rooms above and below the multiple click of typewriters resounded, and messengers came and went with bundles of files. It was a military office, and all the men wore khaki and were supposed to be unfit for active service. A few were unfit; a few had been wounded, but the majority had never left England, and never meant to if they could help it, except to sail back to Canada, a glorious country where, according to Mr Keith, one drank tea at every meal, had furnace heat and blue skies, and where every man was as good as his neighbour, and there were no distinctions except in the number of dollars one possessed.

Anne, who had relations both east and west in Canada, and who had always known a good deal about the country, had loved the idea of working in a Canadian office, but soon had been disillusioned. These office indispensables chewing gum and assuring the admiring English flappers at Gee! they should just see Winnipeg! — that was the life! — and that the Houses of Parliament in Ottawa were *some* buildings, and that all Canadians were one big friendly family united in their love for gum, tea, and the soda-water fountain in the 'drug store' — these statements, and the alternate grumbling and bragging of her fellow-workers had done much to dissipate her prejudice in favour of things Canadian. She knew that she was judging unfairly, and that the scum that comes to the surface in the great cauldron of war gives little taste of real elements of a country, but she was disgusted and contemptuous and did not stop to reflect that other offices equally idiotic were full of equally detestable countrymen of her own.

The smoke added to the stuffiness and chill began to give Anne a headache. She rose and opened a window. A general look of disapproval was cast on her, and Miss Bayly in her chiffon shivered affectedly. Even Miss Wilkinson, methodically licking her forefinger and counting buff slips, remarked after a moment, 'Well, I do s'y I like fresh air as much as anyone else, but fog is fog. Some people are too indulgent of open windows. Consideration is consideration after all!'

'The smoke is rather thick, isn't it?' Anne said deprecatingly.

'Smoke is well known to kill all germs,' Mr Keith remarked indignantly, and unable to bear the sight of Miss Bayly's suffering, he closed the window.

'The English climate let into the house is not at all wholesome. It's not like the dry cold and brilliant sun in Winnipeg,' he said. 'Gee! you should just see Winnipeg at twenty below, and then some, Miss Bayly! But no English fog for me.'

'The Imitationary Force is dreadfully delicate,' Anne said. 'Before I came to this office I used to think Canadians were so hardy. All my cousins seem to be. When do you expect to go out to France, Mr Keith?'

'I am ready to go whenever I am sent,' Mr, Keith said nobly, with a revengeful look in his eye.

'I can't understand any young lady wishing to see more men going to that horrible war,' Miss Bayly said scathingly. 'There's plenty of work to be done at home.'

'Still, we can't keep them back if they want to go, can we, Miss Bayly? If your king and your country need you —' Anne said.

Mr Keith ran a distracted hand through his curling red top-knot.

'If you'll lunch with me at the "Cabin" in Tothill Street — it's not very dear' — he murmured confidentially across the table so as to exclude Anne and the distasteful subject of the war, 'I'll get you that copy of Omer Kame that I saw bound in flowered silk. It's poetry, you know, but everybody reads it, and some of it's been put to music.'

'"Just a Song at Twilight" is one of the sweetest pieces I know,' volunteered Miss Wilkinson, snapping a rubber band round her counted slips, 'and Handel's *Largo*. Of course you don't sing that, but it's grand.'

Anne bent over her task, feeling that the office was unendurable. She had been there for eight months, working from nine to six with an exact hour off for lunch and two free Saturday afternoons in four. She needed the thirty-five shillings a week, and something dogged in her made her hold on. The same mental laziness that made her endure Mrs Hickey and refuse to look for more comfortable rooms made her put up with Department B. She had so little money that she could not afford to do interesting war-work she told herself, and at first it had not been so bad. There had been novelty and even a certain charm in the supervision of the capable Miss Wilkinson and the burly Canadian sergeant-major, who was very polite, and she had been prepared to accept the casual manners of the rest of the clerks as a friendly expression of the new democracy. She enjoyed hearing the life histories of the 'young ladies' and their 'boys' at the Front, though she shrank a trifle from the candour of their confessions, and she tried to be friendly herself. She did not mind the early rising and scrambled breakfasts at the Mimosa Club, the rush to the office, nor, when she got there, the ascent in the crowded lift, and the pushing in the dressing-room for a peg to hang her coat on, and a glimpse into the glass. She was philosophical when her jersey, her fountain-pen, two overall pinafores, and her purse were stolen, as petty thieving was rife and everyone suffered from it. She managed to find the chromatic charms of the dressing-room superintendent interesting, she looked so unlike the sort of person one would choose to look after young girls, and so bad for young officers, many of whom stood about in the passages talking to her in the course of the day.

Anne's work had at first been précis writing vast numbers of letters, and she had become very expert at it before an official with some glimmer of sense and conscience had shut down upon the whole department which toiled forty-eight hours a week to précis valueless documents. The letters had been unimportant, but they were human and often amusing, and there was variety in the work. Anne regretted the change from a small room shared with three pleasant women to the noisy futility of Department B. The task of checking officers' files was even sillier than précising the letters, and Anne hated handling the dirty and ragged papers, and the pretence of keeping a tally of no one knew what. The office became a treadmill, and lately her health and spirits had visibly flagged; but though she was physically tired by long hours and bad air, and bored to tears by the futility, she had not until to-day experienced actual rudeness, and the remembrance of it kept recurring with a shock.

At twelve most of the people in the room went out to lunch. Mr Keith applied a Scotch bonnet to his red head and escorted Miss Bayly in search of food and 'Omer Kame'. Anne snatched an hour of relief in which she could open a window without incurring reproach, and dip into a book which she kept in a drawer for slack moments when the circulation of the files was interrupted.

Her habit of 'making fun', as the office called it, of most things and people in the department, together with an aptitude for becoming absorbed in a pocket Testament, had won her a mixed reputation. Miss Wilkinson thought her no business-woman and unfamiliar with the loveliest pieces of music, but the Testament had convinced her that she was very religious and she respected her accordingly. Miss

Wilkinson had a romantic heart beneath her pink blouse, and she secretly believed that Anne was 'somebody', and admired her, and was flattered because Anne was 'nice' to her. Anne's laughter, her disregard of the office details and discipline that were all-important to Miss Wilkinson's soul, brought a hint of a wider life to the hard-working business-woman who rose at six in the morning to make the family breakfast, who would have found the Mimosa Club a dazzling place compared with the Balham villa.

At one o'clock Anne took her hour off, lunching thriftily at Lyons' or an ABC. She called it 'stoking for efficiency', and had learnt the best combination of cheap foods to support her through the tedious afternoon. Macaroni cheese, bread and jam and a cup of coffee usually made her meal, and she had to force herself to eat it, and often could not succeed, and to the concern of her waitress would pay her bill and leave the food untouched. To-day she idled in the Embankment Gardens throwing crumbs to the seagulls who ambled along the wall on their ungainly kid legs. The fog had lifted, the air was less oppressive, but it was not a cheerful day. At two o'clock she was back in her place facing the worst hours of the day when lassitude of body and mind made sitting upright a torment and the checking papers unbearable.

At four o'clock two young women dressed in brown holland and red caps came in from a restaurant and carried round tea made very strong and noxious in a vast pot. Anne welcomed it as a means of rousing herself from the torpor induced by macaroni and boredom. There was a general scramble to surround the waitresses and buy up their stock of disagreeable biscuits at three a penny. Sometimes they were sold out before they came to Department B, and then there were lamentations.

Anne, sipping the black brew that tasted like lye, began to feel a faint amusement in her surroundings. Work not supposed to stop at tea-time, but there was a general slackening none the less, and tentative flirtations progressed more openly under the genial influence of biscuits and the witch-like potion. Miss Bayly let Mr Keith feel how cold both her hands were, under the outraged eye of Miss Wilkinson, who had strict standards as to the behaviour of perfect ladies and gentlemen, and did not consider that this came within the license of 'a bit of fun'.

Several ladies left their places to cluster round a tall, fair boy reported to have escaped recently from Germany, a newcomer to the room. He looked ill and anxious, and refused to disclose his story, whatever it was. Miss Marsh, a vivacious brunette in black velvet and amber beads (Miss Bayly's hated rival because she too could talk of theatrical matters professionally and belonged to a summer resort troupe called the Purple Pierrots), paid visits about the room volunteering to tell tea-leaf for- tunes. Her entertainment was very popular, and presently she seized Anne's cup.

'Oh, what a queer fortune, Miss Carey!' she exclaimed. 'I see a legacy, my dear, and several presents, and three fellows at least — you are a one! — and a complete change is coming in your life.'

'Well, nothing to do again, Miss Carey,' said Peters' unpleasant voice. 'Now, Miss Marsh, you're busy I know, so hurry to your place like a good little girl. Will you show me exactly how much you've done to-day, Miss Carey.' He lolled beside her chair, staring with insolent familiarity into her face.

Anne glanced casually at him as if he were some curious specimen.

'What you don't seem to understand is that you've got to do as you are told in this office, Miss Carey,' Peters said in a surly voice, leaning over her and putting his hand on her shoulder as if he had some idea of emphasising his words by a half-playful violence.

Anne started up, shaking him off in a flare of rage.

'Take your hand off. I'll report you to the Sergeant-Major. You don't know what you're doing,' she exclaimed in a shaking voice.

She escaped from the room with too much haste for dignity, and she was trembling so much when she encountered the Sergeant-Major in the passage that for a moment she was afraid of giving way to tears. She pulled herself together, avoiding this ignominy.

'I regret it very much, Miss Carey,' the Sergeant- Major said, looking perturbed. He was a big man who liked peace, as he had shown by his aptitude for remaining out of the war, and he was sentimentally inclined towards women as he had recently married his second wife, a very young typist. 'I am sorry Peters was annoying in his manners, but otherwise he was within his rights. He is inspector this week.'

'I have told you that he was insulting,' Anne said furiously. 'It's outrageous to allow a man like that in the same room as women. He ought to be arrested. I shall report him to Colonel Brainerd, or whoever is the head of this vile place. If any of you were real soldiers it would be decently managed.'

'Please don't report him, Miss Carey,' the Sergeant-Major said in visible anxiety. 'I ask you not to. There are reasons why you should overlook this unfortunate incident. I assure you that Peters will apologise and that you will not be troubled again.'

'That's true,' Anne said with sudden quietness, 'because I've no intention of staying here another day. But if I could send that man out to France I'd do it. The soldiers in this building ought to turn in their uniforms and borrow petticoats.'

'Well, I'm sure your sex have been as brave as any,' the

Sergeant-Major said with a worried attempt to be gallant. 'But, Miss Carey, if I tell you that Peters is in serious domestic trouble which accounts for his — his having taken something to drink — will you as a favour let the matter go no further?'

'Canadians and Australians are always in domestic trouble,' Anne said contemptuously. 'It's their bad habit of having three or four wives apiece. Good-bye, Sergeant-Major. I've never been in a Government office before, and I hope never to be in another as long as I live. Don't be afraid, I shall not speak of that little horror. But I advise you to encourage him to go to the war. It might turn him into something decent.'

She shook hands with the S-M and walked down the passage, and rapped at a door marked *Mr Mallison. Private.* She supposed the civilian head of Department B who had engaged her should also accept her resignation.

A soldier opened the door for her. Mr Mallison sent him messages and called him his aide-de-camp, feeling quite military. Mr Mallison could see her. He was seated at his desk, a thin, sleek man with spectacles and a retreating forehead and chin, who greeted her with unctuous jocoseness. Tact was his forte and 'human uplift' and 'the urge to betterment' his hobby. He was an Englishman, but an apostle of a type of American culture exemplified by a gentleman with sandals and long hair, whose portrait hung over his desk.

'Ah, Miss Carey, so you have stolen a moment from 'the cares that infest the day' to seek a word of mental intercourse. How wise. And what message can I give you that will put you in tune with the universe? Do the wheels of your little world need oiling? Remember that we ourselves make our own sunshine, and can always share it with a friend.'

'I have come to resign,' Anne said directly. 'Good-bye, Mr Mallison. You have always been very considerate.'

'Resign?' Mr Mallison said, looking patient and surprised. 'You must not do that so suddenly. Is it some little friction or jealousy in your work? The sense of the infinite, carried into daily life, must be greater than small daily frets. Take a day to reflect. The responsible citizen does not act on impulse but on reflection.'

'I'm leaving now,' Anne said. Her decision was taken and she began to feel an exciting sense of freedom.

'The regulations require you to give a week's notice in writing of your desire to resign, stating your reasons for the proposed step,' Mr Mallison said, impressively official. 'Address the letter to me and it will be placed before the proper authorities, who will then release you. But I beg you to reflect. This is momentary nerve-strain I am convinced. To yield to such impulse is weakness.'

Anne smiled politely.

'There is generally a reason for nerve strain,' she said. 'I am going without writing a word to anybody. I'd feel guilty if I added a word to the mass of silly rubbish that fills this office. If I wrote a letter it would circulate through the building for weeks, being checked, and minuted, and observed, and trimmed with scissors. It's much simpler to walk out.'

'But, Miss Carey, if you leave without warning you forfeit a week's salary,' Mr Mallison said, perturbed into directness.

Anne smiled at him again, but her voice was serious, with a poignant hint in it as she said, 'Mr Mallison, I am so thankful to go that I don't mind even that. I've spent the most horrible months of my life in this office. I haven't one pleasant recollection of it. There is no real work done in any part of it. The men are slackers, and some of the women are — well, curious! I must have been mesmerised to stay so long. No one with any self-respect would be here for ten minutes.'

Mr Mallison blinked rapidly and looked as if he were going to sneeze; he gathered support from a hasty glance at the oleographed calm of Elbert Hubbard.

'Feminine exaggeration, and I am afraid — temper,' he

said blandly. 'The undisciplined sex. Let me suggest a simple mind exercise. Say over to yourself resolutely —'

'Good-bye, Mr Mallison,' Anne said.

She dressed in the deserted cloak-room thankful that it was for the last time, and nodded a farewell to the chromatic supervisor.

The dim street seemed spacious and beautiful to her; the fog had cleared away and stars pricked the dark sky, cut by remote, infrequent searchlights. Anne was free; the burden of life in the office had been greater than she had realised, and she said bitterly to herself that it was like recovering from an illness to get away from those people. She could regret no one of them. In six months anywhere else she had always made warm and sometimes intimate friends, but experience in this Canadian office had left only the hope that she would never again see anyone she had ever known there.

'How adorable to be out of a job, and a week out of pocket — and free,' Anne said, rejoicing. Then she remembered Miss Wilkinson who had invariably been good-tempered and patient, ready to teach newcomers the ridiculous routine, and not too unwilling to have the window opened. She would send her a new song — new to Miss Wilkinson, but tried and trusted, all about roses in a garden. Impulse made her turn back towards the gloomy Thames-side prison — so it seemed in the prospect of unfettered tomorrow — from which she had just emerged. It would be churlish to vanish without a word to Miss Wilkinson, who in varying shades of pink had met the punctual day with an unfailing cheerfulness and a special greeting to Anne. She would go back. When she re-entered the room the entire staff was in readiness to spring towards the door the moment the liberating six o'clock whistle blew. There were still a few minutes to spare, and everyone continued some pretence of work, but actually, as Anne well knew, nothing was being done, and pens and pencils, indexes and files, were safely locked away. Her appearance created a mild excitement among the jaded women and piebald soldiery as she had rudely called the refugees. Miss Marsh remarked admiringly to her neighbour, 'Well, I must say Miss Carey looks distangy in her costume and furs,' and Mr Keith whispered humorously to Miss Bayly, 'Gee! Her Royal Highness has got a fine colour as the result of to-day's little cataclysm with the Q-M-S!'

Miss Wilkinson, unbending from her stern business attitude as she usually did in the last half-hour of the day's work, was sorting out the contents of her drawer and humming loudly, occasionally informing someone in semi-recitative that she would be w'iting when the d'y was done. She shook an admonishing finger at Anne.

'Naughty girl,' she said playfully, 'to stay out of the room so long and not tell me you had permission from the S-M to go home early. He had to come and tell me himself. Naughty girl!'

Anne drew her aside and told her she was leaving.

'I am sorry to say good-bye to you, Miss Wilkinson,' she said. 'Thank you for your patience. I don't know how you put up with everyone.'

'Oh, Miss Carey, you are too kind,' Miss Wilkinson said, blushing with pleasure. 'I knew you didn't take to the work and were wasted here, but I've liked your company. Some of the young ladies are not very well brought up, and that's a thing I'm not used to. But often and often I've said to myself, "Miss Carey is beautifully brought up, and anyone can see it, but she's not the business kind." And sorry as I am you're going, I do truly hope your next engagement will be more congenial. A writing job I should say would suit you, you seem to write and read so much.'

She shook Anne's hand. 'I know what it is to be artistic, and that's what you are,' she said earnestly. 'I've a brother just the same, in an architect's office, and always wanting to be painting portraits. And you see what I am myself about singing. I could leave my work any moment of the day for it, only it wouldn't be right to do so.'

Anne rather hastily disclaimed any ambition to be artistic, and then the whistle went, and the room sprang instantaneously to its feet and made a plunge towards the door. Miss Wilkinson slipped her arm through Anne's and they followed the crowd more slowly. All along the parallel and transverse passages doors were opening to let eager and tired people pour into the mainstream. The air was vitiated, and the glaring lights and high-pitched, cumulative chatter struck the nerves like a blow. Anne watched the scramble for the lift down to the dressing-rooms — B was the top floor — and the dismay of those who were left over for 'next trip, please', with wonder that already she felt detached from it all. Miss Wilkinson insisted on 'seeing her off' before going to put on her own things. Anne wedged into the descending lift among a mass of tired and unaired office humanity, caught a last glimpse of her smiling, valiant face and rose-coloured blouse as she waved a cheerful farewell. She was glad that she had gone back.

London was wonderful. In wartime, with its feeling of steadfast concentration, perhaps more wonderful than ever before. The darkness of the streets, the lamps few and dimmed by green paint, fascinated Anne again. The taxis with their blurred lights, the cavernous, lumbering drays and unlit buses were vehicles of mystery, and the masses of buildings showing no gleam took on the solid form of a vast forest at night; high over all flashed the incessant wings of the searchlights. Anne went out of her way to walk through Dean's Yard. The ghostliness of the cloisters and the outline of the Abbey against the sky rested her tired mind. There was a pale brightness over the river.

The exhilaration of the morning that had been rudely but perhaps not unjustly shattered returned to her as she strolled along Victoria Street and struck into the crooked ways that lie behind the Stores. They were full of Australian soldiers making for a popular canteen, cheerful giants, always polite to women.

Anne thought of Petunia Garry with a speculative interest as to how Mrs Bridson would take her, recalling her beauty with a vivid pleasure. She might really write a play for Petunia that would bring them both success. Meantime she would have breakfast in bed tomorrow, if she could get round Mrs Hickey …

In a tiny cross-street she came upon a Salvationist giving a little company of ragged children physical drill in the middle of the street. She had an oil-lantern burning on the pavement, and she clapped her hands and swayed her body vigorously, singing all the time she worked. The children, armed with small dumb-bells, responded with enthusiasm, enjoying it immensely, and lifting their voices with a will.

"'My sins which were many were all washed away" (bend from the waist, children, knees stiff) "When Jesus came into my heart,'" sang the Salvation sister, beating time. The children bent and straightened themselves and clapped their dumb-bells together, warming themselves by the exercise, the light of the lantern striking on their pleased faces, their voices following flatly the flat, high voice of their teacher.

> My sins which were many were all washed away
> When Jesus came into my heart.

One little fellow sang manfully, his action with the dumb-bells quite out of time, but full of an intentness and joy that made Anne smile. He tried hard to do what the others did without much success. No one minded. He sang as loudly as anyone, and evidently the religious feeling was the thing.

Anne watched. She could not see any child without sympathy, and something about this waif touched her. She stood looking at his efforts, wondering if anyone petted him, inclined to kiss him, grime and all.

The hymn stopped abruptly. Dumb-bells were stacked on the pavement beside the lantern, and the Salvation sister gathered the children round her to pray. She put her arm around the little chap, and he wriggled from it and touched his dumb-bells longingly.

'No air raid can hurt us, children,' the Salvationist said, 'God is so close.'

London was wonderful, Anne thought again as she turned into Belgrave Road.

4 Melancthon

Anne had breakfast in bed next morning, and for several mornings in succession. She did not get up at all in fact, but lay without sufficient energy even to read, each morning saying she thought she would get up in the afternoon, and every afternoon deciding that it was not worth the trouble.

Mrs Hickey was so far amenable that she allowed Alice to take her up her breakfast, a cup of tea and a slice of bread and margarine, and Maquita used her precious lunch hour to dash back to Belgrave Road to make soup for her and take her the papers, and tell her amusing incidents of her day's work. Maquita was in a department of the War Office that concerned itself with wound gratuities, and she enjoyed herself thoroughly and was always suspecting and foretelling the most thrilling events on the Western Front from what she imagined she heard or saw in her office.

'I don't know in the least who he *was*, my dear,' she would say mysteriously, in reference to some fragment of conversation that she had half overheard between two generals in Whitehall, 'but he gave me the feeling that he *knew*.'

Anne roused herself when Maquita came in, or at night when Lynette Mason and Mrs Arnold and the others climbed up to her room to ask how she felt, but for the rest of the day she was content to lie idle, sleeping a little and conscious of the overwhelming relief of not having to go to her office.

She had a long letter from Mr Mallison advising her to take a week's sick-leave and then to return to her duties, which however humble must be carried on, but she did not trouble to answer it for the present. Nor did she write to Thomas at Folkestone.

At the Mimosa Club she was missed, and after the fourth day of her absence, Mrs Bridson waived her personal prejudice against acknowledging Miss Gilroy's existence, and asked her about Anne.

'I am sorry to hear that Miss Carey is in bed ill,' Mrs Bridson said with some concern in her dignified condescension. 'I hope that she will soon be better. You might tell her that I asked for her — Mrs Bridson.'

'Oh! yes, I will,' Maquita responded cheerfully. 'But Anne isn't exactly ill. She's really only suffering from Canadianitis. It's horrid, but she'll get over it.'

'Canadianitis? I am afraid I do not quite understand,' Mrs Bridson said questioningly.

'I mean she has been working in a most horrible office with most horrible Canadians, and it has got on her nerves,' Maquita explained with a giggle. 'Now that she has left she'll be all right. I daresay she'll be up tomorrow or next day.'

'Canadians horrible! I have never heard such a thing said before,' Mrs Bridson said, stiffening indignantly. 'My second cousin was Governor-General in Canada some years ago, and he always said that the people were most respectable — most!'

'Ah, but I don't suppose he was bullied by sergeants who had had too much to drink,' Maquita said with an irrepressible burst of mirth.

'Bullied by sergeants! A Governor-General and an earl!' Mrs Bridson exclaimed. The depths of Miss Gilroy's barbarian ignorance had never been more fully exposed.

'Oh, well of course he wouldn't be,' Maquita agreed.

'But do you mean to tell me that Miss Carey — a lady — has been exposed to such a thing? How shocking.' Mrs Bridson began to go purple.

'Anne had bad luck,' Maquita said more soberly. 'I know lots of nice Canadians and so does she, but they happened to be the other sort in her office, and she wasn't at all happy.'

'I don't approve of these rough offices for ladies, war or no war,' Mrs Bridson said with decision. 'Nursing, yes, that is a woman's profession. But the idea of Miss Carey being spoken to by a sergeant. It is most shocking.'

Maquita repeated this conversation to Anne with considerable embellishments, and took her a copy of the *Spectator* at the same time, lent by Mrs Bridson as being light to hold, and an excellent paper.

When Anne had been the best part of a week in bed, Mrs Hickey could be quelled no longer. She arrived in her bedroom one morning after Maquita had gone, armed with brooms and pails and cloths and cleaning apparatus, her eyes flashing, her black top-knot askew, announcing that sick or well, lodgers had a right to have their rooms cleaned, and God help her if she could put up with the dirt of the place any longer.

'But let you lie still,' she said in a threatening voice to Anne, pulling at the blind with an ill-temper that sent it up with a violent jerk and locked it inextricably at the top. 'Let you lie still in bed, since you're ill, and Alice and I will clean round. God knows the room needs it after this length of time. I could lie in bed myself, the dear knows I'm tired and sick often enough keeping this house decent, and the price coal is and people that onreasonable with their hot water. Drat this cord, whatever's been done to it, it's caught now. Fetch the steps, Alice — fetch the steps, ye poor stupid thing,' she bawled into the ear of the poor, deaf slattern who had followed her into the room.

Anne sat up in bed shrinking from the rush of cold daylight in her eyes and the shrill voice of her termagant landlady.

'Mrs Hickey,' she said hurriedly, 'you can't come into my room till I get up. You can clean it when I am better. Please take away all those things at once.'

'I'll not then,' Mrs Hickey declared, flapping and jerking

the blind cord till she brought the whole thing down on the floor. 'I'm a decent woman, and I keep a decent house, but it's no thanks to my lodgers if I do. Will I leave this room another day, full of dust and dirt as it is, and the carpet near ruined with ashes from the grate? I will not then! Ten pounds I paid for that carpet in Victoria Street, and for all the care it gets you might as well have a rag rug. The dear knows you've been in bed long enough. I don't want lodgers that's always in the house. I let my rooms on the understanding that you and Miss Gilroy would be out the whole day, and I could keep the rooms clean and decent. I don't want lodgers that lie in bed all day, asking for trays to be carried up to them by them as is far less able to climb stairs. I've had enough of it, so I have!'

'Will you stop talking, Mrs Hickey?' Anne said angrily. 'Go out of my room. You are extremely impertinent. I made no agreement with you to be out all day, and this room is mine as long as I choose to pay for it. I'll give you a week's notice now, and for Miss Gilroy as well. She is not likely to come back to you this time, and it is not very good for your house to behave as you do. Now will you please leave my room?'

'I'll not leave your room till I've brushed the carpet and dusted round and washed the woodwork, and so I tell you,' shrieked Mrs Hickey, her thin, sharp features flushing a violent red. 'And I take your notice, and if you'd leave this minute of the day I'd be pleased to see you go, you and Miss Gilroy — untidy as she is. I've lived in the best families, and I know how to behave if anyone does, let alone how others should behave to me. Was I in Hamilton Place for six years — did I live in a castle in Ireland housekeeping for a peer — is it Madeline Duchess of Swanage comes to ask how am I getting on, and what class of young ladies I get, because she could send me titled people doing war-work who'd be glad and thankful to get into a house that's kept as clean as any house in Mayfair — what class of lodger, have I got just now —?'

Here Alice came in panting a little from toiling up from the basement with the steps, which she set up against the window, and Mrs Hickey's speech was interrupted while she adjusted the green blind and scolded the servant. Alice, looking cold and cowed, was an elderly woman, a little lame and very deaf, who believed that Mrs Hickey kept her out of charity when no one else would have put up with her disabilities. The patient creature was overworked and underfed, and slept on a mattress on the brick floor of the scullery, tormented with cold and rheumatism. She knew that Mrs Hickey was 'quick-tempered', but the incessant scolding voice fell unheeded on her ears. She had the quick observation of the deaf, and now she saw that Anne, who was always kind and considerate to her, and had given her a warm jersey and a raincoat, looked angry and upset.

Anne pointed to the door and motioned Alice to go, and the woman, after looking from her employer to Miss Carey in a frightened way, went.

'Now Mrs, Hickey,' Anne said very quietly when the blind was put up, 'you will please leave my room — I am going over to the Club this afternoon, and you can do as you like then. I don't want to hear anything more. I'll have the blind drawn half-way, as it was. Thank you.'

'You're a hard young lady, that's what you are, a hard young lady,' Mrs Hickey said, looking at her fixedly. 'I try to do the best I can for you to keep you comfortable. I work my fingers to the bone to keep this house clean, I go out in the rain and get coal. Do I want my lodgers complaining that I don't dust properly, and that they never get any hot water in the taps? God knows I do my best. I've lived in the best families — six years in Hamilton Place — and you give me notice, you and

Miss Gilroy, and leave my rooms empty, and how will I pay my rent and taxes without lodgers? I'll go to the poor-house and take Alice with me, the poor, decent creature, oppressed with cold.'

Mrs Hickey's voice having grown higher and more tremulous was now extinguished in a burst of tears, and she departed belowstairs to seek the comfort of a little more Twickenham port.

It was thus partly owing to Mrs Hickey's long-threatened outburst having at last come off that Maquita, rushing into the Club drawing-room before dinner, found Anne seated in front of the fire in one chintz armchair — the one that tilted — talking with great friendliness to the Hon Mrs Bridson, who was seated in the chintz chair which was sound. On the sofa Miss Spicer was displaying a nearly completed woollen jersey to Petunia Garry who had just arrived and was looking a trifle out of her element.

'And the border can be in any pretty contrasting shade,' Miss Spicer said in her finished little manner. 'I must show you the stitch if you are fond of knitting, Miss Garry.'

'Oh, thank you so much,' Petunia murmured gently. 'Yes, I do like it. I am good with my hands.' She spread out her rather thin and sallow hands, with long fingers and tapering nails, on her knee, and looked at them with childish complacence. Like a child, too, Miss Spicer reflected with some interest, she seemed not to notice that they needed washing. The poor child showed other signs of neglect too. She seemed very young and very delicate, but Miss Spicer shrewdly suspected that she was more childlike in appearance than in mind.

'Oh, there's Miss Gilroy,' Petunia exclaimed, joyfully running to meet her. 'I've come — I've got a room here. I saw that nice Mrs Templeton and told her that you and Miss Carey knew me. Wasn't it nice finding Miss Carey here?' She looked sweetly at Anne.

Maquita was enthusiastic in her welcome, and after congratulating Anne on being well enough to get up and come to dinner, she went off to see Petunia's room with her.

'Who — ah — is the new Club member?' Mrs Bridson asked Anne majestically. She had taken no notice whatever of Petunia while she was in the room, although for the last hour both Anne and Miss Spicer had been talking to her, and Anne had attempted to introduce her, but had only succeeded in making Mrs Bridson give a frigid nod.

'I don't know her very well — she's Miss Garry — Lady Malloch asked me to be kind to her,' Anne said artfully.

'Malloch — that will be Sir Eustace Malloch's wife?' Mrs Bridson said with interest. 'In the Foreign Office, or is it the Admiralty, Honoria? You must know Eustace Malloch.'

'Very well indeed. I remember him in Scotland — such a fat little man on the moors. Foreign Office, but insignificant.'

'Possibly politically,' Mrs Bridson admitted coldly. 'But the point is that Miss Garry comes to us with some sort of introduction. That is not insignificant, it is a matter for thankfulness, I consider, in these haphazard days, when one is expected to ignore all social distinctions — most undesirable in my opinion. I am glad to know that Miss Garry is vouched for by Lady Malloch. She was one of the Dorset Shelburnes.'

Her interest in her own assertions carried her ruminantly down to dinner without further questions being put to Anne, and Petunia was accordingly admitted to the circle of Mrs Bridson's acquaintance. She treated her with decided stiffness all the same, not quite satisfied with her hair, her walk, her apparent dislike to washing her hands, her inexplicable smile, and her accent — unplaceable rather than wrong — all of which points she observed one by one. But with Sir Eustace Malloch floating in a muddled fashion through her brain it was some time before the honourable lady made any adverse comment even to Honoria Spicer.

Anne was not exactly in a position to be idle, although she had an invitation from the younger of her twin aunts to spend an indefinite time with her at her house in Norfolk. Without considering this alternative — except as an emergency — she decided to take two or three weeks' holiday. She felt affluent with a bank balance left over from Christmas presents, so she dismissed the petty anxieties of life — which Anne could do readily — and set about enjoying the fresh air and faint, infrequent sunshine of London mornings in early spring.

A schoolboy in holiday time knows something of the glorious freedom that Anne felt every morning, when Maquita and all the other workers were hurrying to their offices and she could turn her steps to the parks, but only the victim of futile drudgery such as Anne's had been could fully appreciate the joy of Kensington Gardens at ten o'clock in the morning.

She was lonely, but not to the point of sadness, merely aware of her isolation, and London is friendly and companionable to this form of solitude. She found amusement in the children playing in the Gardens under the eye of their nurses or elder sisters, and taking their fathers for a walk on Sundays by Peter Pan's statue and the shallow where the ducks fed and where the swans would presently parade their grey babies with anxious pride. She liked to discern the mist of green deepen over the trees.

'How strange to live so close to the tulips as that,' Anne remarked one morning, watching a diminutive person shaped like a mushroom wildly escaping from authority into a jungle of shrubs, to be hauled back ignominiously and slapped by her nurse who was pushing a pram with an infant in it. The child did not cry. She hesitated, looked with regret at a red tulip that called to her to pluck its glowing head off, and then trotted sedately along the path in the wake of her nurse and baby brother, accepting her retrieval calmly. Adventure and misadventure seemed to find her prepared. Her solid little person keeping to the paths of rectitude presently, however, met the impact of a high-spirited Aberdeen terrier, frolicking ahead of his master, and evidently expecting such small fry as the mushroom child to clear the way for little dogs pretending to be express trains. The mushroom child collapsed forwards, and a startled wail smote the air. Anne ran to pick her up, but the dog's master reached her first, and was setting her to rights and admiring her pretty boots with so much tact that a second howl was suspended half-way, while a pair of small arms clasped him tightly round the neck. Anne and the nurse reached her simultaneously.

'I'm so sorry my terrier frightened her. His only excuse is that he's not much older than she is,' the dog's owner explained to the nurse, and Anne recognised the voice. 'He's only one and a half.'

'Miss Sheila's two,' the nurse said, and retrieved her dumpling charge a second time, putting her for safety at the other end of the infant's pram. 'And there you'll stay, Miss Sheila,' she said, wheeling it off.

The infant resigned herself and waved a cheerful small fist. Anne laughed, and turned to speak to her friend of the taxi-cab.

'Miss Carey,' he said, having recognised her with evident pleasure. 'And how are you? I'm so glad I've met you. My wife was going to call, and I stupidly never took the number of your house. Still, I meant to go and ask for you from door to door! Are you better?'

'Much less sleepy,' Anne said, gravely looking at him with frank interest, and finding that her memory was at fault in some particulars — he was younger-looking than she had thought, for one thing. 'I apologise for that night. You must have thought me almost imbecile. I never thanked you — I don't know your name.'

'You owed me no thanks, but in any case you were very polite indeed,' he said, smiling at her. 'Why not sit down in the sun for a few moments if it's not too cold? Or were you walking?'

They sat watching the ducks and the children, Anne making friends with Nemo the terrier — who was scolded for capsizing a lady — and thinking that something pleasant and unexpected had been added to her holiday morning. Presently she said, 'I still don't know your name?'

'Dampier,' he said. 'Meebes didn't happen to mention it to you?'

'I've never seen Mr Meebes since the party,' Anne said. 'Anything Dampier, please?'

'Philip,' he returned. 'I'm glad you haven't been back to Simon's house. Do you often go?'

'I've only been once, and I'd never seen him before,' Anne said, wondering why he expressed himself so definitely. 'I doubt if I'll ever go again. I'm not Mr Meebes' "type", as Maquita says.'

'No, you're not,' he said drily. 'Miss Gilroy is the tall, dark girl with the astounding vitality, isn't she? Nice to see, even in this age of super-women. Our splendid bus conductresses and window-cleaners and land-girls are a hefty lot, but Miss Gilroy's nervous energy seemed to me remarkable.'

'It is,' Anne said. 'And when she really *is* tired and it flickers, if you want her help in any way up it pops again in a moment. But you seem to scoff a little at "our splendid women", and I'm one of them — more or less — anyhow I work — so I resent it. Do you scoff?'

'Far from it,' he assured her. 'At their Press notices, perhaps. But that is not their fault — altogether.'

Anne laughed. She said, 'To return — is Mr Meebes a friend of yours? Why were *you* at his house? He's awfully queer, isn't he?'

'Oh, old Simon's a foreigner,' Dampier answered lightly. 'Among other things he writes, and he does some work for a *Review* that I am supposed to edit. Actually I turned it over to someone else at the beginning of the war, but I retain a friendly interest in it. Simon writes remarkably well. He's doing some very sound articles on the basis of the coming peace.'

'Of course you write too,' Anne said, light breaking upon her. 'You write plays, I remember. You wrote *Melancthon*. You are P M Dampier — Thomas and I read it together, and I loved it. And *Mnemosyne* — those little poems. They were horribly sad.' She did not say that she found it exciting to know a 'real' writer, but she felt an interest in literature — that she had told herself, in connection with a letter to Thomas, was war-killed — begin suddenly to revive. The author of *Melancthon* had a distinct place in her memory. Her face kindled. 'Do you know you are one of the three people I've always wanted to meet,' she confessed, half making fun of herself. 'Barrie, Galsworthy, and P M Dampier. Then I dropped out Galsworthy.'

'That seems a pity,' Dampier said gravely. 'He's one of the few sincere writers in England.'

'Well then, he's a little hysterical or something over the war. I can't bear his present manner,' Anne said. 'And of course I never should meet him or Barrie either, and if I did they wouldn't speak to me. I don't know how I came to meet you. I liked your play so much.'

Dampier flushed faintly; although he was amused by her enthusiasm he was pleased too, and a little touched. It seemed to him very, very young and ingenuous to take an interest in authors as authors. They were an egotistic, tiresome breed to him, and he avoided them as much as possible at his Club. They either told you carefully rehearsed impromptu stories that were good enough, or else they sat in anxious and jealous silence afraid of losing money or reputation by giving away an idea or a phrase.

'I am glad you like it,' he said, his sensitive face almost shy.

'You make Melancthon so human, so alive. I found myself getting more and more interested in his ideas. And the scene with his mother was wonderful. I used to read French plays with a funny little French governess who cried her eyes out over *L'Aiglon*, and would sit mopping her little wet face and sobbing out to me, "Continue, continue, I enjoy it when my heart breaks." I was like that — I mean I couldn't read out loud any more of it to Thomas,' Anne said, recalling her ardour with shining eyes. 'My heart broke — and yet I enjoyed that play.'

'You are dreadfully flattering,' Dampier said, 'or dreadfully sentimental! What else did you read with the French governess?'

'Everything — she thrilled with rapture over *Cyrano* too. She was drowned and speechless over his death in the convent garden,' Anne said. 'But let's talk about you. Are you writing now?'

'Nothing,' he said. 'I feel as if I could never again. But perhaps after the war —'

'Perhaps, I know,' Anne responded. She looked at him critically, and his sad grey eyes met hers, studying her face with no less interest.

'P M Dampier,' she said. 'And your first name is Philip. Of course your second one is Melancthon. Philip Melancthon Dampier, isn't it?'

'It is not,' Dampier replied.

'Oh, I'm disappointed. It ought to be. It would suit you. If I knew you well enough I'd call you Melancthon — because you look so melancholy,' she said, irresponsibly pleased with her own jest. 'Why do you?'

'The war, perhaps — if I do, but I don't,' he said lightly, but he looked at her quickly as if searching her face. He looked as if he were about to ask her a question, but he changed his mind abruptly.

'Will you come and see my wife?' he said as he walked with her towards her bus. 'She's back in town now. Any Sunday. I'll write the address so that you'll have no excuse for forgetting us. Do come.'

He scribbled in his notebook, and tore out the page. 'There — and as you're having holidays, you can't tell me you're too tired to use your one precious day.' Anne had told him of her dramatic departure from the office. She laughed.

'I wouldn't tell you that. I want very much to come, thank you.'

'That's right. Next Sunday then?'

'Yes — I'd like it,' Anne said.

'Don't pick up another office job till you're feeling quite fit,' Dampier said. 'They're all ridiculous. I know, because I'm in one myself.'

'Heavens! I must live — or think I must,' Anne protested. 'Mrs Hickey will turn me out soon if I don't show some signs of earning my living. At present she's very humble because Maquita and I nearly left her last week, but it won't last.'

Dampier, looking curiously at her, thought she resembled some delicate and spirited little bird. He had an impulse to close his hand gently over her warm and shining feathers, and remove her from all sordid necessities. The likeness seemed real to him for a second, then he laughed.

'Queer joke, life,' he said.

'I love it,' Anne said softly glowing. 'I'm so curious — I'm so *surprised* by it!'

'You must bring Thomas to see us when he's in town,' Dampier said irrelevantly, looking at her face.

'Yes — oh yes,' Anne said, suddenly feeling a little flat. 'Thomas would be delighted.'

'And you'll recognise Nemo again if you meet him in the Gardens?'

'I will,' Anne said, stooping to pat the little dog. She added under her breath as her bus drew up at Exhibition Road, 'Good-bye, Melancthon,' and went home feeling well pleased by her little adventure. She would write and tell Thomas that she knew P M Dampier, and that she was going to his house.

5 Petunia Garry

Petunia Garry within twenty-four hours settled down in the Mimosa Club as if she had been born and brought up in it. In a week she knew more about its affairs than the oldest inhabitant — probably more than Mrs Templeton herself, from whom she had ascertained the names of her married daughters, as well as the number, names, and ages of their children. She knew which of the servants had steady young men, and which of them kissed a new khaki hero every night off as they parted in the area. She knew that once a number of Mrs Templeton's clients had sent her a round-robin protesting against the regular routine of dishes in the menu, and that the foundress and owner of the Club had promptly invited all the signatories to leave for good within twenty-four hours, and had enforced their departure — smiling and inflexible — in spite of abject apologies on the part of several of the ladies. Mrs Templeton did her best, a generous and efficient best. Anyone who didn't like it must go. There was no discussion. The ladies had gone, some in tears of repentance. It is possible that she let these creep back after a time. Petunia even knew the name — and imagined she knew the age — of the completely inconspicuous lady who worked for Queen Mary's Needlework Guild. She knew that Miss Spicer had once had a beautiful and highly trained voice, and that it had gone completely after a throat operation in her twentieth year, and that Miss Spicer still could not bear to discuss singers or singing. She knew, of course, that the Hon Mrs Bridson was nearly related to a Lady of the Bedchamber and her name and rank — everyone knew that, Mrs Bridson saw to it.

All this and much more Petunia imparted to Maquita and Anne in her odd pretty way at dinner or afterwards.

She did not seem to be curious or gossiping, but she had a sympathetic imaginative interest about every person round her, unusual in a girl of her age (or indeed of any age), and a vivid unemphatic simplicity of description. It was a mental gift, Anne afterwards decided, and had very little to do with the heart. Petunia did not sit about the Club much or show any great disposition to be friendly with the other members. On the contrary, she seemed to acquire information about people by a sort of insight on a most cursory acquaintance. She was lazy and got up late, often missing breakfast altogether and, it is to be feared, taking scarcely a schoolboy's interest in her toilet, as far as soap and water were concerned. Lip-salve and powder played a more important part in Petunia's toilet. She was a mixture of ignorance and experience of worldly and half-worldly knowledge and dreamy imagination. She could lose herself in a book — crude fiction or real poetry — and forget her meals entirely, rousing herself dazed and pale with the intensity of her interest hours later. Once, when Anne took her to the Opera to hear *Tristan and Isolde*, she was delighted, and queerly intelligent in her criticism. She looked extraordinarily happy while she listened to the music, and her unconsciousness gave her a new beauty. Sometimes Anne asked Petunia to go out with her in the morning, and once when they were together they met Dampier walking with another man, his dog at his heels. Petunia recognised him at once. 'That's a friend of Simon's,' she said. 'I saw him the same night that I met you. I never forget a man's face, do you? I like him — but he's too old.'

'He's not nearly as old as Mr Meebes,' Anne said.

'Poor old Simon,' Petunia said. 'It doesn't matter about him, he has such a young spirit.'

But Petunia did not really care for the parks. She liked shop windows, and would spend a whole day studying clothes and dreaming them her own. She had a few shillings a week to spend apart from her living expenses, and her chief passion was to buy what she called a 'cammy', an elaborate affair of cheap lace and pink ribbon. Putting this on alluringly under a transparent blouse, she would sally forth after dinner to the 'pictures', or to a theatre. Men amused her, and as all those she knew, with the exception of Simon, were at the war, she endeavoured to 'pick up' others. To her friends at the Club she spoke of her failures and successes with *naïveté* and an equableness that had a touch of humour.

'I look round the theatre till I see a nice-looking man sitting alone, and then I sit beside him if I can, or in front of him. And I drop my bag or my hanky so that he will pick it up. Then we talk. Then he says will I have coffee or chocolate — and we do. Then he sees me home — but always on a bus. No taxi for me,' Petunia said, with a shrewd look. 'And I never go to my own door, but always somewhere near. And he usually wants to kiss me good night, and make an engagement for next day. And I always say to call at eleven, and I push him out of the porch because my aunt will be so cross! It's great fun,' Petunia said childishly, 'Sometimes they aren't — nice — of course, but I'm accustomed to that. And sometimes they're such dears, and so respectful. Captain Douglas tonight, for instance, he said, "I want to kiss the dear little roses on your cammy" — and he did.'

It was no use remonstrating. Anne and Maquita were made to feel foolish if they did so, and Petunia opened astonished, amused and mocking eyes at them. She 'meant no harm', and was 'always in by eleven'.

'She's a guttersnipe,' Anne said disgustedly. 'And a year or two older than eighteen I'm certain. If it wasn't that she has a strange worthwhile streak in her I'd never try to do a thing for her. Anyhow we can't do much.'

When she wasn't at moving-picture palaces or the cheaper theatres Petunia, much curled, powdered, and as prettily dressed as her wardrobe permitted, betook herself up to Simon Meebes' house. This made Anne more uncomfortable than her other excursions, but Maquita laughed at the anxiety, and sometimes went with her. Maquita had a vagabond nature, as migratory as a gipsy's, and casual entertainment, fresh faces, fresh scenes, noise, gaiety, excitement were necessities to her. She was very popular and was constantly off with young officers on leave, to dine at the Café Splendide or in some Soho place, or on excursions out of town somewhere to assist at a concert or theatricals for a hospital. But just now, as things were, leave was rare, and Maquita had no admirers to share with Petunia, so she mended her clothes and wrote letters for a change when Miss Garry went to the cinemas nearby, and did not want to go to the house in Clifford Street.

Maquita expressed great admiration for Mr Meebes, and spent a good deal of time trying to impress his cleverness and his kind heart upon Anne.

'I think he's remarkably queer,' Anne would say bluntly.

Maquita was not in the least in love with Simon, but she saw him in a romantic light, and the sense of contrast between her own surroundings and his rather heightened the illusion. She really believed it when she explained to Anne that Simon was actuated by the simplest motives of artistic philanthropy when he gave to one girl the means for violin lessons, and to another for a course in acrobatic dancing, and to a third an interest in a manicure establishment, and to a fourth pretty clothes to wear when she interviewed theatrical managers.

'What about Petunia?' Anne asked. 'Is he paying her bills?'

'He's lending her two pounds a week while she's out of an engagement,' Maquita said. 'You'd lend it yourself, so would I, if we had it. We'd take it too, if we had to. This is the Twentieth Century. Isn't it better for Petunia to be here than knocking about in the slums? Don't be stuffy, my dear.'

Petunia herself gave a different explanation of the two pounds a week. 'Simon is a trustee of mine in a way, you know,' she said. 'He has put my mother's jewels into a sort of insurance place where they allow me so much money a month on them, and pay it to me through him. It's not very much, but I can just pay Mrs Templeton with it and manage. Simon is going to get me some clothes soon. He says I must have a warm coat and a smart hat before I begin my lessons. But I'm to rest for a month first.'

'Your mother's jewels?' Anne said. 'But you ran away from home, didn't you?'

'Yes, from my stepmother, when I was sixteen, but I took my own mother's jewels because they were mine. Some of them I had to sell, but Simon made me invest the rest. They are not extraordinary, of course, but the emeralds are very good.'

'What about your father?' asked Anne.

'Oh, he has searched for me high and low,' Petunia answered readily, 'and twice I was very nearly caught because I met some friends of his coming out of his Club in Piccadilly. I'm glad I've got such sharp eyes. I flew into the traffic in the middle of the street just in time, and I was almost run over. A policeman took me by the arm and shook me, but I wasn't recognised. And do you know that very policeman was a boy I used to know. He was once a footman at my uncle's house. But he didn't know me, luckily.'

Petunia looked at Anne and hesitated. 'Anne, you'll never tell, will you, but of course Petunia Garry is not my *real* name. My father is a very, *very* well-known general. He's at the war now.'

Petunia would not say any more just then, but a few days later she came to Anne with shining eyes, her face suffused with suppressed excitement, holding a paper in her hands.

'Anne, I *must* tell someone, and you are such a dear you'll keep my secret, because it would be so *awful* to go back to that woman. But look at this — this is my father.'

Anne looked at the newspaper portrait, which in spite of its appearance of having been executed in coal and water, managed to convey the impression of a clever and distinguished face, and read beneath the picture the account of a brilliant piece of work successfully carried out by General Sir Algernon Eliot, VC, KCB. She felt a thrill of pride herself, purely patriotic as she read, and could not wonder at Petunia's excitement.

'Never tell,' Petunia begged her. 'But Phyllis Mary Eliot is my real name. He looks a great dear, my father, doesn't he? And so he is in some ways, but he's entirely under that *dreadful* woman. And she hates me.'

Her face became sullen and vindictive for a moment, but cleared again as she studied the newspaper picture. She seemed rather to fear that she had been indiscreet in confiding her secret in Anne, because she begged her again several times that day to be sure never to mention it. Anne, ashamed of having been a little sceptical at first, now was almost convinced that Petunia was telling the truth, and that she did dread discovery. It was all very queer, in Anne's formula. If Petunia's people had any sort of position it seemed incredible that she should have succeeded in hiding herself from them for three years.

Maquita advanced a theory that was fantastic but not impossible, and she and Anne presently accepted it as true.

'You know that Petunia has a *chi-chi* accent, Anne. Not very bad, but quite noticeable to any Anglo-Indian at once. 'Bing' Colvile — the boy at Simon's that night — was simply certain of it, and he's lived in India. I'm not quite sure what it means myself,' Maquita said candidly, 'but it's either that you've played with the natives, which isn't done, or perhaps that you are partly native yourself. I don't say that Petunia *is*, exactly. But she was born out in India when her father was stationed there, and lived there, by her own account, much longer than most white children do — till she was almost ten. There is something half-Oriental about her. Look at her arms and legs — they are not an English shape. And her nails are dusky sometimes.'

'She's certainly not a Mahommedan,' Anne said with a sudden giggle. 'They wash the body five times a day.'

'But her nails are dusky,' Maquita insisted. 'And those beautiful, clear, liquid eyes — just like Simon's,' Maquita stopped suddenly. 'Oh, I am horrid to tell you — but Simon's grandmother was a full-blooded Indian princess, he says. I think she was just native. And perhaps it is a touch of it in Petunia that appeals to him. I *think*,' Maquita said, sinking her voice confidentially, 'that Petunia's mother was perhaps native, or partly so. That would account for a lot, or perhaps she is an 'indiscretion', but so beautiful and so nearly white that her father insisted on looking after her.'

'He hasn't done it very well,' Anne remarked.

'It would also rather explain her stepmother's aversion,' Maquita continued. 'She has a girl of her own now, and two little boys. That would be a reason why they would just allow her to disappear.'

'Petunia has told you more of her history than she has me,' Anne said, 'but possibly there is a far-away colour touch somewhere. Certainly she's a mystery. Three parts chorus girl and one part heathen princess.'

The Oriental theory took hold of them, and they found numerous little things about Petunia that seemed to bear it out. Her tranquil and candid acknowledgment of some of the horrid and avoidable facts of life; her profound absorption in books in which she forgot food or sleep; her half-cynical, half-innocent revelations of the seamy side of wage-earning that she had known in her struggles as a chorus girl, and the unquestioning acceptance of her present security; her poise and calmness. Maquita and Anne decided that all these qualities combined to make an Oriental total, apart from odd little physical characteristics that showed.

With the unexpected appearance at the Club of Captain 'Bing' Colvile — always called the Boy — beautiful in the red tabs of a Staff job on the Whitehall Front, the chorus girl in Petunia became uppermost. She was off with him from morning till night, or, to be exact, from luncheon time until midnight or later. His military duties did not seem to interfere much with his amusement, and the gravity that weighed upon most people in those critical days left his airy spirits untouched. Petunia was equally care-free and went blithely out, and bought herself, not only the hat and coat of which she had spoken, but a variety of frocks as well.

'Simon has an account at Nesbit's,' she told Anne, 'and of course he'll be paid back out of my mother's money.' Petunia now was as happy as possible, and looked extravagantly pretty. She began to touch up her eyes and her lips again, a practice she had abandoned since coming to the cloistered quiet of the Mimosa Club, and she had her hair shampooed with henna till it became several shades lighter and there were red glints in her mop of curls. Sometimes it amused her to bring the Boy to the Club to dinner, and she insisted on sitting in her usual place, making Maquita feel resentfully that she looked a grub beside a very dazzling butterfly. The Boy was a clean, athletic young fellow with a frank face, and a wound stripe to his credit that excused his red tabs. His intelligence did not go beyond musical 'shows', but his good manners impressed Mrs Bridson favourably.

'Of course, Honoria, he provides a chaperon when he takes Miss Garry about?' she said to Miss Spicer. 'He is distinctly a gentleman, and not only in the Guards but on the Staff as well.

Excellent, for so young a man! But Miss Garry is decidedly lacking in what I would call a proper sense of dignity. Lady Malloch must of course know all about her, but does it ever strike you, Honoria, that she has at times, well — almost — a *theatrical* look?'

Mrs Bridson spoke in a hushed voice and looked fearfully round her. 'Am I mistaken or does she sometimes use paint and powder? A very vile habit in a young girl.'

'Oh, my dear Charlotte,' Miss Spicer said, a trifle impatiently, 'look about you, and you'll scarcely see a female creature of any age who isn't thickly powdered. I'm certain there isn't a woman in this dining-room who hasn't a powder-puff concealed about her. Including Dolly, who presses the vegetables with her thumb as she hands them.'

'It may astonish you to hear, then, Honoria, that since my nurse powdered me after my bath as a baby, I have never known its application,' Mrs Bridson said loftily.

'It does not astonish me,' Miss Spicer said serenely, 'you are a very simple woman, Charlotte, in your personal ways, and you have a skin that does not require cosmetics. But you must know that other people use them. Can you recall Lady Glenlemon's face, always so thickly powdered that it never failed to remind me of a freshly whitewashed fence, with such old and battered woodwork beneath that flakes always peeled off immediately? She never dared to wear a veil. It caught the wreckage too much. How her poor grandchildren disliked kissing her! Miss Garry is a foolish little girl to interfere with her natural beauty. It is really quite a lovely little face.'

Miss Spicer sighed. She did not take to Petunia, but youth captured her.

'I am inclined to speak to her myself,' Mrs Bridson said with determined kindness. 'I do not believe she has anyone to point out her errors of taste. For Lady Malloch's sake I shall speak to her — very kindly, of course.'

'I shouldn't,' Miss Spicer said. 'I am inclined to think sometimes that Miss Garry could point out a good many things to you and me, Charlotte.'

'I confess that I fail to understand you, Honoria.' The Hon Mrs Bridson stared at her in complete disaccord, and dropped the subject. She found no opportunity for some time of speaking, however kindly, to Lady Malloch's protégée, for Petunia was always on the wing like a true butterfly.

One Sunday afternoon Anne, in response to an agreeable little note signed Rose Dampier, walked over to Montpelier Square to tea. She felt a rather pleasant excitement at the thought of seeing 'Melancthon' again, this time in his own home, and of meeting his wife. 'Rose Dampier' was a name that sounded to Anne very capable and clever. Her note had somehow suggested a busy woman. Anne wondered if there were any children. She hoped so, possibly a baby. She liked a house with children.

There were several people, but no children, in the large, rather charming hall into which she was shown. The tiled black and white floor was half hidden by red rugs, the white, prettily curved staircase was carpeted in red, and there were a number of green plants about, all combining to give an effect of gaiety. There was comfort, too, in the low chairs and the many-cushioned settee drawn close to the bright fire.

Dampier came forward at once and seemed really pleased to see Anne. He interrupted his wife's good-byes to a friend to introduce her. The other guests, it seemed, were all on the point of departure. Anne was late, having walked up from Belgrave Road. Presently she found herself seated alone before the fire with Dampier and his wife, fresh tea having been brought.

Rose Dampier talked a great deal, rather quickly, and in a pretty, tactful manner, as if she felt that her visitor might be shy. Anne liked her at once, but found it a little difficult to put much variety into her own share of the conversation since she was given such small chance to speak. Anne was apt to hold herself aloof from sudden friendship, but she was not shy, and in this case she had no impulse to draw back. Dampier had attracted her interest from the moment her dizzy gaze had seen him at Simon Meebes' house, and her subsequent impression of him in Kensington Gardens had made her look forward with quite undue interest to meeting him again. She was prepared to like his wife and his house, his children if he had any, and any of his friends she might meet. She wished he would talk to her now, and she listened for his infrequent remarks feeling absurdly disappointed that the author of *Melancthon* was completely in the background in his own house.

Mrs Dampier was a graceful woman with untidy black hair, and very white hands that she moved incessantly, and a rather deprecating and appealing way of referring to herself, that conveyed to Anne that she was far from strong. She had the manner of a petted and physically small woman, but actually she was solidly built, and her bright colour gave no indication that she was delicate. She had the sort of complexion that tends to 'run' and become a little untidy in a high wind, or if exposed to too hot a fire, spreading unevenly and too vividly over her face. But a glass screen protected her from her own fire, and Anne thought her rather lovely in her blue dress with its touches of fantastic Chinese embroidery, in the bright setting of the black and white and red hall.

Dampier sat back in his chair wearing an expression that was beginning to be familiar to Anne — 'surprised to find himself not bored' she described it later, looking at them and apparently enjoying all that his wife had to say. She brought his name in a good deal. 'Philip is so fussed if I am ever ill.' — 'I wanted to nurse at the beginning of the war but Philip wouldn't hear of it.' — 'I can't tell you how often I've been packed away from London during the raids. They don't alarm me, but of course in spite of oneself one's nervous vitality suffers, and Philip is so afraid for me and the children.'

Here Dampier got up and fidgeted with a pipe on the mantel, suddenly looking perturbed.

'They're most horrible for women and children. I'd clear you all out of the raid areas if I had my way. And by the way, aren't the boys late?'

'Oh, have you some children?' Anne asked eagerly. 'I hope I shall see them.'

'Two boys,' Dampier said, smiling at her. 'They are out to tea, but should be in by this time.'

'Oh no, Philip, not till six o'clock,' Mrs Dampier said gently. 'I told nurse six would do. Yes, we have two rampageous children, as you shall see. Seven and five, and almost too much for me already.' She sighed.

'They'll soon be off to school,' Dampier promised. 'And here they are now.'

A moment later first the terrier and then two little boys in blue coats and caps came charging into the room in the highest spirits. They stopped suddenly at the sight of Anne, while Nemo frisked and sniffed round her and then made a tremendous fuss over his master.

'Oh, visitors — what a nuisance!' the bigger boy claimed candidly.

'Rowland, I'm ashamed of you,' his mother said severely, 'Where are your manners?'

'Well, you said so yourself yesterday, Mummy,' the child said, pulling off his cap and advancing politely to shake hands with Anne. 'What's your name, please?'

'My name is Anne. Don't you like visitors?'

'Not if they stop us playing,' Rowland replied with perfect frankness. 'Do you know that Anne is the name of Grannie's housemaid in Scotland? We say "Anne, Anne, the watering-can" when we want to tease her. It esasperates her.'

'Rowland, what a very rude little boy you are,' his mother said seriously. 'This is Miss Carey, and she won't come and see you again if you say such rude things. Michael, where is your cap?'

The smaller boy pulled his cap off his curly head and put up his face to Anne to be kissed, a chubby little fellow scarcely past the baby stage. She put her arms round his fat little body and laid her cheek against his hair, delighting in the fresh touch of his face as she kissed him.

'Micky didn't drink his milk at tea,' Rowland announced, flinging his coat off, and stooping to snatch at Nemo's tail.

'Rowland, no tales of your brother,' Dampier said warningly. He was watching the boys with amusement but with an odd detachment as if he found it hard to believe they had anything to do with himself.

'That's not tales,' Rowley began, but a look checked him.

'I was quite polite,' Micky said hastily, looking at his parents while Anne helped him to unbutton his coat. 'I said, "No, thank you, we are not allowed to drink strange milk." I don't like milk, and you said so, Mummy.'

'There, Rose,' Dampier said. 'You'll get a nice reputation as a crank if you put such ideas into the children's heads.'

'I was only speaking to nurse,' Mrs Dampier said. 'London milk is *so* risky. Off you go and get a picture-book, children. Perhaps if you are very good you may stay here.'

The boys ran to a bookcase in the corner and began to dispute over the choice of a book, Anne watching them with pleasure shining in her eyes. They resembled their mother remarkably she thought, and she could see no trace of Dampier either in the brilliantly sturdy and healthy Rowland, with his apple cheeks and yellow-crested head, or in the infant cherub with the heavenly expression, who now laid a book of Bible stories on her knee, somewhat to her embarrassment.

'Oh, we aren't going to have that book,' Rowland shouted. 'Micky just loves the Bible and I just hate it. We're going to have fairies, not angels, Micky. You put that away!'

'Shan't. I want to ask Miss Carey one picture,' Micky said imploringly, struggling to retain possession of his book by pushing it and himself bodily into Anne's arms.

'Do let me, Rowley, just *one* picture!'

He turned over hastily till he came to an illustration of Christ reasoning with the learned men in the Temple at Jerusalem.

'Do leave me alone, Rowley! There, Miss Carey, and what I want to know is a great puzzle. Was Jesus Mr, Mrs, or Miss?'

'Michael, look at your boots all over Miss Carey's dress!' Dampier interrupted hastily, and Micky, overcome with confusion at the dusty patch Anne's skirt displayed, ran off to fetch a brush, while Anne and Mrs Dampier laughed helplessly.

'Come back soon, please,' Mrs Dampier said prettily as Anne said good-bye to her. 'We shall love to see you.' Her smile was very cordial.

'Yes, do. Me and Micky like you,' Rowland volunteered, letting himself be kissed.

'You are looking better,' Dampier said to her at the door, restraining the boys from opening it and speeding the parting guest by almost pushing her out. 'What about work? Looking for it, or still resting?' His eyes looked at her sad and intent.

'I begin to look tomorrow — alas,' Anne said. 'I feel lazy still, and I'm ashamed of myself. Apart from the fact that I have to pay for my existence, it seems shocking to be idle just now, when all our men —' she stopped hastily.

'I wonder if I can do anything for you. What have you thought of doing?' Dampier asked kindly.

'Anything but a Government office,' Anne declared. 'But I haven't bothered to look about yet. I shall tomorrow.'

'You'll let us know what happens?' Dampier said.

'Oh, yes,' Anne said gratefully. 'And I've loved coming to-day. The children are darlings.'

'They are very noisy,' Dampier said. 'Micky should have been a little girl. If I can help you in any way, Miss Carey, please come to me. I know numbers of people who have invented intricate war-work for themselves, and I think they perhaps could be of use to you. Anyhow, come back and see us soon.'

Anne walked home in a mood of mixed feelings. New acquaintances had been few lately, and apt to be transitory — mostly girls like herself, leading a latchkey existence in other people's rooms. She liked the feeling of a family and a house. What dears the small boys were, and how sweet Rose Dampier had been. And Melancthon — she had never known anybody so kind. She insisted on that, refusing to acknowledge a faint sense of chill, a tiny blunting of the edge of her interest in Dampier after seeing him so completely domesticated.

'I wish he had talked to me more,' she said to herself, dissatisfied. His quiet voice lingered in her mind. She wanted to recall every word he had spoken to her.

'I am as bad as Maquita,' she thought. 'I'm imagining that he is what she calls 'simpatico'. Or that he would be if — oh, now I'm thinking in the terms of a typist's romance. After all he is married, very much so. They are dears, and I am lucky to know them,' Anne wound up in a glow.

She found tumult at the Mimosa Club when she walked in to supper. She was late, but that did not matter as the food was cold, and somewhat scanty on Sunday nights.

Everyone was already in the dining-room. Anne took her usual place and heard from Dolly that Maquita was out, and then she observed that Petunia was in, and that at the other end of the room at a table close to Mrs Bridson's she was entertaining some friends. Anne looked and was startled.

There was the Boy rather flushed and talkative, and Simon Meebes, sleepy and feline and hushed, and a lady in a dark red velvet dress with a voice that was slightly hoarse and which, though not loud, penetrated the room.

Petunia was looking radiant in one of her new frocks, a shimmering brownish-gold, cut in semi-evening fashion and marvellously becoming. The party were drinking champagne — in the Mimosa Club, on Sunday night. Dolly's eyes were popping out of her head. But it was not the fact that there was a party; it was not the champagne that chiefly startled Anne. It was the lady in the wine-red dress. There was no mistaking her position in society, or rather out of it. It was candidly proclaimed in every line of her opulent figure, in every richly tinted hair of her head, in every modulation of her slow, hoarse voice. In Paris they could doubtless have softened the classifying word. They have words that indicate the delicate nuances — perceptible to the Gallic chivalry — that distinguish members of the oldest profession. England could only allow her a brutal word.

Anne could see that Miss Spicer's back was as rigid as the Hon Mrs Bridson's at their proximity to the creature.

The lady of the wine-red dress was not even beautiful, her face was plain, her features were fair and heavy with a pinky, roughened skin. Her dress was tight-fitting, cut low, and with very short sleeves displaying slightly reddish arms. She wore no jewellery and little make-up, yet the revelation of her classification was devastating. She might have been a German or a Swede, but she spoke Cockney English, and they called her Reggie.

Anne was at first indignant that the Boy had not protected Petunia from her company, but then she reflected that Reggie might be a friend out of Petunia's mysterious past. She was hardly likely to be one of Simon's pretty ladies. Simon liked them much younger.

She wondered what had induced Petunia to bring these people to the unpretentious Mimosa Club where there was neither good food nor amusement. She suspected a silly plot to shock 'the old cats', as Petunia in private called the Hon Mrs Bridson and Miss Spicer.

But they were not the only ones shocked, Anne learned the next morning. The lady who worked for Queen Mary's Needlework Guild, and who was consequently just as particular as if she went daily to tea at Buckingham Palace, had declined to sit in the same room as Petunia's guests. She betook herself, chilly and hungry, to bed, where she stayed herself unsatisfyingly with biscuits until the comforting expedient occurred to her of a hot bath. She had had her weekly one the night before, but she felt that she could excusably indulge in another and account it a virtue in the circumstances. She must wash away the stain of Reggie's red velvet. The little person washed, and it was a moral rite, not an extravagance.

Mrs Templeton was always out on Sundays or it is possible that the champagne might not have appeared. But Dolly could not refuse to produce a corkscrew, and they presented her with the golden cork and drank out of tumblers.

'This is a funny old mausoleum you've got into, Petunia,' Reggie said hoarsely, looking round her with a glass of wine in her hand. 'Can't say it would agree with me. How about that little hotel in Tottenham Court Road? How about it?'

She began to laugh in an infectious, hoarse gurgle.

The Hon Mrs Bridson rose, eyeing the Boy stonily as he attempted to bow to her, and led Miss Spicer from the room. At Anne's table she paused.

'I should be glad to speak to you upstairs, Miss Carey,' she said portentously.

Anne presently followed her.

6 Ladies Must Talk

'Mrs Templeton shall be advised of this tonight, however late I sit up,' Mrs Bridson announced in an outraged voice, and gasping, from the stairs. 'Such a *creature* — within these walls! Miss Carey, where in the world did that child pick up such an acquaintance? That woman is worse than merely vulgar. She is disreputable!'

'Petunia is very ignorant,' Anne said with misgivings. 'But she ought to know better than to bring those people here.'

'The poor child,' Miss Spicer exclaimed with sudden feeling. 'Can we do *anything* for her?'

She walked to the fire and thrust the poker nervously into the dying Sunday night coals. 'I haven't tried to influence her, but how can I? A dull old maid, with no life left in me! A young thing like that — so pretty as she is!'

'I am amazed at that young Colvile,' Mrs Bridson said, sinking almost unconsciously into her favourite chair. 'And I cannot make out the fourth member of the party at all, but he is certainly old enough to be that girl's father.'

Anne refrained from mentioning Mr Meebes' name, and she had not disclosed the fact that Petunia's Lady Malloch was not one of the Dorset Shelburnes and thus exposed the girl to Mrs Bridson's relentless condemnation. She felt that Petunia required whatever shelter was available, even false pretences. If Mrs Templeton requested her to leave the Mimosa Club it would not be much of a surprise if she betook herself to the society of Reggie, or, what Anne feared more, threw herself wholly on the compassion of Mr Meebes, who had a strong attraction for her, in spite of her half-mocking way of constantly alluding to his age.

'Oh, well, after all, having her friends at the Club shows that Petunia is very open and nice about everything,' Anne said, speaking lightly. 'It is as if she took them home, isn't it? Because she has no home. The champagne can't be her fault.'

'You are right, Miss Carey,' Mrs Bridson said weightily. 'It is only that shocking woman. I could forgive the rest, but that she should *dare* to come here! She cannot be — she did not by any means *look* — reformed!'

'You and I had better go to bed, Charlotte,' Miss Spicer suggested.

'I intend to speak to Mrs Templeton tonight,' Mrs Bridson reiterated.

'Very well, my dear Charlotte, in that case you will have to go down to Claygate where she is staying with her married daughter until Tuesday,' Miss Spicer said severely.

'How unfortunate,' Mrs Bridson said. 'I wonder,' she added, looking from one to the other, 'if, in her absence, I should act? Should I go to that woman and turn her out of the Club? I am tempted to do so, very tempted.'

Anne hid a smile.

'I am sure Mrs Templeton would do no such thing,' Miss Spicer said. 'How would you do it, Charlotte? I dread to think what that young woman might say to you. She looks capable of Billingsgate. And that voice!'

'If one maintains one's dignity one is apt to overawe that class of person,' Mrs Bridson said. 'But perhaps you are right, Honoria. Yes, let us go up. Do I hear them coming?'

An almost comic expression of dismay appeared on her face, and she rose hurriedly as someone approached the drawing-room door, but it was only Lynette Mason.

'Such a day at Penge with that dreadful teething baby!' she grumbled in her weak, high voice. 'My brother's come home, and is in hospital in Bristol, so Laura, my sister-in-law, has gone to him. And *I've* had that baby for thirty hours on end — just bawling!'

'I hope your brother isn't very ill. What a relief it's not a wound,' Miss Spicer said kindly.

Lynette yawned, a long, tired yawn, and sank wearily down on the sofa.

'*How* am I to go to bed?' she asked desperately. 'I'm so tired.'

'Come along, I'll help you before I face my Sinn Fein landlady,' Anne said good-naturedly, putting an arm round the exhausted young aunt, whose weekends were so little amusement to her.

The drawing-room was accordingly empty when Mr Meebes, Petunia, Bing Colvile, and Reggie came upstairs. Reggie promptly went to the piano, and a powerful but ill-used contralto voice pealed through the Mimosa Club. It brought Dolly and the other servants to listen in delight on the stairs. Reggie sang in Italian, proud of the fact that she produced a truly remarkable volume of sound, and with no more idea of restraint in her singing apparently than she had in anything else. She made dramatic gestures as she sang, and she had to break off sometimes in hoarse fits of laughter, in which both the men joined — the Boy uproariously.

Petunia trilled a little, without words, in the choruses, but her smile was frigid. Petunia was not of the type that cares for a divided attention, and Reggie was behaving altogether too much as a monopolist to please her. She sang a little shrilly, her dark eyes looking fixed. Simon Meebes, sitting in Mrs Bridson's chair and smoking a cigar, glanced at her occasionally with a quiet, amused expression. The Boy thought Reggie's performance 'simply topping', and applauded every turn. Petunia admitted to herself suddenly and jealously that Reggie in her tight red dress had a good figure, erect and rounded. But her hands were coarse, and her neck too thick, and she was singing out of tune. The Boy was very silly to admire her. She was sorry that in a good-natured moment she had asked Reggie to meet the Boy and Simon. But of course once upon a hard time that Petunia wanted to forget, Reggie had been good to her.

That was in a little hotel in the Tottenham Court Road, and Petunia had been in a plight, and but for Reggie — she gave Reggie a certain gratitude still, and after all, she reflected complacently, the poor old dear was pretty well past her best. Men didn't really admire her, and she wasn't getting any more good chorus engagements, only small suburbs, and provincial tours. Poor old Reggie. Petunia's face cleared into a soft amiability again, and Simon Meebes, with a comprehending smile, watched her go over to the mirror and preen herself.

In the glass Petunia caught sight of Anne slipping down the stairs, and she called her to come in, and ran out and seized her by the arm.

'Simon wants to speak to you,' she said, improvising glibly. 'Do come in, like a dear.'

Anne came in, and Reggie kept both hands on the keys of the piano, and gave her a cheerful nod in response to Petunia's introduction.

'Glad to meet any friend of the Baby Runaway's,' she said affably. 'Do you sing? How's this for Sunday night in the Old Homestead?' and she burst into a syncopated version of Mascagni's *Ave Maria*, that was very funny.

Simon rose with his sleek, silent grace, and pressed Anne's hand in a soft, moist palm. He began to talk to her in his confidential manner, with an evident intention to interest her, and presently Reggie left the piano and seated herself on the arm of his chair to listen. Petunia turned to Bing, no longer jealous. Who could be jealous of Anne, who walked in Kensington Gardens and liked looking at babies and trees every day of the week, when she might have been considering clothes in shop-windows or on smart ladies in the streets, and picking up a man to amuse her? No, Anne was not a person to be jealous of. In Petunia's view she had no possible chance of being anybody's rival. Hence she genuinely liked Anne. They all talked together about the war, and Reggie made some sound remarks. But at ten-thirty Petunia's party came abruptly to an end with the switching off of the Club lights which, an inflexible rule of economy, were all extinguished at that hour. No one ever stayed in the public rooms much after ten as a rule, and candles were permitted in the bedrooms.

The Boy lit matches, and he and Reggie romped down the stairs with outbursts of laughter and many jokes. Mr Meebes followed silently, with his arm across Petunia's shoulders, urging her to bring Anne up to Clifford Street, and promising to drive them home in a taxi. Petunia refused to be persuaded, even when the Boy joined in with entreaties, and Reggie with jeers. The Boy begged for permission to call next morning at eleven, and was told to come if he liked. He and Reggie began to sing one of her 'jolly little choruses' as they banged the door after them.

It was a memorable night in the annals of the Mimosa Club.

'I'm going over to sleep with Maquita,' Petunia announced, slipping on her coat which hung in the hall, and preparing to accompany Anne. She was fond of doing this, although Maquita did not exactly encourage it. Her bed was too narrow for two, and Mrs Hickey made a point of charging two shillings whenever Petunia spent the night with her — a serious consideration to poor Maquita. She put her arm through Anne's and squeezed her excitedly.

'There's going to be a jolly good row tomorrow, isn't there?' she said. 'Did you *see* Mrs Bridson and all the other old cats looking at us? I expect they wanted some of the fizz.'

'I don't think much of your friends for bringing it,' Anne said.

'Reggie won't go out to supper without it,' Petunia said instantly.

'Why did you bring her? Petunia, you have no right to do things like that. This isn't an hotel,' Anne said.

'The Boy often comes,' Petunia said innocently. 'And I'll tell you about poor Reggie when we get in.' She sighed gently with mysterious implication.

Maquita was making cocoa over Anne's fire, already in her dressing-gown, with her splendid black hair streaming over her shoulders. She was intensely excited after a day with some friends in the country, and she talked so much for some time that neither Petunia nor Anne could get in a word.

'But, my dears, I've met *the* man,' she wound up dramatically. 'When that happens you *know* it. We liked each other *at once!* A naval doctor, not even good-looking. But so *simpatico*. I shan't tell you his name, but you'll both meet him very soon. There is no doubt this time.' Maquita bent her brilliant, flushed gaze over the cocoa and stirred it with a button-hook.

Anne, wrapped in yellow silk, sat on the floor in front of the fire, so used to these flights from Maquita that she scarcely listened. She stared half-dreaming into the flames, shaking out her light, fair hair which scarcely passed her shoulders. It was as silky as a baby's, and 'obliged her' by waving a little, but she thought little of it, and greatly admired Maquita's mane.

She wanted to think of her own day; of her visit to Dampier's house, and of Rose Dampier and the children. She wanted to recall everything that Dampier had said to her, and to see if in retrospect she got that faint sense of chill. It had been such an unreasonable thing, that slight, definite feeling that Melancthon, surrounded by his family, in his own house, was remote in every possible way from her. Of course he was: she knew him very little indeed, but he had gone out of his way to be kind to her. She had liked him so much in Kensington

Gardens, but now she could only see him amused by the little boys, silent, detached. Still, he had come with her to the door and had asked her to come back again to Montpelier Square. They had both asked her. Rose Dampier, in spite of a touch of languor in her manner, had been cordial too. Anne repeated to herself, 'I am lucky to know them!'

'And, my dear, I knew from the moment I went in — you know how intuitive I am — that there was *someone* in the house of special interest to me. "Agnes," I said, "is Tom back?" — I used to be so fond of him,' Maquita said, pouring the cocoa into three cups.

'Let me tell you about Reggie,' Petunia broke in with plaintive eagerness. She told the story with the vivid detail of colour and setting that was her gift. It was a long story of theatrical adventures, but the girls became absorbed in spite of themselves. It was squalid, but as told in Petunia's imaginative language, exciting somehow. Petunia, it seemed, doing quite well for a first engagement, had come to an obscure theatre in London. With some other girls of the company she went to a cheap lodging-house somewhere off the Tottenham Court Road which called itself the Grand Casino Hotel. Reggie was in the hotel, out of a 'shop', but under the protection of a man with whom she was very much in love, and in consequence financially safe for a time. Reggie had 'gone gay' at fifteen, but Petunia added hastily, 'Of course, she's all right now — quite different.' Her lover was doing a mystery turn at one of the West End halls, and making a pot of money, with which he was generous.

'Reggie had — oh — lovely clothes!' Petunia said, her eyes narrowing with envious recollection. Sometimes he brought a pal along to supper with him, and Reggie asked Petunia up to her room, and they had tinned foods of strong flavour, and 'funny drinks'. Petunia got to know one of his friends very well. He was 'really a gentleman', and was also doing a music-hall turn with a violin. He was twenty-four, and the mere description of his good looks made Petunia pale with emotion. Her hand shook as she put her cup down.

'Why weren't they both at the war?' Maquita asked sharply.

Petunia was incoherent, but evidently both Hannibal the Mystic Man (in private life Mr Dick Dempster) and Mr Dennis Percy had successfully evaded military service. One fine day they both disappeared from London, without any sadness of farewell to Reggie, and left no address. Later, it was known that they had gone no further than Brighton, but not alone. Two ladies accompanied them. The story minutely filled in, as emotional as Petunia knew how to make it, followed a reasonably true line up to this point, but though Maquita and Anne were necessarily unaware of it, just here the narrator reversed the rôles played by herself and Miss Reggie da Costa. That lady had been philosophic — possibly case-hardened — over the affair, but Petunia, thinking herself madly in love with the defaulting Mr Dennis Percy, had cried herself into a state of chorus incompetence that led to her prompt dismissal, and had then swallowed half a bottle of opium pills, the property of another young lady who experimented in drug-taking, and had hysterically announced her impending doom to Reggie. (In Petunia's version it was she who had saved Reggie's life, nursed her through scenes of misery and degradation, and finally removed her to a single room in Fitzroy Street, and supported her by selling all her possessions one by one till she owned no single thing but what she stood upright in.)

That bit of Petunia's experience was all seamy side. Her face looked pinched at the recollection of it, and the two girls listening shivered at the picture of moral and physical squalor. They felt only admiration for Petunia's pluck and loyalty. Petunia spared them no details. The scenes in the poor little hot room, the inadequate washing conveniences, the lack of air and food. Sickness and hysteria, and semi-starvation, and outside the noise and dust, the incessant turmoil and staleness of a crowded London street in August. Anne was indignant with that terrible woman in the tight red dress, and compassionate to Petunia — poor little girl, what she had been through!

'Anyway she got better,' Petunia said. 'And then we both got work and I lost sight of her. But it's funny how you like people you've been able to do something for,' Petunia uttered with one of her flashes of insight. 'So I couldn't help asking her tonight. She is *quite* all right now, though she once was a 'fairy'. You can tell, if course, but people ought to be charitable. I don't mind old Mrs Bridson, and old Aunt Spicer, and the others — oh, they *did* want some of our fizz — but I don't want to do a thing Mrs Templeton would mind —'

'I'll just take the liberty of coming in, as you'll never hear me knock above all your own voices,' Mrs Hickey announced, appearing with suddenness in their midst. 'Well, I declare to goodness it's only the other young lady from the Club, come to spend the night. Mrs Pocock, the poor old woman just beneath you, Miss Carey, had the strangest notion that she heard a man's voice in your room. "No harm, of course," she said, "one of Miss Gilroy's brothers, I'll be bound, but it's late for all this talking" — sure I knew it was only yourselves, but to satisfy the poor thing I had to come up —'

'And to satisfy yourself,' Anne said indignantly. 'I'm surprised at you, Mrs Hickey. That poisonous, gossiping old creature is always hearing what doesn't exist. It is time you knew better. I'm ashamed of you!'

'Did you really think there was a man here, Mrs Hickey?' Maquita said with mocking concern. 'How disappointing for you. Another time, perhaps —'

Mrs Hickey burst into a flood of apologies, artfully mingled with abuse because they talked so late and kept the light burning, and the fire in, but young ladies, of course, could neither think of a poor working woman nor of an old lady below them who couldn't get her sleep at all if she didn't get it early, and for her part she believed that keeping the lights on till all hours attracted air raids and nothing less, but little had she ever expected to be accused of a bad mind. She knew a lady, and a good young lady, when she saw one, surely to the goodness —

Mrs Hickey was fearsomely dressed for bed, but over various flannel garments she had thrust on a man's old overcoat entirely out at elbows and grotesquely ragged at the pockets. This was her dressing-gown, and was also assumed in moments of stress when she went into the area to browbeat or abuse a tradesman. Her pyramid of black hair had slipped sharply to one side, giving her a look of rakish abandon, and her ill-tempered, snapping eyes were lit with evil fires. Her tongue ran on in a whine of apology and complaint.

'You're really a wicked woman, Mrs Hickey,' Anne said with a chilly calm that always exasperated her landlady to further flights. 'But after you've looked in the wardrobe and under the bed you can go back and tell old Mrs Pocock all you've found. Please be quick as we are all going to bed.'

Mrs Hickey twisted her thin features into a sort of bitter smile.

'I'm sure I won't do that, Miss Carey, and I regret that ignorant, poor woman downstairs. She was dreaming, that's it. I'm sorry, but you won't be burning my light too late now I hope.'

She removed herself, and they heard her loudly assuring the suspicious Mrs Pocock that of course as she, Mrs Hickey, had told her, she was entirely mistaken. It was just the young ladies sitting up very late, burning the expensive light, but no more harm than that!

Mrs Templeton, wise woman with a mind as calm and ample as her calm and ample body, heard upon her return from Claygate of the terrific occurrences of Sunday right at the Mimosa Club. Mrs Bridson could hardly believe it when she saw her smile at the recital. The little lady who sewed for Queen Mary refused to credit her eyes when she saw that Petunia was not forthright turned out of the Club door. The other indignant, curious ladies debated resigning 'if such things were allowed to go on'. But no one resigned. The historic precedent of the ladies who had left the Club never to return debarred them. Besides, they were pleasantly thrilled.

Mrs Templeton spoke to Petunia privately, suggesting that Sunday night was a poor one to show the Club to her friends, and that notice should be given before she asked guests to a meal, as otherwise there was likely to be trouble with the servants. The matter of bringing wine in was against the Club rules, and of course would not be repeated. Mrs Templeton's rules did not exist to anybody's knowledge in black and white, but she occasionally referred to them as positively as though they were the Constitution of England, and never failed to make the impression she desired. She then added firmly and unexpectedly, 'And now, my dear Miss Garry, I think you should find some work to do. One of my rules is that people using the Club must be employed in some way. What about some war-work, if you are not going back to the stage just now? Ask Miss Gilroy about her job at the War Office — you'd like something of the sort, wouldn't you?'

Petunia fancied going daily with Maquita to the War Office very much indeed, and upon being consulted, Simon Meebes approved of the idea. By all means do war-work for a time, till theatrical — and other — matters grew more settled. He himself was going back to France and couldn't arrange yet about singing and dancing lessons for her. With his help and Maquita's personal influence Petunia got a clerical job at twenty-five shillings a week in Maquita's department. She bought herself several new 'cammies' and blouses and a pale pink sports coat, and trotted off happily to Whitehall every morning.

Anne herself began to look out for some work, but she determined to choose reasonably this time, and nothing immediate offered.

Petunia's assorted guests of Sunday, her defiance of the rules that governed 'nice' people ceased suddenly to be the absorbing topic of the members of the Mimosa Club. They came face to face with the tragic in life, and that put Petunia out of their minds.

7 Miss Pratt and Miss Denby

Two ladies, entirely engulfed in war-work, had spent the winter at the Mimosa Club. Miss Pratt was described by Anne as 'one of those little miaouing women', and the description was apt. Her voice had the quality of plaintive miauling, the exasperating, thin, high note of a complaining cat. She was small and, in spite of good clothes, meagre was the only adjective one allowed her. Her hands were claw-like; her slightly red nose sharp, and her restless eyes shallow and cold.

Ordinarily she lived with her companion, a Miss Denby, in a Bayswater boarding-house that labelled itself private hotel, and served a quiet and refined afternoon tea every day in the drawing-room. Miss Pratt was known to be 'comfortably off', and she was not without a certain sharp desire to make fun of some of the others in their shifts to keep up appearances. Her acid remarks were sometimes amusing, but more often spiteful. It was a meagre life, and Miss Pratt had a meagre mind. She had relations — in this also, more fortunate than many of the refined and forlorn ladies who are carried along the great stream of London life. Sometimes a brother turned up in London and took her out — in a taxi, not a bus — to dine and to go to a theatre. Then her companion got the only holidays that fell to her lot.

In the summer they paid visits together among other members of the Pratt family. Miss Denby, who had been her companion for sixteen years, was much older and made no attempt to appear more youthful than her grey hair and worn face allowed. She was a tall, quiet woman, self-effacing but not servile, and she took the place that Miss Pratt assigned to her with some dignity and complete patience. She appeared not to notice the letters or papers on the breakfast-table till she was invited to do so, and she usually spoke only to second and support her employer. She had a pleasant, gentle manner, and she wore quiet gowns and was fond of fan-like Medici lace collars. It was known that she was an Admiral's daughter and had 'always' had to work for her living, just as it was known that Miss Pratt was the daughter of a rich Midland tradesman, who had made his money rather too late to educate his daughters. The victims of Miss Pratt's tongue said that it was easy to see which was the lady.

The two called each other Marion and Gertrude, and some tie held them together. Miss Pratt adopted a spoilt-child manner, and was fond of saying petulantly that Gertrude 'wouldn't let her' do certain things 'just as if I'd really be too tired!' Miss Denby was certainly necessary to her.

Like most people in their position they knitted through the first year of the war, with occasional efforts at Belgian relief. The second year they did Red Cross work and made hospital supplies. In the third year they packed parcels for prisoners and cut out and sewed chintz comfort bags for convalescent soldiers. The fourth year found Miss Pratt suffering from a common form of war- workers' vanity, the desire to tell people how very little she had been able to do. She responded eagerly to the flattering comments, 'But you've done so *much*! You have taken up so many things, and you are so devoted. It is wonderful.' Miss Pratt's nose would then grow pink with excitement.

'Oh, it has been so little, but this year it's to be soldiers' clubs and canteens,' she announced importantly. 'Three days a week we shall begin work at six in the morning, cooking breakfast for hundreds of men, and three days a week we shall cook the dinner, and wait, and do shifts in between. Sunday we'll free-lance — just help out other people. And of course we must live near our work. We shall move to Victoria.

We are sorry to go, but we can't afford the *time* it takes to get anywhere from Bayswater!'

It was thus that Miss Pratt and Miss Denby came to the Mimosa Club. No one saw much of them because they were always rushing away from meals to take extra duty in one or other of the places they worked in. Miss Pratt often said, with her half-important, half-childish giggle, 'Gertrude is so afraid that I won't be able to stand it,' but she apparently throve on her hard work.

When they came in tired at night Miss Denby would kneel down to pull off Marion's boots, and then prepare her hot bath before she took off her own things. Then, neat and erect as possible, she would come down to dinner in her black dress with the Medici collar, and the touch of pink that she was fond of at the waist. She was unvaryingly tranquil, with a gentle formality that neutralised her into 'Miss Pratt's companion', and hid any individuality she might have possessed. Anne Carey, who sat near her, sometimes thought that Miss Denby was like a figure on a film which gave an illusion of life and action until you remembered that you could not hear the voice or touch the hand of the semblance, whose real self existed thousands of miles away perhaps. Anne, musing on the lot of the working spinster, thought that the likeness to phantoms thrown shadow-like on a screen could be found in many cases.

Miss Pratt talked a great deal about 'my soldiers', and told a number of vivacious anecdotes of the canteen. She found the work exciting, and in her life the mere sight of men was an emotional impetus. Miss Denby's interest was quieter. The Hon Mrs Bridson turned her back on Miss Pratt, but would have been gracious to her companion had Miss Denby's loyalty allowed her the faintest separate interest. But to Mrs Bridson's condescension she returned the same gentle, formal greeting that she had for everyone else.

One rainy night, a few days after Petunia's party, they both came into the Mimosa Club very wet and muddy, and as they toiled wearily up the stairs Miss Pratt's miauling voice at its most complaining pitch urged Gertrude to be quick about her bath, as she was so dreadfully cold. Miss Denby did not respond with her accustomed readiness. Instead, she sank into a chair in Miss Pratt's room and sat huddled up, clasping her umbrella and staring before her. Her hat was a little crooked, and she was very wet.

'I'm tired,' she said heavily.

'Gertrude, are you ill?' Miss Pratt said sharply, because she was frightened.

Miss Denby did not answer. She stared in front of her, and Miss Pratt ran out into the hall, and finding Anne on her way to Lynette Mason's room, begged her to come in because Gertrude seemed to be ill.

It was apparent that Miss Denby was very ill. They got her to bed and sent for hot-water bottles and hot soup, and after a time the look of unnatural strain on her face relaxed a little, and she urged Marion to go down and get her dinner. Anne offered to stay with her while Miss Pratt dined, and she lit the fire and bathed Miss Denby's ashy face with eau-de-Cologne. Miss Denby refused to let Anne brush her hair, and lay with it unbound, streaming over the pillow. Later in the evening mounting tide of fever gave colour to her grey face, and a doctor was sent for. He promptly sent for a nurse.

'I don't like it,' he said.

Miss Pratt clung weeping to Anne, begging her to stay with her, so it was after midnight when she got back to Belgrave Road. Sickness terrified Anne. She knew little of it, and had a nervous dread of sick people, but for this very reason a wish to ignore a cowardice that she despised forced her to offer to do what she could for Miss Denby next day. She hated doing it, but she hated more feeling herself a coward.

'It is so horrible, so stupid,' Anne said fiercely to herself, clenching her hands. 'I won't be. I must do anything I can do.'

Miss Pratt continued to cling tearfully to her. Miss Denby was alarmingly ill.

At midday the doctor gave his verdict almost brutally to Miss Pratt. He was rough and overworked, and he wanted to give all his time to the soldiers.

'Meningitis, and too late to move her to a nursing-home. No doubt she caught it in the canteen; plenty of germs about Flanders mud. She has been prepared for it by weeks of over-exertion and exposure. If women had more sense, our fighting men would have a better chance. There is no hope. All we can do is to try to relieve her suffering.'

Miss Pratt was overcome. She whimpered in a suppressed fashion that occasionally broke out into violence.

Anne had to coax her out of the sick woman's room. But she insisted on returning, and her sobs reached Miss Denby's ear. Her faint voice that seemed to come from beneath crushing fatigue checked Miss Pratt.

'Do let me have my room to myself, Marion, I must rest! How plain you look with your hair untidy. But I'm too tired to do it for you. Why don't you go to bed? I am so tired.'

A second nurse came in that night, and Anne sat up with Miss Pratt in a sort of dreadful dream, fighting with herself silently and longing to escape to her own quiet room. 'Why should I be here — I'm not their friend,' a voice within her said rebelliously.

'I *have* to stay — I have to see if I can stand things,' another inward voice replied with desperate stubbornness.

She heated milk, and made tea at intervals, and soothed Miss Pratt, coaxing her to drink hot milk, or to close her eyes and rest in her chair. Sometimes she helped the nurse with Miss Denby's bed.

Miss Denby lay in one position as if a tangible weight of exhaustion rested on her. She complained if the nurses tried to smooth back her hair, moaning that they hurt her head. The tangled grey locks gave her face a wildness that it had never worn before. Though she was constantly given opiates she remained semi-conscious. Towards midnight she began to talk in an incessant monotonous murmur, but quite distinctly. Anne found herself following with a painful intensity the gradual revelation of a solitary woman's life, related in a voice faint under its burden of unbearable fatigue.

'I don't grudge the work — not that — for the soldiers. But it's harder on women who have no men at the Front. Yes, it is, Marion. You can't really share, and the soldiers know it. I am old enough to have sons at the war, Marion, and so are you almost. It would be wonderful to have a son ... we lead unnatural lives ... women can't — they shouldn't. Boarding-houses, always, always strangers' houses. It's so dreadful. It would have been easy to take a little house in the country and adopt some children. Belgians ... that would be women's work. I can play with children. I listen to them laughing in the gardens ...'

'She is delirious, poor Gertrude,' Miss Pratt whimpered, choking.

'No, not delirious,' the sick woman said with terrible sharpness, 'but dying. I'm telling the truth — the truth. You still believe that you'll marry, but you won't now. You never meet any men. There is no one. But we could have had a home, we could have made some poor child happy — only we were too selfish. It is horrible to spend one's life in a boarding-house. And your relations are so dull, and so common. I mind that most. But I'm a coward. I've worked hard all my life, and now I care only for safety, a roof, food. I get that from you, Marion. I'm too old for dangers, but someone said "live dangerously", and that would be better.'

Her voice sank, and Anne shivered in the silence of the room. Then Miss Denby seemed to realise Miss Pratt's presence again.

'Don't cry because I'm dying, Marion. Crying makes you look so plain. I used to wish sometimes that I might never see you again … Oh, I'm so tired! It is wrong to be forced into a dreadful paid position like this. You shouldn't have so much money. It's not right to be able to buy another woman body and soul — body and soul — body and soul.' She repeated the words over and over till Miss Pratt could have screamed.

Anne was shaking, her cold hands locked.

'I have terrible thoughts. It's because I'm dying … poor little Marion, you get nothing out of life. It's all so empty, so dreary. All false, all wrong and silly. I've had enough of life. I'm glad to die.'

The room was dark except for the shaded light in one corner, and the fire burning with a purring, low flicker. Occasionally someone came to the door and whispered, but the house was still and fearful. There seemed to Anne to be no living thing in the world except the fire in the grate and the bodiless voice that murmured and sank.

The thought of Dampier came into Anne's mind with a sudden rush. If she could speak to him, what release and sanity there would be from this relentless room of death. Anne held out her hands for help, and in spirit tried to get force from Dampier's strength. He could shield her from the terrifying things that seemed to possess the world. He was so certain, so strong. She hid her face in her hands, pressing her fingers hard against her aching eyes, and thinking of Dampier's face, his eyes, his quiet voice.

'You must help me,' Anne found herself saying in wordless, hurrying violence. 'I *need* you to help me.'

In the sudden calm that followed it was almost as if she could feel him in the room. She kept her eyes hidden.

At dawn Miss Denby's voice ceased, and Anne, stirring tiredly, remembered an old custom, and crept to the window, opening it wide 'to help her soul away', she thought confusedly.

A yellow fog was rising from the river, and the struggling sun presently shone ghost-like on the fire and seemed to put it out. It was then that Miss Pratt's companion lifted her head from the pillow and spoke for the last time.

'Marion, I die, I die,' she said in a whisper that had a thrill of triumph in it, and with that cry she lay back and ceased to breathe.

Anne through aching tears thought 'Death is not so frightening after all.'

✖

'All out!' called the keepers of Kensington Gardens.

'All *out!*' Their voices came rather harmoniously from the distance, but were a trifle impatient as if they were anxious to get home to their teas. They hurried about chivvying stragglers towards the late gates, and locking the early gates with a great deal of fuss and importance, alarming the children into a scurrying run by their nurses' sides, and cynically advising lovers to 'pay a bit of attention there!' They shouted '*All* out!'

Anne, disappointed of her intention to wander along the budding Flower Walk into the park, proceeded along the pavement on the Bayswater side, and near Lancaster Gate turned into Victoria Road, and cut across the grass. Officially it was dusk, but the sky was full of light still, and the flush of sunset lingered in its singularly clear blue. In the chilly sweetness of the park there was a delicate message of spring. Anne was insatiable to breathe it, to smell it, to absorb some part of the provocative, disturbing life pushing and breathing round her. She drew a long sighing breath. The hour was exquisite in its cold purity.

She was moved by no definite intention as she walked slowly across the park, only a desire for the free air, and to be as far away as possible from the Mimosa Club. She felt that she could never eat her dinner there again; never bring herself to enter its doors. She had overcome her repugnance enough to go and ask if she could do anything more for Miss Pratt — when she woke at two o'clock from a long sleep — and had heard with relief that she would not be called upon further. A Pratt brother had been telegraphed for, and had promptly appeared, and taken matters in hand. Poor Miss Denby's worn body changed into a semblance of profound peacefulness, had been removed to a mortuary chapel, and Miss Pratt was with her brother at his hotel. Mrs Templeton told Anne this, holding the girl's hand in a comforting clasp. She was indignant with Miss Pratt and a little anxious about Anne, but she said nothing, only her kindness made itself felt.

Anne had been walking about most of the afternoon, and earlier had found herself in Montpelier Square. She hesitated on the side across from Dampier's house, strongly tempted to go in and find comfort with friendly people and a fire. But her hesitation turned to a decisive 'no' as it flashed into her mind that she might possibly be ill herself, or carry infection to the children. She was not nervous on her own account, but she walked away at once. It did not matter much where she went, but she was impelled to wander. The shock of the night had left her with a restless feeling of almost physical pain, a sensation so new to her that she was half convinced that she could get away from it by action. The streets and pavements had wearied and depressed her. Evidently it was not in crowds that the cure lay. But the faint, cold haze that gathered in the hollows of the park, enfolding trees and lovers in a growing mystery, the wide serenity of it all began to soothe her.

Anne had come to two decisions during the day; to move away from the Mimosa Club and Mrs Hickey as soon as she could find a room elsewhere, and to marry Thomas within three weeks. She thought of her resolves in this order. She couldn't endure the Club any longer. Not all Mrs Templeton's kindness could efface the memory of Miss Denby and Miss Pratt — Anne saw the companion as an intolerable, piteous creature when she thought of the past night. And her patience with Mrs Hickey had reached breaking point. That insufferable antagonist with her perpetual hostility and suspicion — she had greeted Anne with the strongest expressions of disapproval of her 'night out' — would have to break a new lance with a new lodger over the carpet and the cleaning and the coals. Anne would pay her, and pack and be done with Belgrave Road.

And she would marry Thomas in three weeks, when he got eight days' leave, because Thomas had written in manifest excitement to say that at long last his limp and his short sight didn't matter to anybody, and he was going out to France, his heart's desire, in the beginning of May, and would she marry him. He was only ASC, but he was going into danger, he hoped — Thomas didn't express himself so crudely — and he wanted to crowd as much experience into life as possible, while he was sure of it — comparatively — in England. Thomas, in short, was emulating the example of many young men whom he had admired and envied at the beginning of the war. Most of them had left young widows. Anne had a faint sense of anti-climax — everything seemed to be late in arriving. But she was not sufficiently herself to see things with her usual poised amusement. Life was so short. She would marry Thomas, and get some work, and carry on somehow till he came back. Then she saw things rather less clearly, because Thomas to her knowledge had no money. She wouldn't tell her brothers of her marriage till it was accomplished. They thought Thomas so ineligible as to be ridiculous. Her sister-in-law was caustic on the subject.

'They think I can live alone, and work forever,' Anne thought, smarting with resentment. She sat down on a bench, and pulled out Thomas's letter and read it over. She liked his firm writing and his tone of anxious manliness. He sounded protective. She would marry him whenever he liked. She felt as impulsive and inconsequent as Maquita. She was used to the idea — a vague one — of marrying Thomas, and her decision brought no great reality to the thought with which she had often played. She liked Thomas very much, and she knew him comfortably well. There was no one else.

Anne sat staring before her, conscious that she was a little cold, and that the mist was creeping and folding more closely and damply among the trees as dusk fell. The hoot of taxis and buses, the lights springing up, pale lemon globes in the half-light, all seemed the expression of that sadness that she was trying to forget. Thomas slipped suddenly from her mind. She thought instead of Miss Denby, of her dying voice. When she had been pressed beyond bearing that poignant murmur, it had not been the thought of Thomas that had come to her support. Anne jumped up hastily and stumbled among a flock of sooty, coughing sheep following their shepherd across the park, in her effort to escape from the restless pain that held her again. The startled animals bleated and plunged, and Anne waded through them to a laurel- bordered path outside a keeper's cottage. Down the path came frisking an important little dog, responsibly taking his master for an evening stroll. Anne's heart missed a beat. But it was not Dampier's dog. His master following close behind at a great stride looked like a Bolshevist artist from Chelsea, with shaggy hair and beard, and hands thrust into his pockets, a pipe jutting from his mouth, and an umbrella jutting at right angles from beneath his arm. Anne, between relief and surprise, found herself curiously disturbed. 'As if there was only one puppy in Kensington,' she said, like a disappointed child.

Dampier, as it happened, was walking towards her. They met five minutes later.

Anne, in a new panic of feeling, wanted to pass without speaking. Instead, she found herself with her hand held in his, stammering, 'Oh, I *wanted* to see you!'

8 Searchlights

Melancthon turned and walked beside her, the abstraction of his face breaking into an expression of eagerness as he looked at Anne.

'You do crop up unexpectedly,' he said. 'I was just thinking that the park was chilly and depressing, and that nowadays one never saw a friend in London, and that I'd go to my club and try and forget the war. A lot of men at the club are specialists in ways of forgetting the war. They concentrate on their dinner, and only think of the war in so far as it stops the supply of caviare from Russia, and special delicacies from other countries, and so spoils the menus. There is a remarkable man, Serracold. I was almost deciding to dine with him to hear him talk of the probable unfortunate effect of the war on the French wines. He's extraordinarily interesting on wine.'

'Men's clubs are so sensible,' Anne said.

'You are satirical,' Melancthon said. 'But what about your club?'

'The Mimosa?' said Anne. 'Well, of course it is not a club in a man's sense, it's a semi-charity to give poor people who think they are a little too exclusive for ordinary boarding-houses the illusion of privacy and comfort. It is honest, and keeps the poor ladies' expenses down to the minimum. That is a great deal. But the illusion of the name wears thin!'

'That sounds bitter,' Dampier said, looking at her in surprise. 'Are you so tired of everything? The war is pretty hard on you, isn't it? It's hard on women.'

'I saw a woman die last night,' Anne said — 'of the war.'

'That was dreadful.' Dampier's sympathy was quick. 'Is it too cold to sit for a moment? Tell me about it.'

'That's all. I didn't know her much. She overworked in canteens and things, and suddenly collapsed and died. I sat in her room all night with her friend, but we couldn't do anything. There were nurses. She talked most of the time, in a queer, wandering voice — like a spirit. She talked about her life,' Anne said in a quivering voice. 'And it seemed as if she couldn't remember one happy thing in it. Just dreariness. She sounded glad to die.'

'You shouldn't have been there,' Dampier said emphatically. 'Was there no one else?'

'Her horrid little friend wanted me to stay, I knew them both a little. How could I refuse to stay with her? I wouldn't *let* myself,' she added fiercely. 'Oh, I hated it — but — it sounds silly — but I want to know how I can stand things. I can't be always shirking. I won't let myself.'

'I don't believe you ever shirk,' Dampier said. '

'I do, and in a way that no one knows,' Anne said. 'I won't get to know people — not well — and in that way I shirk all their bothers — not exactly on purpose. But I'm not generous to tiresome strangers like Maquita. She will do anything for anybody.'

'But you will do everything for one person — or for a few — some day,' Dampier said quickly. 'You'd never save yourself for one minute if someone you cared wanted you.'

'Wouldn't I?' Anne said sombrely. 'I'm not sure. I ought to like more people. I'm lonely enough often, yet I want a lot. Oh, I'm greedy. I'd rather take than give.'

'That is untrue,' Dampier said. 'I can see that you are fastidious in your refusals.'

He dug little holes in the path with his stick and carefully filled them in.

'Did you feel me thinking of you last night?' Anne asked. 'It was suddenly, when everything seemed unbearable and crushing, for Miss Denby, for horrid, sniffing Miss Pratt — oh, for all the world. I shut my eyes and tried to remember you. You seemed a sort of rock somehow.'

Anne looked candidly at him.

'It was a great liberty to take,' she said, her tired face flashing into fun. And then added under her breath, 'But I meant it. I wanted you so much.'

'I wish I could have helped you — you child!' Dampier said.

He got up abruptly. 'Too cold here. Come along.'

'I must go back,' Anne said vaguely.

'I wonder if you would dine with me,' Dampier said, hesitating. 'Rose is in bed with a cold, and I was going to my club. But let me take you somewhere instead. What do you like — the imitation food of the West End or the disguised starvation of Soho?'

The little Soho restaurant which Anne chose was gay with pink lampshades and bunches of flowers. The painted panels on the walls of sophisticated pierrots, and stout cupids, and convivial ladies and gentlemen were sufficiently unlike the tranquil dullness of the Mimosa Club. The people dining at the tables too, mostly young officers and pretty and very admiring girls, all cheerful and talkative, in no way recalled Anne's usual surroundings. Her natural gaiety crept back, and she smiled across at Dampier, her cheeks delicately flushed. She was a little uncertain of this adventure, for an obscure reason which might have found expression in some such phrase as 'Oh, I don't want anything to be *spoilt!*'

Dampier was contented and eager. He wanted to be kind, and he felt protective, and she interested and stirred him. Anne would have been astonished to know that he thought her beautiful. But she had her moments of beauty.

'White wine, of course?' Melancthon said teasingly. 'All women like nice, sweet, sticky white wines. What shall it be?'

'I really like Chianti — red — best,' Anne said gravely, 'as this is an Italian place, because of the red and green tassels on the bottles.'

'Ah, they won't have those in wartime,' Dampier said. 'But we'll try it if you like. Not a success,' he said a few moments later when the vivacious Teresa, daughter of the plump proprietor, had brought it.

'I don't mind,' Anne said uncritically, but Dampier called the waiter.

'The wine is not good,' he said.

'Ah, we have many complaints,' the waiter said philosophically.

'It is certainly not "old Chianti",' Dampier said.

The waiter leaned over confidentially, with a wary eye on the *padrone*. 'Not very old,' he admitted, 'Chianti made in England.' His smile was sympathetic as well as cynical as he bore off the bottle. He returned with the wine list, from which Dampier made a second choice.

'Ah, voici les Gothas!' the waiter remarked casually, as he put down the bottle, and as he spoke the distant bangs of the warning maroons sounded.

A shock of attention went through the restaurant. Everybody looked tense for a moment, and one young soldier stood up as white as paper, with a distraught expression. A brother officer dining with him pulled him back into his seat, and the two girls at the table began at once to talk with forced gaiety.

'I should take you home,' Dampier said anxiously to Anne. 'I daresay I could get you safely there in twenty minutes if there's a taxi about. We generally get half an hour's warning. That would be best I think.'

'Please don't bother about me,' Anne said. 'But you'll be so anxious about your family. Do try and get back to them. And poor Mrs Dampier is ill too.'

'I'll try for a taxi,' Dampier said, but at the door a policeman stopped him.

'Inside, sir. They're here.'

There was nothing to be done but sit through it, and in a moment it seemed the faint distant booming gathered force as the nearer guns came into action, and the night was filled with a continuous crash of fire that shook the street and made windows and tables rattle. Some of the guests availed themselves of the proprietor's invitation to retire to his cellar, whither he led his wife and a brood of children. But most people went on with their dinners in apparent calm.

Anne was not nervous, but she fancied that Dampier must be worried about his family.

'You must just fly home the moment it's over, and never mind me,' she urged.

'I shan't do that,' Dampier replied. He was mentally contrasting Anne's composure with his wife's frantic nervousness, and was suddenly aware that he was grateful to her for not making a scene. Dampier had married a womanly woman, who made many scenes and took care that he was in all of them. He noticed that the other women in the restaurant were almost as calm as Anne. Rose in their place would have given way to tears or hysterics. He smiled suddenly at Anne, a deeper feeling underlying the amusement in his eyes as he said approvingly, 'You are really very good. Almost as if you liked raids.'

'I don't,' Anne said.

There came a lull, which lasted so long that Dampier was able to telephone to Montpelier Square. He came back looking relieved.

'All well so far, and Rose hasn't minded it as much as usual,' he said. 'I've never heard it so loud I think.'

He insisted on Anne drinking a liqueur to steady her nerves.

People began to go, although the 'All clear' hadn't come through. Apparently it was safe enough. Dampier paid the bill, and they set out to look for a taxi.

The air had a slight mist of smoke from the guns and the smell and taste of powder. The streets were deserted; neither cat nor taxi saluted them. Every now and then Anne trod sharply on a fragment of shrapnel on the pavement, but there was no sign of damage in Soho.

'It's over, I expect,' she said.

'I'm afraid we'll have to walk home,' Dampier said, vexed. 'You'll be very tired.'

'Not a bit. But you mustn't come with me,' Anne said. 'Please, please do go and look after your own people. The raid may begin again. I shall be all right. I'll go along Piccadilly and through the park.'

'So shall I,' Dampier said. He put Anne's arm through his and held it lightly.

He spoke as lightly. 'If you want friends, Anne, count on Rose and me. I want to be your friend whenever you need one. Will you remember?'

'Yes,' Anne stammered. She found herself saying confusedly, 'I've made up my mind to get married in three weeks. Thomas is going out to France. He — he wants it.'

'Oh,' Dampier said drily, 'you're unfashionable. The war brides are all getting divorces by this time. Better wait till the war is over. It will be — soon, now. Why this decision?'

'It was partly — oh, last night I thought of it,' Anne said, 'or rather last night I realised how miserable women are all alone. Latchkey ladies, letting themselves in and out of dismal rooms, being independent and hating it. All very well for people with gifts and professions, artists or writers. But for us, the ordinary ones, a latchkey is a terrible symbol. I must be old-fashioned and domestic at heart — I couldn't bear to be like poor Miss Denby.'

'There's time yet, isn't there?' Dampier said. 'And possibly a bad marriage is better than no marriage for a woman. But — be sure, if you can be.' He spoke with a touch of bitterness. 'Consult somebody first — not that advice is any good. Have you aunts of any sort?'

'Of two sorts,' Anne replied with humour. 'I have twin aunts — which isn't at all common, and their names are Maxima and Minima! I'm going to see Aunt Max tomorrow. She's head of the Lodge School for girls at Campden Hill. The other head-mistress is her affinity, and they call each other Paul and Veritas — Aunt Max is Veritas. She's horribly truthful.'

'Where's the other twin aunt?' Dampier said.

Aunt Minnie lives in the country. She isn't married either, but she hasn't got an affinity. She cares only for translating German books. She's much queerer than Aunt Max. I know so many unmarried women, and they're all queer — that's why I *won't* be them,' Anne said in a panic.

'You mustn't marry for that reason,' Dampier said in an odd voice. 'You're a little bit overwrought after last night, and no wonder. But the world isn't all maiden ladies, or hasty, better-than-nothing marriages.'

'You're laughing at me. You think I'm sentimental. So I am,' Anne said unexpectedly. 'So would you be if you lived at the Mimosa Club with herds of women. We can't help it. You've no idea how silly women are. They exaggerate or else belittle everything. They exaggerate their illnesses, and the bargains they get in shops, and everything that men think of them or say about them. I'm curious. I want to know how I can stand life. Women seem so silly. I always hope I won't make a fuss if I get woven into a pattern in a colour I don't like — blue when I'd rather be red, or green, or white! What good does complaining do, and how can we help it?'

'You're a contradictory fatalist,' Dampier said. 'Why do you lament over the frustration of a woman like Miss Denby if no one can help anything?'

'I'm a confused thinker,' Anne said. 'But I have an idea about life. That I wouldn't complain at least at the consequences of my own acts — I'd try not to. But I'd like a lot of life. I'm greedy. I lament over Miss Denby because she seemed to have had *nothing*. That frightens me. Perhaps she wanted things, and tried — and was beaten all the same.'

'Most of us are beaten all the same. But you and Thomas must be more fortunate,' Dampier said gently.

A brilliant wing of light swept across the sky, and another travelling from the opposite direction met it with a swift intermingling; from all parts of the horizon suddenly sprang the searchlights, crossing swords, clashing soundlessly in the empty spaces above the earth. The park was lit up by their sharp flashing blades, making a magical pattern and rhythm, melting, withdrawing, intricate, radiant.

'If it wasn't the war, how marvellous we would think it,' Anne breathed. 'It's a magic sky, isn't it?'

'Anne, you're magic!'

Anne scarcely knew if she heard the whispered words, for a crash that was the unmistakable crash of a bomb smote the air. The searchlights shut off, all but two long intersecting rays, narrow and remote, that travelled restlessly, searching in one direction, and the guns began again.

They were in the middle of the park, and Dampier felt Anne tremble as if she were cold. He led her to a seat beneath a tree, blaming himself for having left the restaurant before the 'All clear' had sounded.

'Won't the tree attract the raid — like lightning?' Anne said, laughing nervously.

'I hope not. It seems safer than the open ground in case of shrapnel,' Dampier answered. 'It may be just another little spurt before they chase the Gothas off. Anne, you're cold.' He possessed himself of her hand, slipping her glove off. She did not resist. Her hand lay in his, and their eyes met in a sudden, long alarmed gaze.

'Oh, don't,' Anne whimpered weakly. 'I don't want you to!' But her voice was lost as he lifted her close to him, and even while she tried to resist she knew that she was mad to feel him kiss her.

'Oh, you are sweet,' Dampier said with a break of passion in his voice. 'I love you, Anne.'

Anne, caught up into a new and fiery element, and strung from head to heel with quivering nerves, hid her burning face and closed her eyes against Dampier's breast. She could feel his heart beating wildly. In an instant they separated and walked on, shaken and amazed.

The Gothas were chased away in that final outburst of guns, and presently the noise grew intermittent, and ceased. The searchlights blazed their white trails along the sky and made the park as bright as noonday.

Anne and Dampier walked silently towards the gate. Anne's tumult dying down left a sharp feeling that was not wholly distress, but her prevailing emotion made her say suddenly and passionately, 'Oh, I wish you had not kissed me. Now it's all spoilt.'

'Don't say that, Anne.' Dampier spoke heavily. 'Don't regret it. Things will be just the same after this. Don't let it make any difference. I have been abominable.'

'No,' Anne said, faintly smiling at him. 'I — let you.'

'You were too strong for me. I was overpowered. But I'm not a philanderer, Anne. Believe that,' Dampier added with a touch of irony. 'But if you read novels, specially war novels, you won't be able to believe that. You will know "what men are".'

'What are they?' Anne said slowly. 'Very much like women?

I can't bear this nonsense of women tempting and men betraying. We meet half-way, I think. This is a war incident. It's nothing more. You can't pretend to care about me. You don't know me. It's the raid and the searchlights.'

Dampier looked at her in a way that made her put out her hand hurriedly as if to implore him not to speak.

'Let's be honest, Anne. I won't torment you again, but let us be honest with each other tonight. I love you. I want you more than anything in the world. But if you marry Thomas, I'll be the best friend you've both got.'

Anne was silent for so long a time that Dampier glanced at her anxiously. Her face was white, and she was walking blindly, stumbling sometimes against the metal hoops that fenced in the borders of the grass.

'It wouldn't be honest to pretend that things will be just the same after this,' she said.

'No,' Dampier said, 'but I'll never worry you, Anne, by word or sign. Don't go away because you won't trust me.'

Anne sat down on one of the green chairs near the gate. The searchlights were fewer and dimmer, and from the street came the valiant bugling of the Boy Scouts — All Clear.

Anne slipped her hands into Dampier's, and his pulses began to quicken. She crept against him.

'Hold me just a minute,' she whispered recklessly. 'I'm pretending all sorts of things, but what I really feel is joy.'

'You're tempting me, Anne. Come away with me,' Dampier said in a strained voice, holding her.

'I want to,' Anne whispered with a sob of excitement. 'But I won't. I won't. I can't.'

From that stubborn refusal Dampier, urgent and lost, could not move her. Presently, in compunction, he ceased to implore her, and they walked silently to her door. Anne, fumbling for her latchkey, let it slip out of her nervous fingers on to the pavement, and Dampier picked it up and opened the door for her.

In the faint beam cast by Mrs Hickey's guttering candle on the hall-table, Anne hesitated, rather white. Their eyes met, and Anne, in a childish way, held up her face, to be kissed, leaned her cheek against his for a moment, and was gone.

Dampier, angry and touched, felt that she was ridiculous.

He strode home across the park, alternately exalted and depressed. Dampier was forty-one, and he loved his wife, but he had never been in love with her. She had fallen in love with him, and they had been married. It is not only women who marry for a home. His feeling for Anne had taken him unawares, and amazed him. Was it passion or was it love? He felt it in every nerve, and his mind, his heart, whatever the interchangeable parts of him were called, were full of her image. Beneath the current of shifting emotions — shame in his disloyalty, joy in the new deeps of his capacity to feel — and the thrill of the triumphant male in the response of the woman, the least fine of his emotions — there was something strong and solid. Dampier said to himself that friendship lay at the base of the thing simply. Anne was companionable — the rest——

He broke off undeceived.

'I'll stick to friendship — if she'll let me,' he said.

He knew that he could not.

9 Thomas

Punctually at four o'clock the next day Anne presented herself at the door of the Lodge School on Campden Hill conducted by her aunt, Miss Maxima Carey, and her partner, Miss Mollond.

Miss Carey and Miss Mollond were friends, partners, and soulmates, and in the utmost privacy they addressed each other by the names of Paul and Veritas, consistently living up to what these names seemed to them to imply. They guarded both the names and the characters attached to them with jealous precaution, but it need hardly be stated that the secret was cherished and exploited by every schoolgirl in the house. In the dormitory discussions, indeed, the ladies underwent a change from the austere, religious and overflowingly sentimental women that they were, to something a thought rakish. It would have distressed these dignified, earnest women very much to know that their chosen names for each other, which were in their minds beautiful, symbolic, and almost sacred, were bandied about with levity among the young creatures whose characters they prayerfully tried to mould.

Paul and Veritas were highly educated women and admirable teachers, and their school had a deserved reputation, but they reserved so much of their personality for themselves that they had very little left over for the schoolgirls, and unconsciously presented a conventional mask to them of which the children were quick to feel the unreality. They were 'funny, brainy old things', but they were not beloved. Schoolgirl passion vented itself on the younger teachers in the house, and gifts to the principals were perfunctory offerings, while they were laid in worship at other feet.

Anne knew both sides of the Lodge School as she had been a schoolgirl there as well as a niece. It had sometimes been a difficult double position to fill because she was anxious to be loyal to Aunt Max who was very kind to her, and she was afraid of seeming priggish or sentimental in the eyes of the other girls. Perhaps it was a tribute to her diplomacy that she had been very popular with the schoolgirls and well thought of by the principals as a sound if not a brilliant student. Her refusal to go on to the University was a matter of serious displeasure to her aunt.

She had not been up to the Lodge for a long time, and she looked about the budding garden with pleasure. Her remembrance of early morning wakings at Campden Hill was full of the wind in the trees and of bird notes. Birds in this town garden seemed to sing more than anywhere else she knew. The house was a square and solid structure, made uglier than it once had been by the addition of two red brick wings, a dormitory and a gymnasium at either side of the grey stone main building. A little party of girls who had probably been to the dentist or a picture gallery preceded her into the house in charge of a governess. One of them, staring curiously down the drive, waved an impudent hand. Anne waved back and laughed.

The maid who admitted her was new and did not know her. She went to see if Miss Carey had returned from church, and Anne waited in the grey-walled drawing-room which was so cool in summer and so much too chilly now. It had what Anne called a 'university emptiness' about it, rather charming if hundreds of other rooms had not followed the same scheme. There were only two pictures on the walls, both small, brightly coloured modern landscapes, one hung low over the chimney-piece, the other behind the piano on which stood a single yellow bowl. A table bore numbers of the *Hibbert Journal*, the *Spectator* and the *Church Times*, and the bookcases at either end of the room held 'books that were literature, in bindings that one could handle with pleasure', to quote Paul. There were old blue candlesticks, and a few flowering plants, and some chairs of a good period covered in chintz. A black cushion was placed at one end of the settee, a yellow one at the other. This marked the determination of Paul and Veritas to be modern. It was not a room that had grown. It was a room that expressed itself by exclusions. The one concession to war emergencies was the gas grate, upright, barred and blatant, that filled the white-tiled fireplace.

Aunt Maxima came in and Anne felt acutely as she had felt before how unsuitable was this setting of space and careful colour to her real personality. Aunt Max was large and hillocky in shape, with a moon-like face and round brown eyes magnified by rimless glasses. She belonged actually to the class and period that crowds the top of the piano with photographs of the family babies, admits chairs of all sizes and shapes, and a multicoloured carpet, knows nothing of plain wall-spaces or the value of a yellow bowl reflected in mahogany, and would let the dog snore by the fire and sniff for crumbs round the generous tea-table. But the caprice of fate had determined that Aunt Max should be diverted from her natural path that lay through plush chairs, antimacassars and crumbs, with rioting, spoilt babies and indulged dogs about her feet, and had decreed for her this bleak intellectualism, with a yellow bowl and blue candlesticks as 'notes of colour', and a soul-mate who rejoiced bleakly in these things.

'My dear child!' Aunt Max exclaimed, planting firm hands on Anne's shoulders. 'It is good to see you.' She kissed her critically.

'Pale! Are you getting proper food?'

Anne was answering this and similar questions when tea and Miss Mollond came in together. Paul, who considered her as a niece as well as an ex-pupil, kissed her tepidly and turned to Miss Carey.

'Such a wonderful anthem, Veritas,' she said impressively. 'A boy with the quality of a great singer: *As Pants the Hart*. And the prayer of intercession most moving. If you could have been with me to feel it!'

Anne hid a smile. Paul had been to Evensong at the Abbey which was a spiritual debauch in which she and Veritas indulged every day, together or singly. Evensong at the Abbey, followed by a comfortable tea, sustained them through all the trials of school life.

Miss Mollond was dark and small. Her hair was drawn plainly back from her keen, extremely earnest face, and her want of physical stamina often made Aunt Max very anxious. At such moments Paul would talk solemnly of the duty of carrying on bravely one's appointed task, and speak brightly of 'nothing being different, if she were taken', and the big woman, shaken by sobs, would gather her frail affinity into maternal arms and promise humbly to try and be as trusting as Paul. These scenes, however, belonged to their inmost secret life, together with the endearing phrases 'dear one' and 'my saint'. Paul was a saint to Veritas. Officially their manner to each other was brief and dry. Paul, too, wore rimless glasses.

'We have sent for you, Anne,' Aunt Max said when the bread and margarine of a war tea had been removed, 'to offer you the First Form. So many parents want to send their little girls back to us as day children that we have decided to have a class for children from seven to ten years old again, and we should be glad to make you the Form Mistress.'

'You are not qualified by any degree, of course,' Miss Mollond said, 'but you have a natural gift for teaching young children which we think is of much more value. Quite a gift. You should make use of it, Anne. But, dear, your aunt will talk it over with you. I must go and change. Good-bye, my dear child. I hope soon to welcome you as one of the staff.'

'You will lie down and rest for half an hour, Paul dear,' Veritas cried anxiously. 'To please me! I insist.'

'If the Sixth Form essays will permit,' Paul promised, with a quick, patient smile.

Anne could teach little girls, and had sometimes done so for a few days at a time to help the school in an emergency, but she was not sure that she wanted to do it as a regular thing. The offer came as a surprise. She considered it while Aunt Max explained and enlarged on the duties that she would be expected to undertake. She must do something, Anne reflected, even if she married Thomas. The Lodge School would relieve her of further necessity to look about her either for work or for lodgings. It would fill her time, and her thoughts, and the idea of teaching the children attracted her very strongly.

'You may live out, if you prefer it,' Aunt Max said. 'But of course I hope you will come up here and occupy your old room. You will be perfectly free out of school hours, and will have your own latchkey.'

'I'll wear it round my neck like a millstone,' Anne said, and in the face of her aunt's concern asked her for her opinion on an immediate marriage with Thomas. Aunt Max was firmly and utterly against it.

Anne left her, promising to think it over, and to talk it over very seriously with Thomas. In any event she undertook to become the Mistress of the First Form for the summer term, beginning a week hence. She went away feeling that if she married Thomas, and if she lived and taught at her aunt's school till the war was over, and till Thomas could support her, that life would be cut and dried and doubtless quite simple and secure in the future.

There need be no chance encounters, no walks across the park, no kisses under the searchlights. She rebelled suddenly against the security which had seemed to her so desirable.

'A young gentleman called for you,' Mrs Hickey informed her as she let herself into the over-cleaned house in Belgrave Road. 'At five o'clock. I told him you'd be at the Mimosa Club for your dinner, so he's there waiting. Such a lovely-looking young gentleman in khaki — the very one you've a picture of in your room. Glasses, and a sweet, good face.'

Mrs Hickey's laudatory tones suggested a taste of her favourite consolation.

It must be Thomas, arrived in his usual fashion without warning. Anne could discuss matters with him at once. She ran upstairs to change, hurrying over it because she had kept poor Thomas waiting so long already, and in the spinster-ridden dullness of the Mimosa Club drawing-room of all places.

But Lieut Thomas Watson had spent two of the pleasantest hours of his life in that room. Arriving at five o'clock at the Club, he had asked for Miss Carey, as he had understood from the voluble Mrs Hickey that Anne was already there. The plump-cheeked Dolly had at once said, oh, yes, please to come in, and she'd run up and tell Miss. Dolly thought he had said Miss Garry, and being used to the number of Petunia's admirers, blithely informed her that a gentleman who hadn't given his name was below.

Petunia had stayed away from the office because she was going out to dinner and wanted to review her wardrobe and add roses and bows of ribbon in unexpected places. She had accomplished this to her satisfaction when Dolly brought word of a visitor. She went down, and the mistake was soon explained, but Petunia begged Thomas not to go. Dear old Anne might come in any minute, and meantime they could have some tea. The room for a wonder was unoccupied, and there was a small fire burning. Thomas and Petunia took possession of the two chintz arm-chairs in front of the fire, and Dolly brought in tea and thick bread thinly spread with jam — sixpence each — and they began to enjoy themselves very much.

All men were profoundly interesting to Petunia, and after a dullish week she glowed in the softest colours for Anne's young man, as she called him. Thomas was dazzled by the beautiful, interested face that she turned to him, and deeply flattered by the attention she gave to everything he said. He was soon telling her happily of his interest in the literary side of the war, and Petunia was shuddering over his quotations from the poems of Siegfried Sassoon. Anne refused bluntly to hear anything by Sassoon or even Rupert Brooke, and indeed her interest in all writers which had once been eager had seemed to die out since the war. This had troubled Thomas greatly. It had been their chief bond of interest — how glowingly Anne had once responded when he wrote her tremendous letters, full of Keats and Shelley, detailing his impressions of Italy (Genoa, Milan, Florence, Rome, and Venice in a month). Now she scarcely wrote, and never of war poetry. Thomas had sometimes wondered bitterly at Folkestone if after all they were suited to each other.

How different Miss Garry seemed. There was real response in her bright dark eyes (by Jove, they were enormous too) and absorbed face lifted towards him as she stirred the meagre fire. Petunia was genuinely responsive. Poetry and a young man together excited her. Thomas expanded visibly. He left the literary side of the war and talked of himself modestly but with some interest. Petunia was dangerously sympathetic. Thomas began to feel that he had never met a really feminine woman before — not the kind to inspire a poet anyhow, but Miss Garry would inspire anyone. Nothing cold or casual, or efficiently self-contained — like war-workers who put off sex as they put on uniform, and made themselves hateful objects to men like Thomas — about her! Thomas became fluent and confidential, and even amusing. He taught Miss Garry little bits — suitable bits of course — of camp songs, and was delighted when she sang them to him in her sweet little low voice. They sang together, scarcely above a whisper, and laughed a great deal.

'Oh, here's dear old Anne,' Petunia exclaimed, 'We must stop being so foolish!'

She subtly implied that Anne was beyond the sweet, pliable years of foolishness, and would be stern to them.

'Anne dear, Mr Watson has been teaching me the dearest Canadian soldier songs he learnt at Folkestone, and all sorts of others. Such fun! I must go now. I'm going out to dinner with Captain Somers. You must meet him, Anne — he's a great dear.'

She said good-bye to Thomas, thanking him with soft warmth for teaching her his songs, and hoping to meet him again. Then she vanished, leaving an infatuated young man, pierced with jealousy of Captain Somers.

Anne in her old powder-blue frock was looking a little pale and thin, by no means at her best, and Thomas felt that the casual friendliness of her greeting was in sharp contrast to Petunia's fascinations.

'We can't dine here,' she exclaimed abruptly at once. 'What about a Lyons, Thomas, or some other small place where we can talk?'

'Let us go to Soho,' Thomas said. 'I know lots of jolly little places there.'

Anne agreed, thinking how regularly Thomas produced in her a feeling of anti-climax. What was it in his serious, conventional character that always brought him in second?

'I was caught in an air raid last night in a Soho restaurant,' she said lightly. 'So for luck we won't go to the same one.

How is it that you are in London? You said you'd be coming in three weeks, in your letter.'

At dinner she jumped restlessly from the subject of Thomas's equipment for France to say with an abruptness that startled and annoyed him: 'How stupid it is that I have nowhere to see anyone except over a café table. Not to own even two rooms is inhuman! If I marry you, Thomas, have you enough money to get me a comfortable flat with room to turn round in, and talk to people in? Otherwise I don't think it's worthwhile.'

Thomas looked so genuinely hurt that she turned off this speech with a joke. But she had expressed a conviction. Her mode of living was becoming impossible.

Thomas raised the point of immediate marriage, but Anne felt the feebleness in his tone, and beneath a faint smart of pride, was glad. Her decision of yesterday had melted like snow wreaths. Face to face with Thomas it seemed ridiculous. She saw with sudden clearness that married to anyone as tranquil and unambitious as he was she would forever be shouldering responsibility, forever be pushing him to effort. Some women liked that sort of thing. Anne felt she hated it. The lover, the husband, the child that sometimes possessed her dreams receded further than they had ever been before. She looked at Thomas critically. He was a pleasant-looking young fellow, with a rather small, close-set mouth, and candid, innocent eyes. He had very nice tastes, and a strong sense of duty that had kept him plodding away at dull and distasteful home jobs without complaint, when a more ambitious man would have worried the authorities into giving him a better billet. Thomas had made earnest and repeated efforts to get to the Front but always so respectfully that they had scarcely been noticed. His going now was not really due to any special effort on his own part. Thomas was never conspicuous. Another machine was going out to France, and Lieut Watson was going out as part of it.

Thomas looked at Anne and remembered that she was a year older than he was. It was too much. Eighteen, he thought, was the right age for a woman to marry. The poets seldom wrote about women much older than eighteen, Juliet and Beatrice indeed were much younger. He didn't at all like the women in modern poetry. He thought the young poets whom he greatly admired in other respects coarse and untrue in their writing about women. Thomas was essentially old-fashioned. Anne was very interesting; he had always admired her, but he began to remember his resentment over her brief letters, when Folkestone had been very cold and wet and dreary, and he had wanted a letter. No, she had not treated him well for a long time. His sense of injury grew. She was not a bit good-looking, and she looked positively ill and old after that wonderful little Miss Garry, with her shining foreign eyes and her captivating gentleness and interest. Anne owed him a little interest at least after his months at Folkestone, and in the face of his immediate departure for the Front. But she was eating her small portion of chicken and tired lettuce drenched in vinegar with a remote, withdrawn air, making no attempt whatever to talk.

'What fellow were you dining with last night, when you got caught in the raid?' Thomas demanded carelessly and crossly.

The scarlet wave that swept Anne's pale face amused him first, and then roused an obscure jealousy.

Anne laughed, astonished that his voice sounded angry when he repeated the question; but the colour in her cheeks was slow in subsiding. He persisted and she parried. It would have been simple to tell the truth, but Anne suddenly saw half a dozen reasons against it. She at last told more than the truth.

'I was with the Dampiers, if you must know,' she said carelessly. 'I've told you about them, Thomas. They want to meet you. We might go to tea there on Sunday — he wrote

Melancthon, do you remember? Philip Michael Dampier?'

'Oh,' Thomas said, appeased. 'But haven't they got a house? Why on earth come to a place like this?'

'The cook was ill or something,' Anne said easily. 'People like a change from their own houses sometimes. Let's have *sbaglione*, Thomas, it's a lovely eggy thing done in white wine, simply delicious.'

They had *sbaglione*, and special coffee — which was a little more like burnt india-rubber than ordinary coffee — and cigarettes, and became quite friendly together again.

But deep down in Anne's heart, like a little chill pebble, lay the lie she had told to her straight and decent Thomas, and it hurt her. Why had she lied over such an ordinary thing, Anne guiltily wondered.

They discussed the future, and agreed that a hurried marriage would be unwise. Thomas's family, it seemed, were against it as well as Aunt Maxima. They would wait and see. In October perhaps. Thomas had only eight days before going to France.

Anne shopped with him and for him all the week, and at night he insisted on dining at the Mimosa Club in order to see Petunia. Thomas fell in love with her with a completeness that surprised and gratified him. He felt himself one of the romantics, and remained doggedly faithful to Anne.

On Sunday afternoon — Petunia being in the country with Simon Meebes, Maquita and some others — Thomas reminded Anne of her suggestion to go to tea with the Dampiers.

Anne hedged, but Thomas urged it. Anne was excited and wretched, as much over the unnecessary complexity she had made of what after all had been largely accident, as over the prospect of seeing Dampier so soon again. With difficulty, and with hot waves of colour, she told Thomas the facts of her dinner alone with Dampier as they walked up to Montpelier

Square. Thomas was frankly astonished.

'Why on earth didn't you say so!' he exclaimed.

'I — I thought you'd mind,' Anne said unhappily, dropping a second pebble into her heart to take the place of the one she had just lifted.

'I think it was all right — as it happened — by accident,' Thomas said with meaning. 'But you're a queer one, Anne.'

'I don't mean to be,' Anne said in a trembling voice. 'I'm pushed into things sometimes.'

'Well, take care of that sort of thing,' Thomas said vaguely. 'The war's a damn good excuse to too many people.'

He recalled with disquiet Anne's deep, startled colour.

The Dampiers' domestic interior reassured Lieut Watson that here Anne had the kindest of friends. Rose Dampier was more animated than usual, and was looking well and pretty, talking to a woman friend whom she evidently cherished. She made room for Thomas on the sofa beside them, and was gracious to him. Dampier, holding back a brace of cavorting little boys with one hand, placed a table near Anne and handed her tea with the other, as grave, as friendly, as detached as he had ever been. The air raid had been the merest episode as she had said, Anne concluded, and a feeling of safety and happiness returned to her. Nothing need be spoilt.

'I *must* ask Anne a question in my Bible book,' shrieked Micky, wriggling out of his father's grasp to swarm over Anne.

'Who avented the sign of the cross what Nanny makes — like this?' Micky demanded, waving a hand mysteriously up and down his white tunic.

Anne looked helplessly at Dampier, who said firmly, 'Micky, don't bother Miss Carey. You'll learn all that when you're older.'

'Oh, never mind then,' Micky said carelessly, 'I expect it was the same people who avented God.'

'God wasn't ever avented,' Rowley said contemptuously. 'He made hisself. Micky's foolish.'

'You are not to bother Miss Carey,' Dampier said again.

'Anne isn't a bit bothered,' Micky said, stroking her cheek with a sticky finger consideringly. 'She likes us.'

Anne's eyes met Dampier's for an instant, then he crossed the room to talk to Thomas, leaving the little boys to riot over her. Two young men presently came in who looked up to Dampier so devoutly that he was embarrassed as well as amused.

'You must go and see Carmichael — everything is in his hands,' Anne heard him saying. 'I never even look in at the office.' Evidently the young men had some interest in Dampier's *Review*. Probably they wished to write for it.

Dampier left them when an older man, announced as Sir Charles Dampier, came in. Anne hadn't connected Dampier with a family — apart from his wife and children. His older brother was not in the least like him. He looked like a sailor, fresh-coloured and alert, with thick dark hair and observant bright-blue eyes. He was keen and businesslike where Dampier was dreamy and shy. Anne learnt that he had been in the Navy, but had retired as a lieutenant to go into business in the City. He had retired from business after making a good thing of it, and was now giving his services to the Admiralty. Rose Dampier told her all this as she detached the boys firmly, and directed them to go and speak to their uncle before she took them off to bed. They went, but galloped back again hot and boisterous to demand that Anne should put them to bed.

'Nurse is out, so Anne must do it,' Rowley shouted, digging his elbows into her knees and pressing a glowing cheek against her face. 'We wish her to, so she must!'

'It would be too much to ask!' Rose Dampier murmured, looking doubtfully at her, and with pretty hesitation. Dampier interposed.

'Most certainly not, boys. Off you go at once. Miss Carey has had far too much of them, Rose!'

The boys went obediently, after rapturously kissing Anne, and within ten minutes had capered back in dressing-gowns and slippers to insist that she should 'see their room, and say good night in bed.'

Anne, who had risen to go, captured Micky in response to a plaintive appeal from Rose, who took possession of Rowland, and followed her up to the nursery.

There was room to put the children into their cots, under nurse's second-best hat and their own old jerseys and morning shoes, but actually there seemed to be no other free space in the nursery. It was a large, pleasant room, but from the high brass fender thickly hung with small drying garments to the top of the big press, it seemed to be used as a dumping-ground for everything in the house that no one specially required. Anne, who was orderly and dainty by nature, was shocked. The confusion was dreadful to her; toys, garments, boys' clothes, nurse's clothes, even piles of clean linen, biscuit boxes and medicine bottles everywhere. She wondered if the same discomfort ruled elsewhere in Dampier's house.

'Nurse is so untidy,' Rose Dampier remarked plaintively, collecting the stray garments from the boys' beds, and thrusting them hastily into an overflowing wardrobe. 'Excellent, but no method.'

'You left the clean wash in here, not Nanny,' Rowland said reproachfully.

'And Daddy's coat to have its buttons sewed on,' piped up Micky.

Rose tidied a little by moving the things somewhere else, and gently shepherded Anne back to the drawing-room.

Dampier seized a moment to speak to her alone.

'Are you getting married, Anne?' he asked swiftly.

'No — not yet,' Anne said coldly.

'Do, Anne, do,' Dampier urged. 'I'm sure it's the best thing after all.'

Anne looked at him to see if he were laughing at her, furious with him, but his expression was baffling, only it held no laughter.

Anne turned away, and Dampier remembered her angry eyes.

'I won't go to the Club,' she said petulantly to Thomas when they were in Belgrave Road again. 'If it's Petunia you want to see, ask her to come out somewhere with us or take her somewhere alone. I'm tired.'

She felt sore and angry still, and had a desire to cry. The second visit to Dampier's house had ended in an impression of alienation and coldness. She flung the gibe about Petunia cruelly. She felt that she cared nothing at all for Thomas, but she wouldn't give him up to a little vampire like Petunia Garry.

The latter had not returned to the Club, so Thomas was content to dine elsewhere, and he and Anne bickered miserably all the evening.

Later, thinking things over, Anne relented. Poor Thomas, why should he not see all that he could of Petunia — and have all the time that she could spare him — if she so greatly charmed him? Anne did not care herself. She made a point of urging Petunia to go about with them, and found herself, with a certain degree of amusement, sometimes making herself scarce. They had quite a happy, friendly three days together, Thomas becoming more and more enchanted. Then he went to France.

A week later Anne wrote suggesting that their somewhat tenuous engagement should definitely be declared at an end, and Thomas acquiesced with suitable reluctance. Soon afterwards he began to write to Petunia. She read his long letters, which were frequent and ardent, aloud to anyone who cared to listen to them, with apparent interest, and often left them lying about, by which Dolly no doubt profited. But her own letters in reply were few and brief. The written symbol held small vitality for Petunia whose demands required speech and touch, and Thomas was to her already a shadow.

Anne continued to send him regular and friendly letters together with his favourite literary weeklies.

At night she lay awake and thought of Dampier. She was surprised and uneasy at his hold upon her. She fought against it, ashamed, but the thoughts persisted.

10 A Knight of Leicester Square

Latchkey Ladies — using the term in Anne's, not in any Leicester Squarish sense — move about a great deal. Not to Biarritz, or Nice, or Paris, or Rome; not even to Bath, or Cowes, or the North. Ascot and the moors have no meaning for them. But they seek the variety of Pimlico and Chelsea and Bloomsbury; the finer air of Bayswater and Hampstead. They occupy tiny flats in Chancery Lane and the Inns of Court. The cheaper parts of the Embankment and the purlieus of Belgravia and Mayfair know them too. There is not a street leading from the Strand to the River where, above offices and warehouses and committee rooms that deal alternately with swine fever and children's country holidays you may not flush a brace or more of these same latchkey ladies nesting together near the housetops. Their knowledge of landladies, of lodging-housekeepers, of 'manageresses' of all grades is profound. Their latchkey is the symbol that admits them to a dreary intimacy with the habits and ways of these people who, for a fee, hand over the metal seal of liberty to eat and live and die unregarded. Unregarded that is to say only in the sense of awakening no warm pity or interest. Curiosity, comment and intrusion of the baser sort are common, and are a frequent cause of the ladies taking wing to other parts. Hope will spring eternal, variety is never impossible in London. You can change your ill. Latchkey ladies do so remarkably often. Theirs is not the monotony known to the married of always fitting the same key into the same lock.

About the time that Anne betook herself up to Campden Hill to teach the First Form under the extremely superior development of latchkey lady personified by Paul and Veritas, a wave of change broke over the Mimosa Club. The Hon Mrs Bridson went with her friend Miss Spicer to Southsea, leaving her address — on a visiting card — with the astonished Anne, and a pompous but kindly meant invitation to let her know from time to time how she got on. Maquita, overhearing this weighty speech, instantly volunteered in the most gushing terms to write to Miss Spicer every few weeks in order to sketch her future career in the Pensions Office, and also Petunia's theatre conquests. Miss Spicer, admiring her wicked ease of manner, tried to subdue Maquita's pealing laugh in vain, but Mrs Bridson merely turned a dull and chilly eye upon her. It had never quelled Maquita's irrepressible cheerfulness and did not do so now.

'To leave *that* young woman is no matter of pain to me,' Mrs Bridson observed to Miss Spicer, but Honoria sighed a little. Southsea might be warmer than London, and a pleasant change in the spring, but she doubted if in the select *pension* to which they were committed she would find anything as fresh, as vital and as satisfying to some need in herself as Maquita, Anne and even Petunia Garry, half guttersnipe, half mystery.

Maquita, who welcomed any excuse for a flitting, gave Mrs Hickey notice the same day as Anne did, and not all the tears and revilings of that irate tyrant could shake her glad determination to go. The cast-down wretchedness of Alice, the poor deaf drudge, at their departure hurt them more than all Mrs Hickey's mixed railing and regret, and Anne could hardly bear it when the downtrodden creature, coming in with the hot water at night, stood with tears dropping down her cheeks to say in her toneless low voice, 'Oh, Miss, don't go! We've never kept a lodger so long. Give Mrs Hickey another chance — she's a quick-tempered woman, but she's not bad.' The girls ransacked their limited wardrobes to find something that would be useful to Alice. She was grateful, but she wept openly under the red and baleful nose of Mrs Hickey when they went. Petunia joined Maquita in a boarding-house in

Holland Park Road; Lynette Mason went to Penge to her brother's house for the summer, suddenly developing an affection for the howling baby, who, it seemed, was very fond of her and would go to her in preference to its own parents. Mrs Benny Arnold's anxieties about her husband ended in the news of his death. A sister came and took her away to the country, numb and broken but strangely calm now that the worst had happened.

So the little group of the winter broke up, and new people flowed into the Mimosa Club. Petunia as spring advanced shirked her office more and more, sometimes for an hour, sometimes for a half-day, sometimes for a day. Simon was out of England, and the two pounds a week that paid her lodging and laundry were unsupplemented. Her income from the war-work she did not do diminished till she could not even buy a new 'cammy' with it. Maquita grew anxious and remonstrated, but Petunia was unperturbed.

'I don't like the old office, Maquita dear,' she said amiably. 'I'll get Simon to sell some of my mother's jewels when he comes back and pay back what I borrow from you. Oh, I do love the hot sun, and the shop-windows.'

She walked about London in one of her dream-moods, forgetting that she was shabby, and surveying the shops uncovetously. She even forgot to look at men. The mysterious side of her queer nature was in possession of her for the time, and there was something childish and sweet in her expression. She walked with her little chorus-girl swing from the hips, her hands in her shabby old ulster pockets, for once blankly unconscious of the effect she was creating. Fancies flitted across her mind. She imagined the winged boy of the Piccadilly fountain impatient under the desecrating hands of the workmen, who thus late in the war were caging him in wood. Perhaps he slipped down at night into the basin itself and played with the floating petals left by the flower-sellers.

Funny little fantastic boy, in the dim street lights. Perhaps he flew like a moth to the Park … Possibly the parks indeed were alive with the released spirits of London at night-time.

Petunia surveyed St Paul's and the Temple, and shared her scrappy meals with the pigeons. But at dusk she flitted like a moth to the shop-windows.

She was lost in dreamy admiration of some sketchy draperies of silk and ribbon, tantalisingly shown beneath the heavily shaded lights that war precautions demanded, in a Leicester Square window one evening when a man stopped beside her, stared intently at her profile, then into the window, and finally went on. In a moment he turned back, and stood beside her, gazing into the shop-window. Petunia had not noticed him before, but she became aware of him now, and something that had slept in her awoke. She cast him a small, sidelong glance, and saw beneath a Staff cap a square-set face staring hard at the frivolous garments of the window. Actually her profile reflected in the glass was absorbing his attention. Petunia stood still.

There is plenty of meretricious romance in Leicester Square or thereabouts — every hour of every day and night, London being what it is, and Leicester Square being where it is — one almost said where she is! But occasionally a pure spring of real romance may jet up without warning from a trodden and unlikely bit of earth. Robert Wentworth, wondering impatiently what in heaven and earth the girl could see in those tawdry rags in the window labelled 'Undies for Air Raids', to keep her standing so long, was a romantic survival, and Petunia was to learn to the full what pure romance could do for her.

Of this both he and she were naturally unconscious. Robert was not the type of man who studies feminine shop-windows with any pleasure, and when Petunia moved off — with her little chorus-girl swing and a jaunty look from under her three-cornered black hat — he stepped beside her and spoke to her. Her response, which was ready and theatrical, her tripping walk, her play with her beautiful eyes, her voice — not Cockney or common, but odd — dismayed him, but only superficially. For in the window-glass Robert was sure he had seen midmost June, the end of the war, the clearance of the tangled and dreadful dreams that had had him at their mercy for months and months, the beginning of all knowledge, and in short, love.

He had always known that love would come to him like that. Like a thunderclap he meant. Later on he was vague about the place of his meeting with Petunia and much ashamed of the underclothes. Petunia, with her malicious sense of humour, told some of his friends.

He saluted her stiffly. 'May I walk a little way with you?' he asked, and added very formally, 'I want to explain to you — ah — that I don't usually speak to people without an introduction. I hope you will not misunderstand me?'

'Oh, don't you?' Petunia said innocently. 'I always do. I think it's the best way. There are so many people you can never be introduced to, aren't there?'

'I must talk to you. You are not like anyone I've ever seen. Will you come and dine with me? I'm not an adventurer — I mean nothing that isn't absolutely all right,' Robert declared.

'I ought to ask my mother first — and, anyway, I ought to change,' Petunia said, hesitating.

Robert eagerly overruled both these objections; girls did as they pleased in the war; he was sure they knew some of the same people, anyhow, and he'd drag someone up to present him properly. Petunia consented to dine at the Piccadilly Grill.

Robert liked the way she walked in and took her place without the slightest awkwardness of either too much or too little knowledge. His own sisters, who were brought up in the country, always entered a restaurant as if they were children being taken out for a treat, looking round with timid smiles for the direction of the man of the party. Petunia was perfectly simple, and her little delicate airs at table pleased him too. They talked. Robert told her his name, his age, which was thirty-one, of his poems and the music he composed, his sisters' names, and what a stodgy crowd his relations were — Pallisers and Wentworths and Ames-Ferrers, all bishops and squires and Cabinet Ministers, all Conservative, all High Church, all been-on-the-land-before-the-Conquest people, you know. Robert, the head of a large family of sisters and aunts, owned a house in town, a place and some villages in Slowshire, and meant to live on the land and be a model country squire — keenly interested in modern music and literature — after the war. He wanted to marry, of course, soon.

He did not tell her much about the wound and shellshock that had only lately released him from hospital, or of the very little work he was fit to do in Whitehall which had lately promoted him to staff-major and pinned the DSO on his tunic. He kept from her as yet the haunting misery of his dreams, but as he looked at her charming, changing face, over which expression rippled like wind-blown sunlight over a cornfield, a growing jubilation shouted in his heart that he had found safety and sanity and the rapture that he had longed to feel in this self-possessed little chorus person picked up at dusk in Leicester Square. Robert didn't say that. He said — to himself — 'This glorious girl — this darling — this delicate wonder. But I won't allow her to curl her hair like that! What teeth, what a lovely line her chin makes,' and much more, silently, and to outward appearance sitting a rather grave and stolid young man in a blaring, glittering restaurant that does not usually conduce to self-restraint.

Petunia Garry told him that Petunia Garry wasn't her real name, but refused to disclose it, and spoke of her father, the VC brigadier-general. She told him many details of her childhood that alternately saddened and delighted him. And she added hesitatingly, 'I said something about my "mother" to you just now, but I am staying with an old friend of my real mother's, that's all. I am so lonely that sometimes I call her mother.'

Petunia's eyes filled with tears, and Robert, terribly moved, could hardly resist pressing her hand.

They talked till the restaurant closed, and then Robert drove her round the parks in a taxi, talking still, and asking her endless questions, fascinated. He was an idealist, and he would not so much as touch her hand.

She told him she lived in Clifford Street, and showed him Simon Meebes' house. The taxi stopped at the door, and Robert stared at her, thunderstruck.

'But I know the fellow who lives here — I hope to goodness you don't. What do you mean, Petunia? What is the right address?'

Petunia gave him a long, frightened look. 'No, it's not where I live, of course,' she said in a low voice, 'but I do know Mr Meebes. He's in Italy now. I only said his house because it was the first address that came into my head. I meant to get out and run home when you had gone. Oh, I have learnt to be afraid of men,' she added in a whisper, hiding her eyes.

Robert could not speak for a moment. Then he said desperately, 'Oh, haven't I shown you that you can trust me, you poor little hunted child! I will try again to show you that you can trust me. You will let me see you again? You will be quite frank and honest with me, won't you?'

She let him drive her to the boarding-house in Holland Park Road, and next evening when he called to take her out to dinner he met Maquita. She did not strike him as old enough to be addressed as mother by Petunia, but Miss Garry had forgotten having invented that little fiction by this time, so she was unembarrassed.

All that Major Wentworth had told Petunia about himself was perfectly true; many other things she divined for herself with that sure instinct that had disclosed the facts and characters of the Mimosa Club to her. Robert was plodding and stodgy like his relatives, with a touch of imagination to leaven the lump — but a touch only. He was snobbish to the inmost fibre of his stolid being: the Wentworths, the Pallisers, the Ames- Ferrers, and the like, were not only the salt and bulwark of England, they *were* England. But a streak of fantastic idealism lightened that lump also. A Wentworth couldn't marry beneath him, but he might, conceivably, raise someone not in any of the proper books to a condition so like the product of the blue and red books that she would be received without question as 'one of ourselves'. The thought absorbed him. He meant to marry Petunia. He was not stupid, and he was soon convinced that Petunia was not in any of the books, after she had laid claim to relationship with several well-known names, and had been easily tripped up. He knew her pretty well — in one way — when she imparted to him that her name was really Phyllis Mary Eliot, and that Sir Algernon Eliot, VC, was her father. His laughter was incomprehensible to her, and she sat looking very much offended, till he said, 'My dear child, think of something *much* better than that! Poor old Algy may be a brigadier-general, but it's the fun of this bally old war that he's only thirty-seven, and I've known him all my life, and he's certainly *not* your father!'

After that she obstinately maintained that Petunia Garry was her real name, and that her parents had both died since she had run away from home. Robert couldn't make head or tail of it. He was persuaded that she was hiding her real self and her real history under the compulsion of some overpowering fear.

He was determined to marry her, but to discover and marry the real Petunia. He undertook this task in a manner so methodical and yet so discreet that Petunia was simply bewildered by it. He studied her from morning to night in every phase. He introduced his friends to her and made up parties for the opera and plays, and questioned them as to the impression Petunia made on them. In no case was it ordinary. He examined Petunia as to her opinion of his friends, and was delighted by her clear, definite little grasp of them, the warped and egotistic Bohemians that he knew, as well as the men who were simply friends of his own class. He watched the effect of music, of dancing, of colour on her, and rejoiced that she was sensitive to all forms of beauty, with a natural discernment. He made her talk to him by the hour, and he tried to seek out all the people that she had known at the Mimosa Club, to wrest their most fleeting impressions and knowledge of her from them. He harried Maquita, questioning and cross-questioning her. He had calmly called her by her Christian name from the first, and she reciprocated.

'Really, Robert,' she said to him one evening, when hours of his psychoanalysis had driven her nearly insane, 'I'm accustomed to be taken out to dinner by men who take some interest in *me*, but you simply drag me over and over the old ground of what I do think of Petunia Garry. I think she's a vampire, if you must know it. She exhausts me.'

Robert made Petunia introduce him to Anne, and he found the Lodge School, and after writing notes to Anne three times a day, took her out to dinner finally. Warned by Maquita's outburst, he did not at once mention the only subject the world held for him. He plunged into it suddenly.

'You know, of course, that Petunia is a liar?'

'I shouldn't say so,' Anne said, startled.

'She is, poor little darling, almost congenital. She does not even remember what she says from one day to another. She isn't logical. She has a streak of genius in it all, none the less, feeling, power, imagination. She will be great, creatively, some day. But what makes her lie? What — what?' Robert asked. 'Some fearful motive that has almost killed her soul — but not quite.' Robert helped himself to more wine, and he already had quite enough.

He poured out his hopes of finding the real Petunia hidden under all the falsity; he enlarged on his conception of the gem-like purity of her soul and mind.

The voice of many bishops in the family spoke in his voice when he said reverently, 'Whatever is true or false in her stories, she is only nineteen now, and she has seen a very hard side of life. God has been very near Petunia to keep her safe.'

He spoke in sincerity, and if he hadn't been drinking a little too much Anne would have been sympathetic. As it was, she said after a pause, 'Petunia — have you ever thought of it? — is like a salamander. She lives in the fire because it's her own element.'

When he thought it over Robert decided never to forgive Anne for this remark, but at the moment he let it pass, because she made a suggestion immediately afterwards that took his attention.

'Mr Simon Meebes knows Petunia better than we do, perhaps. Why don't you ask him about her history? He's in Italy, I believe, but he'll be back if it gets at all dangerous there.'

Anne liked Robert's honesty and his tremendously high ideals, but his persistence bored her, and his snobbery, his determination to prove that Petunia had recognisable blood in her made her angry.

Meantime Petunia herself was half pleased and half bored.

'Robert treats me so respectfully,' she complained to Maquita. From the day she met him she had left the office definitely. That had been the subject of a tirade to Anne and Maquita once when he had asked himself to tea with them.

'You two put Petunia in an office — a Government office! Petunia, a delicate child, half gossamer, half poet!' Robert stormed.

'She needed the money,' Anne said sensibly.

'I am in an office,' Maquita said.

'So was I,' said Anne.

'You and Anne, yes! You don't mind it, it doesn't hurt you!' the infatuated Robert cried. 'But Petunia, all nerves, all sensitiveness to what is ugly and sordid! The idea of thinking *Petunia* should make money! How you could do it, Maquita!'

'Simon Meebes advised it, and Petunia would do anything he said,' Anne said maliciously. 'And she stood it very well, and flirted with the clerks.'

Anne went away disgusted. Maquita took Robert with good-tempered laughter.

To go out with Robert and meet his friends Petunia had to have clothes, and Major Wentworth, who couldn't buy them and give them to her — according to his code, not hers — solved the difficulty characteristically. He presented Petunia with a bank-book, and introduced her to the mysteries of its use. He settled a considerable sum of money on her.

'Whatever happens, dear, whether you love me and marry me or not, I want to have done that for you,' Robert said.

Petunia was not really mercenary, and she was touched.

He helped her to choose her clothes, and they were so various and so pleasing that it would not have been human if Anne and Maquita had not envied her a little.

Robert was in love more deeply every day, No vulgarity, no cheapness, no failure diverted him from his quest for the ideal he was sure existed. And he required Petunia to love him before he married her. The very facility of her response, her eagerness to meet emotion with emotion, put him on his guard. She gave him imaginative sympathy, but her heart seemed as elusive as a drop of quicksilver.

He searched for it until he puzzled and wearied her. He made love to her, and she met him half-way, but couldn't understand him.

'What is it you want?' she asked him one day frankly, like a child. 'I don't want to marry you. You have given me enough, and you are so good. I will live with you now, if that is what you want.'

Robert told this to Maquita, touched to tears by what he thought the highest imaginable point of Petunia's confidence in him. Then he laid his head on his arms on the table and groaned.

'She didn't know what she said!' he cried.

Maquita did not contradict. She began to admire Petunia. She was neither greedy nor ambitious.

Petunia, half enjoying herself, half tired of Robert's incessant attention — Whitehall saw him less than ever — made her escape from him one afternoon by one of her otter-like mental wriggles that furnished him with perpetual psychological interest however much they annoyed him, and went up to the garden at Campden Hill to see Anne. She had a letter from Thomas Watson in her brocade and tortoiseshell bag which she wished to read to her, but as Anne declined to hear it she put it away and began to talk of Robert.

'He's a great dear,' she said in her usual phrase, and with her unfailing perception, 'but he's a little dull. I don't love him, Anne. I see how good he is, but he never makes me all excited inside. Once I was in love — oh *fearfully* — so I know. Did I tell you about Dennis, Anne, and how I tried to poison myself in the Grand Casino Hotel because he went away?

That was terrible, but do you know I want to feel it again, and Robert can't make me. Even the Boy could a little, and Simon — if he wanted to. But Robert tries too hard.'

The story she had told of Reggie da Costa and herself now reversed itself, and Anne could not doubt that this time Petunia was telling the truth. She made the sordid little drama live again, and her eyes burnt with memory.

Anne spoke with all her force.

'Petunia, put all that out of your mind, it's over. And how can you always be talking of Simon Meebes as if you wanted him to make love to you? You *can't* — an old, horrible, vicious beast. Use your common sense. You couldn't love a man like that; you couldn't think of it.'

'I'd know how to keep him all to myself. I wouldn't give him all that he wanted, like that red-haired Lorraine,' Petunia said sullenly, craft and desire making her exquisite face immemorially old.

Anne felt sick. She spoke coldly and lightly. 'If you really don't want to marry anyone so attractive and decent as Major Wentworth, and you don't care for the family places and the family pearls, and the family dinners with the Pallisers trailing their early-Saxon roots behind them, then you ought to say so, Petunia, and let him go.'

'Let him go! I can't *make* him go,' wailed Petunia, exasperated. 'I've offered to live with him. That might make him go — after — and he cried about it. I'd like to live with him — he's a great dear, and then I needn't meet his mother. She looks so stiff, and Robert says she's the stodgiest of them all. But he won't. I believe he's in love with me.'

'He's remarkable,' Anne said. 'You'll have to love him, Petunia.'

'He'll make me, I suppose,' Petunia said, preparing to leave.

'I do like him. But he's too respectful to me, Anne. Would you like it — a man to be just as respectful when he's alone with you as when there are people in the room?

The wooing of the respectful Robert went forward all the same.

11 The First Form

'"He had a dream that he saw a tree filled with angels",' Anne dictated slowly aloud to the First Form, walking round the room to see that pencils were properly held and exercise books in the correct position on the desks. The dozen heads bent laboriously over their task, and then lifted to fix attentive eyes on Anne.

'"Filled with angels", comma,' Anne repeated, '"their starry wings tangled among the boughs".'

'I think angels is an awful shame. It's such an awful hard word to spell,' grumbled a small Scotch voice, and the smallest child in the Form, Lucy Nevil, aged seven, tossed back her long, uncannily heavy black hair and raised a defiant face.

'Oh, you can spell angels as well as anyone, Lucy,' Anne said placatingly. Lucy, as clever as paint, and easily the match of girls of ten and eleven in the class, was as prickly as a burr.

'And think what a lovely dream that was for Blake to have. You'd like to see a great wide-spreading green tree filled with angels, with shimmering, feathery wings, wouldn't you?'

'What else would wings be made of but feathers?' Lucy demanded disagreeably.

'Skin,' volunteered a literal child called Edith. 'Bats' wings are made of skin.'

'Angels with skin wings wouldn't be very pretty! Pooh! I'd rather dream of going in swimming,' Lucy declared.

'Sign your names, and Elizabeth may collect the books,' Anne said hastily, returning to her own seat.

'It's me to collect to-day,' Lucy said, springing up. Elizabeth, a firm, placid child, dealt with her promptly, pressing her back into her place, and seizing her dictation book.

'I'd be ashamed,' she remarked in stern rebuke, 'you're seven years old, and you act like two!'

She collected the books with neatness and despatch and placed them in a pile on Anne's desk.

'In five minutes,' Anne said, 'Miss Mollond is coming in to hear you say your Bible verses. I hope you all know them well.' She ignored a muttered, 'Oh, blow, I hate the Bible,' from Lucy, but catching a guilty meaning look passing between the other little girls, she asked, 'Well, children, is anything wrong?' and waited expectantly.

The Form fidgeted. Then the literal Edith spoke.

'There's something we don't want to say in our verses.'

'You astonish me,' Anne said, wondering for a moment where Paul in her zeal had led them. 'Can you tell me what it is please, Elizabeth?'

Elizabeth sprang to her feet, her face crimsoning, but meeting Anne's look with honest eyes.

'We think it's an undecent word,' she said bluntly. 'At least it's very funny. "Out of the mouths of babes and *sucklings*—"?' She sat down very red.

'Dear me, how silly of you,' Anne said. 'To begin with, there's no such thing as an undecent word, Elizabeth, and you are never to think so again. Some words, like some clothes, are unsuitable if you use them in the wrong places. For instance, I don't say, "Oh, look at all the little sucklings in Kensington Gardens" when I see the babies there in their prams, but that's all that "sucklings" means — little babies that aren't big enough to eat mutton and potatoes, so they live on milk. It's an old-fashioned word, but I had no idea you'd be afraid of it.' She left a stricken group to Miss Mollond.

Anne was enjoying her work at the school very much, and the small liberations such as not having to bother about landladies or laundry bills, or where to find a lunch that she could afford gave her a pleasant sense of affluence. She liked waking up in her comfortable little room to a view of the garden and the sound of birds, and the tireless vitality of the schoolgirls, their immense preoccupation with themselves and the affairs of the school amused and stimulated her. Even the affectionate personal interest of Paul and Veritas was rather pleasing after a long period of solitude. She took a wicked amusement in overhearing their solicitous speeches to each other and in witnessing the small, sentimental exchanges of their devotion, which they were less careful to hide from Anne than from other members of the household. Their daily rest with hot-water bottles at their feet, and literary works calculated to uplift the spirit in wartime in their hands; their pilgrimages to the Abbey for Evensong; their little apologetic surprises for each other in the shape of frugal but 'different' buns for tea, were all observed by Anne with pleasure.

Actually she was pitiless in her disparagement of a friend-ship that flowered in rank sentimentalism, but it was quite tolerable and amusing when she came fresh to it, and Paul and Veritas treated her generously, and enabled Anne to open a bank account. She had a good deal of time to herself — more than that she had a free hand in the management of her Form. Its rules, hours, lessons, were all in her hands and could be varied from day to day as she chose. Except for a Bible lesson with Miss Mollond, and class singing with another mistress, Anne had complete charge. The two Principals had a theory that small children were best in few hands, and they had formed a very high opinion of Anne's abilities as a teacher. Anne never could see why. She had no particular method except as she said 'suddenness'. No child was ever bored by her.

Most of her little girls were day pupils, produced by smart nurses and governesses at nine o'clock in the morning, and tucked into motors for their return home at one o'clock. Two or three of them, however, were boarders at the school, generally with an elder sister.

Anne had various duties in the school in the afternoon and evening, overseeing study and practising, and turning out dormitory lights. She became a craze among the older girls. Tribute was laid at her door — literally; flowers, booklets of poems, chocolates, and frenzied notes of love. Young people in bathrobes, smelling damply of soap, waylaid her to kiss her good night. She laughed at them all, but continued beloved. The school had been without any object of devotion for a long time, young mistresses having mostly betaken themselves to war-work, and elderly makeshifts having been appointed in their places. Anne filled a long-felt want. The school was thrilled to its being.

She adored her own little girls, twelve of them, individually and collectively, and they provided her with endless problems. In effect she could not actually love each child, but she almost did so — even Lucy Nevil who, at seven years old, had a hard and intolerable character, but a brain of such sharpness and ingenuity that she dominated the Form. She was the youngest product of a Scotch professor's family, each member of which was marked by extreme cleverness and complete self- satisfaction. They lived in London, where the professor maintained them by teaching, but felt ineffably superior to all English people. Lucy recounted the habits and opinions of her family faithfully day by day, drily holding them up for admiration.

She also kept a sharp look-out for waste of any kind in the schoolroom. One day she produced a matchbox full of pen-nibs that she had patiently — and secretly — retrieved from the waste-paper basket, taken home and washed, and now flaunted as possessions. She was immediately envied by the rest of the Form, but an acute discussion arose as to whether they were hers or Anne's. Anne ruled for Lucy, but said that searching in the waste-paper basket was not a pretty habit, to which Lucy sharply replied, 'Is waste a pretty habit?'

'Now we'll have drawing,' Anne said, returning to her room as Miss Mollond left it. She began to place a pot of daffodils and two little blue jugs in position, while the children dragged their seats about and got out their drawing-boards. They loved this.

'May we talk?' they said, and as they had had half an hour of severe restraint, Anne said yes, a little, but not all together.

'In the middle of Miss Mollond,' volunteered Joanna Spencer, a very plain, stolid little girl who had wept for two days with shyness upon first entering the Form, but who now was Anne's most loyal support, 'in the middle of Miss Mollond, I had to ask to be excused. I met Miss Carey — the Principal, not you of course, in the hall. She said, "Joanna, what are you doing here?" I said, "I came to get my handkerchief" — the plain truth.'

Joanna subsided, labouring a daffodil.

'My pencil is awful uncomfy,' complained Lucy. 'Could you sharpen it, please?' As Anne took it in hand, she said, 'Yesterday was Mummy's birthday. Duncan, that's my brother, he's nine, gave her a bottle of ginger-beer. Daddy gave her a five-pound note. Elsbeth, Christine, Maisie and me — and I — gave her a manicure case, an awful neat little thing, not very dear.'

'That was a lovely present,' Anne said.

'Yes, all our family gets lovely presents on birthdays,' Lucy stated. 'Duncan got a dog once. We thought it is a West Highland, but when it got ill the vet said it was just dog. Another time Elsbeth got a kitten — but it wasn't a very long-lasting kitten.'

'What happened to it?' Joanna demanded.

'It died,' Lucy replied with reticence.

'Oh, how dreadfully not fair!' came an indignant ice from the corner. 'Miss Carey, Margaret's *ruling her daffodil!*'

Half a dozen artists left their places to crowd about the culprit who faced them defiant but ashamed, and held out her ruler at once.

'I *must* rule,' she wailed with trembling lips. 'Miss Carey knows I can't draw.'

Anne dispersed the critics and soothed Margaret's nervous anguish over the lesson, while the Form settled into faint buzzing conversations by little groups of neighbours.

'I may be an only child,' Elizabeth Percy was presently heard saying bitterly on a rising note of extreme indignation. 'Yes, I may be an only child, Mary Tracy, but I am not *at all* spoilt. If I do have a room to myself, other people's things are in my bureau drawers!'

'Violet Lake is spoilt,' observed Joanna, referring to an absent member with heavy deliberation, and rubbing out with a wet finger. 'She sleeps with her mother every night, and if she chokes on a crumb she is kept in bed for a month about.'

'Cook says we can't have any more jam for tea till the end of the war, so *we're* not spoilt,' remarked the precise Edith.

'I think Edith looks very proud, Elizabeth, don't you?' Mary Tracy said in a low voice.

'Yes, Mary, indeed I do,' Elizabeth returned with equal caution. Edith, prim and aloof, was not popular.

Mary Tracy was Anne's favourite of all the children, and she found it difficult sometimes not to adore her openly. She was a chubby little girl of eight, with bobbed hair and brown eyes that were dancing out of her head with fun and impishness. She was as clever as Lucy and more gifted, and where the infant Scot was a scrap of flint, Mary had a heart of gold, and vivid sympathy. Her speaking voice was rich and soft, and she could recite charmingly, but it was her gurgling laugh, her endless quaint little ways that Anne loved.

'Now we'll run round the garden twice,' Anne said when the drawings had been inspected and criticised, 'and then we'll each choose a piece of poetry to read out loud — very nicely — and tell the others why we like it. And then we'll vote for which of us all chose best!'

This was a favourite way of having a reading lesson, except with Lucy, who always insisted on reading from an old volume of Burns belonging to her father, words which she was too small to tackle, though she read well. When Anne came to her rescue Lucy curled her lip at her English accent and never failed to say, 'I'll ask my Daddy the *right* way, and tell you tomorrow' — which she did.

After poetry reading Anne ordered out copy-books for five minutes, and sat looking consideringly at her class.

'Helen is well enough to see some of her friends to-day,' she said, 'so I am going to take — oh, I couldn't take ten at once,' as all the hands went up. Helen was one of the smaller children who lived in the house; she was at present in the infirmary recovering from a slight operation on her throat, and her friends were always clamouring to be taken in to see her.

'Three will be quite enough, and it must be her special friends, I think. You are not a special friend, are you, Lucy?'

'No, certainly not,' Lucy said emphatically. 'In school I don't like Helen; but I don't wish her any harm, and I would like to see what sort is the infirmary.' Her small, pointed face with its frosty blue eyes and the heavy weight of black hair falling round it looked positively witchlike.

'I don't think that's a good enough reason,' Anne said.

Joanna, Mary and Elizabeth were chosen, and Edith was put in charge of the Form — Anne well knowing that Lucy would take instant command when the door closed behind her — while they trooped out in joyful excitement.

Outside the schoolroom door Mary slipped her fat arms tightly round Anne's neck and kissed her rapturously.

'I love you, and I want to call you Anne,' she whispered. 'Just once — you are such a darling, Anne.' Anne could have eaten her.

They were very solemn in the infirmary where Helen, rather white and strange to them, was tucked comfortably into a big chair painting fashion plates. They smiled at each other, but with constraint. Elizabeth the ready and blunt was the first to find utterance.

'*Helen!* Are you sitting up, and able to paint? None of the First Form think you're going to live!'

The ice melted.

12 Groping

Anne tried to feel that she was content. She was in much better health than she had been for a long time, and the routine of the school was good for her nerves. But below a surface calm, her manner of poised amusement with the doings of the world, that her aunt gravely felt indicated a lack of depth of her spiritual nature, her mind was exploring deep waters. A sense of waiting was always at the back of her consciousness.

'Some day I'll plunge,' she said to herself.

She thought of Dampier, and lived over again the experience of the air raid and dismissed it from her mind with impatient self-contempt. She thought that he too must resent what had happened. Then she argued impatiently, 'How much I make of a kiss. It shows how little I know of that sort of thing. How Maquita would laugh — and Petunia!' She wanted to see Dampier again, but she could check this wish by the recollection of what she angrily called his patronising advice to marry Thomas and be done with it. As a married woman she would cease to interest or disturb him. He probably thought marriage was all a woman needed — any sort of marriage. Anne thus graded Dampier down to a very poor sort of character, and herself to nothing better, and satisfied herself that the incident was closed. Then like a flame would spring up the knowledge that something definite lay between them, ready to live again.

She never failed in her weekly letter to Thomas, and she felt more tenderness towards him than ever before, now that all feeling of duty was at an end. Thomas, in any personal relation, had slipped from her life completely. He was just one of the Army out in France, for any one of whom one could never do enough. Anne wrote him pages about Petunia, what she wore and how she looked. She had no more idea of deceiving him about Petunia than about herself. She was ministering to Thomas's hunger while he was 'out there'. Once back in England he could cope with the situation himself.

Thomas knew all about Robert Wentworth and his determination to find that his Undine had an ancestry as well as a soul. The simple-minded Thomas wrote back, 'I don't see why it matters if he loves her. She is too good for him, and I hope she won't marry him.'

July came, and several things happened. School closed, and Anne wrote a little play for her Form round *The Pied Piper* which they rehearsed with much joy in the garden, and finally played very seriously and with great success before the school and a group of admiring mothers.

It was an open-air performance, and Mary Tracy was an irresistible piper, so chubby and frolicsome that the grown-ups as well as the children would gladly have followed her. She led her band in and out among the trees, singing a little clear tune and waving her beribboned pipe. Lucy was an elderly rat — her own choice — which looked as if it would gladly bite any baby in its cradle, and held a spirited and highly disagreeable dialogue with the Piper before it permitted itself to be led into a border of delphiniums — which was the sea — and so destroyed. Joanna was a weeping matron, her ugly little face screwed up faithfully into a realistic representation of a mother's woe, and Helen, who was tiny and fair, was the little lame boy who limped behind the other children and was shut outside the magic door that opened in the mountains. Anne had a wholesome belief in happy endings, and in her version the little boy discovered that by holding a blue pebble in one hand and a yellow pebble in the other and singing a song the door in the hillside would fly open and all his playmates would come trooping and tumbling out again unhurt. And so they did, with shouts of joy, and their hands full of presents, toys and flowers for him and for their parents. Oddly enough, among their number could be recognised a transformed old grey rat, jumping at the very head of the procession, with a set, determined face, and a mane of black hair waving over its frock, and a fat and jolly Piper, disguised as a skipping small girl with bobbed hair, with her arms round the shoulders of her two best friends.

The children loved the play, and the mothers were complimentary. Two of them then and there invited Anne to become their resident governess, with forty pounds a year and good holidays. Anne gratefully declined.

Just when Anne was busy over the play, Rose Dampier wrote saying that she and the children were off to Scotland for the summer, and that Philip was going to live at a golf club and come up to London every day, as he couldn't take a proper holiday, and would Anne dine with them before they closed the house next Wednesday?

Anne wrote regretfully that she couldn't manage it, but might she run in and say good-bye one afternoon? She made her visit an early one, and hurried it over, and did not see Dampier, but was unreasoningly nervous all the time lest he should come in.

In July Robert Wentworth announced that however well Maquita Gilroy might stand it, Petunia could no longer live among the squalors of the Holland Park boarding-house. Petunia was far too fine and delicate to be thrown any longer with such people as she met there, and besides the singing and dancing lessons that she was taking — under his supervision — tried her. She must have country air.

Unfortunately, as his mother declined to meet Petunia, and regarded Robert's ravings on the subject of her hidden soul and shining physical perfections as part of the lamentable results of shell-shock, the family place was not open to her. He had, however, a godmother, Lady Emily Airth, who had always interested herself very much in Robert, and from whom he had learned much of the idealism that dwelt side by side with, and a little exceeded, the snobbish elements in his nature. Lady Emily welcomed the thought of looking after Petunia for him for a bit. She was piously intrigued by the problem of finding her soul and her pedigree — if either existed — and promised to do her best to gain the girl's confidence and affection. Accordingly Miss Garry was taken by Robert to stay at the exquisitely kept little house in Sussex. She was welcomed generously, and instructed to call the plain-faced lady in the mushroom hat and large calm boots Aunt Emily. She was tactfully shown — later — that to take a bath every day and to keep her finger-nails in good order was essential in the rank of life to which it appeared to be the whim of Providence and of Robert to call her.

'Poor, poor little darling,' Robert said in one of his outbursts to Maquita when Lady Emily disclosed to him that Petunia had defective ideas on the subject of personal cleanliness. 'She does not even know how to take care of herself!' He was desperately pitiful over what Miss Garry must have suffered, lacking even this elementary knowledge of the pedigreed.

'No,' Maquita agreed, and added because she was tired of Petunia, who owed her thirty shillings and a camisole, and very tired of Robert, 'but she really has had every chance to learn. Hot water at the Mimosa was only a penny in the geyser after all. And she borrowed my nail-brush and manicure scissors and never returned them!'

In July Anne was offered a flat in Chelsea for a pound a week, and as it was big enough for two she joyfully accepted it, and asked Maquita to share it with her. They moved in, and filled it riotously with flowers and a kitten.

It was Anne who found the kitten on a wet evening in Sloane Street, caged with a number of others in a box at the door of a miscellaneous live-stock shop. While the other kittens were mewing piteously or lying in a torpid heap Anne's kitten was valiantly trying to climb the netting of the box and was extremely interested in its own efforts and repeated failures. On Anne's poked-in finger it laid a trustful and enquiring paw, and Anne, with a melting heart, went in and bought him for half a crown. She named him Pimlico after his presumed birthplace, and carried him home inside her coat, his cold, alarmed little feet sticking needle-points into her shoulder, and his faint voice uttering 'Wee wee,' like the little pig. He was so small and weak that he could scarcely stagger across the carpet or drink the warm milk in his saucer by the fire, but he was as valiant as a tiger — which he resembled as far as stripes went — and sat so close to the bars of the grate that he singed half his whiskers off.

Maquita and Anne delighted in his minute yawns, in the hunching of his back and his waving tail as he imitated a camel in the face of danger, and when he went to sleep compact and warm between Anne's hands she rolled him in a bit of blanket and put him into a chintz work-bag which she hung up on the door out of harm's way. That became his bed where he slept half the day as well as all night. He was known to visitors as the chintz kitten, and like the true love in the poem, he had the hearts of his mistresses, but his own after the manner of cats he kept to himself.

Anne enjoyed keeping the flat in order and having tempting dinners ready for Maquita at night, and she had no anxiety now about money because Aunt Max was making her an allowance of ten pounds a month. 'It's not exactly a retaining fee,' she said frankly, 'because I can quite well afford it, and I think you should have something for a time at least. But of course, Anne, Paul and I — Miss Mollond and I — both hope that you will go on with your school work in the autumn. We are making no other appointment in the meantime.'

Anne felt that she need not worry about the future nor come to any immediate decision in regard to the school. Paul and Veritas were really old pets, she thought with some compunction, and she had done nothing to deserve their kindness. The children were no trouble to her; she seldom even prepared a lesson for them. It was play really to teach them. But the sense of waiting for some approaching change outside of herself, some decision to be taken, haunted her.

'Soon I won't be fit to associate with good people like Paul and Veritas, much less the children, shall I, Pim?' she found herself murmuring aloud to the kitten one day as she tried to darn Maquita's best silk stockings with his paws darting at her thread.

Her own words startled her as much as if someone else had uttered them. She jumped up uneasily, wondering where her thoughts had led her.

✻

In July Lynette Mason wrote to say that she was going to marry the temporary curate at Penge in two months' time, and Mrs Garden announced in the *Morning Post* the engagement of her second daughter Sophia Grace to Captain the Hon Paul Clifford Price, MC, RFA.

Anne was reading this announcement when she got a letter from Mrs Garden telling her of the engagement, and how happy Sophy was, and how happy she was in consequence, and would Anne come to tea with them to meet 'Cliff' on Sunday at Brown's Hotel where they were for a few days.

Anne admired Mrs Garden without criticism. She wished she could take from Sophy the possession of her mother. Mrs

Garden was a woman of charm, one of those rare women who while putting themselves and their own affairs always and acutely first, can yet remain delightful alike to women and men. Her grace, her speech, her lively sense of fun, even her affectations seemed perfect to Anne. She was full of intrigues and complexities; each step in life was a move in a well-planned campaign; she did nothing without a motive. From borrowing a house to marrying her daughters she was incapable of stupidity or uncertainty in her methods. She made use of everyone and of every circumstance, and yet radiated careless charm. She was insincere a thousand times to one sincerity, but beneath it all she was capable of real affection. And if Mrs Garden could ever have been perfectly candid with herself she might have admitted that Anne was possibly dearer to her than Sophy. She made no comparison, but she loved Anne and was never bored by her. Sophy always bored her — dear Sophy, who was now going to marry so well, and so soon, if her mother had her way in the matter.

Anne found the Gardens' sitting-room on Sunday charming with flowers, and crowded with people whom Mrs Garden almost knew. The cream of her acquaintances were there, most of them with titles, some decrepit, some bright and newly minted in the most recent British Empire design.

Mrs Garden, vivacious, supple, with a sort of frosty golden beauty, guiltless of make-up but essentially artificial, was being everything to all men, and much to some women. She sounded affected as she said, 'Oh, dear little Anne,' in a surprised voice, but her kiss was warm. She had no time to give to her, of course, and Anne, having kissed Sophy and shaken hands with a firm-looking, short young man in uniform who was presented as 'Cliff', sat down beside an old lady who was so thickly powdered that her eyes looked sooty and her lips blue.

'It's no use at all,' the old lady said with great suddenness, but looking quite mildly at Anne, and not moving a muscle. 'As I was sayin' to Captain Price, you might just as well sell it. I have done so. One can't keep plate without the servants to clean it. And where does one get 'em nowadays? I can't. Sell the stuff, that's all.'

Anne agreed, whereupon the old lady abruptly left her seat, made her farewell to Mrs Garden, who was so attentive in walking to the door with her that Anne knew she must be of importance, and vanished.

Anne turned from following the old lady with her eyes to accept a cup of tea from somebody, and the next moment she recognised Dampier. The look she gave him was unconscious, was fleeting. 'Now — what?' Anne's eyes seemed to be asking with a tragic wonder.

Dampier sat down beside her for the rest of her visit.

'Do let me come and call on you and Miss Gilroy and the kitten,' he said pleasantly before she got up to go.

'Yes, come,' Anne said.

✳

On the last day of July Thomas died of influenza at a Base hospital in France. Anne heard the news a few days later on a Saturday night by letter from one of his sisters. They had had two telegrams, but they had been delivered together. 'Gravely ill,' and 'regretting to inform' Thomas's mother that he had succumbed. Maquita was away for the weekend, and it was raining hard outside. Anne thought of death, and Thomas. She lit the fire for comfort and sat by it very quietly with Pimlico sleeping on her lap. She had lost a friend.

The little knocker on the door lifted sharply and dropped. Anne went into the narrow hall and admitted Dampier without surprise. He sat by the fire with her and smoked cigarettes, and she talked of Thomas. She was sad, and tears wet her lashes. Dampier did not say much, but she was conscious of his sympathy. He held her hand for a moment when he left, and Anne looked into his troubled eyes. When she had heard him go she sank down into the chair before the fire and cried again with sadness for Thomas, and yet with a turbulent gladness at the back of her tears.

13 Decision

Dampier had not been able to stand the golf club for more than a week, even though he merely slept and breakfasted there. The sight of men who thought of nothing but their game and discussed it in all sorts of possible and impossible aspects even at breakfast, to whom the state of Europe and the anxiety of England appeared to be unknown, angered him unreasonably. Instead of rejoicing that some of the old stupid spirit of the Englishman survived in the midst of a perishing world, Dampier, finding himself extraordinarily irritable, departed from the golf club to rooms in London.

He fell into the habit of dropping in upon Anne and Maquita in the evening, smoking by their fire while they talked. They looked upon a fire as part of the luxury of a flat of their own, and would scarcely ever declare that it was too warm for one. And indeed it was wet and chilly that summer.

Dampier liked Maquita immensely. The almost unintelligible swiftness of her speech and her sparkling vitality amused him, and he found himself listening for the sharp, high shriek of laughter that cut into argument and finished it with the completeness of a knife cleaving an apple. Maquita knew nothing of repose, nothing of silence, nothing of a continuing relationship in talk that carried itself on from day to day. She was new every morning — or evening — and twice as sudden, but she was stimulating.

Dampier liked Pimlico rather less, especially when that intrepid hunter insisted upon regarding the backs of the chairs as of numerous Alpine heights, and himself as a chamois, taking terrific leaps from jag to jag, and clawing fiercely at each halt. Anne professed seriously to worship the little gutter-cat she had rescued, and Pimlico certainly added surprisingly to her happiness. He appealed to her as all small animals, human and otherwise, did, and she found something touching as well as amusing in the boundless life that animated his little furry body. It was a miracle that she could study by the hour.

Dampier's feeling for Anne he did not put into words, or even into any precise thought. He had himself well in hand.

Sometimes they all went out to dinner and came back to coffee in Mulberry Walk. If Maquita was out, he sat and talked to Anne in a warm, friendly intimacy. Once Anne was out and he waited for her to come back, and laughed at Maquita's headlong narration of the history of Robert and Petunia. Petunia, he said, had his complete sympathy, and he thought that if after marriage she tripped up among the Anglo-Saxon roots of her relations-in-law, Robert would only have himself to blame.

Maquita went away for a week, and during her absence Dampier stayed away from the flat. Anne concluded that he was out of town himself, or else that he was carefully considering her reputation. That he should go away without telling her, or be scrupulous of her position without first asking her if she wanted him to be so, hurt her. But the night after Maquita got back she went over to Tite Street to see a French friend who had a studio there with her brother, and presently Dampier turned up.

Anne looked at him mutely, and saw before he told her that he had been ill. He said it had been nothing, the usual touch of 'flu that no one escaped, and his heart was a tiny bit crocked. The whiteness and lassitude that fever leaves was on him, and Anne, looking at him, thought of Thomas, and her heart stood still. She knelt down beside him to stir the fire, and, still mute, laid her cheek for a moment against his hand. Then she vanished into the kitchen to make coffee, and returned gaily babbling all the news of the week, including, as she put it, a parent's fond anecdotes of Pimlico.

As they talked, Dampier's depression gradually left him, and a suppressed excitement followed it. His face was slightly flushed and his eyes were alight. He took extraordinary pleasure in Anne, in watching her, and in listening to her. Again he thought her beautiful. She was not particularly clever. She talked without any brilliance. She had no very strong views on the position of women, or the chaos in Russia, or the future of the theatre, a matter which keenly interested Dampier. She disliked most theatres, and most English actors and actresses. In many things she was, as she admitted, a confused thinker, but there was, none the less, a capacity to come directly to the heart of a thing in her, and a simple straightness of mind. She had, too, the quality that she felt so strongly in her little Mary Tracy, but of which she was unconscious in herself, a communicable ready warmth, a lovableness that lit her like a small gentle wood fire fed by twigs and bits of bark, and sweet-smelling fir-cones. Dampier liked his analogy of a wood fire to Anne. He added to himself, a wood fire out on a heath, in the open air, not vulgarised by the use and setting of a house. A little clean fire built for a particular, private worship, and extinguished after — no never that, kept perpetually alight, under the free sky.

'Anne, come away with me,' he said suddenly, without moving his position as he sat back in the one big arm-chair the flat possessed, but fixing his eyes intently on her. 'You and I have fenced enough. It's all very ridiculous. Come away with me. We want each other, don't we — don't we?' he insisted.

Anne, curled into the corner of the settee opposite to him, did not move. 'Yes — that,' she answered in a low voice, her eyes meeting his. They exchanged a long look.

'Then nothing else matters,' Dampier said. 'Oh, I know the interminable arguments. So do you. We needn't go over them. Let us go away together, Anne, for as long as we can manage. Do!'

Anne smiled faintly. Dampier was not proposing to break up his home for her or falling into heroics of love. She was glad of that; she could not have contemplated such violence. The adaptability of both of them to modern life was unquestioned, she thought ironically.

She was not so sure when Dampier rose and held her. There was passion beneath his dangerous gentleness as he kissed her. Excitement flamed over her at his touch and made her tremble. She clung to him weakly.

'Say you'll come, Anne, say it, darling. We've wasted so much time already. Oh, let us be happy together.'

She struggled against him, and a sense of calamity seized her mind for a minute. She pushed him away and dropped into a chair, shaken. The terror passed.

'You'll come with me?'

'Yes, yes,' she whispered desperately.

Later she listened while he suggested different plans, half acquiescing, half in a dream, but roused herself to refuse anywhere in London.

'I don't like it either,' Dampier said doubtfully, 'but London is safest of all.'

'We must be in the country together,' Anne said, kissing him. 'I couldn't bear anything else.'

Then he remembered eagerly that he knew a farm-house on Exmoor to which they could go.

'I'll telegraph the first thing in the morning,' he said, possessed and eager. 'Oh, I wish I could carry you off tonight, this minute, Anne. We'll tramp over the moors, darling — can you tramp, or are your feet too little? Anyhow I'll tramp, and I'll carry you if you get tired. And we'll lie on the heath in the sun. And we'll light a fire of oblation,' he added whimsically.

They had fixed their plans pretty certainly by the time Maquita came breezily in. She snatched Pimlico, who was sleeping the sleep of a just kitten full of warm milk, with his small blunt paws and his tiger's head resting on the fender, and placed him against her neck, her chin digging into his back, an annoyance that he much resented. But as he was too sleepy to unsheathe his claws he merely uttered a plaintive squeak, and Maquita, relenting, put him back by the fire.

'Anne's going off to stay at a farm in Somerset for a week. She's looking as pale as cotton down,' Dampier said rather awkwardly. 'I suppose you couldn't manage to go with her, Maquita? Mulberry Walk in August is not ideal for fresh air, and you two girls are too fond of sitting over the fire.'

'Well, I like that. And who sits over our fire with us?' Maquita asked without rancour. 'No, alas, I've just had a week's holiday and I can't take any more till September. I'm not a million-billionaire like Anne. How long are you going for, my dear?'

'About a week,' Anne said hastily, trembling inwardly.

'Lucky child — and very sensible. I can't complain, after a rapturous time in Sussex. But I'll mind the flat and Pim till you come back,' Maquita said. 'When are you going? What's the address?'

'I'm advising her to take shipping, or in other words a train, to any little station, with no more luggage than she can carry in her hand, and then to find a farm she fancies,' Dampier said. 'But as Anne can't believe how much any farm would like to have her, I'm going to send her the address of some people who used to put me up when I went fishing in the Barle. It's a remote place — sure you won't be too lonely?' he asked Anne.

'I don't think so,' Anne murmured.

'The farm people may be dead or gone to the war since I was there,' Dampier said reflectively. 'But I'll wire and find out for you.'

Anne said that he was awfully good — to Pim's ear, as she knelt over the fire.

'But you must be going into the heart of Lorna Doone's country — how wonderful!' Maquita exclaimed briskly, recalling her favourite book.

'Well, if I am,' Anne retorted with spirit, 'I am not going to read the book. I haven't read it, and I won't read it.'

'I shall send you a copy tomorrow,' Dampier declared.

Days of hidden excitement, half misery, half exaltation followed. At one moment Anne seemed to herself despicable and Dampier merely selfish and irresponsible, and she was tempted to fling herself upon Maquita for protection, to force some power outside herself to save her — from what? The next instant nothing seemed to matter in the world but to yield utterly … She could not speak. Her nights were broken. She woke from troubled dreams in a maze of fear sometimes. And outwardly she went quietly ahead with her plan for a week's holiday.

✕

Anne looked out of the train windows and wished nervously that the landscape would not slip past so quickly; that something would delay the train at the stations at which it stopped for a fraction of a minute, as it seemed. She wondered what she was doing; for what had she cut herself adrift so completely? Her mind ached with self-reproach as she recalled Maquita's unsuspecting, affectionate farewells. She had wept in her bed the night before, and if Maquita had happened to come in she might even then have drawn back. Anne was no adventurer, but to-day she had no desire to draw back; indeed it seemed impossible that she should resist the inner compulsion that urged her to the thing she was doing. She was afraid but eager. And somehow beneath all the emotions to which she was vibrating like a violin — curiosity, dread, desire — lay the security that with Dampier, or for him, she feared neither principalities nor powers.

She had caught sight of him at Paddington, and she knew that he was in the train. At Taunton she had to change, and here presently Dampier joined her in her carriage, carrying a bag and his coat, and a thick cup of a station tea for Anne.

He filled the whole scene for her. She met him with a face bright with joy.

They had a carriage to themselves, and Anne made him share the tea because it was so horrible, and when they had finished it the train was ready to make its friendly and leisurely farewell to Taunton station. It began to drift slowly along through lanes full of poppies, past cottage gardens gay with phlox, and larkspur, and roses, and exquisite summer fields green or golden, and far hillsides of bright red clay, turned and ready for a new sowing.

Anne's eyes were fixed on the colours and shapes she could see from her window, but presently her hand stole out to find Dampier's and reassurance. He bent his head to kiss it before he took her quickly into his arms and put his lips to hers as if he could never let her go.

'Say you are happy! Look at me.' He turned her face till she looked into his eyes and smiled with an expression that satisfied him.

They sat soberly enough apart as the train in its wandering local way drew up at a charming station that looked as if it had just taken a prize at a flower-show, so wreathed and scented and gay was it. A fresh-faced, amiable woman got in between them with a basket of eggs. She was full of cheerful

Devonshire chat, but she got out a station further on, to Dampier's relief, as he had something that he wanted to say to Anne.

'Darling, that little ring you wear on your right hand, put it on this,' he said, touching her left hand.

'That? Oh, I can't. What does it matter?' Anne said, startled.

'It matters very little, except to save you possible annoyance. Cottagers are a curious tribe,' Dampier said. 'Put it on, dear.'

'It's my mother's wedding-ring,' Anne said, drawing it off slowly. 'It won't feel right on my other hand. Perhaps that's symbolic! Marry me with it, Philip!' She dropped it into his hand impulsively.

He kissed it and her as he put it on her left hand, and then he exclaimed in a low voice:

'If that were my real marriage! Anne, why didn't you come sooner?'

'Why couldn't you wait?' Anne retorted in a whisper. To her hidden face he said:

'Am I brutally selfish to you?'

'If you are, I want you to be,' Anne answered.

One or two country people and a fisherman got out at their station, and Anne stood breathing in the fresh, delicious air full of country smells with a holiday joy rising above the deeper excitement that possessed her. Dampier looked round for Lock the farmer — Farmer Bob he called him.

He was waiting with a two-wheeled yellow trap, and he welcomed Dampier and shook hands with Anne heartily. There was no other visitor at Brambleway Farm he told them, and the Missis would be glad indeed to see them. She did like to have a tell with visitors, the Missis, it was a regular fad of hers, what you might call a hobby.

The farmer was a lean, ruddy man, lame with rheumatism but full of cheerful talk. He was willing to let Dampier drive 'the finest horse on Exmoor', adding that his yellow trap was the smartest trap on Exmoor, and a moment later volunteering the information that the black and white collie that galloped ahead of them was the finest sheep-dog on the moor.

'Ah, there's few on the moor has better judgment in picking a horse, or a dog, or cattle than Farmer Bob,' he said with a childish innocence in his boasting. 'Better health may they have since I slept in damp sheets at Bampton Fair and caught my rheumatism, but not better possessions. And you'll judge for yourself if the Missis can make the best butter and the best cream you ever tasted, sir and ma'am!'

It was Anne's first introduction to the frank West Country good conceit of itself. She listened with great interest to Farmer Bob's drawling speech. Dampier made her button her coat up, and tucked a rug carefully about her, and they set off smartly up the road, Farmer Bob from the back seat giving directions as to the turnings.

He and Dampier talked, but Anne said little, delighting in the sweetness of the lanes and content to put her hand on Philip's knee to share her feeling with him. They began to climb long, gentle hills, the road a mere track between high banks thick with fern and honeysuckle and planted on top with close-growing beech hedges. At a steep bit of road Dampier gave the reins to Lock and he and Anne got out and walked slowly up to the top.

'I see you're a good walker, ma'am,' Lock said approvingly to Anne. 'I once was that myself, but Bampton Fair did for me. Whipper-in to the staghounds I was. It's very hard after being so flippant in your youth to be crippled in later years. There was never one on Exmoor more flippant than I was. And to think I never missed the fair for twenty-eight years, and got no worse out of it than a drop too much cider, and then to be treated so with damp sheets. A house I relied on too! It's a cruelty, nothing less.'

Anne could scarcely follow him, but she gathered that flippant meant energetic rather than a light way of taking things.

As they reached the higher ground a wide country spread before them, the folding and changing moors flowing endlessly towards the sky, the hills a patchwork of fields divided by hedges and straight deep lanes, and dusky with heather. The horned sheep raised surprised and mildly challenging faces as they passed, and a tiny Exmoor foal jumping and playing about its staid, rotund little mother lifted its hoofs in the air and leaped imaginary rivers, as infantile and innocent as Pimlico.

'It's no use, you can't steal him,' Dampier said, laughing at Anne's longing expression. 'Besides, he'd hate a fire and saucers of hot milk.'

Dusk gathered, and the moorland wind was keen in their faces. Anne began to be a little cold, and she pressed against Dampier's arm very silent.

A few minutes later he lifted her down at the door of the low-built, stone farm-house, where Mrs Lock stood waiting in the porch to receive them, and he felt a shiver run through her that touched him with sharp tenderness. Presently she was following Mrs Lock up an enclosed and ladder-like stair into a low-ceilinged bedroom fragrant with cleanliness and moorland air. She had washed and changed and brushed her shining fair hair when Dampier came up to tell her that supper and a magnificent fire, better than anything at Mulberry Walk, were waiting for her downstairs. It struck her suddenly and acutely that she had never before seen Dampier look utterly happy. His face was almost strange to her. It gave her a sense of power, and the same feeling of sharp tenderness that he had felt for her as he lifted her out of the dog-cart.

'I feel like Eve Victorious,' she said, smiling at him, but speaking with a break in her voice. 'But I suppose I look like a wind-blown wanton! Do I look like — that? I must — in spite of my ring. I'm sure Mrs Lock can tell.'

'You'll be smacked, Miss Anne, if you talk wickedness,' Dampier said, kissing her, and quoting a speech of her old nurse to her when she was little.

They went downstairs and feasted over the fire on what seemed luxurious Devon fare after the London rations. Farmer Bob sent them in some special cider that he asserted was as fine as any cider made in England, and in fact a match for champagne. It was pale and sparkling like Anne's hair. She coloured into the delicate radiance that Dampier loved, and the claims and questions of the world outside the farm parlour dropped away from them both.

※

She carried her lit candle up the enclosed and ladder-like stair, sheltering it with her hand from the draught as she opened the door of their room. The whole world seemed dark and silent, lit only by the beam of the candle she held, and filled by the beating of her heart. She sat on the edge of the bed and vaguely noticed that Mrs Lock had hung her yellow silk dressing-gown beside Dampier's dark blue one on two hooks in the wall at the foot of the bed.

'It's all very queer,' Anne thought in a dream of unreality. She was like some little boat, tossed on the tide beneath an immeasurable sky. She had lost all sense of her personality, and the beating of the tide and the sound of her heart were one.

'This is the end of all I've known and believed till now,' she thought confusedly. She blew out the candle.

※

She woke to sunlight blowing through the muslin window curtains, and farmyard sounds coming in; the noise of a heavy gate swinging back and a man shouting to his horses as he guided them into a field; ducks and hens about the front porch, and in the distance the bleating of sheep and the joyful barking of a collie. The cottage room was fresh and charming with its wallpaper of small coloured flowers, and two blue-painted chairs. Anne looked at her yellow dressing-gown hanging beside Dampier's blue one. From either wall at the sides of the bed a royal couple fully crowned gazed in oleographic splendour at the occupants of the room. Anne could hardly bear the dignity of their hard, globular eyes; they made her blink.

She pulled the sheet over her face, listening to the country sounds outside the house.

'It's all very queer, isn't it?' Anne murmured.

⁜

They changed their plan of tramping across country and sleeping at a different cottage each night. Instead they remained at the Locks', spending the whole day out on the moors, taking food with them, or walking to another village and getting a meal at a cottage. They amused themselves like two children, picking blackberries and whortleberries, and every day at some time Philip found a chosen handful of sticks and dried fern and beech twigs and made a smoky little fire ending in a ring of ash. It was part of his ritual of worship.

Anne was such a Londoner that the most ordinary country sight gave her extraordinary pleasure, a rabbit scudding out of the ferns at her feet, or a lost lamb helplessly trotting down the road forgetting to bleat for its mother while it ate a new sort of flower and looking half anxious, half pleased at the sight of Anne. She spent half an hour trying to catch the lamb, with its anxious face spread with mud, but rickety as its four legs appeared, and aimless as were its evasions she could not succeed in getting near it, and it finally splashed into a big puddle under a gate, baptising itself all over with mud this time, and she gave up the chase.

She joined Dampier where he lay laughing at her on his back on the heather in the hot sun.

'I've got a whole handful of larks to myself,' he said, 'and you haven't got one lamb. Listen — when one of my larks leaves off, there's another all ready to carry on.'

The curlews whistled over the hedges like men, a sweet, distinct phrase, repeated and repeated. They rose swiftly into the air with their young broods, a shower of harsh notes shaken rapidly from them with the sound of a cable being paid out. It recalled the sea and ships. Dampier and Anne, hand-in-hand, watched their tireless wheel, and the drifting uncertainty of the young, circling after their parents and crying.

'I'd like to be a curlew, to know how it feels,' Anne said. 'And I'd like to be a rabbit jumping through the heather, and a red deer hiding in the fern, planning how to escape from the hunters, and a great heavy cart-horse ploughing the land. I'd like to be able just to taste life in all those ways, and in hundreds of human ways. We never get enough of anything.'

She laid her cheek on his hand.

'If I could keep it there for ever,' she said. 'But you must leave me.'

She heard the note of woe in her voice and instantly changed, determined to live in the moment.

'I adore your hands, Philip. They're so kind, and so strong. Do you know the only thing I can remember about my father is how big and safe his hand felt when he took mine in it?

I was a miserable, nervous little child, brought up by my brother and his wife. My mother died when I was two, and my father went out to East Africa and died there years after. But I remember he came home once and took me for walks, and nothing could frighten me when he held my hand.'

'I remember my father in a different sort of way,' Dampier said grimly. 'The speech that lives in my memory is one that he made one day when I ran into the room where he was quarrelling with my mother. "Cut, you little hound, before I break your neck." I must have been about five at the time.'

'Tell me about you,' Anne said suddenly curious. 'I know nothing at all except the little things you've sometimes told me.'

Dampier looked at her narrowly. 'Then it is possible that the divorce scandals of forty years ago — nearly — can die out at last. They are equalled by this generation certainly, but not excelled.'

'What do you mean?' Anne asked.

'A lot of horrid family scandals belong to my people,' Dampier said. 'Actually I believe sheer bad temper and selfishness lay at the bottom of most of it, rather than vice, but that's enough to wreck a family. We had a dose of vice too no doubt.'

He told her something of his early history; of a home made wretched by the extravagance and vindictive bad temper of his father, of his mother's indifference to her children and passion for amusement and escape; of the desire of each for freedom at the expense of the other, and the use made of the children as miserable little pawns in the game. The divorce suit had been a very famous one with a number of 'features' that had enthralled the public for weeks, and upon the judge's refusal to give a decree to either of the parties, Dampier's mother had gone off to America with a man considerably younger than herself, and had died there a short time after.

His father spent most of his time abroad and killed himself by overdoing life in general and failing to stand up to an attack of pneumonia.

The four boys were taken by an aunt and adopted her name as soon as they were old enough to decide the point for themselves. Of the four, the youngest died as a school-boy, and Miles, who was younger than Philip, had been killed at the Gallipoli landing. Philip had been wounded in France the first year of the war and had been pronounced unfit for active service after it. He and Charles alone remained of the family, without first cousins or near relations of any kind. There was a place in Cornwall but it was permanently let. Dampier filled in the bare outlines with touches that reproduced vividly for Anne the desolate years of his childhood. He spoke half ironically, and without bitterness, but the pain had bitten in.

'And when I grew up I was sure that most of the trouble of life, Anne, could be avoided by keeping clear of women. The aunt who brought us up was a kind, good woman, and I have never been grateful enough to her, but she was not a soft person — not lovable exactly. That's what you are, my little Fire, but she wasn't. I kept my appointed course without any adventures, I daresay, simply because I wasn't interested. I had an idea of never making any woman unhappy — which I might do if I married her — and of never bringing children into the world who might conceivably be as unhappy little beasts as I and my brothers.' Dampier made a long pause.

'Then —' Anne said.

'Then came Rose,' Dampier said drily. 'I gave up my idea. She wanted to marry me, I think — goodness knows why. I had an older woman friend — my mother's friend she had been — and she decided that I was to marry, and to marry Rose. Arranged for us both to stay with her in the country, got up expeditions, left us alone — oh, the usual things. Women are so clever. I began to like the thought of marriage and a home of my own of course, and soon I liked Rose very much. I loved her in a way, and there are the boys. Can you understand, Anne? Now there is you. Oh, you didn't teach me to like you. I felt you across the room that first night, and I've been fighting you — but not as I should have done — ever since. You're everything to me, Anne, and I — I can't be free at their cost.'

'No,' Anne said, thinking what his freedom might have meant to her. 'Never mind, I won't complain. We've got happiness now.'

'And I am happy at your cost, Anne!'

'Look at me,' Anne said. 'Am I unhappy? Let us stop using such a word, or I'll be unforgivingly angry with you. I love you, my dear. We have now. Who has more?'

14 'Un Bonheur Caché'

'Woman is the working partner, even in a murder — even if she is murdered herself, I mean,' Anne contended. 'Very likely, if we knew all, she deserves it. I can hardly believe in victims, they seem as unlikely as Amazons. More unlikely, because some of the Waac officers are ferociously enormous Amazons. Their feet take up a whole Tube station. I don't believe that women get anything like a fair show economically, but morally they usually get more than they deserve.'

'Hear, hear,' Dampier said ironically.

He lay on his back on the moor basking in the sun, and Anne, with elbows digging into the heather and her face in her hands, lazily harangued him. It was their last day at the farm, but they had promised each other passionately many more such days in the future.

'Woman is not a victim unless she wants to be,' Anne pursued. 'Even when she kills her baby and blames the man, the fault is her own.'

'Aren't you hard on your sex?' Dampier asked.

'Oh, I wouldn't be *hard* on those women,' Anne said in a soft, startled voice. 'You can't think that? I only mean that we take refuge in our own evasions. We aren't educated to be truthful. I told Maquita lies about coming away with you, of course. I had to. I told Thomas a lie once, about that time I dined with you in the air raid. I'm glad I confessed it later, but I only did *that* because we were going to your house, and I thought he might find out. I don't suppose you have had to tell a single lie about me — men are protected by the social system and their own code of silence.'

'The actual telling of a lie is the least part of it,' Dampier said.

'I know,' sighed Anne. 'But it's the part I mind most. I have to lie to Mrs Lock and Farmer Bob. I don't see a free moment in the future, and my real instinct I *know* is to be honest.'

'It's the system,' Dampier said. 'All very ridiculous. We're victims of an impossible rule of life, but it's less trouble for the community to appear to submit than to break up the law. Each of us finds his own way out.'

They lay silent, scarcely a sound breaking the stillness, except the larks poised above them, a flow of subdued, late-afternoon melody pouring from them, and the sheep cropping steadily behind the bank which made their resting-place. A golden beauty brooded over the moor, and the divine air enclosed them. Anne rolled over on her back closer to Dampier where he lay with his eyes fixed on his 'handful of larks'. She studied his quiet face and thought exultantly, 'How happy he looks. I can make him happy as *she* cannot', the inevitable consolation of the second woman which pierced her sometimes as sharply as a sword.

'If I ever had a baby,' Anne said after a time.

'Yes?' Dampier asked in a lazy voice. 'A little girl with fair hair all in a fuzz like yours.'

'Oh, no, a boy,' Anne said quickly. 'I've chosen his name.'

'Would you like a baby, Anne? Because you love all amusing small things, or because it would be mine — or because it would be yours?' Dampier asked.

'Ours,' Anne said laconically, staring at the wreathing smoke of gipsy fires on the hillside.

'That's why I'd like her, darling.'

'Him,' Anne corrected firmly. 'I'd call him Mark. That would describe him nicely, and the situation, don't you think?'

'Mark Antony?' Dampier said.

'Marcus Superbus,' Anne amended.

Dampier built his fire before they wandered home by the lanes deep-set in fern and honeysuckle and beech hedges that sheltered them sometimes from sudden showers. He drew a circle thrice with a twig of oak, and laid a light handful of spine turf and dried heath as a foundation; then he built up a mound of small beech boughs and brown fern and bits of bog-wood, and lit it. Some of his twigs were green, and it burnt slowly, the blue smoke thin and faint in the sunshine blowing waveringly in their faces. His fire ended in clear flame and clean, hot ash, and he scattered it carefully.

'It's quite out, but it's warm still,' Anne said, holding her hand over the white circle. 'If I'm that fire, dearest, and you put me out some day, only you can ever light me again, you know. Do you like me to talk sentimental like a real heroine? Only it's horribly true.'

'My God, I love you, Anne,' Dampier said savagely holding her as if he could break her in pieces. 'I'll keep you alight.'

✖

London, Maquita, Mulberry Walk and Pimlico were exactly the same to all appearance when Anne got back after her week on Exmoor, but she felt so changed herself that she almost shrank from inspection, sure that her very aspect was different. She kept her secret joy like hoarded treasure in her heart, but she felt convinced that she must betray it somehow if Maquita questioned her. But except to say how awfully well and pretty she was looking, and do tell me about Exmoor, my dear, as soon as we have time for a quiet talk, Maquita took no notice of any transformation, and rattled on as usual about her own doings.

'P M D hasn't been once to see me since you went away,' she volunteered. 'It's you he likes, Anne, there's no doubt of that.'

Anne, pleased at her own quickness, reminded Maquita that he had not come near the flat during her absence either, and agreed that he was very careful of their reputations, or his own, and that possibly he might turn up that evening. She knew indeed that he would, by arrangement.

Maquita, it seemed, was now 'tremendous pals' with Louise and Bastien Duval, the French students in Tite Street, and they were coming round after dinner, if Anne wouldn't be too tired? Anne, dressing with particular care for Dampier, said carelessly that she was far from tired and would love to see them. She thought she meant it, but later on in the evening when Dampier was there, and the young French people, and they were all talking and arguing and laughing a sudden rage fell upon her, so swiftly and so secretly that she found herself clenching her trembling hands in her lap, and felt her cheeks flaming. She wanted Dampier alone, away from all these people. He was hers — hers only. These noisy, giggling people were intruders between them. It was intolerable. The reaction after her week alone with him was almost unbearable. She found herself speechlessly near tears, and was just able to reach her bedroom on some abrupt excuse of rain blowing in through the window when they overflowed. She controlled herself in an instant, but the realisation was sharp that all the world had a right to intrude between herself and Dampier.

'It is indeed a most charming little place,' the French boy was saying as she re-entered the sitting-room, looking round him with critical eyes that approved the black furniture and cream-coloured panelling, and the pleasant bits of china of a careful Chelsea interior. 'One would be inclined to say upon entering, "Ah, 'un bonheur caché'", n'est-ce pas, monsieur?'

Dampier laughed agreement, and looked across to Anne, and suspecting her wet eyelashes, he was suddenly and savagely overcome by the same feeling that had seized her. She must be tired too, and seeing no opportunity for a moment alone with her, he got up to leave, and succeeded in driving the French couple off as well, in spite of Maquita's protests.

Anne and he thought of the phrase again, and used it many times. Chance gave it meaning, for Maquita was suddenly summoned North to her family by the serious illness of her mother, and Anne remained alone at Mulberry Walk. The intimacy of the Exmoor week was resumed, in hours stolen and fugitive of secret happiness. It was not a companionship unbroken by misunderstandings and quarrels; Anne was surprised sometimes by an impatience and irritability in Dampier that went almost as quickly as it expressed itself, leaving a remorseful tenderness towards her, and sometimes by unhappy moods of her own, a looking-back, criticism, that filled them with mutual reproach. But their hours of pure content outnumbered the others, and their need for each other grew. Dampier became miserable if he was kept by his work from seeing Anne for two days, and Anne was restless till he came again. She was frightened by her dependence on him. He was the whole of her life. Outward things seemed the merest shadow of reality beside this *bonheur caché*.

She decided that she would go back to the Lodge School, and gained Dampier's half-approval. He wouldn't hear of her living up at Campden Hill, and Anne had no wish to return to the house, but Paul and Veritas had always been willing that she should live elsewhere, and come daily to her work if she preferred it. Dampier rather urged her to take up no work at all, but Anne was firm on two points. She would continue to work — certainly it might not always be as a schoolmistress she conceded — and she would not let him give her anything whatever. Dampier, who had been very tentative and fearful of her feelings in some suggestion about the flat, never made any such proposal directly again, though he tried in a dozen ways to get round the point.

Then Anne came into a legacy. Thomas Watson's sister wrote that Thomas had left half of his savings to his mother and half to Anne, and they sent Anne's cheque now with all their love. Mother would write, but she was still so weak and shaky that they saved her anything in the way of a trying letter, but Anne would understand how really glad they all were about it, because dear old Thomas had always thought and talked so much of her. A cheque for £250 fell out of the letter. Anne declined it. She wrote a loving and incoherent letter to Thomas's mother, full of real feeling, and begged to be allowed to give it to Thomas's sisters. But the Watsons wrote again that dear Thomas's wishes were sacred to them, and sent back the cheque, and this time Anne deposited it in the bank. Anne had never even known anyone who had got a legacy, outside of books. She drew out twenty-five pounds to send Maquita, and left the rest untouched. It made her feel very safe.

She went up to the Lodge School one day to arrange about her return at the end of September and found Paul and Veritas labouring under some grave emotion. They looked flushed and preoccupied, and were inconsecutive in their conversation. Something had deeply moved them, but what it was Anne could not arrive at. It was not the war, not entirely at any rate. Though it was a holiday they had not been to Evensong at the Abbey, and for tea, which was carried in by the cook, an ample person who looked equally portentous and solemn but as if she enjoyed strong emotion, there was nothing to eat but two Marie biscuits apiece. Even these were left untouched by Paul and Veritas, who kept looking at each other with nervous, troubled eyes.

'You remember Emma,' Paul said with great suddenness and severity to Anne, 'Emma Bradshaw, that *nice* parlour-maid?' She blinked her little dark eyes anxiously, and nervously removed and replaced her glasses.

'Yes, my dear Paul, it will be best to tell Anne, I think,' Veritas said with a look of relief. 'But it is exceedingly difficult to — to compass the matter in words.' Having made this helpful beginning, she stopped.

'Emma has behaved disgracefully,' Paul remarked with finality.

'But we are particularly thankful that it occurred — if it must occur at all — in the holidays,' Veritas interjected.

'Thankful indeed!' Paul said deeply. 'We are most fortunate in *that.*'

'She seemed such a good, decent, refined girl,' Veritas said, obviously recapitulating what she had said many times that day. 'Such a pleasant voice; almost a lady, in fact; and she had a Bible beside her bed too.'

'Is Emma going to have a baby?' Anne asked.

'No, not going to. She has had a baby — here — last night — *in this house,*' Veritas burst out.

Anne looked at them slowly, an odd coldness at her heart. 'You must have known,' she said very gently. 'Didn't you see or know? Poor Emma. Is the baby all right?'

'Had we known, she should not have stayed in this house, but most certainly we guessed at nothing of the kind,' Veritas said. 'Cook admits *now* that she suspected it. She should have come to us and said so at once. But that class is unaccountable. Yes, I believe the child is healthy. Emma was removed to the Lambeth Hospital this morning.'

'How could she have concealed it?' Anne said. 'She must have been quite unfit to work very often.'

'She did conceal it — completely,' Paul said sharply. 'And it was quite by accident that I went upstairs late last night, and — and heard Emma moving about her room. Cook, who is sleeping in the basement, came up and fortunately knew what to do, and we sent for Dr Jones. He was scarcely required, but we were determined to do what was right.'

'As for being unfit to work,' Veritas said. 'She was angry because her plan of smuggling the child out of the house to her sister was frustrated. I believe she would have been able to keep the whole affair from us. That class is not the same as we are. Physically and morally they are coarser.'

'Physically they are much braver,' Anne said. 'Look at the dreadful fuss our class makes.'

Paul and Veritas ignored this, looking uncomfortable.

'What is most shocking about the whole thing to our mind is,' said Veritas, 'that it is not — not — the outcome of a love affair. There is nothing of — ah — *Airly Beacon* about it, or Hetty Poyser.'

Anne hated literary allusions, and she said rather roughly, 'But there was some man?'

'I asked her — I earnestly begged her to tell me his name,' Paul said. 'Her reply was the most morally shocking thing I have ever heard. "How do I know who got me into trouble?" she said. "Except that it was one of those lads in khaki along the Embankment." Those were her words. Emma, that nice girl that we thought so highly of!'

Anne caught sight of Cook in the kitchen-garden as she went out, and turned to speak to her.

'Cook, does Emma like her baby?' she asked abruptly.

'Oh, she do indeed, Miss,' Cook returned emphatically. 'Emma was a light one with the men, but she's a born mother. If that one that come last night had been a lawful child she couldn't have been prouder of it. Laughing over its little hands as pleased as Punch when they took her to the hospital. And it was the loveliest baby ever you saw, curly hair, fine little hands, and the two eyes leppin' out of its head as if it would speak to you.'

'Will you give her this to help her buy it some clothes?' Anne said, giving Cook some money, a little awkwardly. 'And is Emma all right?'

'Oh, that's the strong girl,' Cook returned.

Anne went home shaken by the story of Emma. Paul and Veritas had put her out of the house at the first possible moment, when she might as easily have remained there and been looked after by Cook. That was their judgment of an incident as old and as ordinary as human nature. Over a lawful baby they could have rejoiced and sentimentalised. An unlawful baby and its mother were somehow ugly and unclean objects to be put out of sight. Even 'England's Need of Men', the Bill for the Protection of the Unmarried Mother, and Baby Welfare Week — in all of which subjects they took a patriotic interest — had failed to touch their inbred belief that marriage was the one warrant of motherhood. Anne pondered over them; they were Average Opinion, and there it was.

She went to see Emma and found her as decent and nice-looking as ever, with no evidence of either guilt or shame about her, unless a becoming flush were such evidence. She spoke very quietly. She was not anxious about the future; her sister in the country was very fond of children and would look after her baby for her. She might go back into service, or she might go into munitions — if the war kept up. She was well and strong.

'Having a baby is no such great thing to make a fuss about as they tell,' Emma said out of happy experience.

She exhibited the baby with open pride. Anne, who had never seen a newly born infant before, failed to recognise its beauties from Cook's enthusiastic description, but its tiny stretching and yawns fascinated her. This 'inch of experience' was a man. The thought of Mark clutched at her heart.

She said nothing of the episode to Dampier.

✕

In October Robert Wentworth's family capitulated, and promised to welcome Petunia Garry into their bosom, and accordingly Lady Emily deposited her with a mixture of regret and relief at the town house in Manchester Square, and preparations for the wedding, to take place in a few weeks' time, were set on foot. It was to be a very quiet wedding, without announcement or advertisement of any kind, because whatever Robert had discovered about Petunia's origin and relations did not warrant social publicity at least. No date could be fixed or mentioned, no church chosen. He saw to everything himself with immense secrecy; no Gretna Green elopement, no morganatic marriage of a reigning sovereign was ever more carefully plotted. But on the other hand no society bride had ever a more splendid trousseau. Robert interested himself in every detail of that also. Petunia was sketched and photographed, and artists designed creations for her, and invented fashions, and she was fitted and matched and measured for hours every day. She became a passion with the Wentworth family. Mrs Wentworth kissed her at breakfast and at night, and insisted on being called Mother, and on making her hot milk over a spirit lamp before she went to bed, because she must keep her strength up. The three sisters tried to put on their hats at the same angle as Petunia wore hers, and wondered why they looked so different.

Petunia escaped from them all one day and came to see Anne, flinging her hat down and curling herself up on the settee with evident relief. She was astonishingly improved, and of course very well dressed. Lady Emily had conquered her accent and her chorus-girl swing, and she now carried herself beautifully, and spoke with sweetness and purity. Her hair was smooth and parted like a Madonna's, but very smartly dressed, and she was wearing some of the Wentworth jewels. A remarkably perfect bloom had been secured from a somewhat ragged and uncertain stock, but in the pruning and tending Petunia had evidently suffered. She was thin and pale to the point of delicacy, and so languid that Anne scarcely recognised her.

'You know how I used to love new cammies, Anne, from those common little shops, and how I envied Sophy Garden her ordinary little pink and blue evening frocks?' she said pathetically. 'Well, now that I get all my things from Paquin and Poiret and Drécoll I simply don't care for anything. I'm just worn out standing for fittings, and I am always posing for artists. Robert has some lovely photographs of me,' she added, brightening. 'I'm supposed to be quite a coming London beauty, you know.'

'I don't see why you shouldn't be,' Anne agreed, laughing at her. 'But don't let that stodgy family suppress all the life out of you.'

'Oh, no, but they are great dears,' Petunia said affectedly. 'But I long to get away sometimes, even from Robert. He's so good that I can't help loving him, but I matter so much to him that it's tiring. It's the greatest fun to be back with you, pigging it again together.'

They were at lunch when Petunia made this speech, and Anne stared at her, rather taken aback.

'You never pigged it half as well as in this flat, my dear,' she said coolly.

'I'll be very rich now, of course,' Petunia said complacently. Evidently her memory did not carry her back to her lunches at the People's Dairy or A B Cs in her office days at the Mimosa Club, much less to her experiences in the Grand Casino Hotel, or the room in Fitzroy Street with Reggie da Costa. In other respects her memory was retentive.

'When will Maquita be back — I'd like to see her,' she said, evidently for some purpose that she did not at once disclose to Anne. She added carelessly, 'Does she ever see Simon? Is he in town?'

'I haven't an idea,' Anne said. 'You surely don't care whether he is or not?'

'Oh, no,' Petunia said indifferently. 'Robert won't allow me to say I know Mr Meebes. He disapproves of him. But it would be rather fun to see him again. If Maquita was here, I could arrange it with her. I think I'll telephone and see if he's at Clifford Street — you wouldn't come up with me there, Anne?'

Anne refused point-blank, and begged Petunia neither to telephone nor to call. 'It would be a terribly wrong thing to do. Don't think of it. Don't think of him again,' she urged. Petunia readily promised that of course she would not, and Anne was convinced that when she left the flat she would go straight to a telephone box and ring up the house in Clifford Street.

'Petunia, you have to remember that everything you do matters immensely now. You haven't only got yourself to consider — you simply cannot see Mr Meebes, or go to his house.'

'No, of course not,' Petunia said, looking crafty and offended. 'But, dear Anne, will you let me stay all night with you? Do please, it's such fun to talk about old times together; do you remember how old Mrs Bridson hated me? And I am so sick of calling Mrs Wentworth Mother, and thanking her for that beastly hot milk.'

It was impossible not to laugh, and Anne consented to keep her if the family would allow it. Petunia had her own ways of getting permission. She telephoned to Manchester Square and left a message with the butler to say that she was spending the night with Miss Carey in Chelsea, and would be back in time for luncheon next day. She came back to Anne bubbling with excitement. Robert could not object because he liked Anne enormously and thought her 'worthwhile' (Anne expressed due gratitude for this testimonial), and also because he did not know the address. Petunia began to throw off the shackles of Lady Emily and Manchester Square, and her old vagabondish self peeped out as a period of liberty stretched before her. She went singing into Anne's room, and emerged after protracted counsel with the looking-glass with her lips and cheeks touched up very cleverly, and the merest hint of licence about her madonna-like hair, having just added the accent needed to make her appearance immediately striking.

'That horrible hot milk makes me paler and paler,' she remarked. 'I have to swallow it because Mother stays in the room till I do. And it is good of her to make it, but oh, when I am married! I'm going out,' she added jauntily, 'and I'll bring in something nice for dinner and we'll have a picnic, and a good talk by the fire. Ta-ta, old dear.'

Anne protested, and coaxed and offered to go with her, but Petunia defeated her ingeniously and went off. She decided that she would not accept responsibility for Robert's Undine, but she could not help a little anxiety when seven and eight and nine o'clock passed and her guest did not return, At that hour she let Dampier in.

'She's such a little fool,' she confided to him. 'Of course, she's gone to Clifford Street — if Mr Meebes is in town.'

'Meebes was lunching at the Club,' Dampier said drily. 'He tells me he has bought a silk business in France, and is going to import ladies' clothing on a large scale.'

'I'll have to go and get her,' Anne said, starting up. 'I don't know what fascinates her in that man, but she'll ruin her life if Robert knows she's there. I'm sure he wouldn't forgive her that. He trusts her now completely, and he hates Mr Meebes.'

'Meebes is not a very wholesome character. I won't have you entering his house, Anne. Let her alone. Robert should be able to look after her,' Dampier said.

'Let me go,' Anne pleaded.

Dampier yielded reluctantly. He drove her up to Clifford Street in a taxi, and saw her admitted to Simon's house, but very nearly two hours elapsed before he saw Meebes himself come out, find a taxi, and put the two girls into it. Dampier was boiling with rage.

Petunia and Simon had just returned from dining at some odd little place known to the tribe of Meebes when Anne arrived, and they were upstairs in the smoking-room. Anne was shown into the drawing-room, and kept waiting for a considerable time, in growing indignation and nervousness.

Lorraine, the red-haired shop model who had sketched Petunia the first night Anne had met her, came in presently, and stared sulkily at her without recognition at first. Then she seemed to connect her vaguely with the house. Anne smiled at her. 'I met you here once — you were drawing Miss Garry.'

'Oh, that's it, now I remember you,' the girl said. 'Yes, she wasn't very smart that night! Now she comes to Nesbit's and buys the Paris models off me, and *they're* hardly good enough for her! Going to marry some young swell with more money than sense, I daresay.'

'She is upstairs now,' Anne said earnestly. 'Will you be so very kind — could you, as you know the house — go and tell her I'm waiting for her.'

'Not me!' Lorraine said, a spasm of jealousy crossing her face. 'I'm living here, and I don't mind telling you I am, but I don't go upstairs till I'm told to. I know Simon.'

'Of course you do, Lorraine — wise girl,' Mr Meebes said, entering the room with his cat-like tread. 'Run along up now, dear — or come, we'll all go together to the smoking-room. How do you do, Miss Carey — a pleasure!'

'Where's the girl you picked up in Piccadilly Circus, Simon?' Lorraine cried in her surly voice.

'Lorraine, you're rough tonight, dear. Don't be a jealous tiger, you haven't seen her for a long time. Petunia is in the smoking-room. Come along,' Simon turned in his low, soothing voice, patting her arm affectionately.

Petunia was looking brilliantly lovely and blazing with excitement. She laughed at Anne when she wanted her to come home. Just one more cigarette, just one more Caruso record on the gramophone; she hadn't seen dear old Simon for such an age, and she'd soon be married, and oh, so good. She imitated the stodgy Wentworth sisters with their common-sense shoes, and their hats worn well back on their heads. She had discarded her finer feelings completely. It was obvious that she wanted Anne to leave her, but that Anne obstinately determined she would not do. She felt that she hated Petunia almost, and the house seemed abominable to her, but she heard herself chatting amiably to Lorraine and Meebes, and hid her impatience because it was useless to do anything else.

It was Meebes himself who at last urged Petunia gently to leave, by volunteering to call a taxi for them.

'Miss Carey looks as if she suspected me of kidnapping you on the eve of your wedding, but I have no sinister designs at all, dear Miss Carey,' he murmured caressingly. 'I am glad to see this dear child so well and so happy.' Lorraine gave Petunia a venomous look.

'I'm glad you came, Anne,' Petunia said soberly in the cab with a sudden return to her more responsible manner. 'I would have stayed all night at Simon's — in spite of Lorraine.'

'You're mad,' Anne said coldly, and Petunia instantly laughed, and said, 'Anne, I was only joking, of course.'

She displayed her ruby earring broken and stuffed carelessly into her bag, but was incoherent as to how the accident had occurred. Robert would be angry, she feared childishly. She departed the next morning, pale, delicate, and serene, and Anne was glad to see her go.

She and Dampier spent one of their happiest evenings together after this visit.

'I am so thankful I love *you*,' Anne said to him. 'I might love Simon Meebes — or the righteous Robert — or both! But I don't. Oh, you are my whole life,' she added in a different tone. 'I can't live when I don't see you. I am an empty shell. I love you, beloved and dear.'

15 Petunia Married

The affair of the earring proved to be a great annoyance to Anne. Robert was at her door the next morning just as she was setting out for Campden Hill, in a state of intense excitement, demanding that the flat be searched from top to bottom for two rubies missing from Petunia's drop. Why Anne and she had not had the common sense to search immediately they were dropped until they found them — he had the grace to stop and apologise when he saw Anne's cool and astonished face. He was awfully sorry, but they were family things, and Petunia treated them as carelessly as if they were beads from Liberty's. They must be found.

'I was not there when she broke it,' Anne said truthfully. 'She only told me about it as she was leaving, and she seemed to think it was all right.'

'She caught the earring in a curtain,' Robert said, fuming. 'There, that must be the curtain, and the stones slipped down into the back of a big chair — that one, I suppose. Well, perhaps you'll let me look.'

Anne handed him the keys of the flat. 'Of course,' she said. 'You may take the place to pieces. I am sorry that I am obliged to go out as it looks suspicious, and if at any time you find me living in guilty splendour, you will know that I have secretly sold the two rubies and am living on the proceeds. Leave the keys with the caretaker, will you, when you've done? But seriously, Robert, Petunia had the earrings in her bag, and it's probable she lost the rubies elsewhere — in the street or the taxi perhaps as she went home.'

'She thinks they are here,' Robert said fussily, diving into the chair back and discovering with open disgust the usual fluff and crumbs harboured in such corners, but no rubies.

'Petunia is such a child that all she will say is that anyhow she has enough jewels! Every one of those stones is historic in our family, but I can't induce her to feel responsible for old things.'

'Then why not give her Liberty beads?' Anne asked tartly.

'My wife must wear the family things, and take the same pride in them that we do,' Robert said stiffly.

'Petunia used to talk of her mother's jewellery. Does she not take care of that?' Anne asked, not without a touch of malice.

Robert gave her a curious look. 'Oh, there was very little. It had to be sold to repay some liabilities,' he said hastily. Anne concluded from this that Simon's allowance to Petunia of two pounds a week — and otherwise — had been repaid by Robert.

She went off in an angry humour to school, and her Form did not fail to note her ruffled condition.

'You look awful pink to-day, Miss Carey,' the unerring Lucy remarked, fixing her sharp blue eyes on Anne's face, and, *sotto voce*, she added, 'You can tell, can't you, Joanna, that she's very cross by the way she rings the bell.'

To which the loyal Joanna replied, 'Miss Carey is never cross, unless we deserve it.'

The First Form remained pretty much as it had been in the spring, with one or two changes. The proud Edith had been moved up, and an extremely pious little girl named Josephine had taken her place. She was a great trial to Anne, and a source of mingled admiration, envy and distrust to the other children. Josephine's mother was passionately interested in temperance and missionary work, and her daughter aged ten had declared her intention of becoming a missionary as soon as she was good enough. She was already far advanced in goodness. She had given up sweets during the war, and all sugar, 'except what my mother thinks I need for my health', and her pocket-money went to the support of a Chinese mission known as the Bird's Nest, which received unwanted

Chinese female babies and brought them up to be Christian women. Josephine talked tirelessly of this mission, and of little Ching Chang, heathen babe now baptised Emily, for whom she made clothes and had stood godmother. The Form was fired with an ambition to own, jointly or separately, a Chinese infant kept in a Bird's Nest.

The day of the rubies incident Anne caught Josephine taking up a collection for this object, and promptly interfered. The children were playing in the garden at the time, or rather were supposed to be playing, but instead the whole class was gathered in a group round Josephine, chattering as busily as starlings.

'I can give a shilling — it's all I've got,' Elizabeth was saying with some hesitation.

'That would be a great waste, *I* think,' from Lucy, taking a leading part as usual.

'The poor heathen children won't think it a waste when they get the benefit,' Josephine said in stern rebuke.

'Sixpence would be enough,' Lucy persisted in her hard, logical little voice. 'And keep sixpence for yourself, Elizabeth. If you don't do that you'll just be asking your parents for money before you ought to.'

'I wish I could buy a dear little yellow Chinese baby for myself,' Mary Tracy said ardently, clasping her hands and hopping about in her excitement. 'I'll ask my mother to. I'm almost sure she will, Josephine.'

'You can't have one sent from China — certainly not — the cold would kill them. You must leave them with the kind missionaries to learn about God in the Bird's Nest. You can only work for them and pray for them in England,' Josephine said piously.

'I'll pray for them,' Lucy volunteered unexpectedly. 'But I can't give any money. I only get threepence a week, and things is awful dear in London.'

'We're going to get a baby of our own soon. We've seen about it already,' Joanna announced in a low voice, her ugly little face alight with importance. 'You can all come and see it, I daresay, when it's born. It's quite time we had another; our old baby is two and a half, and not nice at all now — he breaks every toy we've got.'

Here Anne descended upon the group and ruthlessly nipped Josephine's budding organisation of a Form missionary society.

She found Petunia awaiting her at Mulberry Walk when she got home, looking rather conscious and uncertain.

'Robert has turned your room inside out, but of course he can't find the rubies,' she said. 'It's so tiresome of him. I've got enough left for anyone — far more than most people have.'

'Robert suspects me of stealing them, and it is not an agreeable position to be in. I wish you would find them, or tell the truth about them,' Anne said sharply.

'They are lost,' Petunia said quickly. 'It was in that hotel where I dined with Simon; he had a private room. Afterwards he — he tried to kiss me, and I put up my arm to prevent him — and — well, the earring got broken.'

Anne was rather sad at this confession.

'Well, convince Robert that they aren't concealed in this flat, please,' she said. 'It was abominable of you, Petunia, to lie about it. I have every right to be angry, and as for Robert, his mania about his family, and his mania about you, make him horribly rude, to say the least of it. Don't tell me anything more about last night. I'd rather not hear.'

To her surprise Petunia's eyes brimmed over with tears, and as she wiped them away, looking helplessly at Anne, they gathered more thickly and rolled down her cheeks.

'I'm ashamed and sorry about last night. I wish I hadn't gone to Simon's. Promise you'll never tell Robert, please promise,' she said in a quivering voice. 'I don't want to hurt him, and that would — fearfully. I do love him, I can't help it. I laugh at him, but I respect him. He is so good to me, and so patient. He is dull, but I love him in spite of it.'

Her tears fell faster. 'I don't want to be married, Anne. I'm afraid of it. I think it's much easier just to live with someone you love, and then go away when you get tired of it. But Robert isn't like that, and when I marry him I am going to be everything he wishes.'

Her emotion was sincere, and Anne believed her. She had never seen Petunia shed a tear before, and she looked softened and grave as she sat there. Here was perhaps the glimmer of the soul that Robert so patiently sought.

'I'll be lady of the manor in Slowshire,' Petunia added presently in a more familiar strain. 'Robert says all the children in the lanes will curtsey to me.'

Three weeks later she was married in a small church in Bayswater, with nobody present but Robert's near relations, and — representing the sole friends of the bride — Maquita, just returned to London, and Anne. They were not there by Robert's invitation, as he had made it abundantly clear that, as his wife, Petunia must drop all her former acquaintances and find her friends among his people who were all in the right books. He thought that she might as well begin on her wedding-day. But Petunia, in an outburst of affection, had begged them both to come to the church, and Maquita said they would do so to annoy Robert. So they went.

The bridegroom did not look at them as he strode in, white and tense, supported by a brother officer, and stood waiting in an agony of nerves at the altar. Petunia managed to be a little late in spite of the Wentworths, and she came up the aisle on the arm of Lady Emily, who was to give her away, looking self-possessed and beautiful, with a sort of pale, dashed brilliance, wearing a ruby-coloured cloth dress and sables. Lady Emily, with ostrich feathers on her mushroom-shaped hat, and square silver buckles on her large, excellent shoes, wore half a dozen wolf-skins slung variously over her black satin garments, and presented so voluminous and imposing a spectacle that it was not easy for Anne and Maquita, who were on the wrong side, to see round her to the bride. But Petunia was determined to see them. She dodged behind Lady Emily, and gave them a welcoming smile, accompanied by a slight, airy wave of the hand.

It was the last chorus-girl gesture Anne ever saw her make. She left that finally behind her on her wedding-day. The ceremony was as brief as possible, and after the relations had gathered round to sign the register, Robert led his wife down the aisle to the motor at the door. He still looked pale and dazed, and did not show any signs of recognising Petunia's friends, but she threw them another smile and a kiss, and Lady Emily came up and introduced herself and spoke very pleasantly to them. Otherwise they were ignored, and Robert's family trooped out of the church looking remarkably stodgy, undeniably well bred, or at least 'long bred' Maquita said, and lugubrious in the extreme.

Petunia had been married under the name of Wilhelmina Amy Rivolta, which might have been a good or bad name as far as it conveyed anything, and which was presumably her real one. That was all that they ever discovered about her origin; Maquita later had some vague tale that her father was a cashiered officer serving in the Foreign Legion, and another vague tale that he was a sergeant at Chelsea Barracks, but there was nothing substantial to go on, and all surmise died with her marriage to Robert. Petunia Wentworth was an unquestionable member of society.

Anne felt a little sad after the wedding; there was something safe and enviable about marriage, and she did not share Petunia's view of it. She and Petunia should have been in reverse positions. She did not say that to herself; she had only one real regret, that she had not sole claim on Dampier's time. He had gone to Scotland to bring back his family to Montpelier Square. Anne felt a sharp unsubmission, that was not jealousy or remorse but a compound of both, when she thought of Rose and the little boys.

She went to see Mrs Garden in the afternoon of Petunia's wedding-day. She had a house in Cowley Street, Westminster, and Sophy, who had been married early in September with a good deal of elaboration, and had parted from her bridegroom almost at once owing to the exigencies of active service, was living with her. To Anne's joy Mrs Garden was alone, and no one came in to spoil the long, delightful talk they had together by the fire. Mrs Garden petted and coaxed Anne as no one else wanted to do, placed in solitude as she was. There was no affectation in her affection for her, though she had very little time to spare from the duties it pleased her to pay to society to attend to affairs that were really close to her heart. To-day she welcomed Anne with all the warmth and grace she would have produced — lacking the real spontaneity and feeling — for a peeress, and she was the mixture of mother and girl-friend that Anne so adored. She laughed over the First Form, the odious character of Lucy, and the dreadful piety of Josephine, Anne's methods of handling an epidemic of deceitfulness, and an almost incurable passion for eating rubber erasers and the celluloid covers of a blotting-pad owned by Joanna amused her equally. She made Anne talk of herself, but the greater part of her life was so secret now that Anne was reticent. One word broke from her as she was leaving, and though she tried to speak lightly, there was anxiety in her eyes as she waited for Mrs Garden's answer.

'If I behaved simply villainously, and Sophy couldn't know me, and everyone turned their backs, would you still be my friend?'

'You could never behave so villainously that I wouldn't be your friend,' Mrs Garden said.

'Oh, do you mean that?' Anne exclaimed. 'Some day I might ask you to do something for me — would you?'

'Anne darling, I wouldn't do more for Sophy, you know that!' Mrs Garden said. Anne clung to her, kissing her, in a blaze of gratitude.

'I may not ever ask, but I feel safe if I've got you,' she murmured.

Mrs Garden was a little disturbed, and her wits were quick. She made a point of seeing a great deal of Anne that autumn and winter, but she found her quite happy and tranquil always, and discovered nothing, and in her busy life she soon forgot her misgivings.

Dampier came back without his family. Rose was fearful of raids, now that the Germans were desperately pushed, and preferred to stay where they were less likely. He and Anne spent several weekends in the country together, and had long walks and fitful intimate talks, but Anne obstinately refused to speak of the future.

'There is only now,' she would say, and for a time they left it at that.

The Armistice was signed, and in time for Christmas Rose Dampier and the children came back to London.

After Christmas Anne's tenancy of the flat in Mulberry Walk came to an end, as the owners, relieved from the fear of air raids which had driven them to the country, wanted it back. Maquita, never a stayer, had some time before betaken herself to a studio in Bloomsbury Square, whither her French friends Louise and Bastien Duval followed her, and a somewhat rackety *ménage* was carried on there.

Anne and Dampier sighed over the loss of the little flat; it was their secret garden, a *bonheur caché*, and it held memories for both of them. Anne found another flat in Chelsea, but this time in 'Buildings'. It was in common parlance a Cattery, with mostly dim elderly ladies as tenants. There were male cats living there as well, but they were many times outnumbered by the females, each of whom appeared to keep a pet parrot, or canary, or bullfinch, whose cages on a fine day adorned the window so that the pets might benefit by the fugitive rays of sun. The approach to the Cattery was the worst part of it. It was built round a large concrete courtyard which appeared to have undergone some volcanic upheaval, and presented a surface of fissures, hills, and deep depressions that held the rain like dewponds. Fat pigeons gurgled and whirred there, and one lady opened her windows to throw out crumbs and let the pigeons fly into her room, making them her pets. Morning and night when Anne went out and came in she met the dim ladies exercising Pekinese dogs, or mixed terriers, and one aired a large half-Persian cat in a red Morocco collar, with a haughty air of exclusion. She wore a brilliant figured-silk cape, and smelt of spirits.

Anne — to match the other tenants — of course had Pimlico, now well grown in wickedness and knowledge, and longing above all things to meet a pigeon in single combat, but she did not air him in the courtyard. Sometimes he went out in her muff or her pocket, a perfect-mannered cat and a quiet traveller in buses. At the gate of the Cattery was a little restaurant for the benefit of the tenants, and Anne told Dampier that it was called 'Meat-Meat', and that at lunch and dinner-time every door emitted a stream of cats padding off to be fed. Actually it was a cheerful little place called The Delphinium, painted bright blue and green, with delphinium china, but Anne could not think of it otherwise than as Meat-Meat.

Her own flat when you got to it was inoffensive, she said, and it was not so dull as that implied. Furnished with Pimlico and her books and flowers, it had a friendly, pleasant air, and the taste of the faith-healer who owned it inclined to simplicity and quite good furniture. Maquita called it the Flattery. Anne had a woman who came in daily to keep it in order, and resigned herself to the volcanic courtyard and the devastating ugliness of living in Buildings till something better should turn up. She could see Dampier here; that mattered most of all.

In the flat immediately beneath her lived one of the few married couples of the Cattery — without children, of course, but slaves to an asthmatic fox-terrier. Their *ménage* interested her mildly as she observed it in her comings and goings. Husband and wife were past middle age, and they called each other Girlie and Darling, and the terrier Jocko. Darling was a big man who walked like an actor with a long stride, consciously dreamy, and dressed in kidney-coloured clothes, with a wide-brimmed tan felt hat, sombrero shape, and a black cloak when it rained. He had longish hair, and often sat at his window writing. Anne thought perhaps he was a poet and modelled himself on W B Yeats, but Dampier insisted that he was a cinema operator or else the local tax-collector. Girlie was mannish, and walked about the court with her hands thrust into the pockets of her tweed skirt, with no hat on her rough grey hair, greeting her acquaintances at various windows with a cigarette in her mouth which she only removed to whistle to Jocko.

Anne thought they hadn't been long married, they were so aggressively domestic, and held such tender conversations in such loud voices in the courtyard, flaunting the married state as it were in the face of the necessarily virgin parrots and canaries and bullfinches in the neighbouring windows. He would call out from the court, 'I shall just run out, Girlie dear, and get you a paper to see what's going on. Back in a moment!' And she appearing at their window framed in geraniums would respond, 'Oh, thank you, Darling, that *is* sweet of you,' and he would stride dreamily off, sometimes unconsciously splashing into one of the dewponds and bespattering his kidney-coloured legs.

In January Anne fell ill with a sharp attack of influenza that passed off quickly in its worst symptoms, but left the usual depression and apathy. Her servant, Mrs Gamble, looked after her in the morning, and did her shopping, and Dampier, in spite of her protests, came in at some time every day. It was holiday time. Paul and Veritas were at Bath, and Mrs Garden away, and Maquita very gay, so that most of the time she was alone. She fought against the physical wretchedness that oppressed her when Dampier came in, and insisted on sitting up on the sofa beside the fire to talk to him, and could even be gay, but when he was obliged to go off because Rose expected him back to dinner, or because he had to take her out somewhere, or was having guests at his house, Anne dissolved in miserable tears, and felt that her position was the hardest in the world. She wanted Dampier to be altogether hers, to be with him always and openly, to know his friends, to be known with him. Actually she had made a bargain with herself neither to feel nor to say these things, to be faithful to her creed that it was futile to dispute the result of a course deliberately chosen. She held to it in her heart, but physical weakness betrayed her sometimes. He had power in his voice, his eyes, the clasp of his hand to make her so happy that no sacrifice seemed hard. She met her reaction alone. She dreaded above all things hurting him in any way, harming his life or his prospects; she was nervous of his constantly coming to see her, not for herself, but for him.

'The Buildings have a thousand eyes,' she assured him; 'someone might know you. Do be careful!' but he laughed at her.

One day he reported that Girlie was ill and that a trail of notices from the front door throughout the building

announced the fact, and begged the other tenants to walk
quietly, not to bang their doors, and on no account either
to ring or knock at the door of 21A. Jocko disappeared; a
nurse in red and grey flitted about, and Darling strode
distractedly out of the courtyard, and hurried back at once
with some requirement a dozen times a day, wearing always
his black cloak, and flapping like a disconsolate raven. Anne,
miserable and unoccupied, found herself taking an almost
painful interest in the drama belowstairs. She hoped very
much that Girlie would get better. Instead she got worse.
Dampier informed her that all the notices had been changed
and were now peremptory. The front door bore the ominous
word 'Operation' in letters two inches long, and underneath,
'Be very quiet, please.' The other half-sheets of notepaper said
variously, 'Serious illness at 21A. Quiet essential.' 'Operation;
do not bang doors.' 'Operation; tread quietly on the stairs,'
and 21A itself was urgent in black and white that no one
should ring, or knock, or leave parcels on the floor.

Everyone was sympathetic, and except for the gurgling
pigeons, there was not sound about the Buildings. Anne
presently heard with relief from Mrs Gamble that the lady at
21A was a lot better, but the notices remained up.

One night a considerable time later Dampier was sitting
with Anne about ten o'clock when two young men who lived
near the roof ran quickly down the long stone stairs talking
to each other in ordinary voices and laughing cheerfully. They
heard a door flung open below, and Darling's voice roaring
like a bull, 'Have you no consideration at all for other people
— for serious illness? Don't you know that we have had a
tremendous operation here, and yet you rouse the house, late
at night, with your noise and laughter!'

His own voice would have roused the dead, much more
a sick woman in the room behind him, but none the less
there was in it the protective note of the savage male for its

mate. The young men were abashed and apologetic. Darling withdrew, banging 21A. Anne and Dampier laughed over it. But she felt more respect for Darling afterwards; in his roar she had recognised the authentic cry of suffering and anxiety. Darling and Girlie shared something precious and desirable. The notices vanished after that, and Jocko returned, but though Darling daily shouted through the window his customary remark about the paper, it was some time before Anne could distinguish Girlie's reply.

She was well again herself by this time, and back at the school, rather white and shaken, and still given to fits of unaccountable gloom. When she told Dampier she seriously debated the more recommended forms of suicide — veronal, the Thames, a gas-oven, or opening a vein in her arm — Dampier refused to smile. He looked so anguished over her feeble jests that she almost wept in her remorse.

'I can't bear it,' Dampier said with an effort; 'you kill my heart, Anne, when you say such things. I feel so endlessly unhappy about you sometimes. I am so selfish. Let us give it all up and go away openly. It will be fairer to you — fairer really to them, in the long run. Someone has to suffer. Why should it all come on you? I can't bear it for you.'

'I am not suffering at all,' Anne said quickly. 'Just because I've had 'flu, and talk nonsense, Philip. We wouldn't be happier — or as happy — if we did what you suggest. Legal proceedings — if they had to be — would kill me — would kill us both for each other. You couldn't bear it, and I couldn't. Your work and your friends are here. Love is the smaller part of actual life really, there is always the day's work — for a man. If we went to America or abroad we'd never have a real home. We'd both be uprooted and strange. Besides, your life, your home are here. They exist; they are part of you. You can no more forget them or leave them behind than your own body. And they were first, Philip, whatever might come later,' Anne said, hesitating, and then laughing a little uncertainly. 'If you and I broke away and lived together, I'd be always finding you remembering it was Rowley's birthday, or wondering how tall Michael had got, and how they were getting on at school, and crowds of little things about them. I can't and won't have it! I won't take on such responsibility.'

'What if I take it? What if I force you to it?' Dampier cried roughly, holding her back and making her look at him. 'Aren't you sick of lies, Anne? I am. Let us lose the world.'

'If we could — only we can't lose the world. It's too small now, too insistent, always jumping up at your elbow and interfering,' Anne said, insisting on lightness, 'And remember how fond you are of those boys, Melancthon, and how much you want them to have a happy childhood. In a divided house that wouldn't be possible.'

She fought against herself in touching on the strongest feeling in his life, his fear of making his children unhappy, and she knew it. 'I'd go away myself and hide, I'd disappear for ever — only the world's too small — out of your life, as they say in movies, before I'd let that happen,' she said, holding him.

'You must never do that,' Dampier said. 'Stay where I can see you — that at least.'

'Don't let us be so frightening. We have now, this minute,' Anne said, kissing him.

Dampier began to talk of his work: he was thinking of taking over the editorship of his *Review* again, and he wanted Anne to give up her school work and become his secretary. That would be one way of having her near him, one way that she could easily and naturally meet his friends. Dampier was growing eager about his writing. He had a long-planned scheme for a book of informal essays, and it began to take hold of him strongly, to his pleasure as well as to his surprise, as he had thought that impulse dead in himself, war-killed.

Anne liked the idea of becoming part of Dampier's office, of seeing him daily in a different relation, formally as an employer. He was amused at her ardour over the literary side of it, and promised that she would soon be disillusioned about an editor's job, and think him guided by anything but the best interests of literature.

'I'll begin at Easter,' she said. 'I've got to give Paul and Veritas a term's warning. I shall at once, though it seems fitful of me not to finish the year. I shall love your office, Philip — and to work with you. But I am not very capable. You may dismiss me with a caution.'

'I may eat you more likely. Don't look at me like that with sparks in your eyes, or you'll burn up the *Review* — and me.'

Anne 'gave notice' that she wanted to leave at Easter, and Paul and Veritas unwillingly, and after lecturing her seriously on the danger to character and life of instability, released her. Secretly the good ladies were confident that the girl had suffered more than she would show by the death in France of young Lieut Watson, and although when they approached this subject Anne quickly warded off all sympathy, they insisted on feeling sympathetic.

'She has sometimes a pale, luminous look that I feel means secret suffering,' Paul said with fond sentiment. 'But of course I think that if she battled, she would be given strength. 'Get work — it is the best of all,' as Mrs Browning says.'

'She is taking up some secretarial work for Mr Dampier, who wrote that remarkable play *Melancthon* which the *Spectator* admired so greatly. They called it the nearest approach to a great drama since Tennyson's *Harold*, and a serious contribution to the study of modern religion,' Veritas said. 'Association with a man of that stamp can only have a beneficial influence on Anne's character. Anne has not a strong character. By resigning at Easter she shows that she takes her duty to the school, and to us, too lightly. I am very much disappointed in Anne. She seems to be restless. She tried half a dozen different kinds of war-work, and dissipated her energies, instead of concentrating on one thing, however monotonous and distasteful. She is like her mother; my brother's wife had charm certainly, but no definiteness.'

'Anne lacks religion,' Paul concluded with solemn emphasis. 'Without that guiding principle there can be no stability of purpose. I wonder that we were able to impress her so little, Veritas. It makes one very humble.'

'I feel convinced, Paul, that your example has influenced her more than we now know,' Veritas asserted ardently. 'Some day we shall see. We must wait.'

16 Poetry Day

Mary Tracy skipped out of her seat, holding her chair with one hand to show that she had not 'really left her place', and waving the other towards Anne as a signal that she wanted permission to speak. Her eyes were dancing, and she nodded her little dark bobbed head, consumed by inner excitement. Before she caught Anne's attention, unfortunately, Lucy Nevil rose to her feet, with a scowl at Mary, and began to address Anne without permission in a high and rapid voice.

'Miss Carey, we've all thought of an awful good plan —'

'*You'll* not tell about it,' the robust Elizabeth broke in, her fair face aflame with indignant reproof, and she dragged the infant Scot down into her place by her streaming hair. 'Be ashamed, Lucy Nevil! We arranged about Mary —'

Anne, turning from the board on which she was giving a small girl a lesson in lettering, confronted a rising tide of feeling, with a questioning air of calm surprise. She said nothing at all, and her little girls subsided, blushing violently and directing ferocious glances at Lucy. A shamed silence descended on the Form, but Mary Tracy continued to rise and sink in her place like a small captive balloon, held only by a thread from soaring away altogether, sinking when she caught Anne's eye, and rising hopefully when she turned away. When Anne presently smiled at her, Mary was up in an instant, one fat arm raised above her head, her eyes beseeching, and her dimples irresistible.

'What is it, Mary?' Anne asked. 'You look as if you were just going to fly out of the window, like Peter Pan.'

'Oh no, dear Miss Carey, I'm not really,' Mary said on tiptoe, and speaking with her soft, rushing eagerness. 'But we have a plan of poetry, if you'll allow it. May we? We want to say our *own* poetry to you on Thursday, instead of learning any. Do let us, oh, do let us.'

'Dear me! how many people can write poetry in the Form?' Anne asked. Every hand was promptly lifted, but Lucy immediately qualified her assent.

'I've not yet written a poem, but I can by Thursday—; if Margaret and Elizabeth can write poetry,' she said, looking with some contempt upon these two rather lazy-minded classmates, whom she could easily outsoar in most subjects.

'That will be very nice,' Anne said. 'I think it is splendid that you can all write poetry. I knew Mary could, but the rest of you have kept it a great secret. I shall be delighted to hear what you have written.'

Broad smiles went round, and Lucy clapped her hands. Then Joanna rose in her place.

'We don't all do it often,' she said solemnly. 'We've made up this on purpose for you. I think it's very hard.'

'Of course,' Anne said cautiously, 'the poems won't be personal — I mean, you mustn't write about each other, or about me.'

'Oh, no,' chorussed the Form.

'In fact,' Josephine said, 'mine is a hymn — a sort of a hymn.'

'Oh, do hush,' Mary cried in an agony. 'It's no fun unless it's a surprise! Don't tell what you've written, anybody.'

'I can keep mine a good secret as I don't even know myself,' Lucy remarked with morose satisfaction.

'You'll have to ask your mother to let you stay up late if you haven't begun yet,' Joanna said. 'No one can write a good poem in two days. Mine isn't very good, but it took a whole week, before tea every day. And then, you have to copy it out. Poetry is hard work.' Joanna moistened her lips and blinked her round eyes, recalling the labour of hours as if by a physical effort.

Lucy looked impressed, but replied with a somewhat sharp buoyance, 'You're not awful quick anyhow, Joanna.'

'I think poetry is easy,' Mary said, jumping irrepressibly up and down. 'I just love it. I write lots and lots.'

On Thursday morning a mixture of shyness and suppressed excitement kept Anne's little girls unusually quiet during the first part of the morning, but they found it impossible to give their full attention, and were inwardly so seething to say the poetry they had 'made up ' that she took pity on them, and after giving them an extra run in the garden, announced that now it was poetry time — much sooner than they expected.

They sat as still as mice, eyeing each other shyly, Joanna's round face suffused by a deep crimson blush.

'I think that as Mary has so much to do with this plan,' Anne said, 'that she must take charge of the Form, and say who is to recite. I'll listen till you've all said your poems, and then we'll talk about them. Hands up, if you agree.'

Their hands went up, Lucy's unwillingly, and only because she fully realised that public opinion would be strongly against her taking the lead in this matter. All eyes were fixed on Mary Tracy, who looked about her with bright responsibility.

'I think Elizabeth Percy first, please,' Mary announced judicially.

Elizabeth, a handsome, fair child, stood up, blushing vividly. She began to recite in a breathless singsong from nervousness, but remembering after the first verse that 'gabbling' was severely criticised, she succeeded in slowing down to an extreme deliberation, punctuated by gasps of alarm.

Baby

Baby, where do you come from?
Out of the misty heights,
Out of the purple mountains,
Did the stork pick you up in his flights?

Or out of the blue-green glaciers,
Or out of the realms of snow?
Baby, where do you come from?
Baby, why don't you know?

Baby, where do you come from?
Out of Fairyland?
Where flowers chant sweetest melodies,
And birds sing on either hand?

Or perhaps you just came down, Baby,
Out of a tree so high
That it seems to me, Baby darling,
It will soon break through the sky.

'Oh, Elizabeth, what a *sweet* poem,' the Form commented warmly as the author collapsed with great suddenness into her seat, bathed in blushes.

Josephine was next, and she stood up perfectly composed, with her usual little patronising smile as of secret, superior virtue.

'Jo is awfully good,' the rest of the Form generously admitted, seeking to explain the faint discomfort she aroused in their minds. Joanna came nearest to the truth of the matter when she stated stolidly, 'Jo talks too much about it.' But they prepared to listen to her poem with deep attention.

'It's rather religious. It's a sort of hymn — a Christmas carol,' Josephine explained.

'Oh, so is mine,' Joanna cried, much disappointed 'I thought I'd be the only one. What a pity. Miss Carey won't like two.'

'Oh, indeed I will,' Anne said quickly. 'And perhaps Mary will let you say yours after Josephine. think two new carols will be delightful.'

Josephine stood patiently waiting, and began at once to recite, giving painstaking expression to every line.

Once was born a little child,
Who was the most meek and mild
Child that ever trod the sod,
For he was the Son of God.

Mary was his Mother's name.
Some time before an angel came
And told Mary that her Son
Should be the Son of God.

Not in palace decked with gold,
Not in castle very old,
Was this Son of Sons born,
But in a manger in the morn.

'Well, that's perfectly true,' Lucy observed with approval while the others applauded with the slight criticism that Josephine always aroused.

Joanna came next; her face was expressionless, and her voice was solemn, as befitted a hymn that had taken a week of anguished effort 'before tea every day' to compose.

'Christmas Carol,' she announced (a little triumphantly, for Josephine had omitted this preliminary), and. began to chant:

On Christmas night I saw
The shining moon high up above me in the sky.
On Christmas night I heard
The bleating of the lamb.
On Christmas night I saw
A light far, far away.
On Christmas night I heard
The church bells ringing.
On Christmas morn Jesus Christ was born,
In a manger, many years ago.

'It seems like as if you'd mixed up Christmas Eve and Christmas, Joanna,' Lucy remarked dispassionately.

Joanna looked anxiously at Anne for approval, and meeting her encouraging smile, sank heavily, but with comfort in her soul, into her place, prepared to take a readier interest in succeeding efforts now that her own responsibility was discharged.

'I forgot to say that I'd made a sort of moral to mine,' Josephine announced obsequiously, rising again to her feet. 'I'd better say it now. It makes a little lesson.' She recited brightly:

> Let your soul blossom as the wayside flower;
> Let kind words shower
> As the raindrops fall.
> Always have a kind smile,
> As the sunshine does the while.

'We had better all remember that,' Anne said drily.

'I didn't think you would allow words to shower while we were in school, Miss Carey,' Lucy cried pertly. But she was abashed by the severe disapproval of the class and sat rather subdued while Mary Tracy announced that she thought she would say her own one now.

She stood up against the wall, her hands clasped behind her, her shining eyes gazing out of the window. Mary had dramatic ability and a soft, charming voice that might be her fortune one day. At the present stage she favoured tragic poems, and Anne prepared herself for something serious.

'My Daughter,' Mary announced. She pitched her voice a little lower than usual, and it rose and fell in a charming cadence as she swayed slightly back and forth, everything but her poem forgotten, a true artist.

I had a little daughter
With a voice like running water
Her hair was like gold;
But now she is old.
Her eyes were brown
But now they have grown dim with the length of time.

She used to ride on a palfrey white,
With a flowing mane and tail,
 And up and down from morn till night
She rode and ne'er did fail.

But she had a greater pleasure still,
And that was watching the old mill;
She would sit and look for hours and hours,
And ponder o'er the great wheel's powers.

Hers was once the fairest face
In all this village old;
But now she keeps a humbler place
Down in the deep dark mould.

Mary's low voice sank to a note of melting sorrow, and she cast a look of enjoyable woe round the room.

She flung her chubby arms wide and let them fall at her sides, then walked to her seat with her head bent, the Form watching this dramatic proceeding much impressed.

In a moment she raised her usual smiling face to Anne. 'All my poems turn so very sad,' she said. 'I'm sure I don't know why it happens, because I never feel at all sad myself. Lucy next — she's sure to be cheerful.'

Lucy rose with a threatening frown on her small face, looking anything but cheerful. 'I'm going to say a wee bit of Burns. I can't write so good as him myself,' she announced modestly.

Every hand was instantly raised in protest.

'Not fair! Not fair! Miss Carey, tell her that's not fair! We said our own poetry,' the Form clamoured.

'If she couldn't make up one herself,' suggested Joanna in a slow voice, looking rather pleased, 'if that's why she has to say a printed poem —'

'That is not why, Joanna Spencer, and don't you say so,' Lucy said, goaded into rage at the thought that her ability to hold her own with the others should be questioned. 'I have written a poem! If the rest of this class can write poetry so can I. And yours didn't rhyme so very much! I said a wee verse of Burns would be better, and so it would.'

'I think we'd rather hear yours to-day, and Burns next time,' Anne said tactfully.

'It's called 'Silvery Billows,'' Lucy admitted wrathfully, 'and there it is! You can see for yourself that I wrote it myself!' She laid a neat manuscript on Anne's desk and proceeded rapidly with her recital.

> Silvery billows as thou rollest on,
> Dost thou bring tidings of my only son?
> He's a young naval officer on the deep blue sea.
> Silvery billows bring him back to me.

'Is that all?' Anne asked, suppressing a desire to smile when Lucy came abruptly to an end. 'It is perhaps a little short, but it is a very nice poem,' she added soothingly.

'It's all I could think of,' Lucy said sulkily.

'That's just what I told you,' Joanna solemnly reminded her. 'I said no one could write a good, *long* poem in two days. Mine wasn't very good, but I took —'

'Next,' interrupted Anne.

A wise little girl called Margaret followed with a 'song' written to her mother, who was in America.

A Farewell

The birds shall carry my message
Through the air to you far away,
The flowers shall nod good morning
From me to you every day.
The ocean a story shall tell,
That I think of you far behind,
And I send all the love I can send
On the fleet wings of the wind.

Helen, a child as quiet as a mouse with very little vitality to spare, surprised Anne by quite a charming little verse.

The Shepherd

The shepherd leaps from rock to rock
And full of joy is he;
He on his homeward course is bent,
As one may plainly see.

His flock though scattered far and wide
By him alone are sent;
And every ewe and lambkin too
Is upon joy intent.

'I wanted to do a little more,' Helen confessed simply, 'but I couldn't think of anything to say.'

Anne assured her that this was the best of reasons for writing no further.

That was all, as the Form was temporarily depleted by illness, but Mary, who was a prolific poet, offered to say another of her compositions to Anne, and skipped up to the desk to lay it before her, painfully and roundly written on a sheet of her mother's best notepaper. She began to recite without preliminary.

Oh motherhood thou strange and mystic thing,
Hiding beneath the shadow of death's wing,

And lurking shed'st a ray of purest joy.
Sweet motherhood the sorrow and the tears
Are all at rest,
And with a smile of purest happiness,
The mother clasps her baby to her breast.

'That sounds like a grown-up poem,' Lucy said crossly. 'I am sure I don't know what you mean by it, Mary Tracy.'

'I'd love to be the mother of a real baby,' Mary said with her jolly smile. 'Dolls only pretend to cry and eat and move. A real baby is fun. Besides, poems don't always mean things. They're just singable words sometimes.'

'Your poems are too sad, Mary,' Joanna said with consideration. 'I like them, but they are very miserable, really.'

'You ought to put a good moral in them to comfort people if they must be all sad,' Josephine suggested in a tone of bright self-satisfaction, morals never being to seek either in her conversation or her compositions.

'I couldn't think of a good moral,' Mary said rather bewildered, 'and I'm sure I don't know why my poetry gets sad every time. I'll try to do an unsad one next.'

'That about your daughter,' Josephine pursued relentlessly. 'You could have said that if her body was in the dark mould, all the same her soul was in heaven, and that you'd meet again some day.'

'But she could only say that if it was a real daughter who was dead, not a poetry one,' Elizabeth objected.

'Mary couldn't meet an imaginary person in heaven, Josephine.'

'Morals are not at all necessary in poetry,' Anne hastily broke in, as the discussion threatened to become complicated.

'In fact they are things you have got to be most careful of, because you run into fearful danger of turning priggish and preaching to people otherwise, and that is a thing no one wants to do of course. But now let us say what we think of all the poems.'

The Form embarked delightedly upon the expression of its individual opinions. Anne suggested that next day they should ask Miss Carey and Miss Mollond to come in and hear them, and the children, interested and excited, took back the poems they had laid on her desk.

'In case we want to alter anything before we say them again,' Mary said.

'You can't alter a good poem in a short time,' Joanna stated gloomily. 'It's hard enough to write one at all, I think.'

'Thank you all very much,' Anne said. 'I have enjoyed every poem, and I think it was a splendid idea. Some of you may grow up to be famous writers, but even if you don't, you see how pleasant it is to be able to write what Mary calls 'singable words', don't you?'

'Do you think I'll ever be famous, Miss Carey?' Joanna asked solemnly, her plain face flushed, her faithful eyes shining with a splendid hope as she anxiously waited for a reply.

'I shouldn't be surprised,' Anne said rather touched as she recalled Joanna's dogged loyalty and patience during a whole week when she had been the single member able to come to school, of a Form devastated by influenza.

Anne walked home thinking of her little girls, and realising that she would be sorry to leave them when the time came to take up her work in Dampier's office. Mary Tracy had her heart. She was irresistible, alike in her clear little mind and in her springing, soft, round body. She had such poetic fancies that she could write 'Eve was so called because she was born in the cool of the day', and 'a cemetery is God's dust-pan', and she had such spontaneous impulses of affection that she would kiss Anne's hand when she took her pencil to show her how to hold it. No other little girl of eight was ever so dear or so remarkable to Anne's mind as Mary Tracy.

But Anne was anxious to be done with the school and to begin something new. It may have been partly what Paul and Veritas called the instability of her character that tempted her to variety of work, but in this instance it was also a sort of physical languor that had hung about her since her illness and which the spring did not help her to shake off. The inexhaustible vitality of the children was a tax on her own strength, and she went home jaded with the constant effort to respond to their demands. In Dampier's office she would have a certain amount of routine, and some quiet hours in the day. She began to long for Easter.

Dampier took her into the office of the *Review* one day and introduced Carmichael the editor to her, and quite a covey of young men engaged in literature who hung about. Anne knew most of their names, and she looked at them with frank interest — a double interest as she thought sharply of Thomas who would so have liked to know them. In most cases their bright eyes were magnified by glasses. They discussed — in charming voices — their own work with delicate, tireless egotism. Obviously they all worked hard. Most of them were married, and all of them needed more money than they made. They were eager in their appreciations, voracious for recognition, a little sad and heavy about life itself in spite of a sort of ready, professional joy in sunlight, work, cats, gardens, and their own sensitiveness, their own reaction to these things.

They amused Dampier; he was very much of an onlooker, Anne thought, watching his cool and detached enjoyment of their talk, but he was genial too.

Carmichael the editor was different from the others. He mixed poetry with political economy, and in appearance he was more like a keen young engineer or businessman than a writer. His thin, dark face was responsive, and his black eyes were strong and alight with enthusiasm. He wore his wiry dark hair cut short and brushed conventionally to one side, and he was immaculately neat. His manner was frank and pleasant, and he spoke with a nice touch of humour about himself and his work. Carmichael ardently concealed an idealism that he suspected of being merely sentimentality. He had fought the first two years of the war and had lost a foot, but Roehampton had fitted him so cleverly that he scarcely ever limped except when he was very tired. His genuine regard and admiration for Dampier won Anne.

Dampier called him John, and did not fail to notice that he and Anne made friends at once.

'*Damaged Goods*,' Anne said in a soft, odd voice. 'No, I wouldn't go to see it.'

'A didactic, medical tract. An encyclopaedia article without a trace of feeling,' one young man said. 'Intolerable on the stage. I'd rather see Grock the French clown.'

'Of course I'll teach you anything I can,' Carmichael assured Anne in reply to a question about the *Review*, thinking that she had a delightful voice. 'I'll be only too happy. The *Review* practically edits itself these days.'

'I put Miss Carey into your hands,' Dampier said. 'Carmichael knows everything that one can know about a paper, technically and otherwise. He's an expert at type-craft among other things, and no compositor could teach him anything. You'll learn the secrets of the trade from him, from tact with a contributor to make-up. John, Miss Carey is your responsibility. Do you think you can teach her to become an editor?'

'That's not fair to Mr Carmichael,' Anne protested.

'You can depend on me to do my best,' Carmichael said with his pleasant smile, looking as if he enjoyed the prospect. Anne met his friendly smile with one as friendly.

'I'm going to like your office,' she assured Dampier as they walked home. 'In a way I'm sorry to leave the children, but I look forward to Easter.'

17 Shadow

Anne said and felt sincerely that she would never shirk any part of life. From the beginning of her relationship with Dampier she had faced certain facts squarely — flinching, because she was sensitive, but with no intention of evasion. Dampier opposed her views, but failed to maintain his philosophy of opportunism in the face of her indomitable sense of what was right.

'Of course you're quite logical,' she asserted, troubled by him, 'but I know what I feel about things. I have a sense of direction — I can't put things into words.'

With the approach of the spring remote possibilities came closer to her, and fear, actual and cold, woke her at night and lived unsleeping in her mind by day. In vain she assured herself that 'nothing was wrong', and again — rather desperately — 'that if — well, if — ' — she would go through it somehow.

Dampier was away for a week at Easter with his family, and Anne, having parted thankfully from her little girls, and escaped from the mild reproaches of Paul and Veritas, remained alone in her flat, clasping and unclasping her cold fingers, and walking about the rooms as if she were caged. The difference between theory and actuality struck her like the blow of an iron hammer. She had to stick to her creed and test it when she was caught in the relentless machinery of life, and every nerve cried out for release.

'It can't happen,' Anne cried to herself in a panic, caged and terrified.

She was resolute not to face what she insisted were imaginary fears. She was tired and nervous; she would take a tonic if she didn't feel better, or see a doctor, but mental suggestion would be best. She summoned up the spirit of her faith-healing landlady. She must feel fit for Dampier's office and her new work. She laughed and snatched up Pim, tormenting him by pressing his furry length under her chin, and then holding him like a ball between her hands till he shrieked in angry protest and leaped away. She would refuse to think about herself at all. 'Youth, health, vigour,' she repeated feebly, recalling a formula of mental healing.

But fear woke her in the defenceless hour of dawn. She sat up in bed and faced it at last, shivering so that her teeth chattered, but valiant. She was certain that she was going to have a child.

She stared into the darkness.

One thought, irrational but sharp, and always at the back of her consciousness, took definite being. Dampier must not know.

Whatever it cost her in intricate plotting, in secret endurance, she would see it through without his knowledge. She could face anything alone, but she felt, with a passion of unreason perhaps, that she could only endure alone. She must think things out, she must lay her plans carefully. She would be secretive; she would find a way. Other women hid such secrets. She had money in the bank, luckily — Thomas's money! Work in the office would be impossible. She must get out of it somehow. She would go abroad; perhaps Mrs Garden would take her to France or to Italy. Or some quiet corner of England might do to hide in. She might throw herself on the compassion of her hermit aunt who lived alone in Norfolk, and was eccentric but kind. But Melancthon must know nothing. Anne repeated it on a sob as she sank into her pillow facing incredible loneliness.

Pimlico, policing the flat in the darkness, sprang on to the bed purring softly, and touched her wet cheek with his paw in delicate enquiry. He snuggled down her shoulder, his purr doubling in intensity as he felt the pleasant warmth, and slept there unrebuked.

Anne watched dawn glimmer through the window, and discover the shapes of the furniture in her room. The light grew and the pigeons fluttered and gurgled in the courtyard; somebody's alarm-clock shrilled for long time, and at last struck six.

Anne, turning and sighing, fell asleep suddenly like a child, her face against Pim's gently heaving side.

She woke late, very tired, but with a reassembly of her forces. She was prepared to face the odds of life. She believed in paying for a thing without regret. But things were very queer, in her own inadequate phrase. She could not quite realise yet — it might not be true.

Dampier came to see her the evening he got back from Scotland with signs of such heavy cold that she forgot her own anxieties in alarm over him. But he was in high spirits over the prospects of his *Review* in the new policy he had laid out for it, and he insisted on staying late to talk about it and his work, and what was to be Anne's share of it, and laughed at her fuss and anxiety.

'You're not to go out tomorrow at all, and you must promise to stay in bed unless you're better,' she begged as he said good night. 'I don't want to see you or hear from you. Do, do be careful.'

He promised, scoffing at her alarm, and she saw him go with misgivings she could not shake off.

A pencilled note from him reached her two days later which added to her anxiety.

'I've reluctantly gone to bed with a cold so shan't be able to arrange about the *Review* for a day or two. Will let you know when things are right.'

She bore the tension of her nerves for another twenty-four hours, and was just setting out to discover on one pretext or another how things were at Montpelier Square, when a telegram was handed to her.

'In great trouble Philip pneumonia can you come Rose Dampier.'

Anne sat on the settee trembling uncontrollably. The room took on a wholly unfamiliar look to her staring eyes, and Pimlico's voice, mewing from the window in his daily excitement over the pigeons, sounded faint and strange to her ears like a cat that was being drowned. She could hear herself gasping as if she had been running.

Philip would die. She had no hope at all. Perhaps he was dying now. She was afraid to go to his house. It occurred that perhaps he was delirious and had spoken her name, and that was why Rose had sent for her. But she quickly remembered that Rose was the kind of woman who would send wildly to all her friends in an emergency. She would probably fill the house with people. Still, it was possible that she suspected Anne of — but no matter. She did not care. All that mattered was to get to Montpelier Square as fast as she could and hear the worst. After that nothing counted at all.

The shelves and pictures in the room began to look less grotesque to her eyes. Pim's voice, trilling soft exclamations over the pigeons, took on an accustomed note. Anne pulled herself sharply together and went out. It was five o'clock. She trembled as she sat in the taxi that seemed to creep through the streets and to make the short distance to Montpelier Square interminable, but she was quite collected when at last the door was reached, and when she paid the driver and rang the bell she was calm to the point of numbness.

She was shown into the smoking-room at the end of the hall where she found the two little boys playing with their toys in front of a bright fire, looking subdued and neglected. They greeted her gladly, but were a little shy as it was a long time since she had seen them, and their faces remained solemn as they sat down one on each side of her.

'Daddy's ill,' Rowley said in a scared, low voice. 'He's got something wrong with his breathing that makes him make a funny noise like a bicycle pump.'

'We're not allowed in our nursery all day, only at night to sleep, because it's just over Daddy's head,' Micky added.

They looked forlorn, and Anne told them that if they were as good as gold and played quietly in the smoking-room their Daddy would soon be well again, and able to play with them. They sat expectantly with their eyes fixed on her face as if they were waiting for that moment to come.

Their mother came in. She wore an old pink flannel dressing-gown and her face was tired, but she seemed brisker and less anxious than Anne had feared to find her.

'Oh, my dear, how good of you to come,' she exclaimed hurriedly, disengaging Micky who made a rush and a leap to cling about her. 'I hope you didn't mind my wiring, but I felt sure I could ask you to do some little things for me. There is so much required.'

'Of course — anything I can do,' Anne said. 'How is Mr Dampier?'

'Oh, my dear, it is pneumonia,' Rose said, her eyes filling with tears. 'The very *sound* of it terrifies me. But the doctor is satisfied so far. We have a good nurse, and are to get a second the moment one can be found — perhaps tonight. Meantime Nanny is helping in Philip's room. There is so much to do constantly in this illness, and I wondered if you would mind helping with the boys, see them to bed and that? I have no one else I can turn to at the moment.'

'Anything,' Anne repeated mechanically. She could have

pushed Rose aside and run from the room crying, 'Let me go to him. He wants me, I must be with him,' but convention kept her tranquil and masked.

She asked questions that Rose answered with a torrent of irrelevant interruptions about the boys' pyjamas, and how she suffered from the low temperature of Philip's room which had the three windows always open, and the difficulty of getting unadulterated methylated spirit that would not block the nurse's lamp under the kettle. Anne, throbbing with desire to see for herself how Philip looked, to touch his hand if only for the briefest moment, strained her ears for any sound from the room upstairs but lost no single detail of what related to him in Rose's rambling talk. He hadn't influenza, but 'straight' double pneumonia following severe cold. The Scotch train had been so draughty, and Philip was always so afraid for her — she was the delicate one — and had insisted on putting his coat over her as well as the rug. Only part of the time — she wouldn't allow it longer. Indeed she had been asleep when he did it, and as soon as she woke she insisted on his taking it back, but she blamed herself dreadfully now because that must have been the beginning of the chill.

'How does he seem, actually?' Anne asked, outwardly patient and sympathetic with an anxious wife, and inwardly terrified that her control would break and her tearing misery betray itself.

Rose said, 'Oh, so terribly ill,' and sobbed, but Rowley unexpectedly supplied a clear picture. Anne, shuddered.

'I peeped into Daddy's room and saw him,' he piped. 'He's sitting straight up in bed with lots and lots of pillows — I've never seen so many pillows — and he makes a loud, funny noise almost like a railway train. And it's 'stremely cold for him with no fire at all and all the windows wide open!'

Mrs Dampier went upstairs again, and Anne gave the boys their tea and then read to them for half an hour before soft-footed, and in Indian file, they crept up to the nursery. Passing Dampier's door, she could hear the painful struggle for breath that seemed to fill the house, and her heart contracted with his suffering. How could she bear not to go to him?

The children were very good and went silently to bed with no attempt to play, and as Anne sat beside them mechanically repeating all the nursery rhymes she could remember, prompted now and again by a subdued little voice, the irony of her position was sharp in her heart. She who loved Dampier — terribly — could only play nursemaid to his children while he lay downstairs, wanting her almost certainly — dying perhaps. Her murmuring voice failed.

"'The King was in his counting-house counting out his money" — I wonder how much he had? — "The Queen was in the parlour eating bread and honey" — was it comb honey or loose honey? — "The maid was in the garden hanging out the clothes" — go on, Miss Carey,' Micky urged in an excited whisper, almost forgetting to be 'very quiet'.

There began an interminable, dream-like week for Anne, when her body lived among outward things much as usual — a prop for Rose Dampier's dependence, and a refuge for the forlorn small boys who clung to her — and her whole soul and personality, the hidden entity that felt and suffered was withdrawn into icy and comfortless space. She looked after Rowland and Micky by day, taking them out for walks and introducing them to Pimlico and her flat, a huge joy because they could make a noise, and chase the kitten with shouts, and then tucking them up in their cots at night, and saying verses and songs till they fell asleep. Then she usually spent the evening with Rose, who could not be continuously in her husband's room and dreaded to be alone. Twice she slept all night on the smoking-room sofa, when Rose was specially nervous.

The days Anne could just endure because there were many things to be done indirectly for Dampier, apart from her care of the boys. The nights meant misery against which she was defenceless. If she slept, she woke in a panic sure that she heard Dampier's difficult breathing becoming more agonised, and sinking to dreadful silence, sure that he was dying. Her own fear too that had come before his illness recurred. Useless to push it into the background; it imposed on unguarded moments.

Dampier was very ill, but he was fighting for himself in a way that helped the doctors enormously. There was danger at every turn, but if he could continue to fight, inches were gained, and at worst he did not lose. That was at first. Then there came a few hours when he seemed to have lost heart for the struggle like a swimmer carried out to sea who throws up his hands seeing no hope of rescue … Rose never left his room, shuddering in a fur coat, and Anne remained downstairs alone, waiting. The children had been sent out of the house with a maid.

Anne concentrated every effort of her body and on Dampier's need. If she could put out any power and reach him he might be helped and held. She poured her energy and will with an intensity that cost physical agony. She fought for him as he had ceased fight for himself.

The bad hours passed, and Dampier rallied and turn the corner in one of those swift changes that occur in the course of the disease. The improvement was marked that Rose, worn out, consented to go to bed a few hours, and Anne promised to stay and awake her at ten o'clock, when she was to relieve one of the nurses.

Anne sat by the smoking-room fire too exhausted physically to eat the food the maid brought, her mind blank, possessed of neither anxiety nor relief, too utterly tired to feel anything at all. Presently her numbness passed into sleep as she sat upright and unrelaxed in a high-backed chair by the fire, her hands rigidly folded in her lap.

John Carmichael, the editor of Dampier's *Review*, was shown in, and crossed the room quietly, not noticing first that there was anyone in the room. When he saw Anne his low-spoken greeting failed to penetrate the coils of soft grey sleep that pressed about her, and he sat down opposite her, observing her intently. Her pose at first gave him pleasure; he thought that she looked like a Verrochio Virgin with her colourless face sharp-cut against the high back of the chair, her fair, silky hair and dress of some rich red texture shimmering in the firelight, and her hands held stiffly before her. Then he gradually realised that he had never seen such tension in a face and figure before; every line was full of apprehension, intolerable strain. It was dreadful in a sleeping human being; most dreadful to young Carmichael in a woman.

He decided that he ought to wake her, and to try to get her to lie down and rest in some easier posture. He was terribly afraid of startling her, but the more he looked at her the more urgent it seemed to rouse her from that death-like unconsciousness in which there was pain and no rest.

Carmichael walked over to the door, opened it, and shut it again with some little noise, speaking Anne's name as if he had just come in.

Her eyes opened widely, and she roused herself with a cry, 'Oh, what is it? Why are you here? Is he worse?'

'No, splendid,' Carmichael answered soothingly. 'I'm so sorry I've alarmed you, Miss Carey; forgive me. I wanted a word with Mrs Dampier, and was shown in here. The maid said she would be down presently. But you were sleeping — I'm so awfully sorry to disturb you. Let me spread this rug over you on the sofa.'

'Philip isn't worse?' Anne asked in a lifeless voice, looking at Carmichael half dazed with sleep.

He noticed her use of Dampier's Christian name, oddly possessive, with surprise.

'He's extraordinarily better tonight. I've just met the nurse in the hall,' he assured her.

'I can't bear anything more,' Anne said in that dead voice. 'I'm in terrible trouble. I thought Philip was going to die.'

Carmichael, startled and uncomfortable, was sure that Miss Carey was half asleep and not fully conscious of what she was saying, but he was afraid to hear what else she might say. She appeared to be completely overwrought. He was certain she was suffering more than the shared fatigue and anxiety of a friend of the house in a time of trouble. He had felt pity for her as he watched her unconscious face, small and tense, with shadowy, closed eyes, the poise of her head so defensive. He was stirred now to extraordinary interest.

'I know you've been an awful brick all these days,' he said eagerly. 'Mrs Dampier has told me all you've done for her. You must be tired out. But I hope and believe Dampier's coming round now. You mustn't worry too much. You're one of the sort that takes things too hard.'

'What else matters to me in the world?' Anne asked, her eyes fixed on his face, her voice low and heavy.

'The impulse to confession almost always requires a fresh ear and a fresh heart.' The words occurred to Carmichael's mind, and he shrank with a nervous distaste from the idea of receiving any sort of confidence from Miss Carey. He was moved by her attitude and expression, but he dreaded what she might say in her overwrought condition. Something that might shake his loyalty to Dampier or lower Anne's own position in his eyes.

Anne dropped forward, her face hidden in her hands.

'All these days I've been nearly mad. Even now he isn't safe. If he dies I'll slip over the Chelsea Embankment in the dark.

I know a place where no one would see. I'll tie the irons out of the kitchen to my wrists, and that will be the best end.'

'Miss Carey, your jokes are horrible,' Carmichael said sharply in a sudden rage with her, and trying to stop her from further disclosure of what he felt convinced was a hopeless infatuation for Dampier. He had a devotion to Dampier himself that made it easy for him to understand a woman's admiration turning to love, but its expression shocked him past endurance.

'I ache to be with him, and I know he needs me more than anyone else,' Anne said. 'But we are apart. Isn't it hopelessly silly?'

'If what you say is true — but I don't believe a word of it,' Carmichael began and stopped. He tried again. 'If it is true, aren't you behaving in a very cruel way to Mrs Dampier? Miss Carey, I know you don't mean what you say. Don't say these things.'

But he stopped, horrified by the passion he roused in the strange, flat voice.

'No, that's just it,' Anne cried. "Don't say these things!" Live them, think them, but hide them. Never say what you really believe and are! But I will say it, whether you believe it or not —'

The door opened, and Mrs Dampier came in looking rested and bright. Yes, things were still going beautifully; Philip's hands actually felt cool to touch.

Women were too extraordinary, Carmichael decided, or else Miss Carey was a born actress or a hypocrite — probably both. He heard her say how glad she was in perfectly quiet and natural tones, and Rose, holding her hands, affectionately said good night and thanked her for the comfort she had been.

Anne hurried a little.

'I must get home and have a good sleep,' she said vaguely.

'I'll get a taxi; it's only five minutes' drive.' But as she walked towards the door with Rose's friendly hand on her shoulder, she stumbled and fell across a chair, and slipped fainting to the floor.

Anne had always fainted without much trouble, but this time she was so hard to bring round that the doctor who came in began to look anxious. When at last she became conscious, he refused to let her be moved even upstairs, so for a third time a bed was made up for her on the smoking-room sofa, and one of the nurses undertook to have an eye on her during the night.

Carmichael meanwhile had slipped off, an unaccountably angry and miserable young man.

Anne slept heavily and dreamlessly as soon as she was put into bed, and rested oblivious of pain or joy, and the household, emerging from shadow, slept.

Dampier had turned the corner and improved slowly, but without any set-back. Rose, who had been remarkable in her self-forgetfulness, now began to realise what she had been through, and she felt a good deal of self-pity. She showed so much anxiety in case her health should permanently suffer, and demanded so much sympathy, that Anne, uncertain of her nerves, gave up her daily visits to the house. She assured herself by telephone morning and evening that all was going well, and spent the hours between idling in her flat or sitting apathetic in Kensington Gardens. Sometimes she took Rowland and Micky out, and they always clamoured to go and see Pimlico and her 'sweet little house', but they had their nurse again at their disposal, so these visits were few.

Dampier saw his brother Charles for a few minutes each day, and in a little while Carmichael was admitted but strictly warned not to talk business. Then Rowland and Micky were allowed to peep in and call out good night and good morning, but they were awed by the paraphernalia of the sickroom, and Micky, shy and frightened of the gaunt, strangely smiling man in bed, burst into a roar of dismay and had to be removed, a proceeding of which he was afterwards much ashamed.

Dampier was shaved and able to sit up in a chair, wearing a new blue dressing-gown in which he felt very smart, when he asked one day to see Anne. She was in the house, and Rose took her to the door of his room, but did not go in with her. The nurse had gone downstairs to her tea, and so Anne saw him alone for a moment.

She held on to herself, but the tears came to her eyes when she saw his familiar eager smile, and touched his thin hand. He had been five weeks in bed, and she thought he looked incredibly ill.

His eyes devoured her face, and all of her, coming back unsatisfied to something shadowed and unhappy in her aspect.

'How are you, darling?' he whispered. 'You've let yourself get thin! I won't have it, Anne.'

'Hush! You've no right to talk. But, oh, you're better now!' Anne said poignantly. He held her hand to his lips, and she dared stay no longer.

She felt comforted when she lay on her settee that evening, pretending vainly to read. Dampier was still in the world, and whatever labyrinth lay before her, that fact alone seemed to lighten her burden.

'It's a terrible thing to care for people,' Anne said to Pim who was purring on her chest, his eyes narrowing with sleep to mere slits of light, his paws curled round her fingers. 'Pim, you little wise cat, you don't love anybody, do you? Your race has learned sense. Grace and manners and wisdom, but no attachments. Oh, you wise angel-kitten — but I don't envy you, Pim. Don't be offended, but I would be glad of a little demonstration when I come in sometimes. And to care for someone yourself — well — it's very queer, Pimlico.'

His warm body on her chest felt responsive tonight. His eyes were pin-points, and the shutters closed over them; his purr sank within him like a little flame, and he slept. Anne was tranquil, giving herself up to a good moment.

She saw Dampier several times after that, but not as it happened alone. Soon he was downstairs again, and once or twice Carmichael came in while she was there, and they talked of the *Review*.

Carmichael looked curiously at her the first time, quickly and in secret, but she showed no embarrassment, nor was there the faintest indication in her manner that what she had said of the feeling for Dampier was true. Carmichael was half inclined to dismiss the recollection — which had haunted him — of her face and her voice, but he could not quite convince himself that there had been no reality in the scene. He observed her furtively, and the faintly shadowed and apprehensive something about her that had troubled Dampier struck him.

He noticed too that she was evasive about beginning work, and spoke with none of the enthusiasm she had shown on the visit to the office. She said she preferred to wait till Dampier could get to his office. That perhaps was natural, since she was to be his secretary, but when Philip himself suggested her starting with Carmichael she quickly made some plausible excuse.

Carmichael was puzzled. He was still young enough as a writer to express himself sometimes in the apt thoughts of other men, and, studying Anne's face, a familiar passage came into his mind.

There was a listening fear in her regard
As if calamity had but begun,
As if the vanward clouds of evil days
Had spent their malice, and the sullen rear
Was with its stored thunder labouring up.

Carmichael's literary imagination was pleased by this quotation, but all that was sensitive and generous in himself made him pity Anne.

There was a listening fear in her regard.

He thought it touching and horrible to be a woman.

18 Aunt Minima

Minima Carey, Anne's other twin aunt, was unlike her sister Maxima in every way. Their lives had been so separate and so different that there was not even a strong attachment between them. They had both gone in for higher education at a time when it was still something of a novelty for a woman, but unlike Maxima, Minima had completed no particular course of study, but had strayed down many diverting by-paths, and had opened her mind to so many different breezes of opinion that her mind had become a draughty, uncomfortable place. As time went on she became a nebulous sort of personality, taking up one new theory after another, and spending much of her time in translating books of 'revolutionary' philosophy from German and French into unprecise English, which harmed no one because long before she finished her translations the original work had been superseded by something newer, which she had to read in order, as she expressed it, 'to keep up with the trend of modern thought'. The rest of her time she spent at her piano, singing and playing, and composing music which she seldom took the time to write down. She was a brilliant player, and her once sweet voice had been moderately well trained, but at fifty odd it was thin and very high, and could not have afforded much pleasure to anyone but herself. This did not affect its owner, who lived alone in her house in a somewhat bleak Norfolk village, gradually becoming more and more of a hermit, solitary and absent-minded, following her own pursuits and for weeks at a time seeing no one but her servants. Her life passed in a sort of odd, unpractical dream that she was going to 'improve' her music, and that one day she would make a translation of some famous book that would be recognised as greater than the original, and that then she would go out into the world of men and women and meet some of the thinkers and writers whose work she admired in an intense confusion. Meantime she played and sang and wrote and gardened a little, and was careless of what she had to eat, and time drifted past, and her black hair turned white.

Minnie was unlike her sister, too, inasmuch that she had no close woman friend and nothing approaching a soulmate. She had once had a burning romance. She had loved a young man on whom her parents had frowned because he was a Roman Catholic while they were Broad Church people. She had been separated from him in the ponderous, interfering manner of the day, and, romantic and ardent, the young people had arranged to elope when the young man was thrown in the hunting field and fatally injured. Aunt Minnie was so far unresigned that she never lived under her parents' roof again, but took her small fortune and wandered about on the Continent picking up languages.

Her father and mother were dead, and her sister Maxima had become Veritas, the affinity of Paul, and head of a girls' school in London, when Minima returned and settled in a house of her own. Aunt Minnie felt no particular need for anyone. She lived alone, contented in a cloudy world of her own.

Once or twice in her life Anne had stayed with her, and had enjoyed it. But she never felt that she made the slightest lasting impression on her aunt's heart. She was too visionary a creature, and had been too long detached from real affection and the habit of ordinary family life. But while her niece was in the house Minima was kindness itself to her. She talked to her quite seriously, with a rather deprecating and shy manner, about vast works of philosophy and modern music. Anne, like all children, expected to be taken seriously, and she greatly admired her aunt's looks.

It was of Aunt Minima that Anne thought when she faced the certainty that she was going to have a child. She meant to meet what she had brought on herself boldly, but at the same time she must throw up as many defences between herself and the world as possible. She would be secret and ingenious to hide herself, and later the child. A hundred plans had passed through her mind. In time the idea of throwing herself upon her aunt in her Norfolk hermitage began to seem the simplest way out.

'Just at first,' Anne said vaguely.

She was almost sure for one thing that Aunt Minnie's mind held no definite blacks and whites, no unalterable standards of conventional morality such as guided Paul and Veritas through their admirably direct lives. At one time or another Aunt Minnie was pretty sure to have advocated the 'right of every woman to have a child', and to have championed the cause of the unmarried mother, Anne said to herself with rather bitter humour. Perhaps she would be willing to put these theories to the test. If so her very vagueness would protect Anne from harassments that she dreaded.

She could not conceive of turning for help to Paul and Veritas. They were good women with a hard core.

She remembered their outraged faces when Emma the parlour-maid had disclosed herself as a 'fallen' woman. They had been very kind to Anne, and in return it would be kindness to them to spare them all knowledge — if that could be done — to keep out of their way, and be thought merely selfish and neglectful. It would not be easy. But her eldest brother and his wife were going for a year to Japan, so that was a difficulty out of her path, seldom as they met. Her younger brother was in Canada, farming in the West.

She longed to throw herself on Mrs Garden's compassion, but she did not dare. Mrs Garden knew Dampier. Anne's desire to exclude him in every way was becoming an obsession. It was self-protection partly; by excluding him she made things easier for herself.

But the difficulty about Dampier was greatest of all. She could not take up the secretarial work in his office even for a time while she completed her plan of disappearance from London. It would be nerve-shaking to see him constantly, and if she were to begin to work before he got back to the office there would be Carmichael to face. She could not. Carmichael and Mrs Garden — she put their names together — she must not see either of them. They both knew Dampier; they both liked her. Mrs Garden loved her, Anne knew.

No, it must be Aunt Minnie. She would perhaps take her abroad; that would be possibly the best plan of all!

Anne suggested to Dampier that she might have the opportunity of spending the summer in Italy: she thought if so that she would like to take it. Then she would settle down into an office again. She hadn't really had a proper holiday since before the war.

Dampier was surprised but on the whole relieved that she was not anxious to begin without him. Another matter was engrossing him. He was better, but he did not recover strength, and he felt so far from fit for work that he decided to arrange with Carmichael that he should carry on the *Review* for at least the next three months, which would bring them to mid-July. After that he would probably be perfectly well again. He was to go somewhere abroad as soon as he could travel — to Spain possibly, to some sunny climate at any rate where he could lie in the open air all day and thaw out his lungs, which he described as feeling stiff with cold as if they had been frozen.

And suddenly the doctors decreed unanimously that he was to put all thought of work definitely out of his calculations for a year, and go to Spain — if the ideal conditions could be found there, which they doubted — or to Italy, or better still to Switzerland, and make up his mind to a life of invalidism for that period.

The shock to Dampier was at first so great that he refused to take the doctors seriously, and jeeringly told them that there was no use talking to him as if he were a rich man. But they meant it. They convinced him that his illness had left him in a condition to slip very easily from life, unless he was willing to accept their advice and try to get back what he had lost. Rose took the news well. She set the thought of her own health aside again, and began tirelessly to talk of climates, and travel, and treatment 'that would be best for Philip'. She enjoyed taking things into her own hands. California was suggested; she jumped at the thought. She had friends living in Pasadena who would be able to tell him all about the life, how best to live, and where. She wrote off at once to them. Before they could reply, the journey was decided and passages taken.

Rose fussed about her clothes and the children's things and passports, and packing, and saw to letting the house all, it seemed, at the same moment, and was in a constant state of confusion and hurry. The children were wildly excited, nurse rather less so but pleased on the whole. The house rapidly took on an air of complete discomfort and insecurity.

In the general upset the patient for whose benefit this was being done came off badly. He felt extraordinarily miserable in mind and body, shaken at the thought of leaving Anne and going so far away. He began to lose the little he had gained and to find it impossible to sleep. He struggled through his depression to persuade himself that he must get to a climate that would restore him to physical fitness, and work, and normal life.

The California decision came upon Anne like a blow that left her dazed. She felt fierce revolt, passionate hostility to Rose, to all the world that conspired against her. She couldn't endure that Dampier should go from her, that the world should divide them. It was all very well for her to plot and plan to hide herself from him, but that he should be altogether beyond her reach if she desperately needed him, out of her very knowledge if he became ill again, away from sight and touch for unending months in a place remoter to her than the Himalayas was the last cruelty. She had seen nothing of him for long now. All their intimate hours had ended on the night he had come back ill from Edinburgh. And now even the stolen seconds they had together were to end. Anne paced the floor in anguish.

She regained her self-control after a night of misery. Ashamed of her ravaged face in the glass, and frightened by her own capacity to be hurt, she did not go out all day.

In the evening she walked along the Embankment, inclined to be cynical over the whispering lovers on the benches, the inarticulate couples clinging silently to each other in doorways. How they would hate each other in a year or two when the romance in which nature clothes physical attraction was over. Especially if they married and had a baby. Anne had seen it often in the bench and park type of lover, particularly in the very young ones. The girl sickly and disillusioned after the birth of her baby, the young husband rough and irritable, both of them inarticulately wondering what trick had been played on them, resentful … but the infant, somehow, a tie.

Anne looked into the water at the place she thought a good one for committing suicide, but with no impulse to slide into the river. Life called to her. She had unending curiosity about it. She wanted to know how she could stand it, the road in front. Other women, countless ones, had followed it. She was eager to know how she would fare, afraid but curious.

She tired herself out before she dared go home. She must sleep or Philip would worry over her worn looks, and she was determined that he should go away without anxiety on her account. She said to herself that after all his going so soon was a fortunate thing for her; it made things easy. In a few months he would be home again, and they would see each other. She had no fear that she might not live. She meant to live. She was vague about the future, as she was vague about most things. She had to live her life step by step, and her perception, her power to see ahead, grew slowly. It was hard for her to break the childish habit of accepting one day after another hopefully, without action of any sort. But thinking out the future, in the vague yet frightened way a child might, she was conscious that she had come to the end of a particular passage of her life; the feeling was overwhelming. Some part of it that had held was definitely over. Deeper than the explanation of natural facts this conviction lay.

'Endings are terrible,' she said drearily.

Dampier was out very little before the day on which they were to sail, partly because the weather was bad and largely because he was hardly fit for it. His incapacity surprised him. He spent an hour or two in his office talking business with Carmichael, and went to bed for two days afterwards, beaten by the noise of the streets as much as by the actual exertion.

Part of an afternoon he spent with Anne in her flat, and somehow anxiety seemed to slip from them and they were happy again in each other's company and could laugh together in the old way over Girlie and Darling scrambling about in the courtyard with Jocko, and the fantasies of Pimlico's behaviour as he surveyed them from the window. Anne's eyes were bright, there was some colour in her face. At the sight of Philip sitting in the big chair her spirits rose absurdly and found it easy to be gay. She could pet him and a fuss over him as she had longed to do all the weeks of his illness. She made tea over the fire a festival.

Philip watched her, responding as he always did to Anne,

and then the dread of losing her assailed sharply. Why had he been such a fool as to consent to go so far away? He would loathe California and its relentless sunlight. Rose and the doctors should not have pressed it; he should have asserted himself, on had felt such deadly physical apathy until to-day. But he should have held out for Italy or Switzerland. Anne checked these half-uttered self-reproaches.

'I want you to go,' she insisted, smiling at him. 'You will come back well, and that is the only thing that matters. Besides, I envy you the flowers, and the sun, and the colour, and it gives value to life to be envied, don't you think? Somebody once told me that the Pacific Ocean smelt like a peach tree in flower mixed with spicy, heavenly other smells that you never tire of. Think of it!'

'I want you to come, Anne darling.'

'That's impossible,' Anne said quickly. 'And you'll like me better when you haven't seen me for ages. Time will go fast. Will you write and tell me about the fascinating American life?'

'I'll write,' Dampier said. 'And I'll like to think of you in the *Review* office, if the Italian summer doesn't come off, or if for any reason I am kept away longer than I now intend. Do you think you'll begin in September? Carmichael will be first-rate to work with, and he will be glad to take you on whenever you want to begin.'

'It's rather absurd perhaps to create a special job for me,' Anne suggested.

'You're no politician,' Dampier returned, smiling. 'But I'll make Carmichael promise to get some work out of you, if that will satisfy you. And I'm a tyrant in my office. Wait till I get back to it.'

He added in a moment, searching her face, 'I feel somehow anxious at leaving you — horribly oppressed. Promise me you'll be safe and well.'

'Of course,' Anne murmured, flushing deeply in the firelight as she bent forward to hide her face against his knee. 'Now don't talk about me. We're not going to waste our snatched day like that.'

'It's waste to talk about anything else,' Dampier said. 'What about money, Anne? Oh, I know you hate the subject, but you must consider me a little in this. I refuse to be put off. Don't you see that I can't go so far away without feeling sure that in this one smallest thing I have taken care of you? You must be unselfish and let me — just in case you need it — in case of an emergency.'

'Yes,' Anne said suddenly.

She yielded to please him, but she told herself that she would not require to touch the sum of money that he insisted on depositing in her bank.

As their stolen moments ebbed, she slipped into his arms and he held her in silence that neither could break.

Then they parted.

✕

Aunt Minima never read long letters; if anyone — usually it was Maxima trying to 'get into touch' once a year with her — was so ill-advised as to send her a closely written sheet, she glanced at the beginning and the end and quite forgot the middle. Anne made her letter a brief request to go and stay with her aunt for a week. She would explain — if she could — when she got there. The reply was prompt, and sounded cordial. She was to come and stay at Tanglewood Cottage for as long as she pleased.

A curious exaltation supported her as she travelled to Norfolk. She was triumphant that Dampier had gone off happy about her, and had started his journey well, and that her secret was still her own. She was hopeful of her aunt's sympathy and help. She was in a half-dreamy, half-excited mood as she drove up to the house. She heard the sound of the piano as the maid opened the door, and smiled because these same brilliant, rapid chords and comet-like trails of notes were so associated in her mind with her childish recollections of visits to Aunt Minnie.

The elderly parlour-maid remembered her and smiled, making her welcome. Anne would not let her disturb her aunt, and entered the drawing-room confident that she would not be noticed. Nor was she. The room was long and low, and the piano was at the far end facing the door, its upright top concealing the performer. Anne sat down to listen, and presently Aunt Minima began to sing *Who is Sylvia* in a piercingly high soprano from which all sweetness had long departed, but in excellent style, and with the assurance of a prima donna. Aunt Minnie, shy in all else, was bold in her musical expression.

Anne found herself irresistibly inclined to laugh.

'Holy, fair, and wise is she,' sang Aunt Minnie.

Maggie brought in the tea, put a match to the grate, and ruthlessly interrupted her mistress's performance by announcing loudly that Miss Anne Carey had arrived and that tea was in, ma'am.

Aunt Minima broke off short as Maggie's message reached her, and rose to greet Anne very kindly, with a shy breathlessness, her dark eyes shining and beautiful, just as her niece remembered them.

'Dear me, you're quite grown up,' Aunt Minnie said half regretfully, looking at Anne as if perplexed. 'And you were just learning to walk the other day. Such a funny, pale little child from India. To see you is to remember time, Anne. It slips by, and I scarcely notice it when I am alone. I am glad you suggested coming to stay. I don't think of asking young people here. There's not much amusement in an old maid's house, is there? And I live in my books and my music.'

She was an odd, incongruous figure with her eager, charming face and her distinction of bearing under an assortment of strange, irrational garments, her slim fingers sparkling with antiquated but good rings, and her slender feet sandalled like those of a prophet in the wilderness. She was remoter even than Anne had expected, but she felt drawn to her. Aunt Minima kept looking at her fully grown niece with a slightly bewildered air that melted into a half-deprecating smile now and then. She found it difficult at first to find anything to say. Later in the evening she began to talk about the family with an almost pathetic eagerness to hear about them, as if she were conscious in a way of her isolation. She was not without a sense of humour, and the mention of her twin sister Maxima and her partner Miss Mollond calling each other Paul and Veritas and solemnly prescribing for themselves a life of admonishment and truth, lit her face with a flash of gentle fun that made her come closer to something young and warm. 'What a curious weakness in my sister,' was all she said.

Anne had determined that the matter on which she had come should be disclosed that night, but when she attempted to approach the subject she found that her courage failed her. Her hands turned icy, and a deep inner trembling seized her. She had no voice, no words. She could just bear the possession of her secret. She shrank with terror from uttering it. The idea of confession, of any sort of appeal to compassion began to fill her with a sick, shocked dismay. Some such thing had seemed just possible in London. Looking at Aunt Minima's quiet face in this formal, tranquil room it appeared a grotesque, a shameless thing to have come at all.

She sat almost sinking under the despair that seized her, but fortunately Miss Carey was not an observant person.

'Did you think it very strange of me to come down here?'

she forced herself to ask at last in what sounded to her a harsh whisper.

'My dear child, I am very glad you wrote to me,' her aunt replied.

'You may not want me to stay,' Anne said incoherently, 'when you know — Aunt Minnie — oh, I wonder —'

She stopped suddenly, and Aunt Minnie said in a gentle, gratified tone, 'My dear, I live alone, but I like to know that my family sometimes remember me. And now,' she added in her soft, abrupt fashion, 'we must go to bed at once. Our candles are ready.'

Anne went up to her room feeling reprieved. By sunlight things would be easier; she would be able to speak tomorrow, or else to make up her mind to go back to London with the silence unbroken. She crept into bed exhausted.

She woke with a prostrating headache, and was unable to lift her head all day. She shut her eyes, suffering too much for any but dazed, inconsequent thoughts, but feebly thankful for a further reprieve. She faintly resented the weakness, but could not struggle against it. In the evening she was better, but too weak and shaken to get up or to say much when her aunt came in half shyly to see her.

And next day she could face things no better. She sat in the sun in the garden while Aunt Minnie, in a smock and a sun-bonnet, did something with a rake and a spade that seemed to be drastic as far as the beds were concerned.

Impossible to speak. How silly she had been. She would go back to London and lose herself somehow there. But she was afraid to be alone. She had been mad to think that anyone could help her; she must be alone, whether she was afraid or not. Women always must be, in her position. It was incredible that she should have thought at all of coming to this quiet, servant-governed house; merely foolish to have relied on a creature so visionary as her aunt; wrong indeed to have intruded on her retired, orderly life. Moreover she — Anne — had no right to ask for anyone's sympathy.

She sat apathetically in the garden day after day, watching the business of life go forward with such definite purpose and gaiety, such promise and profusion. She wondered if she would ever be able to bear the spring again, if she would ever feel happy and free again. She wondered about Dampier — remote already. Everything seemed unreal to her, her own body and mind most of all. What was going to happen to her?

More than a week had passed, when Anne made a resolve as she dressed in the morning that come what must, she would at least tell her aunt exactly her position before she went to bed that night. She nerved herself to it all day, trembling inwardly. Her aunt was not formidable; it was herself she feared. She could act, she could endure, but Anne could not speak.

Her aunt, sitting talking to her with bright, eager eyes, and a face glowing with enthusiasm as she spoke of Bergson's theory of laughter slightly mixed with Maeterlinck's theory of death, gave her an opening by saying abruptly, 'You are looking tired again tonight, Anne, and I was pleased yesterday because you seemed better than when you came. I am inclined to advise you to see my friend Dr Scott — except that I don't believe in advice — because she is excellent at knowing what is lacking in one's food. That is the common secret of most bodily ills. We are what we eat,' Aunt Minnie declared firmly, as if she gave the matter of her own food profound thought, instead of accepting whatever her servants put before her, unconscious whether it was good or bad for her, or even what it was.

'You look run down,' she added.

'It's not that,' Anne said in a low tone; 'but I am not a bit well. I am going to have a baby.' She blurted out the words, her shaking hands betraying her. Her aunt looked at her uncomprehending.

'Anne dear, how long have you been married? How is it I never heard? Girls are very secretive nowadays. Do they even keep their own names?'

'Nobody knows,' Anne began hurriedly, and with the words it flashed into her mind that here was a — temporary — way out. She repudiated it in a breath. 'I am not married.'

The look she had dreaded to see passed instantly over Aunt Minnie's face, a mingled shock and shrinking. She saw the growing dismay and question in her eyes. Aunt Minnie fumbled to express herself, finding a phrase that sounded decidedly old-fashioned in view of her ambition to keep up with the trend of modern thought.

'Is it — is it possible — that you have been' — Aunt Minima's agitation made the next word a whisper — 'betrayed, Anne? Did he promise to marry you? He must be made to. Your brothers —'

Anne's perverse sense of humour made her smile. Olivia Primrose was as near as Aunt Minnie could get to the latchkey life of the present day.

'It's nothing of that sort,' she said. 'But can you help me? Will you let me go abroad with you, or stay here? No one must know. It will be easier away, and I have enough money. I won't be a trouble to you. You needn't even stay with me — if you will only just let me say that I am going abroad with you.'

'But when?' Aunt Minima asked, the look of physical shock deepening on her face almost to disgust, and half consciously drawing a little away. Anne's cheeks burnt.

'In the autumn — October.'

'Oh, perhaps it is not true,' her aunt exclaimed.

'It is true.'

'Anne, you must be married — before — if only — you must consider the child. Your baby, Anne!'

Anne paled.

'Afterwards perhaps. Now I can only think of myself. Don't speak of marriage. There is no question of it.'

'No question? — but this is terrible,' her aunt said, shaken into contact with reality with a violence that almost dazed her after years of detachment.

Anne desperately tried to recall something else she had meant to say.

'Don't you believe in the right of every woman to have a child?'

She saw Miss Carey try to rally to a belief to which she had once subscribed, but she answered confusedly:

'Yes, most certainly, but you seem so strange and hard about it. Of course some women are intensely maternal and regard men only in one way, as the fathers of their children. Eugenically that is sound, I think.' Aunt Minima's wide, perplexed eyes softened. 'It should be a right and rational thing for every woman to have a child — every woman who feels impelled. Is that how it is with you, Anne?'

Relief began to dawn in her face.

Here was a second way out, but Anne disregarded it too.

'No,' she said in a low, tired voice, 'I've always wanted children — some day when I was married, if I did marry. But I don't want this baby. It all seems so frightful to me that I feel as if I were talking wildly while I tell you about it. It's terrible to me because I'm afraid — oh, not physically, that doesn't matter, but in every other way.'

Her frightened eyes searched her aunt's face, charming and confused, on which time had carved so little history, wondering how she had escaped thus easily from life.

'I've been living with a man — for a year past. Because I love him,' she said below her breath. 'He is married, and I always knew it. I knew what I was doing. I don't regret it, and I'm a coward to come and ask for help now. Don't speak about him. He is no more to blame than I am,' she said hurriedly. 'He has gone away from England very ill. He's not even on this side of the world. He doesn't know about me.'

'Ah, one of those overseas soldiers,' Aunt Minnie exclaimed unexpectedly.

'No,' Anne said with a wan smile.

'But I heard about some soldier,' Aunt Minnie persisted, recalling as the vaguest people can do some sort of family gossip, and feeling suddenly assured and practical on the strength of it.

Anne told her briefly about Thomas, and answered a few hurried and reticent questions, conscious that her aunt was striving to see any sort of ethical justification in the affair, but that she was driven back into an inherited and deeply rooted horror, almost as great as her sister Maxima had experienced in the case of Emma. Theoretically — in an ideal society — every woman had a right to a child. The woman who produced her child from motives of love and fulfilment did far more for the race than the woman who became a mother only from a sense of moral obligation in marriage, perhaps. But actually one's own unmarried niece in producing an illegitimate baby was bringing the most obvious form of shame and disgrace upon everyone concerned. Aunt Minnie was profoundly shaken, and for two reasons. She was morally horrified, and unconsciously she was alarmed and resentful at being drawn into the affair. She had lived aloof so long that she had lost the habit of close human contact; it seemed difficult and dreadful to her. She had found sympathy meaningless after the death of the young man she should have married, and no one had called much upon her active kindness in the years of her solitude. She was not hard, simply withdrawn and unreal. But Anne's story troubled her.

She rose with great suddenness and advised her to go to bed in an abruptly gentle voice.

'We'll take counsel together after a night's sleep,' she promised, and she drifted out of the room.

Anne went upstairs hurt and inclined to self-pity except that she had put that out of the way as something forbidden. She was sorry for her aunt too; she had missed everything that made the world beautiful, and her own frustration had taken from her the power to feel strongly. She had not even condemned Anne.

The little she had told Aunt Minima had vividly brought back the treasure of past days: the hours on Exmoor — she smiled as she thought of Philip's ritual fires — odd, stolen moments, and the *bonheur caché* of Mulberry Walk. Anne, driven and afraid, had a sense of warmth at her heart as she lay in bed wrapped in her old golden silk dressing-gown, her arms thrust above her head, her eyes wide with recollection.

Aunt Minima did not entirely fail her. She gardened all the next day, with her sun-bonnet pulled well forward over her face and a long-handled spud working havoc among the young seedlings. After tea she played and sang *La Fille de Mme Angot* for an hour or two, but late in the evening she diffidently approached Anne's chair and sat cross-legged on the floor beside her in a posture she had been taught to assume for the practice of Indian deep breathing. She wore a blue Liberty burnous, and her expression was less remote, more interested and vivid than usual. She spoke in a shy voice.

'You shall have my house for as long as you like, Anne, and no one shall know,' she said. 'That will be better than going abroad where there will be all sorts of formalities and difficulties. I shall tell the servants you are married, and they are both old and discreet.'

'You are good,' Anne said, tears springing to her eyes. 'But I can't stay. I should never have come. I'll manage in London. I had no right to thrust myself I on you.'

'I may go abroad,' Aunt Minnie said calmly, 'but I am not sure. I would like to be a help to you, but the merely physical side of life is rather dreadful to me, and I am afraid I should be useless. Have any friend you like to stay with you. I may be here, but do not count on me. My friend Dr Scott will look after you. I should like to help you, Anne,' Aunt Minnie repeated in a helpless voice.

'You are doing everything,' Anne said, laying her cheek against her hand.

Miss Carey caressed her hair and face a little awkwardly, then got up from the floor murmuring, 'So that's arranged. Stay now, or come back when you like.'

She crossed the room to her piano and began to produce a cataract of sound, stopping suddenly in the midst of a brilliant passage to fall into a sort of waking dream, her beautiful hands resting on the keys, her eyes absorbed.

'But if you love this man,' she said abruptly, 'it is very hard that you should be alone.'

19 Carmichael

Girlie, restored to health, frolicked robustly in the courtyard with Jocko, flourishing her cigarette and shouting to Darling to come out and take snapshots of 'Mummy and her Boy'. Girlie had grown fatter since her illness, and had bobbed her coarse grey hair, which now looked like a mop. She crouched with her arms round Jocko against an angle of the building, and Darling strode out with his kodak and took several pictures of her, after which she took pictures of him and Jocko, and then they strolled about the yard throwing a rubber ball for the dog to fetch, and laughing loudly at his clumsy and rheumatic gambols. They were happy, and happier in flaunting their united content before the eyes of the other occupants of the flats. Their gaiety had the note of advertisement in it, and no one else used the courtyard as a sort of private terrace in their fashion. Darling put a protective arm round Girlie's shoulders and gazed at her in theatrical adoration, and she put her cigarette between her lips with a hoarse gurgle of laughter.

Anne, in a sort of stupor of solitude in her room, shut the window to keep out the sound of their voices which rasped her nerves. She had given Pimlico to her servant Mrs Gamble, and had dismissed that leisurely and gossiping person, and no one came in to disturb her. She was preparing to give up the flat, and she burnt papers and sorted the accumulations of drawers and boxes with a steady, mechanical energy, falling sometimes into a stony quiet with her hands in her lap, her expression withdrawn and remote. She would rouse herself impatiently from such lapses. She sorted and destroyed with a sense of finality. She would never enter this flat again once she had left it; never see the Buildings, or the pigeons, or — and her ghost-like smile was not of regret for the married pair below her — Girlie and Darling again. She was sure of it, and there was relief in the thought.

She deliberately burnt two volumes of Dampier's plays and poems. She had bought them herself before she knew him. She had nothing that he had given her; he had never written her a letter. She watched the printed pages of his books blacken, curl, and burst into flames. A phrase, a word, leaped to her eye, and she spoke them idly aloud in a voice without meaning. Dampier's written words had ceased to live for her. She remembered reading a particular speech from *Melancthon* aloud to Thomas; the very words now smoked and flamed before her eyes. Well, she had not known or dreamed of knowing Dampier then, and now Thomas was gone, and Dampier had come and was gone too. There seemed no difference to her between the silence that had fallen in France, and the silence in California. One was as likely to be broken as the other. It was all very queer.

She was sitting over the fire still, abstracted and lost, when someone lifted the knocker on her door and rattled it in a familiar fashion. She hesitated, but she could not shut out Maquita. In another moment the room brimmed over with Miss Gilroy at her most effervescent.

'Anne, you little darling, what an *age* since we've met, but I'm always so busy. And where is Pim, the angel — not given away? Oh, you are heartless! I have so much to say to you, dear, but tell me all about yourself first. Louise and Bastien and I are looking for new digs. The landlady says the other tenants complain of the noise we make when we have parties, but of course the truth is that we are giving her notice — fed up, my dear. You know, the usual old latchkey life. We want more room too. Louise is doing wonderful work, and she has sold six pictures this spring. Of course I simply won't think of marrying Bastien, though he asks me all the time, poor boy, but I think it's only habit — Frenchmen! — don't you? He's altogether too irresponsible. You know my type is a strong man who *does* things, not anyone I could rule, and *not* one I might have to support! Bastien is just that lazy, artistic kind. No, thank you! And anyway your own race and your own religion do matter.'

Anne got tea while Maquita poured out her news and comments headlong.

'My screw has been raised, thank goodness, it's almost decent now, but our department will soon have to wind up. You *are* lucky not to be in an office any more.'

She was looking well and smart, some of the raised screw evidently having gone into her clothes.

'Who do you think I've just met, my dear — Robert Wentworth, of all people, fearfully pleased and important because Petunia's going to have a baby. It *is* rather sweet of her of course, and I'm sure Petunia's baby will be a darling, but after all, these things *do* happen. Imagine Robert running after me to tell me about it in St James' Street — he is a weird character. "We expect a family in September," he said, just as if it was going to be kittens. I nearly said something vulgar, but I hope for her own sake that Petunia will only produce one Wentworth at a time. Robert says it is a most important event for the County, even if it is a girl, but that he and Petunia have determined from the first that it's to be a boy called George after the King. Petunia is clever. She probably will manage it. Poor child, she's in Slowshire now with her mother-in-law as her guest. Imagine all the beef tea and milk she'll have to swallow.'

Maquita's laugh went off like a rocket.

'This *is* cosy — like old times,' she went on. 'What ages since we've met. It's that absurd school of yours. How is it getting on, and Paul and Veritas? And what about P M D? — does he still come and talk over the fire?'

'No. Haven't you heard? He's been very ill,' Anne said steadily, her lips dry. 'Pneumonia. He's had to go away for a year or more to California. They've all gone — the house is let.'

'Oh, I am sorry,' Maquita said with sincerity. 'What bad luck. I often wonder what his wife was like. You know her, do tell me! He liked you, Anne, you know.' She looked at her.

Anne said nothing.

Maquita chattered on about trifles, but her eyes unconsciously discovered something disturbed in the room, though as yet little had been touched in it. The spirit of it was changed. Anne's tranquil grace which she imparted unconsciously to her surroundings, the impression of her fastidious personality, was somehow withdrawn. The books by the fireplace were shoved anyhow into the shelves, the desk was covered with untidy heaps of papers. A big yellow bowl held anemones that had been dead a week, and there was not another flower in the room. It was a room no longer kept delicately to please its owner, or made festive for a coming. No one cared to look at it now.

'Are you going away for a holiday, or are you giving up the flat? It makes me sad to see it,' Maquita said, looking sentimentally round her.

'Giving it up. One of my twin aunts is taking me to Italy,' Anne announced. 'Of course it's the wrong time of year, but still —'

'But how lovely — how lucky!' Maquita exclaimed, kindling instantly into enthusiasm.

Anne said nothing.

Maquita stopped short and gave her a sharp look.

'Anne ducky, what is it? You are unhappy — tell me. You mind about P M D. Is it that? He'll come back, my dear —'

'Oh, Maquita!'

Her secret broke from her in that single cry of Anne's, and the two girls gazed at each other dumbly. Maquita looked frightened, then her eyes blazed.

'Oh, he couldn't be such a beast!' she said incoherently with bitter rage. Anne stopped her, and for once Maquita was silent while she talked. She was quick enough to accept the fact that she could say nothing against Dampier, that Anne considered herself a fair debtor to life, not a victim. Presently she was looking at her — talking steadily with a kind of pale illumination — almost in envy.

'You with a baby! It will be sweet,' Maquita broke in, suddenly maternal. 'I'll help to bring him up, Anne, or her.'

'Mark,' Anne said, her eyes shining with a new expression, her mouth breaking into a smile. Maquita — suddenly and for the first time — made the thought of this child as a separate entity cross her mind.

'He'll need a lot of money; dear little clothes first, and later school and university. Let's make him a great man, Anne! An explorer, or a wonderful doctor! I'll work like anything and save everything for him. It will be our lifework, caring for that child.'

Maquita's words flew like quicksilver, her expression was solemn and rapt.

'Oh, you are good,' Anne exclaimed, touched by her generosity. 'You'll be nearest to him after me. He won't have any real relations, poor little Mark!'

'He'll be better without them,' Maquita said rather sombrely for her. 'They expect so much from one, and want one to expect so little from them. And goodness knows I don't, but my richest aunt in the world walked me about in the kitchen garden when I was last at home, telling me that she did hope I was saving up for my old age. I told her I meant to be young for a long time yet — but that sort of aunt ages one dreadfully — and that anyhow on fifty shillings a week I couldn't save anything vast for an old-age pension. But she was as full of warnings as an owl. Oh, don't start the world with rich relations!'

'You're a dear, Maquita,' Anne said irrelevantly, envying her the freedom of the world that still lay before her, but still occupied with the thought of the child as hers, her own, and out of contact with material considerations for the moment. She was withdrawn into a little circle of silence, lifted out of the valley of fear into a place of joy. Maquita found it moving to look at her, and tears sprang to her eyes.

'I'll come and stay with you now, tonight. You shouldn't be alone. I can help pack up, at least,' she said impulsively, blinking her wet lashes. 'Oh, Anne, how terrible it is — how wicked — and why do I envy you?' She sobbed, searching for her handkerchief.

'I'm wicked. I'm low and base, I suppose, and I'm going to drag other people into it to suffer, that's the worst of it. Everyone will have to know some day — my family, my brothers,' Anne said, shrinking from her, the illuminated look fading from her face leaving it strained and grey. 'I never wanted to be this sort of person. It torments me. But when other people like me want to kill themselves, I don't want to kill myself. I want to live. I intend to fight to make this baby happy. Afterwards — surely people will be kind. But I dare not think about later. I have to get through *now*. Oh, Maquita, tell me if you think I am mad to try and keep him from knowing anything about it!' Anne's cheeks crimsoned. 'Oh, he must not know. I can bear anything but that. I must hide myself, I must, Maquita! I shall never see him again.' She broke into desperate tears.

Maquita put her arms round her, moved to the depths, but Anne with self-command that amazed her, checked herself in a moment.

'I always say women are idiotic from the second they begin

to have babies, and here am like the rest of us,' she said cynically. 'Yes, you can envy me, Maquita, queer as it seems to say so. I have been so terrifically happy that there is no one in the world I would change places with. I am "out of misfortune's reach" in a way. But do stay with me — do stay.' She clung to her.

It was nearly eight o'clock, and Maquita had just left the flat to fetch some night things when the knocker was sharply lifted twice in succession. Anne, thinking Maquita had come back for something forgotten, hastily opened the door, and John Carmichael walked in.

She was utterly astonished.

The young man's face was set and pale, and he looked horribly self-conscious and nervous. He was not quite clear himself why he had come, but some compulsion had driven him. He had wanted to see Anne again, she had lived in his mind ever since the night at Dampier's when she had slept by the fire in her red dress and had wakened to such wildness of speech. Subsequent meetings had been formal and ordinary, always in the presence of others. They had but added to his disturbance and his desire. He went over and over in his mind the words she had uttered, shutting his eyes with intensity to recall the very folds of her dress, her stiff, pointed fingers, the shadows on her tense face, before she had started in despair to wakefulness. He had gone home excited by her, angry and compassionate by turns, but unable to put her out of his mind.

'But I will say it.' He had wondered ever since what else she might have said had Mrs Dampier not come in at that moment. The thought of the Dampiers made him groan. He knew them well, and what did he know of Anne? Nothing. She was in fault he was sure if there was — Carmichael was ashamed of his thoughts at this point. Anyhow, it was no affair of his; better to keep away. But he wanted to see Anne again. He was sure that she was in a dangerous, perhaps a desperate, mood, and he could at least try to help her.

Carmichael was quixotic, and the tedious disillusionment of the after-the-war world was powerless to break a certain stubborn idealism in his heart. With his reason he accepted the hard facts of life and realised their necessity and truth. In him at the same time a nameless faculty rejected all logic and made certain inconsistencies the truths of life that governed him.

This was his fourth visit to Anne's flat. She had been out or away each time he had called. Now, faced by her coolness and composure, he suddenly felt a fool and an intruder.

'How kind of you to call,' Anne said conversationally. 'How is the *Review*? I've missed it this month. I should love to be working with you, but as Mr Dampier probably told you, I think I'll be going abroad quite soon. Perhaps in the autumn — will you smoke? There ought to be cigarettes about, but I've been away lately, and neglecting things I'm afraid.'

Her indifferent glance about the room scarcely seemed to take in the evidence of the neglect she spoke of, but Carmichael caught sight of the dead anemones, and although he had never been in Anne's room before, this one small detail fixed itself in his mind as unlike her habitual concern about her surroundings. She was oblivious of the little things that had mattered once — he felt that.

He talked as formally as she, stiff and conscious in spite of an effort to be natural, and underneath swayed to the point of dizziness by her presence in the same room. It was unaccountable to him, the more so because he could see with cruel clearness that she looked ill and plain, unlit by any interest. He sat down and rolled a cigarette while Anne pulled the thin yellow curtains across the window. In her face as she turned to stir the small wood fire, Carmichael saw defined the reality of her wild words spoken in Dampier's house. A savage emotion took him. She talked, and he heard his own voice responding to her rather hurried remarks with ordinary indifference, but he was watching the play of her features, every least movement of her hands, and listening to the inflections of her voice which had seemed to him so charming the day Dampier had brought her to tea at the *Review* office, and which now was so poignant to his ears. He realised anew the 'listening fear in her regard', and seemed to see her changed, effaced, frightened. His thoughts ran riot. She was so finely modulated, so sensitive, so delicately made for fun and laughter and the deeper gifts of life — God!

Carmichael threw his cigarette into the grate and sat back, trembling inwardly, his chivalrous sense goading him till he longed to clench his hands and break someone's neck. Anne found him morose and difficult to talk to; she slipped into the big chair that caressed her like Dampier's arm, it was so much his, composedly speaking of casual things and not giving Carmichael much time to assent or disagree. She exerted herself to entertain him almost as if she were anxious to prevent him speaking at all. She wished he would go, but he sat on, his troubled gaze fixed chiefly on the fire, but stealing sometimes half furtively to her face.

Anne considered him critically once, remembering that she had liked him because of his devotion to Dampier as well as because he had been simple and rather humorous about himself among the affected literary young men in the *Review* office. But she thought him tiresome now to come to see her when she wanted to be alone. She wished Maquita would come in and take him off her hands. She supposed he was pleasant and kind and sincere, but she really couldn't be bothered.

'That night at Dampier's,' he suddenly said with a violence that made her start, 'You spoke to me about him. Perhaps you didn't mean what you said, but rightly or wrongly, I can't forget it. You've shaken my faith in him — I thought Dampier was a prince! I'm wretched about you — about Dampier — in hell about him. I looked up to him — laugh at me, and tell me I'm a fool.' He was horrified by the crudeness of his words as the poured out of him.

Anne looked at him without pity.

'I must have been ill that night — we were all so tired and anxious, weren't we? Don't lose faith in Mr Dampier. He is wonderful. Forget what I said, whatever it was. I can't remember.'

'Yes, you can,' Carmichael said roughly. 'And you spoke the truth. Won't you be sincere with me again? I will do anything for you, that is what I came here to say. That's what I want. I wish you would trust me.'

'You are very kind,' Anne said conventionally, 'but really there is no need. Thank you so much.' She averted her eyes.

'You push me back. You won't let me be a friend,' Carmichael said, looking at her intently.

'I can't be bothered with new friends,' Anne said carelessly. 'I'm sorry I'm not in the humour. I used to respond to that sort of thing once. But I've done with it I'm afraid. I'm sorry the grate is so black and powdery. It's because I've been burning books of poetry — Dampier's plays among them — and gibing at myself for what I used to feel. There's nothing in poetry really, unless you have a very comfortable body and mind. Do have another cigarette, you've wasted yours. Maquita Gilroy will be in in a few minutes, she's staying with me just now. I forget — have you met her?'

'No. And before she comes in,' Carmichael said deliberately, 'I want to ask you to marry me. Will you marry me, Anne? I'll take you to Italy, or to China, or wherever you want to go — whenever you like.'

'This is a very poor joke, isn't it?' Anne said evenly, looking very white.

'It would be,' he agreed in the same half-suppressed, even tone, 'but it's not a joke to me. Will you marry me — could you? I am rather crocked by the war you know, but I'm getting fitter all the time. Will you marry me? I'll spend my whole life for you.'

'Of course you are joking. I don't even know you,' Anne said, wounded, and breathing quickly. 'I didn't think you would treat me like this. What do you mean?'

'I mean only what I say, that I think of you and nothing else all day, and I am tormented — ever since that night when you were asleep when I came in. Your face, your voice — they go with me. I do want you, Anne. I ask you to marry me.'

He looked at her with a twisted face as if he were putting great command upon himself not to make some gesture towards her, and his voice struck through her defences.

'I won't, I can't,' she said in a low voice of suppressed passion. 'You are sorry for me. You are trying to be kind to me, and I tell you I don't need it. Go away and leave me. You are horrible. But I can laugh at you — perhaps that is what you mean me to do?'

She began to walk up and down the room, her face rather terrible, half convulsed, and a sound that was not laughter coming from her lips. Carmichael, alarmed and horrified, sprang up and put an arm round her shoulders, drawing her down on to the sofa.

'Anne, my dear, you persist in misunderstanding me. I must be very clumsy. Never mind, I'll go away since that is what you want,' he said in despair.

She subsided, gasping a little, and he knelt beside her, chafing her cold hands and soothing her like a child.

'There, Anne dear, there, my dear, it's all right, you've no business to have hands like ice! I'm going away in a moment — just as soon as Miss Gilroy gets back, but you mustn't faint before she comes. Lie still a minute.'

Anne lay back with her eyes closed, feeling a vague comfort in his touch and in the momentary pretence that it was Dampier come back. Then she sat up, moving away from him, and putting her hands up to her hair.

'I'm sure I'm dreadfully untidy,' she said, returning to her conventional tone with a pathetic effort. She looked sorrowfully at him.

'You mean to be kind I'm sure, but you don't know what you say —'

'I do know,' he interrupted.

'That I have been somebody's mistress — that I am going to have a child?' she demanded very low. Her shadowed eyes searched his face.

'Marry me and let me take care of you,' he said steadily.

'Oh, you're impossibly noble!' Anne cried impatiently. 'You've got some ridiculous social idea or other. Does it occur to you that I don't care a pin about you, that you never so much as cross my mind? That I don't consider myself a victim, and that though I'm unhappy I'm not ashamed, not anxious to be 'righted'? How can you want to marry me? You'll regret it soon enough. There's no question of caring for me. Well, I won't take advantage of your kindness. I feel tempted to, in a way,' she added in a gentler, a less bitter tone, 'because I'm conventional in outward things and I find it hard to face people — to outrage them.' Her head drooped.

'The man who left you is an unimaginable scoundrel,' Carmichael said furiously.

'I am not left,' Anne retorted with bitter pride, her cheeks blazing. 'I've chosen my own way. I've lied well. He — he doesn't know. He won't ever if I can help it. Oh, there isn't going to be any melodrama. I'll keep out of the way, and they shall never know. I can do that now, easily enough. You'll keep my confidence, I know.'

'Jeer at me if you think I deserve it, but marry me from any motive you please,' Carmichael said.

'I believe you mean it,' Anne said slowly, amazement in her eyes. 'But it is impossible.'

'But surely —' he began in agitation.

'Surely things can never begin again? No, never,' Anne said. 'No, never. It is over, I know, I feel it. He may not recover. He may stay in California. I don't know what will happen to me, but in any case he is out of my life as I am out of his, for good. Oh, I know it, I am certain of it. I'm too tired to talk any more,' she said like a piteous child. 'Would you mind going away?'

'Will you be a friend and look upon me as yours? Let me be of use if ever I can — if you ever want me?' Carmichael said urgently.

'Yes, I will,' she said.

'Oh, who will look after you?' he burst out with emotion, taking her hand. 'Let me, Anne. Don't go from me.'

'I'll be all right. I've no intention of killing myself. I don't mean to slip over the Embankment after all. To tell you the truth,' Anne admitted, smiling faintly up at him with an expression that took the triviality and flippancy from her words and made her strangely touching and, Carmichael felt, spiritual, 'now that I've got so far I am curious to see the whole immoral business through. Are you awfully curious for experience, for every bit of life —? Oh, there's Maquita!'

There was a commotion in the courtyard as Girlie and Darling, plunging out for a run with Jocko, collided the narrow doorway with Miss Gilroy, flying in at her usual high speed, and swinging her suitcase. Maquita penetrating, cheerful laugh cut into the mellow and dignified apologies offered by Darling and Girlie's abrupt 'Sorry' and the hysterical barking of Jocko.

Maquita clattered at the knocker and was let in.

'My dear,' she babbled, 'we now *know* Girlie and Darling! I've been run into by the whole family. He's a dreadful-looking cinema actor or something, and surely if you are nearly knocked flat that's an intimate enough introduction! Well, I've got my things, and hurried like anything. Louise isn't pleased. Oh, I'm glad you haven't been alone.'

'Nighty-night!' Girlie's voice called to Jocko. 'Come to Mummy now, naughty Boy! At once, sit! Time for bed. Say nighty-night to the pussies and come in, Mummy's own Boy!'

20 'Mark'

A day of sunlight and sparkling sea becoming hour by hour calmer and bluer as it beat against the cliffs below Miss Carey's house succeeded a week of storm and rain. A warmth that held a memory of summer pervaded the soaked and battered garden, and the hardy yellow chrysanthemums in the wide border at the foot of the garden lifted bold heads, shining against the grey stone wall.

Calm succeeded storm within doors as without. The servants, following the custom of their kind, partook copiously of tea and fortified themselves after a time of unusual stress by frequent little extra snacks of food. They discussed discreetly — because they were discreet and loyal elderly women — the affairs of the house, which had taken a mysterious and exciting turn since Miss Carey's widowed young niece had come to stay. The routine of the house, unbroken for years, had been profoundly disturbed. They talked it over, but without resentment. Indeed they were conscious of a certain enjoyment. They surmised something strange in Anne's widowhood, but they liked her, and they were sympathetic. They inclined to the deserted wife theory, and moralised on men and the cruelty of the world. They refilled the teapot, and discussing yesterday, had only admiration for the young mother. Such self-command, such quietness! Cook plunged deeply into reminisce and Maggie made two more rounds of buttered toast and spread them with a little Gentlemen's Relish.

The day before in hours of storm Anne's baby had been born. Anne herself was the calmest person in the house; Cook and Maggie palpitating in the kitchen, with the pot, the most agitated.

Anne came back reluctantly to consciousness in the quiet house. She did not want to open her eyes, and there seemed no reason why she should make the effort. She was blissfully comfortable, and a desire unformed in words floated vaguely through her mind to remain in this beatific state. If she neither stirred nor thought —

She sank a little way into oblivion again, and returned more nearly this time to wakefulness. But she would not wake yet. Outside there was something frightening, some nightmare that eluded her, but made her afraid, and she was afraid of fear.

She sighed and opened her eyes, relapsing instantly, her lashes dark on her colourless cheeks. But in the momentary glimpse she had recognised that she was in bed in her own room, which was dark, and that beyond, in a little room, there were lights and voices and a stir of people. She was dreamily resentful. Perhaps they might wake her, and she wanted to lie beautifully quiet and untroubled. She could not think who those people could be in that far-off square of light, and it did matter. Oblivion closed over her again.

She had at last come to the end of a long road that had lately led her by dusk along cliffs and beaches, beside a sea that tormented her by its noise and its intolerable eternity, and yet strangely soothed her with a sense of her insignificance, her transience. Anne was significant and terrifying to herself in the enclosure of a room, the definiteness of a house, in those autumn weeks. In the house there were the eyes of the servants and the rattle of Aunt Minima's piano. The rough autumn airs, the thunderous seas whose waters were pricked in the dusk by distant lights, these brought a forgetfulness of the body that was better. Now she had come to the end at last. She knew an amazing relief.

These images of evenings in the buffeting winds and lamp-lit hours surrounded by the rising and ebbing of Aunt Minima's flood of music indoors, formed themselves more sharply in Anne's mind, and she woke suddenly and completely.

'Anne,' Aunt Minnie was saying in a soft, moved voice, 'I want to show you your baby.'

'I had forgotten all about him,' Anne said, astonished at herself, with a quick throb of realisation. 'Bring him to me quickly, Aunt Minnie! Oh, poor little Mark.'

Miss Carey lowered the baby importantly to a pillow beside her, remarking, 'Hours old, and hasn't seen its own mother yet.' She took a soft, awkward pleasure in her new rôle.

Anne examined the infant with a painful excitement beneath her languor.

'Poor little Mark,' she said, touching its cheek.

'Not Mark, Anne, your little daughter,' Aunt Minima corrected.

She saw Anne shrink back as though from a blow.

'Oh, no, I can't — I don't want a girl. Take her away,' she said violently, turning from the child.

'She's a dear little baby, Anne,' Aunt Minima said reproachfully. 'Look at her dark hair — like a little Indian.'

'Take her away,' Anne repeated obstinately in a muffled voice, 'and leave me alone, please. I want to be alone.'

Later in the day she capriciously demanded the child and lay looking at it with sombre eyes.

'Philip wanted a little girl, but not you, you poor little thing,' she thought to herself, and in a sudden passion of resentment that anyone should think her baby unwanted, Anne seized the little thing in her arms and pressed her mouth to its tiny dark head.

'You've no right to be a girl. You've chosen a horrible life,' she said seriously to her. 'But as I'm chiefly responsible, you can count on me. We'll manage somehow.'

She studied the small red face which seemed grotesque and goblin-like but somehow satisfactory because it belonged to her baby, searching for a likeness. She could find none.

'So far you're a goblin, not like me and not a bit like Melancthon,' she advised her, 'but I may love you all the same.'

She felt that she adored her already.

After that Anne was as much absorbed by her infant as even the nurse could wish, though she would utter no extravagant praise. She hung over her, taking perpetual interest in her grimaces, in the clutch of her fingers, and her absurd completeness as a human being on a minute scale. She was amused and cheerful.

'I can think of no name for her,' she would say, perplexed. 'I never meant her to be here at all, of course. I expected her brother Mark.'

She wondered ardently what Dampier would say to her could he see her, but that led to forbidden longings, to be fought down in the still hours.

Aunt Minima was immensely relieved that her house had been so little disturbed, and that she could play her piano without objection from nurse or patient almost at once. She was perplexed that in the circumstances Anne seemed so happy and untroubled; playing with her baby, addressing ridiculous speeches to it, warning it about behaviour and the world, Anne was wholly charming, she thought.

'You are essentially maternal,' Aunt Minima said kindly, as if uttering a truth that surprised her very much. 'Dr Scott thinks you are a perfectly normal woman, and she says that is a very rare thing. The essential woman.'

'The essential savage perhaps,' Anne said with an ambiguous smile.

'Far from that, my dear! You look more like a flower with your little face,' Aunt Minnie said eagerly, a growing affection for Anne making her face glow. 'It's merely that you are the type that cannot flourish physically or mentally without the normal woman's life — children. Now your Aunt Maxima and I are not like that. Intellectual interests suffice us. The other would weary and limit us.' Aunt Minnie was serious and shy. 'I actually think that even without marriage that the other — that what you did — was right, for you.'

'So do I,' said Anne.

'You broke God's law,' Aunt Minima said gently, but as if impelled to say it. Her face flushed up, and she was distressed. She forgot her many rationalistic translations, and when real life was in question reverted quite simply to the early training received from her father, the vicar.

'Or one idea of it,' Anne said. 'But I think each of us has his own law to make and keep.'

She recalled her talks with Dampier, lying on the moors.

'Don't think me callous or unable to feel,' she said with sudden tears in her eyes. 'I am not complacent. I lie here at night and try to think things out, but it's very much of a tangle. At present the sheer relief from all that long, long ugliness seems worth living for. I hated myself. I think now, because I love this queer little thing, and I've forgotten the worst of it, that it was worthwhile, but I'm not really sure. I was afraid, and I was bored. The purpose of life, actually in progress, is hideous.'

'I don't find it so. It's miraculous and efficient,' her large, square-shaped doctor said, entering the room smiling.

'You only watch the process,' Anne said significantly. 'The pain is nothing — I thought women exaggerated, and they do — but it is such a long job to get through alone. Simply boring. Weeks of ugliness. And I hated you,' Anne said candidly, looking up at Dr Scott's large, firm pink face and mannish, short grey hair.

'I'd like to have crept away alone, like a beast in a jungle.'

'You're a primitive woman,' the doctor said pleasantly, 'but, unluckily, civilisation has taken its toll of you too. You would not have come out of the jungle, you know. All the same, I'd welcome more patients with your ideas. You help restore the balance of nature. Women who can't and won't; women who shouldn't and do! I want clinics for common sense, and I'd teach how not to, as well as how to have a family. But to my view every woman with the instinct for a child (and some certainly have no such instinct) ought to have one. That is if she is willing to support it and acknowledge it. That is the vital thing. That makes the morality of it.'

'It is not an easy world to do that in,' Anne murmured.

'Oh, perfectly possible, with common sense,' the doctor asserted briskly.

'Whatever they may think, you're not only an "instinct" all the same,' Anne told the baby later. 'I love you but even now — oh, even now you're not first!'

⁂

The child was small and delicately made, but seemed to thrive well, and Anne recovered excellently, causing Dr Scott to triumph over the rare case of a woman who 'did not coddle her nerves'.

Anne was up and about her room, moving from one window to the other and taking exquisite pleasure in the November trees naked against the silver-grey sky and the small chrysanthemums making a bank of sunlight yellow by the wall at the bottom of the garden, when one morning Miss Carey called to her from the next room in a voice that she tried not to make alarmed.

'Anne, will you come! I cannot wake the baby.'

It was the hour when the child was lifted from her cot and

carried in to her mother. To-day the nurse was out. Anne tried to run, struck with terror, and found that her feet would only drag across the floor.

'Give her to me,' she gasped, 'and get the doctor.'

She took the baby from her aunt's arms and almost fell into a chair. The baby's eyes were slightly open and there was a bluish shadow round her mouth. Anne put her lips to the tiny hands that already felt cold, and pressed the child distractedly to her breast, as if to warm her. Then she laid the little thing across her knees with agony in her heart.

'She is dead, my little baby,' she said, adding frenziedly, 'oh, get someone — do something!'

But there was nothing that could be done; nothing that could make any difference. Dampier's unknown child, the daughter he had desired, had spent a few days as the guest of this troubled planet, and then without warning her tiny heart had ceased to beat.

Anne, after her first outburst, was calm, but she suffered intolerably. She went through the days collectedly with a stoic endurance till the unnamed child was laid in the earth.

On the day that happened, Anne shuddered to see the yellow chrysanthemums at the end of Aunt Minima's garden still making sunlight beside the grey wall.

She lay in her room for a time, unable for any effort, but as soon as she could she tried her best to get about.

'I'll soon be all right again,' she assured Miss Carey, and begged her to practise as much as she liked. Outward things had no power to disturb her. She sat quietly in her own room while Aunt Minnie sang and played in a subdued fashion. One thought revolved torturingly in her dazed mind: 'Oh, why are we made to love so bitterly?'

She was not quiescent; she was digging deep into her own mind and experience trying to find a faith or a philosophy that was more than a mere 'feeling of direction', as she had called it long ago. She began at last to see that the ordinary life of a human being was not just a series of detached pictures opened anew each day to please a child, but a building that required architecture. She had built recklessly with her coloured bricks, thinking mainly of her own delight, and the building had crashed about her. She was not even sure that she could have done differently, but she turned things over and over in her mind trying to see.

Sometimes she lay awake in the darkness or at dawn recalling every instant that she had caressed her living child, remembering the physical touch of her hands, of her head when she had pressed her lips against them. Her baby with its perfect little body gone into nothingness for ever, and she so longed to hold her.

Then at times the loss of the child seemed nothing to the loss that had preceded it. She had an intolerable longing for Dampier.

But the world was altogether empty.

21 Ravelled Ends

Minima was presently called to town by her sister Maxima's serious — and as it turned out, prolonged — illness and Anne chose to go to London with her to join Maquita in rooms.

Miss Carey reached London with relief. She was distressed by Anne's grief over the baby, and she missed the little thing oddly herself, but she thought that on the whole the child's death was a fortunate thing. She wanted her routine of life to continue as usual, after an interruption in which she had been as sympathetic and kind as possible, but the house did not resume its familiar aspect quickly. Miss Carey had felt more helpless than ever in the face of Anne's silent but apparent distress. Aunt Maxima's illness came as a godsend to her twin sister, it was so much less alarming than Anne.

Bewildered and nervous, but full of good intentions, she went to Campden Hill, where she nearly drove the efficient Miss Mollond out of her senses by her unpractical suggestions.

Once Maxima had turned the corner, Minima began to go regularly to the British Museum, where she spent long and happy days. She dropped Anne out of her mind without difficulty, as well as Paul and Veritas.

Veritas, slowly convalescing, turned more and more to Paul for diversion and companionship. Her twin sister, although a guest in her house — in Anne's little room — and the object of great admiration to the schoolgirls, was seldom available as nurse or companion. She had discovered Egypt and Professor Flinders Petrie's work there, and her past philosophies and studies were as nothing to her in the present enchantment.

Paul and Veritas naturally knew a good deal about pyramids and mummies and cuneiform writing, and the contents of tombs, and Assyrian history, and they had attended courses of Professor Flinders Petrie's lectures. Their smiles as they listened to poor Minima's enthusiastic wonder over these things were slightly touched by superiority.

Poor Minima; what a wasted life! No useful work, no lasting friendship, no profound religion — one feared, without presuming to judge! — nothing to give stability or meaning to her days. A mere frittering of her talents, one feared, a selfish seclusion, perpetual new superficial interests sprung from accident, like this turn for Egyptology!

Paul and Veritas saw it very clearly, and noted how untouched by the deeper emotions was Minima's youthful face with its halo of white hair but adding to its charm.

'Your poor sister, dearest Veritas!' Paul exclaimed sadly, unconscious that she was slightly jealous of her presence in the house. 'Hers is a melancholy, unenriched life. How blessed *we* are!'

'Dear Sainty! Yes, yes, indeed!' Veritas agreed, tears of weakness and love welling into her eyes. She and Paul loving God, loving each other, working together for the school, and living full, rounded lives, how blessed they were! Paul bent down and kissed her affinity and partner before setting off for the Abbey service where she meant to return heartfelt thanks. Soon, she trusted, Veritas would be strong enough to accompany her, and then they would offer their solemn and united gratitude that they were allowed to be together for a little longer. Veritas had nearly been taken from her. Before this illness it had been her own frail health that had given cause for anxiety. Now yet another bond united them in the common fear of losing each other.

Paul and Veritas did not mention Anne; her conduct had wounded them too deeply. She had left the school at Easter to go into a literary office, and she had not done so, nor had she replied in any satisfactory manner to their natural questions on the subject. Anne's letters, they agreed, had never been her strong point, but those of the past summer from Minima's house — the Italian trip being unaccountably delayed — where she was apparently content to idle away her days, had been very poor, very poor indeed. They had feared a certain lack in her character always. And — culmination of poverty of feeling and selfishness — throughout her aunt's dangerous illness she had not written at all. She might have offered to help in the school where she could have been of real use. She could and should have displayed some concern. They discussed it; Miss Mollond secretly wrote pointing out Anne's plain duty to her; they tactfully sounded Minima, who was vague as usual, and then by mutual consent they dropped her name.

Aunt Minima suddenly found that her new-born love for Egypt must take her to Egypt, and of course Anne would go with her. It would do Anne's health good, it would cover the failure of the Italian trip, and be an excellent plan in every way. Aunt Minnie blazed with the idea of Egypt. She went to see Anne, nervously prepared for a tragic greeting, and was slightly bewildered because Anne and Maquita were laughing over their tea as she came in.

'Anne, dear child,' she began uncertainly, but Maquita swiftly intercepted further exclamations, and was soon displaying a delighted interest in Babylonian discoveries that roused Aunt Minnie to eloquence. Anne, no longer smiling, slipped a little into the shadow and heard their voices like thin rods striking against each other, making a meaningless noise. She made no effort to follow what they said. Effort became more difficult daily, and she was too tired to care about anything. She felt a growing desire to throw up her hands and sink beneath all necessity for thought. She shut her eyes, and her old fancy of the jungle possessed her again. If she could only be like a wild creature and creep away to hide herself under tangled green things till life seemed bearable again. She could imagine herself lying very still for a long, long time, hearing the stir of life about her, feeling the wind and the sun remotely from her green depths. No voice would bring trouble to her dreamless content, no hand touch her, and gradually some energy might return to her. She might recover her eagerness to live.

'Arabia Deserta, I read that many years ago, most absorbing — Palestine — Egypt! I had thought before of Italy, but it shall be Egypt, and I came specially to say that I shall take you, Anne. We shall study Egypt together. The Tel-el-Amarna period — how engrossing it will be; Miss Gilroy, do you not think so?' Aunt Minima demanded softly brilliant.

Maquita was convinced that no other period could be more absorbing. She looked a little anxiously on Anne's apathy, inexperienced enough to believe in change for a heart that carries an empty place, and hoping Anne would consent to go. Maquita had welcomed Anne wholeheartedly, dashed and strangely nervous at first, but full of affection. When she had found that Anne was much like her old self, outwardly at least, and wearing an old red dress that gave her colour and a fictitious gaiety, she became more natural, and gradually recovered her ordinary quicksilver fluency of speech.

Anne was touched by Maquita's loyalty and warmth, and she could speak a little to her, who knew most of her story. Maquita with all her headlong ways neither questioned nor intruded. She wondered at Anne, thinking her strangely unrebellious against fate. There was nothing bitter in Anne. Maquita felt that in her place she would have been filled with unimaginable bitterness for the rest of her life.

Aunt Minima drifted away, feeling that everything to do with Egypt would be easily arranged, and that Anne, though unresponsive, would recover her spirits and 'get over things' once she was away from England.

She came every day to see her, and things began to shape themselves for departure, vague as she seemed in most particulars.

Mrs Garden came to see Anne perturbed and puzzled. The girl looked very ill, and admitted to having been ill, but Mrs Garden got no further than this. She too urged Egypt, and Anne remained passive in their well-meaning hands.

Sophy Price came to see Anne, patronising her from the plane of the married woman, and eyeing her sharply with close-set blue eyes. Her cold eyes made Anne shiver, but her curiosity, her suspicious questions, were met by a baffling, gentle blankness by Maquita.

Sophy's life seemed to be planned out clearly and pleasantly with 'Cliff' climbing steadily from promotion to promotion, finer houses as 'expectations' from relatives were realised, smarter society, more luxuries as time went on. Sophy was ambitious to have jewellery, motors, fine clothes, and later no doubt, to complete things, a child or two. Anne did not envy her, but Sophy like everyone else seemed to have got ahead of her with her nicely planned, admirable, and possibly amusing life.

There was Petunia too. Maquita had seen her with her sturdy infant — George Wentworth — looking every inch an Englishman like his father, and not in the least guttersnipish or mysterious like his mother. Petunia was becoming the beautiful young society woman that Robert had meant her to become. She was lovelier than ever, Maquita reported, in the radiant approval of the Wentworth family. They considered her son a brilliant personal achievement. Petunia had evidently put away all remembrance of her nomadic, earlier existence, and her fear of boredom if she were permanently tied to Robert, and had settled down. She had seen the wiser way of life.

And Maquita — even Maquita beneath her fine carelessness placed her coloured bricks carefully enough. Her latchkey never passed out of her own safe keeping.

But Anne could feel no envy of Sophy, Petunia, or Maquita.

22 Latchkey Ladies

'Beg your pardon — so sorry,' John Carmichael muttered formally as somebody suddenly swept across his path from a big office doorway, almost colliding with him. 'And what on earth are *you* doing in Chancery Lane?' he added in a very different voice as he recognised Anne Carey.

The meeting kindled an eager pleasure in his eyes, but Anne had stopped with a look of shock on her face, as if ordinarily she shrank from acquaintances. She spoke nervously in answer to his question.

'Oh, I almost live in Chancery Lane. I come to an office here every day.'

'I last heard of you in Egypt, through Miss Gilroy. I hoped you would let me know when you got back,' Carmichael said with reproach.

'Yes, oh, I might have some day,' Anne said hurriedly, 'but I took up some work and it is very absorbing. It has to do with looking after the famine children in Central Europe — Poland chiefly. And though it is only office work, and I am so far away from the reality, I seem to think of nothing else. It takes hold of you. I am hoping to be sent out to Poland soon. There is lots of work to be done among the children — nursing, feeding, teaching — general reconstruction. I want very much to go.'

'Where are you living? May I walk along with you?' Carmichael asked.

'I am afraid I must hurry up to Oxford Street and get my bus,' Anne said, obviously making an excuse to get away from him.

'Let me go with you to the bus then,' Carmichael said in a pleasant, friendly tone. 'You won't make me lose sight of you again for such a long time I hope. Where did you say you were living?'

'I didn't say,' Anne returned calmly, smiling a little.

'But you will tell me? Where is it? Don't be unfriendly,' Carmichael said persuasively.

'I have rooms with Maquita Gilroy in Pinhole Street, Bloomsbury, near the British Museum, just at present,' Anne admitted. 'We roam about from flower to flower for our meals — that is to say from one café to another.'

'Then I convict you of untruth. No bus goes anywhere near Pinhole Street,' Carmichael said, ignoring the latter part of her speech.

'I never said it did,' Anne fenced with a smile. 'I did not say I was going direct home.'

'Will you come and have tea with me, it's just five o'clock? I want very much to have a talk. Please do, Anne. Come and meet my sister, she's with me in the Temple, and she's expecting me back to tea to-day. She is one of the new lot reading law. She would like awfully to know you. Do come.'

'I — I don't think I can. Not to-day,' Anne said, hesitating.

'Please come, Anne. You'll like Constance, and she has a girl friend with her who is as nice as possible, but much too fat. She will be the fattest female barrister who ever wore a wig. She and Constance can't stop talking shop for a moment — they know far more law already than the Lord Chief Justice, so you and I will have to produce counterblasts of life and literature. That's right, come along.'

Anne yielded, and they crossed Fleet Street and turned into the little lane flowing softly in the dusk between the old Temple buildings.

'But I can't talk about literature. I've forgotten how to read,' she warned him. 'I never see any new books. Are you still editing the *Review*?'

'Oh, no, young Mayhew took it over long ago,' Carmichael said without explanation. 'He is doing very well with it. I'm writing hardly at all.'

'And what about Mr Dampier,' Anne asked constrainedly.

Carmichael divined that she wanted to get any mention of his name over while she was walking along in the dark, sheltered from observation. 'I used to hear sometimes — from Mrs Dampier, but I haven't for ages. They aren't coming back?'

'I don't think so. Not yet, anyhow. It must be eighteen months or more since they went, but — as perhaps you know — Dampier had another bad illness the first winter.'

Carmichael made an effort to speak naturally.

'I didn't know,' Anne said in a low voice.

'Now he is very much better, but it is wise to stay where the climate suits him for a bit. And Mrs Dampier likes it.'

'Yes, I am sure it is wise for them to stay in California,' Anne agreed, and Carmichael thought he detected relief in her quiet tone. They turned into a doorway and began to climb a long stair.

Constance Carmichael was unaffected and friendly. Her eyes were clever and black like her brother's, and she wore her hair bobbed, very black and rather fascinating on her round white neck. Her friend Miss Lee-Hope promised to be the chubbiest embodiment of the law likely to be seen about the Law Courts. She was apparently a good deal older than Constance, who regarded her as alarmingly learned, and although she looked like an overgrown baby, and a delicious fat gurgle accompanied most of the remarks made by herself and other people, her chin was firm, and the eyes that crinkled up with laughter were intelligent.

The atmosphere of the shabby old rooms was very pleasant, and Anne was glad that she had been persuaded into breaking through her hermit rule. After tea, as Carmichael had warned her, the embryo lady barristers debated points of law, and he and Anne were left free to talk to each other.

There was something restful to Anne in the easy way Carmichael accepted her presence in his room and talked without the slightest self-consciousness. He was able to express quite simply that he was glad to see her again. He had meant to find her, and here she was. He was content as he smiled across at her. How exactly in the right place she looked in the room that he was very fond of, and he was pleased that she and Constance seemed to take to each other.

She was very much changed he thought in the year and more since he had seen her. She was not changed to the eye, for outwardly she was much the same, and Carmichael found her little air of delicate gaiety, which he had seen when he had first met her, and not again, rather touching. But to the inner perception — and his was swift and sensitive — she was subtly different. He had seen her gay, and he had seen her tragic and afraid and angry — with him. Now there was sorrow behind the eyes that smiled, and beneath her laughter she was pensive. There was, too, a new courage in her pose, and what had formerly been irresolute in her had become certain and strong.

Anne's face in rest had now a sad composure, the expression of an experience which had taken her into deep places. It interested Carmichael profoundly; he wanted to know what she thought and felt. He could only guess at the history of the past year, but he guessed that Anne knew more of life than he did, in spite of his months at the war. Anne wore no tragic air and refused to carry a grievance against life about with her, but her inner history was tragic.

Carmichael thought her wonderful.

'It was odd my tumbling into you like that,' Anne said.

'But lucky for me,' Carmichael responded. 'I meant to give you two months more — till Christmas — and then to make a deliberate search for you — Agony Column, detectives, bloodhounds, oh, everything very thorough. Miss Gilroy eluded me somehow after the day I met her, when she told me very rapidly, in the middle of crossing Trafalgar Square, that you were in Egypt. And you didn't keep a promise you once made me, to make use of me as a friend.'

'I may yet,' Anne said gravely.

'I hope so. Let us walk by the river, will you, Anne, and then if you insist I'll take you up to Pinhole Street by the tram that goes into the tunnel,' Carmichael said.

They had left the lady barristers-to-be by this time, and had emerged into Essex Court.

'I'd like to,' she answered.

They crossed the Embankment and walked slowly along by the river towards Waterloo Bridge.

'Are you happy?' Anne suddenly asked.

'I was going to ask you that. I am going to be,' he answered.

'I am not unhappy,' Anne said. 'I have a queer, *sufficient* feeling of possession somehow, as if in the background of things I owned something which the world might envy me. I don't really feel my days or my hands empty. It is silly, perhaps, because of course I have nothing. Actually, I have lost. And yet — they are there.'

'Of course,' Carmichael said.

'My baby died,' Anne told him below her breath. She stopped and leaned over the parapet, staring across the river.

'I am sorry, Anne,' Carmichael murmured. A sincerity in his sympathy struck her.

'Do you mean that?' she exclaimed. '"How fortunate" is what other people might think.'

Then, moved by some obscure impulse, she found herself talking to Carmichael as she had never talked to her Aunt

Minima or Maquita, as she could not talk to any woman. It was an unburdening of her soul, such as if she had been of the older faith she would have made in the confessional.

Carmichael listened, moved to a desperate pity.

Anne, gazing not at him but at the slow traffic of the river, and speaking in a passionless, quiet voice, finished.

'It is incredible how you suffer in losing a child, even when she has lived so short a time. It is partly anger I think, such time and patience thrown away. Aunt Minnie talked of God, and I used to pray, but if God listened at all, he never answered. I think that an ear for God's voice is a gift of the soul, just as an ear for music is a gift of the body. I haven't it. Do I bore you? You have made me want to pour out all sorts of things I've only dared think in the past year. I don't feel poor — rather rich, somehow.'

Anne added after a pause, 'Not to be cheated by life is what matters most. I was afraid of that. I seemed to know so many people who lived and died in a kind of greyness. That hasn't happened to me.'

They walked on silently.

'Aren't you lonely?' Carmichael asked.

'Rather,' Anne said, 'but I am very busy all day, and I'm teaching myself Greek in the evenings when Maquita goes out. I don't like theatres, or sewing, and I like Greek.'

'You are horribly lonely,' Carmichael burst out sharply.

'Not horribly,' Anne said gently. 'I often forget it.'

Carmichael asked morosely, 'Do you still think of Dampier? Will you go back to him?'

Anne leaned against one of the sphinxes, turning away from him in silence.

'I have a right to know,' Carmichael cried in a voice rough with feeling.

'I think of him sometimes, but I will never go back to him,' Anne said.

'Are you sure?'

'I am very sure.'

'Why, Anne, why do you say so?'

'Oh, it is true,' she broke out passionately. 'He is to me as if he were dead. We are separated by more than death. Once, if he had asked me, I would never have left him. But he did not ask it. He gave up nothing for me.'

It was her only criticism of Dampier, and she had not known that it was in her heart to say it.

'I can never again do what I have done. I am changed too. Oh, things don't come again. If you are happy once, that is all,' Anne said impatiently. 'Stop me talking about myself. I can't bear it.'

'I can bear it,' Carmichael said. 'I am going to talk about you for years I hope. Marry me, Anne, and I'll teach you Greek.'

He took her hands firmly in his and forced her to look at him regardless of the passers-by who loitered to watch this love scene with mild interest.

'I am as lonely as you, and I want no one else.'

'I would be afraid,' Anne said, meeting his determined eyes, 'because the things that separate us would matter more and more later — if you cared.'

'I am not afraid, Anne,' Carmichael said.

'I'm wasting here. I can't write,' he said half an hour later when they found themselves walking up Pinhole Street towards Maquita and a belated supper. 'I'll go with you, Anne, to Poland. There is plenty of real work it seems to me for people with sanity and strength. Writing is foolishness. We'll work together, but we'll marry first. And now, if I consent not to come in, will you promise that I may see you tomorrow?'

'I will promise that,' Anne said, 'but nothing else.'

'That will be enough to begin with,' Carmichael said. He kissed her hand, and smiled into her pale, serious face.

'The world owes you a lot yet, Anne. You'll see.'

Maquita had made cocoa and an omelette that had become smoky and resilient as it was kept warm in the grate. She was sitting over the fire looking pensive, and she announced without reproach that it was too late to go out to look for food, and she didn't suppose Anne felt like turning out again, and so she had decided that they would just pig it at home, as Petunia would say, if Anne didn't mind.

They pigged it quite pleasantly, and Maquita lit a cigarette, still pensive.

'Are you not going out?' Anne asked.

Maquita shook her head.

'Anne,' she said solemnly, 'Stephen has issued an ultimatum. Either I marry him at once or he goes off to South Africa and stays there. He simply refuses to "dangle" any longer. Oh, I simply hate to lose Stephen Martin. He's the very best friend I've got in London, and we do so enjoy things together. He is so *simpatico*. I think he is behaving very badly.'

'Does he mean it?' Anne asked.

'Oh, yes, he means it. That is what is so annoying about Stephen. He says a thing and does it.'

'But why not marry him?'

'Do you know, for a long time I have thought I would,' Maquita admitted ruefully. 'But now that marriage is held to my head like a pistol, I find that I like my independence. I like my own latchkey. Slaves of the key — do you remember, Anne, talking at the Mimosa Club long ago?'

'Get married, Maquita. You will still be able to keep your latchkey,' Anne said. 'It may not be quite the same, but you like change, and you are tired of this sort of thing, really.'

'I'm not tired of omelettes in the grate, and washing my hair in front of the sitting-room fire.'

'Stephen may still let you indulge in these harmless tastes,' Anne suggested. 'I'd marry him, Maquita. He seems to me a very ordinary young man, but agreeably well off. What fun to be rich at last!'

'Oh, I don't think of that,' Maquita cried earnestly. 'And he is not at all ordinary, Anne. That is partly why I'd feel guilty if I drove him back to South Africa. It is not an artist's country, and he would not have fair opportunities there for his work. He is a real artist, and I am sure he will be great. He is so understanding, so sensitive, he has such a sense of humour —'

'I believe you are in love with him. Marry him, my dear,' Anne advised.

'Oh, do you think I should?' Maquita demanded, much interested. 'He is the strong type that I admire, my type, certainly. But tell me what you think. Your opinion influences me so much, Anne.'

'My opinion is that you will be just as happy sharing Stephen's latchkey. Or, since you will be rich, even ringing for the butler to let you in. Oh, I hope you will be happy! There is no one in the world who ought to be happier than you.'

'I feel that I don't want to lose him,' Maquita said slowly. 'But marriage is rather limiting, isn't it? And I don't like to leave you. What will you do?'

'I'll go on learning Greek,' Anne said composedly. 'But I don't know how far I'll get.

Notes on the text

BY KATE MACDONALD

1 The Mimosa Club

Fireside: 'Fireside' was a common element in the titles of family fiction magazines published in the early twentieth century. Maquita makes a little extra money by sending contributions to the column 'Odds and Ends'.

The Hon: Mrs Bridson is the daughter of a baron, denoted by the style 'The Honourable'. She clearly feels her own importance.

Debrett: *Debrett's Peerage and Baronetage* had been published since the eighteenth century by the eponymous publishing house, and is a list of the nobility of England, Scotland, Wales and Ireland, with their family connections meticulously laid out.

Allenby: General Allenby was at this time leading the British Empire Egyptian Expeditionary Force in a campaign to capture Palestine from the Turkish Empire.

bob: shillings.

range: a traditional kitchen range contained one or more ovens, a hob for pans and warming drawers, and usually provided the heat for the entire kitchen as well.

pick one up: to casually spend time with for company, with no sexual connotations.

Queen Mary's Needlework Guild: formerly the London Needlework Guild, headed by Queen Mary, it organised the making and distribution of clothing and fabric items, originally for children's orphanages, but in wartime for the troops.

rent-free: courtiers and ladies-in-waiting to the Royal family would often be granted the use of a property of the Royal Household to live in after retirement, sometimes instead of a pension.

LBC: Lady of the Bedchamber, a lady-in-waiting to the Queen or her daughter the Princess Royal.

atall: Grant is indicating an Irish syntax by joining the two words.

lifeguardsman: a soldier, probably not an officer, of the Life Guards, a longstanding regiment of the British Army.

slavey: an underpaid and overworked kitchen maid, usually in her early teens, although Alice is an old woman.

A S C: the Army Service Corps provided the fighting troops with all their supplies and equipment, an indispensable part of the British Army.

2 Simon's Pretty Ladies

Clifford Street: next to Savile Row and Regent Street, a few streets north of St James' clubland, on the edge of London's theatre district.

Brook Green and Chelsea: Brook Green is in Hammersmith, west of Kensington which was a much more socially precarious address than it is today. Chelsea was famous for its artists from an earlier epoch, such as Dante Gabriel Rossetti, James McNeill Whistler and Augustus John.

nothing wrong: Maquita reassures Sophy that Simon isn't exploiting them.

infantile: in the sense of child-like rather than childish.

from a play: Bottom served by Titania's fairies in Shakespeare's *A Midsummer Night's Dream*.

3 Anne Walks Out

P M: Paymaster.

Omer Kame: *The Rubaiyat of Omar Khayyam*, a translation by Edward Fitzgerald from 1859, a very popular poem following the Orientalist fashion.

brown holland: a plain linen fabric used for working uniforms.

lye: a fat-dissolving alkali, used for cleaning ovens.

Elbert Hubbard: an American anarchist and socialist, who founded an Arts and Crafts commune in New York State, and died with his wife on the *Lusitania* in 1917.

distangy: mangled pronunciation of *distinguée*, distinguished.

Q-M-S: Quarter-Master-Sergeant.

Dean's Yard: a square adjoining the old monastery buildings of Westminster Abbey.

the Stores: the Army and Navy Stores, traditional outfitters for Army, Navy and Empire staff.

4 Melancthon

Melancthon: the name used by the medieval Lutheran reformer Philip Schwarzerdt, as the Greek equivalent of that name, 'black earth'. He and Martin Luther wrote the *Augsberg Confession*, and were the principal instigators of the Protestant Reformation. Dampier's play is presumably about him.

ruminantly: chewing on her own thoughts.

Barrie and Galsworthy: J M Barrie and John Galsworthy were probably the most well-known and successful British playwrights of the war period.

L'Aiglon: a play by Edmond Rostand about Napoleon II; the title role had been created by Sarah Bernhardt in 1900.

Cyrano: the 1897 play in rhymed couplets about the historical figure Cyrano de Bergerac, also by Rostand.

5 Petunia Garry

round-robin: a letter circulated for group signature.

nearly related: closely related.

cammy: a camisole top, normally worn as underwear.

chi-chi: a racist term for a distinctive accent associated with native speakers of English from the Indian sub-continent.

half-Oriental: this archaic term means they suppose that Petunia's mother's family were Indian or from the Indian sub-continent.

Montpelier Square: a residential London square between Harrods and Hyde Park.

6 Ladies Must Talk

Sinn Fein: the Irish Republican party, at this stage in history working for Ireland's independence from Britain.

Mascagni: Pietro Mascagni, a popular contemporary Italian composer of operas.

button-hook: ladies' shoes and boots that were fastened with small buttons needed a special button-hook to unfasten them again.

out of a 'shop': she was an actress temporarily out of a job.

under the protection: being financially supported by a man, probably for sexual rights.

'gone gay': become a casual prostitute.

'fairy': a prostitute.

the area: the basement courtyard in front of the kitchen, through which tradesmen made their deliveries.

7 Miss Pratt and Miss Denby

in their shifts: when they were at their most vulnerable.

Medici lace collars: detachable collars to change the appearance of a plain gown, which would also be washed separately by hand, thus saving on laundry bills. The Medici style was like a half-ruff, standing up at the back of the neck and open at the front.

meningitis: an inflammation of the membranes covering the brain, which in adults can cause rigidity in the body. Miss Denby has caught it before the invention of the antibiotics used to treat it now.

live dangerously: to 'live adventurously' is one of the older 'advices' of Quakerism.

sheep: sheep were grazed in Hyde Park and other Royal parks in London until the 1940s.

8 Searchlights

les Gothas: the Gotha G V was a heavy bomber used for night raids by the German air force in the war.

maroons: a rocket fired as a warning for air raids.

nearer guns: anti-aircraft guns.

9 Thomas

the University: to the University of Oxford.

Hibbert Journal: its subtitle was *A Quarterly Review of Religion, Theology and Philosophy.*

As Pants the Hart: Psalm 42.

10 A Knight of Leicester Square

caging him in wood: the statue of Eros at Piccadilly was covered over with a wooden surround to protect it from bomb damage.

the blue and red books: *Debrett's* (see above), and *Burke's Peerage*.

made love to: mild caressing and kisses, but not sex, which is what Petunia offers when she suggests living with Robert.

12 Groping

Undine: undines are water nymphs who lack souls.

newly minted: many 'war knights' and other new titles were created during the war as a reward for or recognition of significant political, financial or industrial contributions to the war effort.

influenza: the 'Spanish' flu pandemic that killed so many immediately after the war had been widespread in western Europe since early 1918.

13 Decision

Lorna Doone: the novel *Lorna Doone* (1869) by R D Blackmore is the most well-known Exmoor novel. It is also the story of two people whose romance is forbidden by their families.

principalities nor powers: from Romans 8.38; a statement of trust in what is to come.

oleographic splendour: portraits of George V and Queen Mary, and probably of Edward VII and Queen Alexandra as well, of a type distributed in weekly magazines and routinely pinned up on walls as decoration.

dressing-gowns: notice that nothing has been said in these passages to indicate that Anne did not sleep alone. The dressing-gowns convey the information that Dampier was with her all night to the attentive reader, while the publisher and author avoided prosecution on grounds of publishing immoral content.

14 'Un Bonheur Caché'

Un Bonheur Caché: French, a hidden happiness.

Waac: Women's Auxiliary Army Corps, the women's branch of the army founded in early 1917 to free up non-combatant military roles, enabling more men to be sent to the Fronts.

Airly Beacon, **Hetty Poyser***: Airly Beacon* is a short poem by Charles Kingsley from the mid nineteenth century, in which a woman is courted by a man on Airly Beacon and sits there abandoned with his baby. Hetty Sorrell, a character in George Eliot's novel *Adam Bede* (1859), murdered her illegitimate baby. She lived at her uncle Martin Poyser's farm; for Veritas to give the character her uncle's surname might be either forgetfulness (or the author's mistake), or an exaggerated Victorian repugnance for the unmarried mother keeping her own name.

morganatic marriage: a marriage between a high-status man and a low-status woman, which is legal but gives the wife no rights to titles or privileges for her children.

Paquin and Poiret and Drécoll: leading French and Viennese couture designers of the period.

16 Poetry Day

Roehampton: Roehampton House was the base for Queen Mary's Convalescent Auxiliary Hospital, where prosthetics were fitted to servicemen with amputations, and they were trained how to recover the use of the impaired limb.

Damaged Goods: performances of the English translation of the stage play *Les Avariés* by Eugene Brieux were actively promoted from 1916 by the British military authorities, despite an earlier ban by the theatrical censor, for its discussion of the medical and social impact of syphilis as a sexually transmitted disease. The silent film of the same name ran for years during the war period.

make-up: making up a page with blocks of set type and illustrations and photographs.

17 Shadow

she had faced certain facts squarely: this may refer, very obliquely, to Anne's refusal to use contraception, possibly for religious reasons.

a listening fear in her regard: from 'Hyperion. A Fragment' by John Keats (1818-19), and the person described is the Titan Theia, wife and sister of Hyperion.

18 Aunt Minima

Who is Sylvia: a song from Shakespeare's *The Two Gentlemen of Verona*.

Olivia Primrose: the seduced and abandoned daughter of the eponymous vicar, Dr Charles Primrose, in Oliver Goldsmith's hugely popular novel *The Vicar of Wakefield* (1766).

perhaps it is not true: Aunt Minima thinks that Anne may have miscounted the weeks since her last period, which is a rather perceptive thought from this otherwise detached and elderly Victorian lady.

La Fille de Mme Angot: a comic opera about a young florist's romantic confusions from 1872 by Charles Lecocq, which was popular with Victorian audiences because it wasn't risqué.

19 Carmichael

screw: salary.

soon have to wind up: after the war had ended, the War Office and other government departments began to shrink to what was needed for peacetime.

St James' Street: in the heart of London's clubland, traditionally a decorous area where gentlemen would not run.

gibing: sneering, making critical remarks.

20 'Mark'

Gentlemen's Relish: a Victorian sandwich spread made from anchovies with a high salt content.

21 Ravelled Ends

Ravelled ends: deriving from Shakespeare's *Macbeth*, 'Sleep that knits up the raveled sleeve of care / the death of each day's life. Sore labour's bath / Balm of hurt minds'.

***Arabia Deserta**: Travels in Arabia Deserta* by Charles Doughty (1888).

22 Latchkey Ladies

sphinxes: the Thames Embankment is still lined by stone sphinxes.